Praise for The O'Brien Family Novels

"[Cecy] Robson's O'Brien family has the hottest brothers ever! . . . It's impossible not to keep your fingers crossed for an HEA, but the author knows exactly what she's doing as readers hold their breath during this roller-coaster ride of passion." —*RT Book Reviews*

"*Feel Me* is a smart romance with a fantastic heroine, alpha-male hero, sexy times, and sigh-worthy romance, and it should be on your to-be-read list."—*Harlequin Junkie*

"Like all of Robson's books, the characters of Feel Me are complex and dynamic, the emotions are raw and real, and the ending is sweet and heartwarming."—*The Book Disciple*

"You know, I don't think I've ever read a book by Cecy Robson that I haven't just absolutely adored. [*Crave Me*]was no different. She gives you characters you can identify with and a story that enthralls you…5 Stars." –*Two Girls With Books*

"An amazingly touching love story! I LOVED the love in [*Crave Me*]…I am HOOKED on these O'Briens!!!!" –*Romance Novel Giveaways*

"Cecy Robson will once again play your emotions like a concert pianist in her latest novel in the O'Brien Family series." -*Heroes and Heartbreakers*

"This story *[Let Me]* is filled with hope and passion, a really great read. I strongly recommend this book to any romance reader." --*Night Owl Reviews (Top Pick)*

"I'm just going to come right out and say it: I love the O'Brien family!" -*Feeling Fictional*

"Robson proves once again that she can sweep us off our feet with a fun, romantic tale. . . . [Once Kissed] is another must-read. I thoroughly enjoyed this novel."—*Rainy Day Ramblings*

"Devastatingly beautiful, heartbreakingly romantic and emotional, Cecy Robson's third book in her O' Brien Family series just might be my favorite yet." - *My Guilty Obsession*

"*Let Me* by Cecy Robson was a fantastic read. It has equal parts humor, sexy, heartbreak, and romance with a very satisfying ending. Ms. Robson did not disappoint." *-Under the Covers Book Blog*

"Confession: I'm a little obsessed with the O'Brien Family. Addicted, you might say. And this book? Fed my addiction. In the best possible way. I LOVED *Let Me*."*- Give Me Books*

"Make room on your list of book boyfriends for Curran O'Brien! This bad-boy cop is fiercely protective of the feisty Tess, and the sexual tension between these two is off the charts!"*—USA Today bestselling author Lauren Layne*

"WOW!! Just WOW!!! I have to say that Cecy Robson has completely blown me away with Let Me. I'm an avid reader, and I love all sorts of books, but this one has probably touched my heart in ways that no other book has." *-Devilishly Delicious Book Reviews*

"OMG! Robson delivered all the FEELS in a one two punch...If you love loud families, you will fall in love with this crazy, loving family! *Let Me*...read it, own it, love it!" *-Caffeinated Book Reviewer*

"I love second chance romances and when you toss in a huge, crazy Irish family with nothing but love for each other… no one stands a chance against the O'Briens. THAT is what made this romance [*Once Kissed*] a riotous hit with me." *-Addicted to Happily Ever After*

BY CECY ROBSON

The Shattered Past Series

Once Perfect

Once Loved

Once Pure

The O'Brien Family Novels

Once Kissed

Let Me

Crave Me

Feel Me

Save Me

The Carolina Beach Novels

Inseverable

Eternal

Infinite (coming soon)

The Weird Girls

A Curse Awakened (novella)

The Weird Girls (novella)

Sealed with a Curse

A Cursed Embrace

Of Flame and Promise

A Cursed Moon (novella)

Cursed by Destiny

A Cursed Bloodline

A Curse Unbroken

Of Flame and Light

Save Me

An O'Brien Family Novel

Cecy Robson

DEDICATION

To Shirley, for always treating me like one of your own.
Your "little one" will miss you.

ACKNOWLEDGMENTS

I met Killian, my first O'Brien, in *Once Perfect*. When he made an appearance in *Once Loved*, I knew I wouldn't be able to let him go. But when I met his family in *Once Pure*, I knew I was onto something. I just never imagined where this wonderful, loud, completely inappropriate, and loving family would take me.

Finn, Wren, Killian, Curran, Seamus, Declan, Angus, and Ma, thank you. You gave me plenty of laughs, helped me shed my share of tears, and made me fall in love over and over again. I'm sad that we're saying goodbye. I'm honored to have given you the happy endings you all deserve. Mostly, I'm grateful you found your way into so many hearts.

To my fans, who have suffered, cheered, laughed, and swooned right along with me, you'll never know the extent of my gratitude. This family is as real to me as they are to you.

To the usual suspects, Jamie, Nic, Kim, Kristin, Gaele, and now Val, thank you for experiencing the O'Briens with me. From the first draft to the last, you were there.

To my beloved children, this is what family is really about. I'm blessed to call you mine.

CHAPTER 1

Seamus

"Fuck, you're old."

Finn holds up his hands in surrender. "Not that I mean any disrespect, Seamus."

It's what someone who means disrespect always says after he says it.

"Hey," Miss Brenda, a.k.a. the seamstress taking my measurements, snaps. "You want to fight, take that shit outside. I run a classy place around here."

I settle down for Miss Brenda's sake, not that my little brother couldn't wipe the floor with me. I'm tougher than hell, but as a current UFC champion, Finnie could wipe the floor with most anyone.

I don't realize I've lunged forward until I catch sight of our roughly ninety-pound mother glaring at us from the entryway leading out to the bridal showroom, or whatever the place with all the dresses is called.

Now Ma, she could wipe the floor with Finn. That glare is one of her many superpowers and no matter how old we get, it freezes us in place until we calm our shit.

Yeah, yeah, I know I shouldn't start anything here. But that's what me and my brothers always do. We fight about sports, politics, and pretty much anything that pisses us off, whether we think we'll win the round. The fighting Irish? I think they had the O'Briens in mind when they came up with that saying.

When Ma thinks we're ready to behave ourselves, she eases out of the doorway to check on Wren. My little sister is closer to losing her shit than we are.

Wren wanted a small wedding. She should've known she was screwed from the start. There are seven of us to begin with, six boys, plus Wren and Ma, who with a lot of determination and probably more than a little whiskey, kept us in line growing up.

Small wedding? Yeah, right. Wren doesn't have enough friends to match up with the rest of us groomsmen. But she has close to five hundred cousins to fill the pews at the largest Catholic Church in Philly.

"Turn around," Miss Brenda orders. "Jesus. What did your mom feed you when you were little? Steroids? Youz all are going to have to go a size larger to accommodate your freakish chests and long limbs."

"What about our outrageously good looks?" I ask. "Do we have to go up a size for that, Miss Brenda?"

Ms. Brenda ignores me, studying the lower half of my evidently superb specimen of a body. "The pants, we need to go down a size."

"Now, I don't know about that," Finn answers her truthfully. "Not to brag, Miss Brenda, but most of us are freakishly big in other ways, too. If you know what I mean, ma'am."

I try not to laugh when Finn's face turns almost as red as his hair. He'll lie to your face about eating the last donut, staying out too late, and betting on the wrong team. But important things, like size of our manhoods, he'll tell you the truth even it means embarrassing himself in front of a battle axe like Miss Brenda.

She grips her tape measure like some kind of weapon. We've been here less than an hour and we've already managed to piss her off at least four times. She's eyeing us like she's ready to take that tape measure and choke the ever-living shit out of us.

"I'll make sure to leave plenty of room in the crotch," she growls.

"Thank you, uh, ma'am," Finn offers.

"Brenda's Bridals" isn't exactly the classiest place a bride-to-be and company will ever frequent. It's not in the best part of Philly. Like most shops around here, when Brenda's closes, the metal gates come down to protect the windows, doors, and the goods inside. And like most of the shop owners, Miss Brenda walks out to the cracked asphalt parking lot packing heat.

Why would we come to a place like this with all the places to choose from in a city this big? 'Cause Brenda's is local. Her family has been around as long as mine. People like the O'Briens and Ms. Brendas of the city, we take care of our own. No fancy reality TV show is ever going to film around here. That's okay. It's where Philly families will continue to go long after that show is cancelled.

Sure, there's a good chance your wallet will get lifted if you stand too long looking at the dresses in the front window. But if you're ballsy enough to drive here and dare to go inside, take a look at what Miss Brenda offers. No matter what goes wrong, Miss Brenda and crew will make sure you look your best on your big day. Your tux, dress, or whatever, will fit like it was made for you, and everybody who sees you walking down the aisle will know you opted for quality and a fair price rather than glitz.

"When did that shit happen?" Finn asks, pointing at my chest when Miss Brenda swaps out the shirt I'm wearing for a different one, ironed sharp enough to cut me.

I looked down my sternum to the hairs gathered between my pecs. I have definition in my chest, arms, and stomach. I may be a carpenter, but I keep in fighting shape. "When did what happen?" I ask.

"That gray shit." Finn shudders as if it physically pains him to see the hairs that have sprouted.

There are a few grays on my temples, too, but for some reason the chest hair seems to bother him more. "I don't know. A few years ago. It's what the ladies call dignified." They really don't. More to the point, they say things like, "Ride me, cowboy" or "faster, my probation officer will be here soon."

The latter only happened once, okay twice, but in my defense, it was with the same broad.

"Damn, Seamus," Finnie says, snagging my attention. "It's like I'm watching you age right in front of me. If you don't get a handle on it, I may be rolling you out of here in a wheelchair and stopping by the nearest drugstore to pick up a cane."

"Da hell, Finn? I'm only thirty-six."

"Thirty-seven," Wren and Ma call from the next room.

"See, that's what I'm telling you," Finnie says. "You're old. Old people always forget how old they are."

He hops down from the box when the seamstress, who's been eyeing him like she wants to bite her way up his leg, slides the tape measure off his neck. If Finn notices, he doesn't give it away. He's madly in love with his woman, Sol. They're getting married right before Wren.

"Who cares how old I am?" It's what I say, but it's really screwing with my head that I lost a year without even knowing it. I'm going to be forty in less than three years. That can't be right.

Brenda finishes working her magic and leaves, grabbing her youngest daughter by the hair and hauling her out to the showroom. Like me, Brenda didn't miss how she was two seconds away from straddling Finn.

We ignore their rather audible screeching and keep talking. The hair pullin' and all that yelling they're doing, that's good parenting according to how we were raised. "I'm twenty-six," Finn tells me. "I have a woman I'm marrying, and probably seven kids to pop out before I get to be your age." He shrugs. "Sol has good childbearing hips, I think she could do it." He shakes his head. "But you, you're running out of time."

He circles me, taking his time. Good. I might be able to punch him in the back of the head before he has time to react. It'll be a good punch, too. One that might send him stumbling into that rack of pink hats. "I think you've got two, maybe three good years left before your balls shrivel up and drop like stones on the floor." He slaps me on the back. "Don't let your balls down like that, man. You're better than that. So are they."

I think twice about punching him in the face. I have to say, it takes some doing. I only resist, because I like Sol and she'll lose it on me if I mess up his face.

"Me little Finnie is right," Ma says from the door, her Irish accent as thick as the day Grammie popped her out in a potato field.

"He's the baby and already getting married. Promising me grandbabies like a good boy."

He points at her, making a clicking sound. "You know I've got you, Ma."

That did it. The moment Ma leaves, we're throwing down.

Ma shakes her head like people do when all is lost and there's nothing that can be done. "Look at you, Seamus. All strapping male with the strength and charm of an Irish prince." She walks in, her steps slow and steady. It's the same way she walked in when we were kids and we knew we were fucked.

"I just have one question," she says, her voice light as it often is before she strikes. "Are you trying to kill your mother?"

Jesus. Here we go.

She holds up her hand. "Oh, me handsome son. It's a simple question really. Do you want me to die?"

"You want Ma to die?" Wren yells from the other room. She shuffles in with enough white fabric trailing behind her to sail across the Atlantic. Brenda's other daughters, the not so slutty ones, charge after Wren, lifting the eighty feet of material high in the air.

Wren points an irate finger at me. "If you give Ma the big one, you're going to really piss me off. No one—not even me—ever thought this shit would happen," she adds, motioning to layers of dress.

Brenda's daughters, Finnie, and Ma nod their heads in unison. My sister is beautiful. I can say that because it's true, even though right now she looks like a Barbie doll shoved into a giant cupcake. Like me, Wren has black hair, blue eyes, and light skin. If you cut us, we'd bleed Leprechauns that would dance a jig the moment their little feet hit the floor. We're *that* Irish.

Wren's problem is she has a mouth most sailors would run screaming from and an attitude that's even less polite. Let's face it, none of us ever thought Wren would meet a man strong enough to tame her.

I'm happy for her and everything, but right now it sucks balls.

Wren was my safety-net because of her mouth. Finnie was too, because he was the youngest and always in trouble. As far as I was concerned, I had years, no, *decades* before I had to worry about settling down. But life can be a real bitch and here she is waving two giant middle fingers at me now that Finn and Wren are getting hitched.

"So what if I'm not married? So what if I haven't popped out a few kids?" I hold out my arms. "Plenty of women have had the absolute pleasure of sampling the merchandise—"

I wince when Ma slaps me upside the head. She might be five foot nothing, but she has the agility of a cobra and possibly the ability to fly. I'm almost 6 foot 2. How the hell can she can reach me?

"And what happened to all these 'ladies' who sampled the merchandise?" Ma demands.

"I think one is back in prison," Finnie offers. He frowns, giving it a lot of thought. "Larceny and Fraud. Right, Seamus?"

"It's where most of the skanks he dated belong," Wren agrees. "Remember Kenna O'Sullivan?" We all collectively cross ourselves, including Miss Brenda's daughters. "They never did find the body."

"Yeah. She was a nutcase." My voice trails off. I'm not doing myself any favors. Thank God Finn has my back.

"Hey, Shoshana Greenstone was nice. Oh, and her husband was pretty damn understanding when he found out you were banging her."

"I didn't know she was married!" I yell for the hundredth time. "I just, you know, thought she worked odd hours."

Wren grins. "No, she just had trouble finding a babysitter for her kids."

"What about the others?" Ma asks. "The girls have liked you since you were a wee lad."

"I don't know," I answer truthfully, my annoyance making my voice sound gruff. "No one's really ever done it for me." I look at them. "You want them to do it for me, don't ya?"

Wren places her hands on her hips. She may look like a lady, all soft and dainty in those clouds of lace, but she'll never exactly think or talk like one. "You mean besides in the backseat of your truck?" She nods. "Yeah, that would be nice."

Ma leans in. I know what she's going to say even before she says it. "I was younger than you when I pushed out your baby brother onto the cold kitchen floor."

Finn holds out his hand, looking a little green. "Ma, please don't. Miss Brenda won't like it if I puke on her stuff before I pay for it."

"Then you better pay for it," Wren says, knowing it's that time again to tell the divine tale of Finn's birth.

Shoot me.

The birth of a child is supposed to be a good thing, a beautiful thing, filled with miracles, stuffed animals, and balloons. Maybe for most families it is, under the right conditions. But my family doesn't tend to do things the right way. I suppose it's one of the many things that makes us "us." Our hearts are usually in the right place. But the right way for birthing babies means a hospital and under sanitary conditions—not in a kitchen barely big enough for a refrigerator and stove.

I remember that day clearly. Ma was making shepherd's pie, until she wasn't. Her water broke like an extra-large water balloon thrown on the floor by a very pissed off toddler. She started screaming, then Angus started screaming and Curran almost fainted. Five contractions later, Finnie was coming out and there wasn't anything we could do to stop him.

Bastard. I missed my baseball game because of him.

It was something out of the *Good Earth*. Remember that book? It was one me and millions of kids across America were forced to read. I don't recall all the details. Aside from the concubines that seemed to be everywhere, there's only one scene that really sticks out in my mind, and I swear to Christ it will haunt me for the rest of my life. The poor Asian lady excuses herself in the middle of tending a field. About an hour later, she comes back with a baby latched onto her tit and a hoe in her hand. She picks up right where she left off, digging holes and planting seeds, beside her husband who doesn't bother asking what the fuck is wrong with her. To this day, every time I go to a Chinese restaurant, I feel like I should apologize to the Asian women working there on behalf of all asshole men everywhere.

Like the little Asian lady, Ma cleaned herself and Finnie up, slapped him on the boob, and finished making shepherd's pie so we'd have something to eat. It wasn't until everyone was settled at the table that she allowed a neighbor to take her to the hospital. Angus and Declan cleaned up the kitchen and Curran's vomit. As the third in line, I should have done something, too. But somewhere between getting over missing my baseball game and Ma finally leaving for the hospital a thought came to me. That's going to be me. Not the one giving birth. That shit is fucking traumatic. I mean being a parent. A real one. Not, one who'd leave his pregnant wife and six kids to bang his mistress a few blocks away. Like our father had that day.

Seeing Ma give birth like that changed me. Made me want a family rather than simply be a part of one. If I'm being honest, I thought I'd have one by now. Or at the very least, be married to someone without a rap sheet. I've taken it easy for the most part, not even feeling pressured to date. That changed when my older brother and sworn bachelor for life, Declan, met the perfect woman and the youngest O'Briens agreed to forever.

Wren frowns, her smirk gone. "Seamus, what is it?"

I yank at my collar. "Nothing, just hungry."

Finn steps forward, his expression as solemn as Ma's. "Are you sure?"

I knock him on the shoulder and laugh. "Yeah. It's all good."

It's what I say, even though it's not.

CHAPTER 2

Allie

"Yes, Mr. Traynor. Your house will officially be on the market at midnight tonight." I reach for the messages my assistant, Roxanne, passes me. Ten calls, ten possible listings. She texted me earlier, but she knows I prefer a hard copy.

"Coffee?" she mouths as I continue to reassure Mr. Traynor.

I nod, keeping my smile. I learned a long time ago that if you keep your smile, your composure remains intact, no matter the obstacle.

"I know you're anxious, Mr. Traynor. Retirement is an exciting time, but it does mean letting go of the life you've had and starting a new one."

"Yeah, new life," he says, recognizing I hit the nail on the head.

"I promise I'm going to take great care of you. We won't sell unless you're happy with the terms."

Most real estate agents wouldn't make promises like this. I do and keep my word. It's why my company is so successful. That, and because I have no social life.

"You get me. Don't you, little girl?" he asks.

I try not to laugh. At thirty-five years old, I'm long past childhood. But given my youthful features and the large population of seniors I serve, I suppose I seem very young.

"I'll take care of everything," I assure him.

Upon disconnecting with Mr. Traynor, I fall into my chair and fire up my laptop. I've already returned two messages by the time Roxanne returns with my coffee.

"Thank you, Roxanne."

I lift the contract in front of me and take a sip of my coffee before I realize Roxanne isn't leaving. "Is something wrong?" I ask.

She makes a face. I know that face. "Your mother has been calling all morning. She says it's important and that it involves your sister."

There are only three reasons my mother typically calls. She needs help with a business matter, wants money, or wants to brag about my sister Valentina. I handle the first two fairly well. The latter is something I've never grown accustomed to.

God was generous to Valentina. He blessed her with striking beauty, a modeling contract with Wilhelmina, and intelligence that earned her a full scholarship to the University of Pennsylvania.

Perfection is a foreign concept to me. I was diagnosed with ADD and raised in a family that couldn't afford the medication to treat it. Oh, and modeling? Wilhelmina usually passes on women with buck teeth and frizzy hair who don't grow past 5'3".

The teeth I straightened with my first real estate paycheck, and the business degree I earned studying an extra year in college. My achievements never measured up to Valentina's accomplishments. She reigns as queen and her crown remains untarnished even after she slept with the man I was supposed to marry.

My office phone rings. Roxanne and I both stare at it. "That's probably your mother," she says.

"Probably," I agree, watching the light across the monitor blink with every ring.

It eventually stops ringing. Not that it offers me a reprieve. I know I'm not safe. I do my best to ignore the sympathy splaying across Roxanne's features when the phone rings again.

I wish I had the kind of mother I couldn't wait to speak to. But every conversation with my mother is the equivalent of, "Is that what you're wearing? What you look like? Who you are?" Insert a pained groan. "Perhaps it's best to just lay down and die."

My hand sweeps across my forehead in anticipation of my impending headache.

"I'll give you some privacy," Roxanne says, hurrying off.

"Allie Mendes," I say, keeping my voice professional.

"Oh, Alegria, when are you going to stop using that ridiculous nickname?"

"Hi, Mom," I say. I ignore the dig. There's plenty more to come.

"I received a letter about our 401(k) from the financial planner. The one you recommended. Something about investment opportunities. Such an annoying man."

"Tyrese is very good at his job. If he's contacting you, it's because there's an opportunity for you to make more money." Now, I have her attention.

"This is wonderful. He wants to schedule a meeting. You'll be here won't you? You know the family and I don't understand such things."

I rub my eyes. "I'll call him and set something up."

I wait for her to continue, but all that greets me is the gruesome silence that comes with bad news. "Is everything all right?" I ask.

"Everything is wonderful, *mija*," she says. I don't miss the hesitation in her voice or the over-animated tone that follows. "I have exciting news about Valentina."

Valentina and I haven't spoken in years. But our mother has spoken enough for her. I assume things that should be impossible, like she was selected to be the first celebrity in space. Or that she's the new face of Chanel. Or that she's dating a member of the royal family. Never mind. She accomplished those amazing feats before turning thirty.

"Very exciting news," my mother adds, her voice strangely forced.

I make a note to call Tyrese. "Okay . . . what is it?" I ask.

"She's getting married."

"She is?" I'll admit I'm surprised.

It's not that my sister can't have anyone she wants. I just never pictured her marrying *anyone*. She's stunning and so ridiculously elegant, men pant behind her. She loves attention, but becomes bored quickly, moving on to the next celebrity or billionaire playboy. I envisioned her having affairs until she died in a lavish apartment in Paris surrounded by servants and her devoted lover, forty years her junior, weeping at her bedside.

"There's very little time to plan. The wedding is just a few months away." My mother's voice drops to whisper as if she's sharing juicy gossip. "I think the young lovers couldn't wait to start their family."

"Valentina is pregnant?" Aside from never getting married, I never imagined Valentina with children. Kids are "dirty, selfish things." Her words, not mine.

"She didn't exactly say that. But I'm certain she'll bless us with our first grandchild."

"Hmm," I reply, thrilled my mother isn't on one of her "why have you denied me grandchildren" tirades. I scroll through my emails, leaving my mother to her thoughts.

"Honestly, she hasn't given us much time to plan."

I don't want to remind her that Valentina wouldn't allow our family to plan anything. She's likely hired *the* celebrity wedding coordinator and Matt Damon and Ben Affleck are duking it out for a chance to be the ring bearer.

"Aren't you going to say anything?" my mother asks.

Her tone is off again. I wonder briefly if I missed something she said. "Sorry, Mom. I wasn't expecting the news." It's true, but I can't stop my small smile. If this is what Valentina wants, I'm happy for her.

I pull my laptop closer when an email pops up regarding an upcoming closing. "Who's the lucky guy?" I ask.

Another dramatic pause, followed by and something I don't quite catch.

"I'm sorry?" I say.

She sighs. "She's marrying Andres."

The air around me vanishes in a rush. I try to speak. To breathe. For a long moment, I don't manage either. "A-Andres who?"

"The boy you used to know," she replies.

I don't know if my mother is trying to spare me by choosing the words she does. If so, it doesn't work. Slowly, very slowly, a sting spreads across my eyes, expanding like a web to entrap my heart.

I tell myself not to cry. It's been *years*. *Years* since Andres and Valentina betrayed me. But there's that pain, tearing open the stitches I carefully placed.

Andres and I met when we were in middle school. We were the nerds who read comic books and could recite any line from any Star Wars movie. We moved in together right after college, much to the dismay of my family, who would've sworn on my grandmother's grave that I was still a virgin. I worked and paid the bills, while he finished his masters in nuclear engineering and saved enough money to pay for the first year of his doctorate.

We were supposed to get married.

We were supposed to have children.

He wasn't supposed to break my heart.

And now, now…

I start speaking before I remind myself to whom I'm speaking. "How . . . how did this happen?"

My mother senses my sorrow, even though she's not here to witness my tears. "Alegria, you and Andres have been apart for years. What he and Valentina share is very special. He's promised to give Valentina everything a mother can hope for."

This is the final blow she casts and it hurts more than the rest. Andres wasn't good enough when I was with him.

But he's with Valentina now, and the education I helped pay for allowed him to create a nuclear weapon he sold to the military for millions. He's no longer the geek my family made fun of. Like Valentina, he's royalty now.

"When did this happen?"

"The proposal? This past weekend, I believe."

"No," I say, my tone sharp. "When did Valentina and Andres happen?"

My mother's words release stiffly. If she had any sympathy for me it's gone. "They've been together for years," she replies.

Years? No . . . "It wasn't a one-time thing?" Once more, I forget to whom I'm speaking.

"Not if they're getting married," she replies impatiently.

She continues speaking, moving past my feelings and focusing on my sister. I'm not certain how much time passes. All I can think is that I've been kept in the dark for years by my family.

My mother keeps speaking about venues and fittings. How Valentina's wedding will be unlike anything anyone has ever seen. "You know your sister. She will make her mark on this city." She mentions something about an upcoming engagement party and bridal luncheon, assuring me not to worry. "You're not being considered for maid of honor. That would be cruel and Valentina doesn't want to hurt you."

Most of what follows is gibberish, fragmented sentences intended to gloss over what's happened and to keep me silent. I was never good enough for my mother, sister, my family, or apparently, Andres. Today is another reminder.

I don't say anything, attempting to hang up the receiver. My mother is still speaking. I wish she would stop. Just as I wish the tears that flow wouldn't come.

CHAPTER 3

Seamus

I maneuver down 8th Street, while Wren chews my ear off through my Bluetooth. Most people from out of town would have their navigation system on. But I'm not from out of town and only losers and out of towners use their navigation systems in the city. Anyone who's lived in Philly at least five years should know where Termini's bakery is. If he doesn't, he needs to get the hell on outta here.

"Don't forget. Sol wants Finnie to have a groom's cake. She doesn't care what kind and neither does he."

I roll to a stop at the light. "Why can't he pick it out?"

"He and Killian are guest commentators for that big fight on Saturday. They're leaving for Vegas some time tonight. They're also hosting the next few Fight Nights and have to sort through the next batch of contenders."

"That's right."

In the background, I hear her fingers flying across the keyboard at rocket speed. "I'm going to seriously owe you for helping us out," she says. "You wouldn't believe all the stuff I have to do at the office before me and Evan leave for Sweden."

"It's no biggie. I'll take care of you and Finnie."

"Good. The venue Ma picked out for the engagement party has a separate room for desserts. A separate freaking room!" she repeats. "We have to fill it and make it pretty, so try out as many of those little cakes as possible. The place can make their own, but they don't compare to Termini's. Their cake was dry enough to use as bricks and the icing would have made damn good mortar. You feel me?"

"Dry cake, shitty icing. I got you."

More typing, some quick talk to someone asking for Evan's schedule, and what sounds like paper being ripped. I'm tired just listening to her work.

"I need those little bitty cakes," she says, sounding like I don't understand and might screw up. "Stuffed little pastries or whatever. I also need them to be different each time."

"Different?" I ask.

"Yeah, like a theme."

"Theme?" I ask. Okay, this was supposed to be an easy job. Me eating cake and her liking me for doing it.

"Seamus, I have a rehearsal dinner, the bridal luncheon, the reception, and the breakfast the day after, and anything else Ma comes up with. I don't want to look like a cheap ass who recycled the same thing over and over again."

"I can respect that," I say. I stop at a light, waving to two women who stop to admire the goods.

"Ma thinks I have time for all of this," Wren adds. "Like all I do all day is fetch Evan's coffee and write notes up in shorthand. *Shorthand*, Seamus. She thinks that shit still exists."

"Aren't you his secretary?"

"My title is administrative assistant to the CEO of iCronos, moron. Believe me, I do more than order him coffee." She sighs. "Evan's under the gun to finish a project he's presenting to Sweden's Ministry of Health and Social Affairs, as well as to the Regional Medical councils, and I'm helping him. I don't have time to pick out desserts for events I don't want to have. We're running an empire here."

"Evan's out of his mind about marrying you. I thought for sure he'd want the two of you to take care of all the wedding stuff."

"He does," she says, her voice softening. "But this deal is important and we have to wrap it up before the big day so we can actually enjoy our big day. The ceremony, reception, and honeymoon we're planning together. Those are the things we're excited about. Everything else, though . . ." She groans. "I just can't. I never signed up for this blushing bride-to-be bullshit. I wanted to get married on the beach with just us. But no. Ma insists I get married in a church or risk God releasing a plague that will have flying monkeys shooting out of my lady bits. No one needs that shit."

I swipe a hand over my mouth to cover my laugh. As the only girl in the family, Wren is screwed ten ways from Sunday and twice from Saturday. I can picture her waving her arms like she does when she's pissed. "You know when I mentioned the beach to Ma, she asked if I wanted to be responsible for unleashing the apocalypse?" Wren adds. "She asked me that bit of crazy *right to my face*."

"What did you say?" I ask.

"I told her that the second coming doesn't depend on me and Evan getting married in a Catholic church, and you know what she said?"

"Are you trying to kill your mother?" I offer, taking shortcut when I see an accident up ahead.

"Yeah, she did! She even brought up all that fire and brimstone shit. You know that always gets me. I tell you, Catholic guilt can slap you upside the head like a drunk, nasty bitch."

This time I do laugh out loud. "You sound a little stressed, there, Wren."

"That's because I am, genius. Did you know I'd have all this crap to do?"

"Nope," I say, cursing when I run over the mother of all pot holes.

Wren ignores me going full speed ahead. "No wonder so many people get married in Vegas. This isn't natural. All these different events to mark the only big event that matters. Can't I just get married and skip the rest?"

"You can if you want Ma to die and come back to haunt you leading the Four Horsemen. You know Ma's been waiting for this day. Remember when Grammie—God rest her soul—used to pray the rosary?" I drop into my best expression of Grammie, her Irish accent so thick you could spread it across soda bread. "Oh, sacred Jesus, forgive this undeserving and hell-bound child for her many sins and let her find a man deserving of your grace. Do not strike her down with your mighty spirit. Bless her womb as your beloved father blessed your mother's so she may have strapping, intelligent, and dashing boys, in Jesus' name, Amen."

"You remember all that?" she asks.

"Hell, yeah. It was how she said good night."

"True. God rest her soul," Wren agrees. "To be fair, I wasn't the hell-bound child. That was Finnie. I was the destroyer of dreams and all things pure."

"Yeah?" I frown. "I thought that was Grammie's nickname for Curran?"

"No, he was God's answer to birth control. Killian was Damian from the Omen."

"Oh, yeah," I say, turning back onto 8th. "I remember her squirting him with holy water every Sunday before mass, so God would let him in."

"In Grammie's defense, he did look like that creepy kid after the bowl cut Ma gave him," Wren adds. "Angus was 'Gluttony' and a few other of the seven sins, depending on the day. You were Judas, on account of you always ratting us out."

"I remember that much. Hey, what was Declan?"

"Dear boy. That kiss-ass was always the favorite."

"Bastard," we both mutter.

I pull up in front of the bakery and start to parallel park, only for some shithead to try to take my spot. He gets out of the car and so do I. He takes one look at me, gets back in his car, and leaves.

"Did you hear me, Seamus?"

"Nah, some dipshit just tried to steal my parking spot."

She pauses. "Did you get it back?"

"Ah, yeah," I reply like it's obvious, because it damn well is. "What were you saying?"

"I was asking you if you are going to bring someone to the wedding, the rehearsal dinner, and all the other shenanigans I'm supposed to be a part of."

"Do I have to?"

There's a long dramatic pause. Never a good thing with Wren. "Listen Seamus, I know we gave you a hard time the other day about being old as fuck, still being single, and no woman in sight without a long list of baby daddies. But our hearts were in the right place."

"Sounds it," I say.

She sighs. "We just don't want you to be alone, you know? You hear about those spinster women found dead, their faces half-eaten by their twenty cats. We don't want that to be you. We don't want to find you dead, alone, surrounded by asshole cats licking their whiskers."

How did I go from being the reigning stud in the family to my family stressing I'll die a death by pussy?

"Why the hell is it when everyone has someone they need, everybody needs to have someone, too?"

"I wasn't supposed to find someone nice," she replies by way of an answer. "I was supposed to be that spinster, Seamus. I don't even like cats. It was okay for you to be alone, because you're a man and men supposedly have more opportunities."

I turn off my car, because I know Wren isn't done yet. She doesn't disappoint.

"But then I did find someone, proving I wasn't such a lost cause. You hear what I'm saying? If I can, by the grace of God and our dead grandmother—God rest her soul—find someone good and kind, you can too."

"Thanks for the pep talk there, Wren. I'm glad we had this heart to heart." I start to open my door when she stops me with her words.

"Are you trying to kill Ma?"

"Are you seriously asking me this question, *again*? For someone who is trying to help, you're not helping."

"My point is, there is someone out there for you. You just have to find her. Forget all the skanks. Stop spending your weekends watching football at Killian's and eating your weight in nachos. Go to church and find someone. Someone nice. Someone who isn't going to steal my purse."

"It was one time," I insist. "And I paid you back the bills she stole."

"Seamus."

"And the clothes."

"*Seamus*."

"And your panties."

"Seamus! I don't care about all that." She pauses. "Okay, the panties were a big deal, because honestly, what the fuck? But all that aside, I care about you. What's going to happen if you don't find someone in the next few years? Or worse, if you end up with some psycho you don't deserve?"

I slump into my seat, every curse word I know falling into my mouth like a landslide. Wren is feeling a lot of pressure. Finnie's fiancée, Sol, is too. Ma isn't doing so hot, either. They have weddings to plan and a long list of nightmares that I can't possibly relate to.

I don't get their preoccupation with me. They have better things to do. I want to yell at everyone to mind their damn business. Except I can't. Pains in the ass or not, in their own demented way, my family means well. I try to ease at least one worry the best way I know how. I lie.

"You're worried over nothing. I already have someone lined up to bring to all your shit."

Instead of shutting Wren up, she gets more nuts. "Who are you going to bring?" she asks slowly. "Seamus, it can't be just anyone. I don't want any drama. I want a decent meal, say hello to few people, and get the hell out so I can have naked time with Evan."

"Don't worry about it. She's . . . nice."

"When you say 'nice,' do you mean all her tats are spelled correctly, or she won't burst into flames if she walks into church?"

"There won't be any flames," I assure her. "And she's got no tats." I grimace. Now I've gone too far.

"Who is she?" she presses. "This can't be some woman you met at a bar."

Well, there goes Plan A.

"She has to be a decent human being," Wren says, laying it out. "Someone you wouldn't be afraid to tell Father Flanagan you were with the night before."

Shit. Is she kidding? It's bad enough I can't pick up someone at a bar. Now she's expecting someone with morals, too? I was just going to hit someone up on speed dial. But by the way she's acting, it won't be enough to get Wren or Ma off my back.

"I'm bringing the woman I'm seeing," I blurt out.

I know I'm screwed even before she says anything. "*You're* seeing someone?"

"Sure."

"Someone who doesn't deflate when you're done for the night?"

"That was one time!" It was also a joke. We blew up a bunch of adult dolls and shoved them in Curran's patrol car. But we're men and that's what men do to other men at their brother's bachelor party.

"Then who is it?"

"Who's who?" I ask, trying to buy myself some time.

"Who is the woman you're planning to bring to all the events I have to attend so the Four Horsemen don't gallop across the dead remains of my wedding party?"

I look around like she's somehow spying on me from the next building. I used to be a great liar when I was a kid. Don't judge. If you grew up in my family, you had to learn to lie to survive, to have somewhat of a social life, without your mother kicking down a door and dragging you out of an underage drinking party by the hair. But since turning legal, and Ma retiring to Florida, I haven't really had anything to lie about.

"Ah, Georgina . . . Glass." I smack myself on the forehead for being such an idiot.

"Georgina Glass," Wren says. She's not impressed by my Brady Bunch reference. Truth be told, neither am I. "Tell me you're screwing with me."

"Course I am." I scroll through my contacts as I speak to her on my phone.

Most of the women on my list are, by some miracle of God, married. Some are on their second marriages and possibly third. One is on probation, but I think she's doing real good now, learning computers and shit. The hottest one is in prison, but the crazy psycho needs to be there for the safety of Philadelphia and any man in the vicinity with a penis. One, I definitely can't call, because I accidentally made out with her mother. I know what it sounds like, but you ain't perfect, either.

"You're not seeing anyone. Are you?" Wren asks, sounding disappointed and maybe a little heartbroken, too. "This is all bullshit to keep Ma alive."

Sweat gathers along my crown. I start to panic, but try not to let it show in my voice. "Have I ever lied to you? Scratch that. Have I ever lied to you about a woman? Never mind," I add, realizing I'm only digging myself into a bigger hole. "The thing is, I can't really tell anyone."

"You're gay, aren't you? Come out of the closet, Seamus. The rest of us pretty much figured as much. God, I've never met a blue-collar man who obsesses over hair gel more than you do."

"I'm not gay, Wren." In a way, I wish I was. Then I wouldn't have to deal with psycho women. "It's just that . . . I just met this girl. She's real shy and stuff, and I didn't want to put any pressure on her by attending all these family events. We're just getting to know each other. I don't want to scare her off. Hear what I'm saying? This girl is special."

It's a line of bullshit I don't even buy myself. The O'Briens have this thing, a curse if you will, once we get to talking there's no stopping us. Words fly out of our mouths before we give it much thought and next thing you know we're in confession giving Father Flanagan an earful. For the most, part it's harmless and only adds to our rather spectacular personalities. Today, all it does is bend me over a table and give my rock-hard ass a good smack.

"If this girl is so special, how come we haven't heard about her before?"

"Did you hear me? It's new and we're getting to know each other."

"Did she just get out of prison?"

I'll give her this, it's a fair question.

"No, she's a nice girl. A good girl. She goes to church and helps out in soup kitchens and shit."

Wren doesn't believe me and neither do I. Where is such a magical creature found? Not in Philly, I'll tell you that much.

I'm ready to take it all back. Let Wren know this is what she's reduced me to, a lying idiot with a make-believe girlfriend

"And she likes *you*?" she asks.

I should stop right where I am. But I don't. My lie takes on a life of its own. "Why wouldn't she? I'm a catch."

My mouth is out of control. I didn't sound believable at first, but now I find myself getting defensive and needing to protect my pretend girlfriend. What the hell's wrong with me?

Stop speaking, asshole, I tell myself. But here I go, kicking myself in the balls to save Wren and my family the trouble. "I make a decent living," I remind her. "I've got some money put away and I'm the best looking one of us."

"Seamus, I'm not saying anyone wouldn't be lucky to have you—"

"You're not?" Hey, that's kind of nice.

"I'm only saying most of the women you run around with suck, leaving you with nothing but a restraining order and a new security system." She pauses, and as if it pains her, asks, "So, what's her name?"

"I'm not telling you." *Because I don't know my own damn self and Jesus God in heaven, make it all stop.*

"Why? If this girl is so amazing, why can't you just tell me her name or who she is? Is it someone I know?"

"I want it to be a surprise."

"Why?"

"Because few things are anymore." I open my glove compartment, hoping to find that roll of duct tape so I can tape my mouth shut.

"Do I know her?"

"Maybe, maybe not," I say. Damn. It's like I'm possessed or something.

"Seamus, I'm really stressed here. If you're lying to me or playing games, it's not funny. We're all worried about you dying alone and those damn mutant cats munching on what's left of your toes."

"Eh, you have nothing to worry about. I'm bringing someone. Promise." I rub my face, hoping to rub the last few minutes from my mind. "You can trust me, Wren."

"Okay . . . I believe you. Just—"

"Just what?" I ask.

The other end of the line grows eerily quiet before the distant sound of Evan's voice echoes through, dripping with worry and something else.

"Darling, are you all right?" he whispers in his thick British accent.

"Fine," Wren says, forcing out the word and allowing another seep of that tension to cut through the mic. "Just finishing up with Seamus." Her voice is heavy. "Seamus, just pick out whatever you think will look good on the dessert table. If you need anything, call me."

The way she says, "If you need anything," makes me think she's no longer talking pastries.

"I won't let you down," I say, staring at the sign to the bakery.

I mean what I say. Now, all I have to do is fly to Oz and

SAVE ME

swap out some red shoes for a girlfriend.

CHAPTER 4

Allie

"You haven't called your sister."

My mother's voice bellows over my Bluetooth like a looming storm. A very dark storm determined to kill me via a lightning bolt through my heart.

My mother can't be this naïve or heartless. I've been a wreck following the conversation we had the other day. I helped Andres through thick and thin, only for him to help himself to my sister. Mom knew this would devastate me, so why does she keep calling me to discuss all the wedding festivities?

"Alegria? Are you still there?"

"Yes, Mom," I reply. "I'm still here."

"Then why do you seem so distant? Why does it feel like you're not listening at all?"

This is the moment where I express how hurt I am. But different rules have always applied to my sister and me. I'm the sponge, the one they cyclically squeeze dry. Valentina remains the queen. This time, I can't bow down. Valentina wears a very tarnished crown and for once my mother needs to see it.

"This is a lot to take in. This was someone I was once very close to."

"This doesn't change your relationship with Valentina," my mother interrupts. "You'll always be best friends."

If I was driving in the coal regions and not into Philly, I might very well consider ramming down on the accelerator and driving over the edge. This is where my mother always takes me; to the very edge of sanity where all that separates me from men in white scrubs wielding restraints is a minute thread of reason.

My mother's voice continues in that animated and bizarre speech pattern she's adopted over the years, feigning that she's a worldly socialite and not a first-generation Latina who worked at a canning plant most of her life.

"You're worried Valentina will forget about you, aren't you?" she asks.

She doesn't even consider that perhaps I meant Andres. Nor does she acknowledge Valentina and I haven't spoken in years. Valentina knew what Andres meant to me. Everyone did.

I take a breath, gathering courage that abandoned me long ago. "Mom, I was talking about Andres."

It's my last attempt to share what I'm feeling. To show her I'm hurt. Me, the woman who saw past Andres's idiosyncrasies and promised to marry him.

"*Niña*," Mom says. "You knew that was never going to work out."

No. I didn't. Not then.

Traffic eases to a slow crawl. "You used to complain about Andres," I remind her, unable to let the conversation drop. "When we were together, you used to tell me I was wasting my time on someone who wouldn't amount to anything."

"I don't remember that," my mother says. "Did I tell you they're having the wedding at the Montana Elite?"

"Yes, you've mentioned it."

"Oh, don't worry about the price," my mother insists, as if that's the problem. "Andres can afford any reception hall after obtaining his doctorate in physics."

I should remind her I helped pay for that degree, but I don't want to sound bitter. I'm better than that. At least that's what I thought until my mother shared the big news.

"Andres promised Valentina everything she deserves," my mother gushes.

"Great," I say, through bared teeth.

I think I growl. This is what my family has finally reduced me to, a growling, crazy woman who's contemplating biting someone.

"The waiting list for the Montana Elite is years. Did you hear me? *Years*!" My mother happily declares. She laughs. "But, once they knew who the bride was . . . Well, they weren't going to let a celebrity of Valentina's status slip through their fingers, now were they?"

"Heaven forbid," I agree.

Andres isn't the man for me. I knew it when he confessed he'd spent the afternoon in Valentina's bed. As much as it killed me, I couldn't stay with a man who traded me in so easily.

My mother rambles on about Valentina's meeting with the designer who fitted her for the last Oscar ceremony. I shake my head, the motion giving the young women standing in front of a deli pause, as if I'm somehow judging them. I wouldn't do that. But I am judging the situation in my family.

There are several things not allowed in my household. The main one is any negativity aimed at Valentina. The second is to speak up against an elder. It's been ingrained in me and perhaps in Valentina, as well. The difference is, I was berated into silence. Valentina knew how to use her words, so they were encouraged rather than dismissed.

"The cake," my mother says, remembering I'm still here. "Oh, the cake! That celebrity cake boss has agreed to make one with the groom proposing to Valentina in front of the fountain, just as Andres proposed to Valentina at that famous fountain in Paris."

"*Les fontaines de la Concorde*?" I offer. That's wonderful and coincidently where Andres promised to propose to me.

"Yes, that's the one."

Or two, I don't bother to explain.

I say nothing more. My entire family sees Valentina as a hero, the epitome of the American dream my grandparents, immigrants from Honduras, wanted for their children.

"Where are you?" Mom asks.

I'm barely listening at this point, but manage to answer and keep my emotions from my voice. "I'm driving."

"Where to? Valentina wants to see you. Are you available for lunch?"

She can't be serious. "No," I reply, speaking a little too fast. "I have a very busy day."

That's a lie. Today is one of those days set aside for catching up on emails and treating my staff to something nice.

"It's been years since you've seen your sister. What's so important you can't make a little time for her?"

Um, perhaps everything? I'd rather cover my naked body with honey and jump into the closest bear enclosure.

"Work. I told you, I'm very busy. I'll be in the office all afternoon."

"And now?" she asks unable to drop the subject.

"I'm on my way to Termini's Bakery," I say without giving it much thought.

"That's completely out of your way."

"I know," I reply.

"Then why are you going there? Why drive so far out of your way if you're too busy to see your family?"

"It's my favorite bakery," I tell her. "And I wanted to treat my staff to celebrate our success from last week's sales."

Mom doesn't sound excited about my good news. "A little early in the day for sweets, don't you think?" she says, instead.

"What—"

"This isn't a good time for you to gain weight," she snaps, the frustration in her voice as tangible as the cool March breeze flowing through my partially cracked window.

"You have a bridesmaid's dress to fit into and Valentina has enough to worry about."

"For goodness sake, Mom. How many ways can you slap me in the face?"

"*Alegria!*" My mother screams. "I called to arrange a lunch with my daughters. Not to be insulted."

I should hold my ground. But it's not my nature to cause problems. "I have a lot to do today," I respond, attempting to calm.

"No, you have a lot to do for everyone except your family, who should matter most," she adds, coolly. "Explain to me how people who spend the day filing and answering the phone are more worthy of your time than your adoring sister?"

"You want me to have lunch with Valentina," I say. "For what? So you can pretend Valentina and I are fine and this absurd wedding has no effect on me?"

By now, my mother is screaming. "What has gotten into you?"

Years of my family's constant badgering has taken its toll. I want to yell and curse, like I think I deserve to. But once more, I revert to being the good daughter. The one who fills out her family's tax returns, never raises her voice, and maintains her composure. It sounds stupid and weak, and it is, but it's the role I adopted long ago to survive.

I don't want to be cast aside and forgotten. I want a fighting chance at belonging and meaning something to someone. And no matter how pitiful and fragile my connection to my family is, and how imperfect and dysfunctional they are, aside from my career, they're all I have.

"I'm going to Termini's," I repeat. "Goodbye."

It's as much as I manage before disconnecting.

I'll receive an earful from her later and more from my aunts after she's done crying to them. There's crazy and then there's my family. Is there any wonder I feel so alone?

I rub my temple. Today was supposed to be a good day. My business is booming. I can't let my mother and Valentina take that away from me.

The breeze intensifies as I near the bakery, giving me enough of a chill to shut the window. By some miracle, I find a spot right in front of the store. I hop out, my small heels clicking onto the sidewalk and my thick braid slapping against my back.

My Infiniti SUV sits high, and I bounce every time I slip out. It normally gives my clients a giggle. I don't mind. They find it endearing.

I walk into the bakery and wave to Cara Maria, the young woman at the counter. She doesn't notice me. She's preoccupied with the man leaning over the counter. His stance appears relaxed, but there is a coiled energy and alertness lurking beneath, ready for anyone and anything.

As I venture further in, the display of cannoli and fresh baked goods catches my attention, albeit briefly. Something about the man flirting with Cara Maria is familiar.

My attention travels away from the display and fixes like glue on him, lingering longer than it politely should. Dark jeans cling around rather long and impressive legs, skimming the top of what appear to be expensive running shoes. He must be one of those men who run all the time through snow and rain, to maintain his strong, bordering on immense stature.

His musculature isn't that of a weight-lifter or someone I'm certain at one point religiously played football, but it is one that proclaims his athleticism and take-no-nonsense attitude. Broad muscles fill out the tight, dark blue T-shirt, warning those who would dare to start a fight that this is a man who won't go down without taking someone with him.

I know him, I think to myself, and it's not from the cover of some sports magazine. Familiarity and curiosity keep my interest. I can't see his face, but it must be some spectacle of beauty for Cara Maria to be so engrossed by it, and not everything else this man has to offer.

I wander closer, pretending to take in the pastries all while stealing a better look and hoping to catch sight of his profile. Somewhere in the back room, the other workers hustle, preparing what must be a large wedding order. I catch a hint of a four-tiered cake being carefully lifted and carried in the direction of the rear exit. A young man follows, hoisting several boxes in his long arms.

"Thank you," the woman at the counter tells the owner. She pays for an exorbitant number of cupcakes, her joy evident as she turns and hurries out.

"Tell her I said happy birthday," the owner calls after her.

He nods to me as the woman passes. I start to help her with the door, but the big guy flirting with Cara Maria beats me to the exit. "I got you," he tells her, opening the door wide.

I pause, waiting for him to turn around so I can finally see him, only to turn when the owner speaks. "What's it going to be for you today, Allie?"

"I'm not sure," I answer. In the time I turn, tall-dark-and-rock-hard ass cheeks is already back to Cara Maria's side. The owner rolls his eyes, likely annoyed by how much time Cara Maria is spending with him. I can't blame her. I'm practically gawking myself.

"My apologies," I tell the owner. "I think I'm going to need a minute."

"All right," he says, "let me know when you're ready."

He lumbers to the back, evidently to fill another large order. "Try this one," Cara Maria says to Mr. Sexy, her voice now more of a purr. "They're stuffed with whipped cream and messy, but they're tasty."

"Yeah?" the man says, his voice deep and gruff, like many of the blue-collar workers in the city.

"Oh, yeah," Cara Maria replies, a blush gathering on her face as she watches him chew. "They're real popular for bridal luncheons."

"Hmm," he says. "This is good. Can I have another?"

Cara Maria laughs. "Sure. But you better not leave here without buying something."

"I won't. Trust me." He seems to think things through. "Could you make a donut cake?"

"A donut cake?" Cara Maria questions.

I turn quickly to eye the eclairs when he finally seems to notice me. Who *is* this man?

"You know. Like a cake, except instead of layers of cake, there are layers of donuts," the man explains. "Guests can pull off one at a time and eat it."

"That sounds . . ." Cara Maria begins.

Genius, I think smiling. This curvy Latina body was shaped from plenty of tortillas and a few donuts.

"It's for my brother," he adds.

"Which one?" Cara Maria asks with a laugh.

"Good question," he says, laughing with her. It's a hearty laugh. One you expect from a man who laughs often and means it. It's another trait that's familiar, but for the life of me, I can't place how I know him.

"It's for Finnie. His fiancée wants him to have his own groom's cake." He holds out a hand, emphasizing each word. "The best part is, he gets to decide what kind. And my baby brother deserves a donut cake if any man ever did. Oh, and if you can sprinkle some of the donuts with bacon, that would be perfection on plate, if you know what I mean."

The name Finnie catches my attention.

"Bacon for your baby brother?" Cara Maria gushes. "That is so sweet."

"It's the kind of guy I am," he tells her. "Hey Cara, you sure you're married? I could really use someone who thinks I'm sweet right about now."

"I'm sure. But if I wasn't . . ." She gives him the eyes. "I'd sure take you up on your offer, Seamus."

"Seamus," I repeat a little louder than I intend.

"Huh?" He turns around and looks at me. Now, I know exactly who he is.

CHAPTER 5

Allie

The first time I met Seamus O'Brien, I was very young and certain he was wearing contact lenses. His eyes were more like sea glass, reflecting his humor and maybe a little hardship, too. As I did when I first met him, and every time after, I allow his gaze to draw me in, the color and clarity too perfect to be real, very much like the rest of him.

Like most of the O'Briens, Seamus has a reputation for dating many women. He doesn't have to do much, not with that face and body. He simply has to be himself. Perfect dark waves of hair frame features that belong on chiseled marble, as dark specks of facial hair pepper a jawline capable of sanding through redwood.

I smile and . . . not even a glimmer of recognition lights his alluring blue eyes.

Before I can offer him my hand, he turns his attention back to Cara Maria and her tiny and perky body.

"I think Dominick can do a groom's cake." She glances my way, annoyed that the attention he was showering her with was briefly stolen. "In the meantime, try some of our glacés and secs."

"Some what?"

She giggles in that cute way men like that I never quite mastered. "Tiny iced cakes and dry biscuits. Puff pastries," she clarifies when he makes a face at the "dry biscuits" reference.

"All right. For a minute there I thought you were trying to give me some nasty crap my family won't want."

"Would I steer you wrong?" she asks, her voice resuming that tinge of seduction.

Cara Maria has been married for about a year, I believe. Married or not, many women would enjoy attention from Seamus. Goodness. Most women would enjoy sharing the few feet of space that exists between us. Did I mention the man is *beautiful*?

Cara Maria's focus locks on Seamus as if only they exist and this is a romantic getaway, not a bakery with an atmosphere sweet and thick enough to lick. Like a seasoned figure skater, she lifts her hands elegantly displaying the tray of small glazed cakes delicately placed across a silver tray.

"Take your time and try as many as you'd like," she tells Seamus, her tone and stance impressively sultry for a woman wearing an apron dusted with flour. "You can't go wrong with anything you pick. I guarantee your sister will be happy. *Very* happy," she adds with a rather impressive bat of her lashes.

To me, she casts a glare and walks into the back room. I suppose it's her way of assuring she's marked Seamus as hers. Seamus doesn't seem to notice, latching onto the tray with as much enthusiasm as he had Cara's tiny figure.

"Thanks, Cara," Seamus says.

He starts to munch, the first pretty little dessert exploding in his mouth. White cream drips down his chin. He wipes it with the back of his hand. It's only then he realizes I'm still standing in front of him.

"Oh, hey. Sorry. You want one?" he asks. He tilts the tray so I can see the selection.

"No, thank you."

"You sure?" he asks. "They're pretty good. Messy, but the best desserts are."

I tilt my head. "You don't remember me, do you?"

He pauses. A small rectangular piece of cake covered in chocolate fondant and topped with a white bow hovers an inch below his mouth. Slowly, he lowers it, taking me in. "Um. Sure. One of the best nights of my life. Sorry I haven't called, my grandmother died and it's been real hard on me and my family."

"What?" I ask.

"My Grammie, she was real special—God rest her soul—and out of respect for her and all the memories we shared, I've been, you know, grieving and shit."

If memory serves, Seamus's grandmother died when we were in high school. "I don't think you understand," I begin.

"Yeah, I do, and it meant a lot. Sorry I didn't invite you to the funeral. It was a private thing. A family thing. But like I said, you are the best I ever had."

I blink back him, wondering exactly how many times he's used his dead grandmother as an excuse to blow off a one-night stand. I take another gander at him. My guess is probably a lot. "Seamus, it's me. Allie Mendes."

"Allie Mendes," I repeat when he doesn't reply.

His gaze shifts between me and the tray of desserts still waiting to be devoured by his evidently ravished stomach. "I know. How could I forget? You were really flexible and . . . stuff."

"Flexible?" I say.

He wipes his chin again, giving me the once over. "Did I say flexible? I meant hot. Real hot. Scorching hot. My sheets and everything else are still burning." He winces when he realizes he said more than he intended. "You know what I mean." He gives me the puppy eyes, since I'm obviously not attracted to him enough. "Like I said, with Grammie dying, it's been real hard on all of us. I wanted to call. But it's like every time I pick up my phone, I want to call Grammie." His turns up the puppy stare. "And you can't make calls to heaven."

I throw back my head, laughing. The sound is so genuine, I barely recognize it in myself. "Seamus, I assure you we've never slept together."

Confusion appears to rattle his brain. I can practically hear it bouncing along his skull like a ping-pong ball. "We didn't?"

"No," I assure him.

"Did we at least feel each other up?"

I cover my mouth, laughing and loving how it feels. "No."

He leans against the counter and looks at me again. "But we wanted to, right?"

My cheeks burn. Wow. He's a Neanderthal. More looks than charm and clearly more brawn than brains. I grin, certain I've gone insane, because I take his inappropriate and asinine response as a compliment. "I sold you your apartment building," I explain, attempting to let him and likely myself off the hook. "The one you and your brothers renovated."

He frowns, but otherwise says nothing.

"I also relisted it and sold it for three times its value."

It's as if I'm speaking to the row of pastries behind him instead of an actual human being. "I matriculated at your sister school," I offer, trying a different approach. "We attend the same church." Again, nothing. "I taught your younger brothers and sister Sunday school."

Finally, a light seems to go off in the very, *very* dim recesses of his mind. The heat index may be high, but there doesn't seem to be a lot of kindling in that fire.

"Oh," he says. "I know you."

"Good, I—"

"You're Valentina Mendes's little sister. She was *smokin'* and damn, what a body! Hey, she still single?"

So much for the compliment.

I try to smile through the fire burning a hole into my face. "It's funny you should ask. She's actually engaged."

"Good for her. Bad for the rest of us single bastards. But damn good for her."

I think I might actually vomit.

"Hey, you okay? You don't look good." He holds out his hand. "I mean that in the most respectful way possible." He shoves the tray of sweets in front of me. "Here, take one. A little sugar goes a long way. When someone gets hypoglycemic, it's not pretty. In fact, it's fucking ugly. Happens to my brother Angus all the time, which is why he's so damn fat. But that's a different story. I once saw a guy crash face first into a tray of spaghetti at a church social, because he waited too long to eat."

I reach for a small white cake with little pink flowers, thinking there may be something to his hypoglycemia theory. Goodness, I feel sick. "You mean Kevin Velasquez?" I ask.

"What?" he asks, doing a double-take.

"The 'guy' you're referring to is Kevin Velasquez," I clarify. "It was at the Christmas social. You were eighteen at the time. I think I was fourteen." I grimace. "And I was the one serving the spaghetti."

I was also the one cleaning Kevin up afterward, but I don't believe that's worth mentioning. To this day, I still feel bad for him.

"Oh, yeah. It was Kevin," Seamus says. "Poor sap."

At least we can agree there. "He seemed really embarrassed afterward," I say, remembering how he kept apologizing for ruining my dress.

Seamus doesn't seem to be listening anymore, focusing hard on his tray of sweets. It shouldn't disappoint me. But in a way, it does. It was nice speaking with a man close to my age whose home I'm not attempting to put under contract. It's an opportunity that doesn't come often and I've forgotten how wonderful it feels, even if he remembered Valentina long before he remembered me.

I start to tell him goodbye, but then he says something I don't expect. "That was nice of you to help Kevin like you did."

"Pardon?" I ask.

Seamus grins. He knows I heard him. But I wonder if he knows how stunned I am that he's still talking to me. "Even Father Flanagan was kind of like, 'oh, *shit*,'" he says.

"I mean, Father didn't actually say the words. I don't think real priests are supposed to curse. But if they could, I bet Father would've cursed that day. That was one hot mess Kevin made. He puked, too, didn't he?"

I make a face remembering. "Yes, all over the spaghetti and all over me when I tried to help him stand."

"I'm not surprised," Seamus says.

"I know," I agree. "Like you mentioned, he waited too long to eat."

"Not Kevin," he says, knocking me playfully in the shoulder. "I meant you trying to clean him and his mess. You were always doing something nice."

I smile a little, watching him pop another cake in his mouth. For as much as Seamus eats, he must work out like a fiend to stay in the shape he does.

"What about you?" he asks.

"Pardon?" I ask.

"*Pardon*? Did you seriously say 'pardon,' *again*," He laughs out loud, not caring who might hear. "Sweetheart, this is Philly. Not England or wherever the hell 'pardon' is used. I suppose you eat your cheesesteaks with your pinky pointing up."

"Only if the Eagles are down by seven for good luck."

"Yeah?" He smirks at my nod. "Spoken like a true fan. Mostly, I just swear at the TV and threaten to punch the ref in the face, but we all support our team in our own ways."

"In that case, I will very much continue to hold my pinky up during our most dire moments."

"And I'll continue to swear, because I owe it to the Eagles." He thinks about it. "And because I'm fucking good at it."

We laugh. Seamus tosses a rum ball covered with powdered sugar into the air and catches it in his mouth, a rather impressive if not sloppy feat. I point to the eruption of white powder across his jaw. "You have a little something there."

He points to his chin. "Here?"

I make a fanning motion with my fingertips. "Everywhere, if I'm being honest."

He removes a few napkins from the dispenser on the counter and swats at his face as if trying to put out a fire or possibly kill a mosquito. "Better?' he asks.

"Not by much," I admit. I point to a few spots that are more smeared than clean. "If you could just get, no, not there. No, that spot was clean. Yes. No. Ah, perhaps you should ask to use the restroom?"

"Nah, I don't need to go." He tosses what remains of the crumpled napkins in the garbage can and reaches for a clean bundle, handing them to me. "Help a fellow Eagles fan out, will ya?"

I take a step back. "I really shouldn't," I say, clutching the wad against my chest.

He cocks his head, likely wondering why I'm skipping away rather than closing in. I can't fault him. Women likely throw themselves at Seamus, hoping for a squeeze of his patable ass.

"Why not? You still mad at me for not calling you after our hot night of sex and sin?" he asks, winking.

I laugh, and against my better instincts, step timidly forward. As I dab his chin, it occurs to me how much I've laughed in the moments since first approaching him. It feels *good*, natural, and surprisingly peaceful.

"What's wrong?" he asks. "You nervous or something?"

I lower my chin, pausing my movements slightly. "Maybe I am," I admit. "I'm not one to randomly touch men."

"You randomly touched Kevin," he reminds me. "Even the nuns who worked with the homeless wouldn't go near him."

"That was different," I say, focusing on how the small whiskers of his chin scrape against the napkin. "Kevin was in distress."

"No. Kevin was covered in puke and marinara." He groans. "And there you were with a roll of paper towels. Had you been working the salad line you would have been spared and some shit-out-of-luck altar boy would've been stuck hosing Kevin down in the garden with the Virgin Mary looking on."

"I don't know about that," I tell him. My fingertips move across his jaw. The napkins provide just a small barrier between my skin and his. Although I shouldn't take advantage of this moment, I can't help but wonder what it would feel like to actually touch a man like Seamus.

Small lines crinkle the edges of his eyes and a bit of gray streaks along his temples, smoothing his tough exterior with a sense of refinement. If I recall correctly, Seamus is a highly in-demand carpenter who specializes in creating complex and intricate woodwork for the most prestigious homes in the area and restoring old mansions to their former glory. His fingers are deeply calloused, the skin along his palms rough. The physical demands of his job leave his hands like well-worn leather, but his face hasn't suffered a fraction. Each bit I fuss with appears as soft as his full lips.

"I think more people than you imagine would've helped Kevin out," I say, realizing neither of us has spoken."

"Can't say I agree with you on that one," Seamus says, angling his chin so he can better see me. "His own parents left his ass to get the car."

I try to pretend I don't notice him staring. "That's right. I remember. Poor Kevin."

I move to the other side of his face, laughing when I see the powder has somehow reached his earlobe. "How can a grown man make this much mess with one little rum ball?"

"It's a gift. Kind of like Kevin with the spaghetti."

I pull away when I find him frowning. "My apologies. Am I being too intrusive?"

"Intrusive?"

"Crossing a boundary," I explain. "Was I getting too close to you?"

He laughs. "I know what intrusive means, cutie. Believe it or not there's a brain to go with all this awesome manly brawn."

"I'm sorry," I say, backing away. "I wasn't trying to insinuate you're dimwitted."

He laughs again, this time harder. "Good, because I'm not." He watches me as I hurriedly toss the napkins into the small trashcan. "Oh, that's right, you're married. No wonder you're so skittish about touching me."

"Skittish?"

"It means jumpy, nervous," he adds with a wink

I cover my mouth, feeling I should set him straight, except Seamus's thoughts take him full speed ahead. "You married to that special needs guy, right? I must tell you that was real nice of you to look past his disabilities like you did. Most women wouldn't have given him a first date. Let alone promised him forever." He leans back on his heels. "You're a hell of a broad."

I barely keep my jaw from slacking open, stunned. "Are you referring to Andres Costas?"

"Yeah," he replies, as if he couldn't possibly mean anyone else.

I didn't think my day could get worse after my conversation with my mother, then along came Seamus O'Brien. "Andres doesn't have special needs."

"Sure, he does," Seamus replies. "It's nothing to be ashamed of. The little guy did try."

"He doesn't have special needs," I insist.

Seamus frowns, evidently confused. "Are you sure? If memory serves, he couldn't tie his own shoes."

Is it hot in here? No, it's just my flaming face. "He could tie his own shoes."

"No, he couldn't. He wore those Velcro pieces of shit forever."

"His mother special ordered them for him," I say.

"I'll bet," Seamus adds thoughtfully.

"But it's not because he couldn't tie his shoes," I stammer. "He would just forget, constantly frazzled and worried about making it to class on time so he could sit in the front row."

Seamus shakes his head. "I hate to break it to you, Allie, but there was more going on than that. He wore these giant shorts in gym class. They were practically pants. And if that wasn't bad enough, he tucked his shirt into said shorts. Whenever anybody would try to talk to him, he'd quote *Star Wars*, *Star Trek*, Star something. I didn't know what he was talking about. I felt bad about it and always offered him a piece of gum. He seemed to like that."

I should probably be grateful Seamus didn't shove Andres into a locker. Many a tough Philly boy had . . . along with a few tough Philly girls. "Andres is very intelligent and is a member of Mensa."

"Mensa?" Seamus repeats. "Oh, that's that smart people club, right? The one packed with virgins?"

I gasp, appalled. "I don't know about all of them being virgins," I add, feeling this awful need to defend Andres and perhaps myself. "But I assure you Andres didn't have any issues. He was just shy and socially awkward."

"If you say so. Either way, it was nice of you to marry the guy. God knows no one else was going to."

This is one of those moments in time that I should run, run far away, screaming with my arms flailing.

"You okay? You don't look good. No offense," he adds quickly.

"I didn't marry Andres," I admit.

"Good for you," Seamus says, pointing at me. "I always thought he was kind of an asshole. 'Cept calling a special needs guy an asshole just makes you sound like the asshole. Know what I mean?" He doesn't wait for me to answer. "Bastard owes me at least six packs of gum."

Seamus takes another long look at me. "What's wrong? Did I make if you feel bad? I wasn't trying to. If anything, it's a good thing you didn't end up with him. No. A *great* thing. You could've popped out a bunch of nerds quoting Star Trek shit. 'A long, long, time ago, in a galaxy far, far away.' Who the hell needs to hear that every day, all day? Not you, that's for damn sure."

"That's *Star Wars*," I clarify. "Not *Star Trek*."

"Whatever." He bites into a mini éclair, speaking through chews. "I'm telling you, God did you a favor. You're too cute to carry a kid for nine months only for that freak to slap elf ears or some other nerdy shit on him the second the cord's cut. As far as I'm concerned, you got lucky. Think of the loser who ended up with him."

"He didn't end up with the loser, Seamus," I tell him. I look up from staring hard at the peel and stick linoleum tile at my feet. "He's marrying Valentina."

He finishes off the éclair, swallowing hard, shock gathering along his features. "Valentina who?" he asks.

He knows who I'm talking about. "Shit," he says, when I don't bother to reply. "When did that happen? Last thing I heard, Valentina was judging that modeling show in Paris."

"Just recently. The wedding is in a couple of months," I mumble.

I don't know why I'm telling Seamus any of this. I've already been embarrassed enough. But who else do I have to tell?

"He's marrying your sister?" He scoffs when I nod. "I can't figure out who's the biggest asshole. Him or her."

I sigh. "Considering I'm one of the bridesmaids, my guess is that it's me."

"You're kidding? Why would you do that to yourself? If one of my brothers—never mind. They would never pull something that dirty on me." He looks at me quickly. "No offense."

I nod slowly, unable to find the words or the energy to keep our conversation going. I fiddle with my purse strap. "It was nice speaking with you, Seamus. Call me if you need anything."

"Where you going?" he asks when I turn away. "You didn't buy anything to eat."

I purse my lips, realizing he's right. I stop in front of the clear glass display at the center. I don't realize I'm making my way back to Seamus until he nudges me gently with his elbow.

"Look, I don't know what to say to make you feel better except that you're still better off. He was a shithead then and he's a bigger shithead now. And your sister—" He cuts himself off. "She shouldn't have done that to you."

I smile at how he censored his remarks about Valentina. Seamus doesn't know me and he's been nicer to me than anyone in a long while.

"You didn't remember me from the real estate venture I helped you through."

It's not a question. Simply a fact.

"Nope. Curran and Declan took care of it. They're more business-oriented. Me and Angus are more the physical labor behind the scenes kind of guys."

True. What he may not realize is there was a great deal of negotiation and back and forth with the other parties. It was one of the toughest sales I'd ever undertaken and among the lengthiest to complete. But that's not what Seamus remembers. Nor was it all those times we've crossed paths throughout our lives.

"But you remembered me with Kevin," I point out.

"No," he says. His smile isn't wide or playful, yet it lights his eyes in a way that stirs a smile of my own. "I remembered you being nice. People aren't nice anymore. Not as nice as they should be, anyway. You always were. That thing with Kevin, it's just the one I remembered first."

"Thank you," I say, my heart warming. He's right. The world could use more kindness.

He smirks. "So, you taught Finnie, Wren, Killian, and Curran Sunday school?"

I thought we were done speaking. I'll admit I'm happy to continue our conversation. "Yes. I did."

"That must've been a train wreck." He resumes his cake-testing duties, lifting a pretty vanilla cake with colorful sprinkles. "Be honest with me, how many times did you want to send them to hell? You can tell me. I won't say anything." His voice falls below a whisper as if sharing a delicious secret. "Between you and me, how many times did you ask the Archangel Michael to strike them down?"

I laugh, recalling all the times I had to separate his siblings from fighting with other children and each other. "Your family had a habit of getting into brawls. For a long time, they had a rivalry with the McElhanneys. It all came to a head when Georgie McElhanney destroyed Curran's papier-mâché version of Baby Jesus, right before the Christmas pageant."

"No shit," Seamus asks. "I can't fault Curran for that one. That has to be some kind of sin. It may have even been the eighth deadly sin if God had kept going."

"Maybe," I agree.

"Seamus," Cara Maria yells from the back. "The boss says we can do your donut cake."

"Cool," Seamus answers. He scrolls through his phone, jerking his chin in the direction of the almost empty tray. "I'm ordering all these. A hundred and fifty for the engagement party and about five hundred for the reception. The heart-shape works. I have a few bills for the deposit. Just let me know how much I owe you."

Cara Maria returns to the counter, feverishly writing out the order and clarifying the dates and times. She's not quite finished writing when Seamus drops a pile of twenties within her reach. It's been a pleasure speaking with him. But now that Cara Maria and all her loveliness is back, it's as if I no longer exist.

"It was nice seeing you again—"

"Oh, shit," Seamus says, cutting me off and looking intently at his phone. "I forgot about the bridal luncheon. Hey, Cara. Can you add fresh flowers to a display?"

"The decorator can make nice candy ones," Cara Maria answers. "Orchids, roses, whatever you want." She shoots me a dirty look, informing me I need to get going.

I back away slowly, recognizing my time with Seamus is over.

I'm almost to the door when the owner calls out to me. "Allie, did you decide what you want?"

Oh, yes. The reason I'm here. I return to the register, this time keeping some distance from Seamus, who evidently didn't notice me leave.

Somehow, I find my voice. "Two dozen mixed donuts, a few croissants, and one of each of the pastries in the circling display, please."

"You got it, sweetheart," he says. He walks to the front and starts filling the order when the doorbell chimes announcing another customer.

"Well, well, well, look who's here!"

Valentina's voice rings in like a chorus of bells. Except the chorus resides in hell and I'm being burned alive. For a moment, I can't breathe.

I don't have to guess my mother threw me under the bus. I turn around as I feel the color drain from my face. My mother and Valentina stand before me like twins. Creepy, evil twins, dressed in matching ponchos. Valentina's is red and likely Dior. My mother's is powder blue and likely not. Mom is smiling, seemingly pleased with herself. Valentina is smiling, too, feigning an innocence that left her long ago.

There's no escaping these women. I should know this by now.

Like Valentina, my mother is tall and statuesque. I was cursed with the midget genes on my late father's side. Where Mom has shoulder-length dyed black hair and light brown eyes, Valentina has long silky midnight hair almost to her elbows and eyes so green you'd swear saints hand cut them from emeralds.

Of course, because that's not unfair enough, it appears Valentina still weighs the same as she did in high school. She must not eat, or drink, or breathe. If it weren't for her cosmetically enhanced breasts she might look too thin and not like a goddess strolling through Mount Olympus.

She unwraps the poncho like a veil of red cashmere, revealing the plunging neckline of her blouse and giving a generous peek of her fantastic rack.

"*Damn*," Seamus mutters, looking up from his tray of goods to admire Valentina's magnificence. He may not have noticed me leave, but he certainly notices Valentina arrive.

Valentina smiles in that way she does when men stop to admire her, all the while pretending she doesn't notice or care.

"Alegria, aren't you going to say hello to your sister?" Mom asks, her expression as appalled as her tone.

I whip around, unable to face them. This is too much, too soon. "Save me," I whisper, praying to God and all the apostles.

"What?" Seamus mumbles, mid-chew.

Another creampuff explodes in his mouth, spilling the contents across his chin. I cover my face. "Save me," I repeat, wondering what I ever did to deserve this.

"*Alegria*," Mom says, her anger reflecting in each syllable. "Why are you ignoring your sister?"

I'm not ignoring her, I want to say. *I'm just blinded by her spectacular presence.*

"Allie?"

My gaze shifts to the doorway where Andres waits, appearing as blindsided as I feel.

My skin is on fire, creating a waterfall of sweat along my spine. He takes a cautious step forward, then another, stopping beside Valentina and taking her hand in his.

My gaze drops to their entwined fingers. This isn't happening. This *cannot* be happening.

An expensive black Merino coat covers Andres's small frame, giving him the broad shoulders he never managed on his own and the bulk he always longed for. His once out of control curly hair is now thinning and cut close to his scalp and his glasses are long gone.

I'm in a dark brown suit, the long skirt making me appear shorter. The kitten heels don't help. I dress conservatively in front of my clientele. They're older and don't like a lot of flash. But in front of Valentina, I resemble an 18th-century schoolteacher rather than a successful and respected professional.

I don't look like Valentina. I don't act like Valentina. I don't share her high I.Q., I never have. Which is why I wasn't good enough for Andres or my family.

"Hi," Andres says. He glances at Valentina apologetically, as if my presence will somehow inconvenience her.

Her red glossed lips widen into a satisfied smile. She knows she doesn't have anything to worry about. He belongs to her.

"Hello," I reply.

Valentina rushes to me, her speed and movements inhumanly graceful. She throws her arms around me like she would a long-lost friend, not the sister she hasn't spoken to in years.

She lifts me briefly, making a grunting sound as if I weigh a more than I do.

Following an uncomfortably long embrace, she holds me out at arm's length, staring down at me and asserting her apparent superiority. "It's so good to see you, Allie." Her face softens like she wants to cry. "Mom says you don't have a date for the wedding. But don't worry. I'm sure Andy and I will find someone willing to take you."

Andy? I slowly turn in Andres's direction. Lovely.

I suppose it could be worse. *I* could be *Andy*.

"Did you hear that?" My mother asks, beaming. "Your sister and Andy are going to find you someone, so you don't have to be so alone."

They wait, expecting me to thank them. I'd rather stab myself in the eye with Valentina's pitchfork.

I lift my chin, meeting my sister square in the eye. "I have a date," I reply.

"No, you don't," my mother immediately interjects, making me feel worse, because she's right.

I stand to my full height, ignoring how they tower over me, clinging with my teeth to whatever strand of dignity remains.

"Really?" Valentina asks. She tosses back her hair, fighting, it seems, to keep from full-out cackling. "And who might that be?

My breath leaves my lungs with an odd squeak as Seamus yanks me to him, pressing me into his large, firm body. His chin is smeared with cream, chocolate stains the front of his shirt, and he has something stuck between his teeth. That doesn't stop him from flashing a smile with what remains of his pearly whites.

"How's it going?" He smacks my ass and gives it a squeeze. "I'm Seamus. Allie's boyfriend."

CHAPTER 6

Seamus

Allie makes this choked, gurgling sound. Hmm. Maybe she needs a drink. She jumped pretty high when I squeezed her ass. Another few inches and I probably could have caught her in my arms. That would've been good for show.

Hey, she asked me to save her. I'm going to give it my all.

I grin at Allie's stunned face and offer her a wink. *You're welcome, baby.*

I turn my sights back on her family. I recognized Valentina right away. In general, I suck at remembering women, their names, their faces. Only the psychos stick with me, usually because I have to pick them out in a line-up.

Valentina is the kind of woman that is hard to forget. Her legs start roughly below a chin sharp enough to cut my finger on. She's aged two, maybe three months since I last saw her in high school. I'm guessing she's had work done. Whoever the doc was did a nice job.

Hot bod and a face men would kill to caress doesn't mean she gets a pass to dump on her sister. Holy shit. It's like her goal was to make Allie feel like crap the second she sashayed her long legs in here.

"He's *your boyfriend*?" Valentina asks Allie.

Valentina is making like she wasn't giving me the once over. Yeah, honey, I saw you.

"Um," Allie answers, looking to me for help.

Allie isn't that good of a liar. We'll have to work on that if we're going to pull this shit off.

I chuckle, my attention gradually drifting back to Valentina. "I get what you're saying. 'Boyfriend' doesn't sound right, does it?"

Valentina laughs softly like a saint, but her comment is straight up insulting. "It certainly doesn't," she says, like she's apologizing on Allie's behalf.

I laugh, too. More because it's taking a lot for me not to call her out on her bullshit. I know her type.

This is what's called getting into character. It's also called giving it to someone who really deserves it. I kiss the top of Allie's head. "I suppose *lover* is more accurate. Right, babe?" I don't wait for Allie to answer. Unless you count that odd noise she makes. "I was just trying to be respectful, seeing as how you're here with your mom." I wave to Mrs. Mendes. "How's it going Mrs. M.?"

If looks could kill, the glare Mrs. Mendes nails me with would have me six feet under, begging her not to shatter what remains of my broken body. I hang tight to my smile and focus on Valentina, watching the way she takes another gander at the merchandise. I almost stop to flex since she's no longer trying to hide it. Except that will mean taking my hands off Allie and I don't think she'll keep her feet if I let go.

"You're lovers?" she asks, raising her eyebrows and her puckered lips in challenge.

"Yes?" Allie says looking back at me. Shock and fear flickers across her bright brown eyes. I don't have to know her to guess she's ready to tear out the door.

Uh, uh, uh, Curves. We've got ourselves a job to do.

I stroke my finger along her chin, leaving a small trail of powdered sugar. I'm half tempted to lick it off her face. But as much as I want to play up this little scenario, I don't want to risk Allie kicking me in the face. It would blow our cover for sure.

"*You're* seeing *him*," Valentina scoffs, her voice low, but not so low I can't sense her amusement.

Wow. I didn't remember Valentina being this bitchy in high school, but I never really knew her. She was too busy flirting with all the boys whose families came from money. When I dropped out of high school at fifteen to help support my family, she'd walk past me on the street and pretend I didn't exist.

I chuckle. "Yeah. Didn't you hear me the first time?"

That pale color Allie developed when her family walked in vanished when I smacked her ass. I give her round cheek another squeeze. It seems to be working to bring a healthy flush back on her face. What can I say? I'm a helluva guy.

Allie is one of the good girls. I didn't remember her when I first saw her. But that spaghetti incident? You don't forget something as epic as that. Kevin what's-his-face's family probably brings it up every Christmas. Can't blame them. My family would do the same thing if it was one of us. Hell, it might have ended up being the Christmas card that year. We're like that though, sending pictures of us mooning everyone wearing elf hats. It's better than little Johnny dripping snot down Santa's lap cards we get from our cousins.

"I didn't expect this," Valentina says, resuming her supermodel pose, or whatever the hell she's trying to work here.

"Neither did I," her mother says, narrowing her eyes when she sees my hand hasn't left her daughter's rear. "I also didn't expect to see my daughter groped in public."

Allie looks at me at a loss for what to do. *It's okay. I got you.*

I look into her eyes, like only she exists. "Sorry. Allie is just so hot and sexy, I can't seem to keep my hands to myself." Take that, Mamacita.

"Alegria," Mamacita says. "Where did you meet him and why didn't I know about him?"

"Um," Allie says looking back at her mother. "I sold him an apartment."

I think she wants to say more. But she seems to be struggling to speak so "more" doesn't exactly come.

Her mother's scrutinizing gaze bounces from Allie to me. I don't think she likes me. That's weird. Old ladies in powder blue usually do. "Who are you?" she asks. "You obviously know me, but I've certainly never met you."

I can see where Valentina gets her jovial personality. "Sure you have," I tell her. "I'm Seamus O'Brien. My family and yours have attended the same church for years." She looks at my hand like she wants to bite it off at the wrist, then use it to spank my ass for touching her daughter's.

"Oh," Mamacita says, distaste puckering her lips. "You're Aileen O'Brien's son."

The one whose husband died in his mistress's bed. The one with all those children. The one who was made a fool of. These comments and more go without saying, but I sense them in her condescending tone.

I bristle. You don't mess with my Ma. You just don't. I keep my head in the game for Allie's sake and maybe for a little payback, too. "That's right. Aileen O'Brien who singlehandedly raised seven kids and sent them all to Catholic school."

"Not all of them," she says.

For someone who claimed she didn't know me, she sure remembers me and Angus dropping out to keep our brothers and sister in school, and eating more than soup from a can. I smile. "You're right, and now here I am, dating your daughter."

Funny thing, she doesn't seem to like that one bit. "Where did you meet?" she bites out.

"At a bar," I say, only to have Allie cover her face.

"A *bar*?" Mamacita asks, appalled.

"I thought you said you sold him his apartment?" Valentina says, enjoying her mother's grilling behind of mask of well-meaning concern.

"I did," Allie says, her voice growing soft. It's like her family has some kind of superpower over her, capable of making her quiet and meek.

Allie's gaze wanders to the old guy beside Valentina. "No, you sold me the building, baby," I remind Allie. I nuzzle her neck. Just a little to remind her and her family who I'm supposed to be here.

I ease away from Allie slowly, like I had to force myself to stop and drop my voice another tone. "You also sold it a couple years later for a nice chunk of change."

"Really?" Valentina asks. "Tell me more about it." She looks at Allie. "I'm intrigued."

I'll bet you are, sweetheart. Allie doesn't know where to start so, I start for her. "I ran into her at O'Malley's pub a few weeks ago. I always thought she was cute and finally worked up the nerve to ask her out. She didn't want to at first, something about being busy with work."

I look at Allie. "With work," she semi-agrees.

It's the best she can do, so I keep going. "We met at Giovanni's for wings. I wanted to keep it casual and so did she." I laugh, like I'm remembering our very awesome first date. "I wasn't sure it would work out. I mean, I remembered her from church and how she taught Sunday school to my little brothers and sister. I thought she was nice. I just never knew how nice."

I clutch her closer to me when I realize she's slipped slightly away from my grasp. Uh, Uh. I'm on a roll now. "I hadn't planned on another date. I also didn't think we'd close the place down. Now . . ." I make eye contact with her again. "I can't picture my life without her."

Allie blinks back at me and that's about it. The hell? I'm putting on a decent show here. But this woman . . . yeah, we're going to have to work on the lying.

"I take it you'll be at my wedding?" Valentina asks, taking a step forward. "And the rehearsal dinner, as well?"

I flash a big grin. "Damn right. I'm not letting this princess go." I do a double take when the old guy adjusts his weight. "Oh, hey, sorry, sir. I didn't mean a blow you off. Hope you're okay with me dating your daughter."

There goes Allie, making another squeaky noise. It would be cute if it didn't sound so panicked and if she didn't look like she wanted to die. She buries her face in my chest. "That's Andres," she mumbles.

I think I misheard. "You want us to undress?"

She spits the next few words out through her teeth. "No, *precious*," she replies. "I said that's Andres. Valentina's fiancée."

I burst out laughing. "No, shit. Damn. Age was a real bitch to you, wasn't she?"

Sometimes my family and I say things that are little out of line. "Off-the-cuff," some people might say. "Fucking rude," even more will mutter. But that's what makes us *us*, and them *them*, and why we get into fights as much as we do.

Don't get me wrong. We're a lovable, if not sane, bunch. Another day, I might feel bad. Today isn't one of those days. This guy was better off when I thought he had special needs. Now, I just think he's a little bitch.

He frowns. So does Allie's mother. Valentina looks annoyed. Not that I insulted her husband. More like I pointed out what everyone is probably thinking and what she'd rather ignore.

"The stress of my job takes its toll," he snaps. "But it's given me more money than I can spend in a lifetime."

"That's nice," I reply casually. I suppose he wants me to be impressed. If so, it's going to take more than money.

Andres scoffs. "I don't know why I'm wasting my time speaking to you. You're a shell of a man, pathetic at best."

"You think *I'm* pathetic?" I smirk, trying not to crack up. "I don't think Stephen Montessori would agree with you on that one, Andy."

A fresh coat of red flushes his cheeks. Stephen Montessori shoved Andres into a gym locker. I made Stephen let him out. Considering what he pulled on Allie and how he's talking to me now, I should've left him inside. In fact, I should demand repayment for all that gum I gave him to shut him up about Star Wars. Damn. I bet this nerd would beg for a threesome with that green chick from Star Trek if she was available. Nothing against green chicks.

Andres fights to regain his composure after a quick glance at Valentina and his future mother-in-law, using the only weapon in his arsenal. "Insults are all you have. Unlike me, who's made a fortune."

The money thing is getting old, but if he wants to go there, let's go. "You really think you're the only one in this room who's made his share of bills?" I return to stroking Allie's side, this time slower and more like she's naked in bed with me, instead of clothed and standing on linoleum. How about that? She has some seriously nice curves. "This woman handled all my real estate ventures. Thanks to her, I have a few mil to brag about myself, if I was the bragging type." I shrug. "But those who brag about money are those who have nothing else to brag about. No offense," I add. It's what I tell him, even though I want to offend him all over the place.

He smiles with as much warmth as Mamacita. "Is that so? I would love to see your portfolio."

"I bet you would. It's big. Real big if you hear what I'm saying. Thing is, I don't have to whip it out and compare sizes. There's no comparison. Isn't that right, babe?" I ask Allie.

She gives me a look that tells me she understands we're not talking about stocks or whatever the hell. That's right, sweet cheeks. You found the best man, right here, to save you.

My gaze flickers briefly to Valentina who is watching our interaction closely. I haven't quite figured her out. But anyone who steals a man away from her sister the way she did, feels the need to be on top and stay on top. We'll get to her in time. Right now, it's all about Andy Poo or whatever she calls him when she's pretending to like the five seconds he gives her in bed.

"You may claim to be more and have more, but I doubt it," he snaps.

I laugh. I almost feel sorry for him. Almost. "Allie doesn't doubt it. Believe me, I've given her loads to compare."

Andres pales, only to scowl when my glaze flickers toward Valentina. He thinks I want her or envy him for having a woman all men supposedly want. "Considering who you slipped a ring on, it seems you have a lot more to prove to anyone stupid enough to listen." I point at him and make a clicking sound with my tongue. "See you at the wedding shower."

I ignore the "How dare you?" remark from Mamacita and the high-pitched gasp that's sadly from Andres.

"Hey, Cara Maria? You have our stuff ready?" I call to her.

She and the owner were watching our interaction with steadfast interest, if not downright shock. They exchange glances. For a moment, I think Cara Maria is going to rat us out, but she plays along, as does the owner.

"You're all set." She looks at Allie and smiles. "See youz next week."

I release Allie and drop a few bills to pay for her order. It's good for show, and thankfully, she doesn't stop me.

"Ready, sweet cheeks?" I ask, giving Allies' ass another pat.

She practically stumbles out the door. I turn around to her family and grin. Oh, yeah. We've got this.

CHAPTER 7

Seamus

Allie doesn't answer, more or less allowing me to lead her out the door. Her mother mumbles something about not behaving properly in public and something about a fitting. Allie says nothing. I don't think she means to ignore her mother. Like the owner and Cara Maria, she's still in shock. Except Cara Maria recovered a hell of a lot faster.

I follow Allie to her car, a white Infiniti SUV, opening the door for her and then jogging to the other side.

I wait for her to let me in. My truck is two cars behind hers. But I'm trying to make it like we showed up together. It would work better if she lets me in. I knock on the window, pointing to the bakery box I'm holding. The defeat marching across her face like toy soldiers makes me worry she isn't going to let me in. But then, all at once, the locks deactivate.

I carefully place the box on the floor in the back and hop into the front, worried she might lock my ass out. I'm not saying she's terrified or anything, but she's not the same woman who was checking me out while wiping my face. Yeah cutie, I noticed.

My back relaxes into the seat. Whoever she had in here last had long legs like me. I easily slip in, waving to her family, who continue to watch us from inside the store.

Allie pulls away, her gaze straight ahead, driving forward like I'm not even there. "So, what's the plan?" I ask. "You want to drive around until they leave and then you can just let me off back in front of the store?"

I almost get whiplash for how fast she cuts the next corner. She jets down the street, slamming her SUV into park behind a fast food place that has seen better days and likely a few robberies.

Allie is breathing kind of fast. I'm not counting or anything, but that shit doesn't look natural. She's not pale. Not dying. No . . . what's a good word for it? Stable. That's it. She's stable, not much more than that.

She points at me, looks away, and points again. "You grabbed my ass."

"Yeah, a few times," I agree.

I'll admit, I didn't expect her to start off with that. I also didn't expect her to look so pissed. I cock my head, confused.

Her skin goes from pink to red and back to pink like a strobe light. Impressive and freaky, but I don't think she's doing it on purpose. Again, she points, leaving me with the impression she wants to gouge my eyes out with that finger.

"You grabbed *my ass*," she repeats, this time, louder.

"It was either that or kiss you," I say. "But since we'd just met, I thought the ass-grabbing was more polite."

"More polite?" she repeats.

Christ, I can practically smell her blood boiling. "Yes?" I ask, since I'm no longer sure.

Her eyes fly open and she looks at the giant burger sign as if it can somehow help her.

When she finally turns back to me, she isn't any less pissed. "Why did you? . . . How could you? . . . What were you thinking?"

I frown. "You make it sound like this whole thing was my idea."

"That's because it was!" she screams at me. "You pretended to be my boyfriend. *My boyfriend,* who I'm taking to the wedding luncheon, the rehearsal dinner, and the wedding. God Almighty, Seamus. What did you do?"

"You told me to save you," I remind her, speaking slowly. "But now you have to save me, too."

"I beg your pardon?"

Wow. It's like her voice has lost all of its softness and only hysteria remains. Maybe I should have kissed her. She has some nice lips. I'll bet she's really good at it.

"Remember Finnie and Wren?" I ask, forcing myself to focus. "They're getting married. And from what I've seen, my brother Declan is close to getting engaged." I unsnap my seatbelt, getting comfortable since I anticipate a long chat. "I'm getting a lot of crap about getting old, being single, and not having any kids. Believe it or not, it's like my entire family thinks I can't get anyone classy."

"Oh, I believe it," she replies.

Her voice is quiet, but less hysterical. Hey. I'll take what I can get. "I told them I had someone to bring to all the events, the luncheons and whatever. Someone without a prison record, you hear what I'm saying?" I pause, fearing the worst. "You don't have a prison record, do you?"

She shakes her head slowly.

"Okay, good. You seem real nice, too. So, I say it's a win-win for both of us."

"You're insane," she says, and that's pretty much it.

"Hey. This was your idea."

"It was not!"

She's back to yelling, but she catches herself and shakes out her hands the way women do what they can't handle a problem. I have to say, in her defense, I am an extraordinary specimen of male.

"You told me to save you," I remind her, yet again. "Your family walked in. You lost your mind and you begged me to save you. No offense, Allie, but the least you can do is say thank you."

"I was talking to God," she whimpers.

I stretch out my arms. "Looks like God sent me, instead."

She turns slowly, facing the graffiti lined brick wall. The edges are crumbling and Dukane loves Latifa is sprayed in giant pink letters. Hey, I think I know them.

She leans forward, her face falling into her hands as she makes that odd squeaking noise she made back in the bakery. I give her some time, wondering if I should text Dukane and see if him and Latifa are still together.

I reply to a few texts. Mr. Robson likes the woodwork I did in his home office so much, he wants me to redo his library while he and his wife are on vacation. I text him back and set up a time. When I look up from pocketing my phone, Allie is still right where I left her, face buried and all.

"I suppose we should establish some rules," I suggest, thinking I've given her enough time.

She lifts her head. "Rules?" she asks.

"Yeah. Rules. Like no groping below the belt, unless you want me to and maybe some over the sweater fondling in case of an emergency."

"Please explain to me what kind of emergency warrants me being fondled by you over my sweater."

Damn, she's testy. "It could happen. You want to come across as convincing, don't you?" I give it some thought. "I was thinking that maybe for the rehearsal, you can wear an extra pair of panties beneath your skirt."

"For what?" she asks, not letting me finish.

"To subtly pass me to me under the table," I say. "Maybe in front of Andy. I'll clutch them against my chest and give you a wink. Yeah. That'll work."

"*Why?*"

"Because that's what couples who can't keep their hands off each other do."

She blinks back at me. "I take it this is something you've done yourself?"

"Oh, hell no," I admit.

"Then who are these magical couples you're referring to?"

"I never claimed to know any." I drum my fingers. "But I think I might have seen it a movie once."

"Really?" she asks. "Did this movie have a horny plumber who 'accidently' walked in on the panty removing twosome?"

I perk up. "How did you know?"

"Oh, God."

I laugh. "Yeah, that's what she said."

Oddly enough, Allie doesn't laugh with me. "Fine. We don't have to do the extra panty bit. But we do have to make it believable."

She sighs, sad, but in a way that makes me think she's seeing things from my side. "You need me," she says.

"And you need me, too," I remind her.

"Yes. I do." It seems to hurt her to admit as much. It makes me sad. Like I said, she's always been nice. She deserves some niceness in return, or at least some support to get through the crap her family is putting her through.

"Come on, cuteness," I say. "I'm not so bad. Think of me as your new best friend."

Her eyebrows pucker. She shouldn't look so pretty, but she pulls it off just fine. "My new best friend? You want to be friends with me?"

"Why wouldn't I? You've probably spent your life helping people out. People like poor Kevin and probably some others who don't deserve it." I mean Valentina and Andres, though I don't come out and say it. Still, she seems to know. "For once, let someone help you out." I smirk. "Let someone save you."

"Someone like you?" she questions.

She's back to looking the way she did when we first started speaking. Pretty. A little shy. And mostly kind.

"Someone exactly like me," I agree.

I eye her from long braid to funky boots. "You're hot, Alz. But all that hotness has frozen over beneath too much hair and enough layers of clothing to cover a hut."

"You think I'm hot?"

Of all the things she could have said and could have down-right smacked me for, that's the one thing she picks up on. I briefly wonder why. She must know she's attractive. Doesn't she?

"Yeah," I say, my confusion as evident as her doubt.

I frown when she dips her head. Holy shit. This woman doesn't get how pretty she is, which means she doesn't know how sexy she is, either. No worries. She has me now. We'll help each other out, and maybe, just maybe, I can help her tap into her inner panty-peeling seductress locked away in that castle of insecurity. Look at me sounding all metaphorical and shit.

I lean close and tug her long braid. She glances up. "I'm about to tell you something that will probably offend you, and may be slightly inappropriate."

"You?" she asks. "I don't believe it for a moment."

I don't know Allie well, but I get the feeling she's being sarcastic.

I chuckle. "In order for people to believe that we're together, we have to do something about all this."

"All of what, exactly?"

"Nothing major, just your clothes and hair."

"Just my clothes and hair? Really? And tell me, Seamus, what exactly is wrong with the way I dress? It's professional, neat, and expensive attire."

"You're successful. I get it and that's a good thing," I say. "We're going to need to drop a few bills on new clothes. The hair, I know someone who can fix it."

She strokes her long braid as if she can somehow protect it from my evil clutches. "You don't understand. My hair is wild."

"That's a good thing. The wilder the better."

"It defies gravity," she says, as if I'm somehow missing the point. "The only way to keep it neat and under control is to braid it." She speaks faster when it becomes clear I'm not budging. "I don't see anything wrong with keeping it the way it is."

"I do. You look like a Mormon and not the good kind. I mean the cult kind. The one with multiple wives and three hundred kids. The kind that make us Irish look infertile.

Seriously, Allie. You're sexy and everything. But if you told me you're number four of six sister wives, I'd believe you, based on what you're wearing."

"I represent a great deal of elderly clients," she fires back defensively. "If I don't dress a certain way, they might not take me seriously."

"I'm not telling you to change the way your dress in front of your clients."

"Oh, good," she says.

"I'm just telling you to change the way you dress around me."

She twists her entire body to better see and possibly better yell at me. "Excuse me?"

"Oh, and my family," I add. "They're never gonna believe that I fell for you dressed the way you are."

"Would you prefer me in a G string and tassels?"

"Yeah," I admit.

"I may have to kill you," she says.

Believe it or not, it's not the first time a woman has threatened me with death. "I'm only saying my family would believe me dating a stripper over you. I'm not saying you have to be over the top with tube tops and miniskirts—"

"Good, or else I'd have to remind you this isn't the 1980s."

"But you do have to change what you have on," I jerk a thumb behind me, ignoring that the bakery is nowhere near where I'm pointing. "I don't think we pulled off what we needed to pull off with your family. But if you start dressing and acting like you're really into me, they're going to believe it. And better yet, my family will believe me."

"You're asking a great deal," she says. This time, she's the one eyeing me up and down.

I smile. "You asked first."

"I was asking God," she reminds me.

"God was busy, so he sent one of his best-looking angels. That's me, in case you're wondering," I add when she just looks at me. "So, from now on, consider me your very own hot-as-sin guardian angel."

She shoots me a look that says she might actually murder me. I'm familiar with that look. Believe it or not, I get it a lot.

"Seamus, I appreciate what you tried to do at the bakery. But I don't think this is the right course of action. My family is rather difficult, but they're not stupid. I don't see how we'll pull this charade off."

"I told you, we don't have to do any over the sweater action unless it's an emergency." I'm trying to make her laugh. This thing's not so bad. Like I said, we can help each other out.

The corners of her cupid lips lift when she realizes I'm just messing with her. Her reaction tells me two things: she doesn't want to kill me *yet,* and that she realizes I may be on to something. I like to rag on people to the point where some may think I'm dumber than dirt. I'm not, and if we play it right, it'll buy us time *and* get our families off our backs.

"How come you need me as much as you do?" I ask her.

"What do you mean?"

"I mean, why don't you have a man? How come you're not married? Why haven't you squeezed out a few kids?"

"I could ask the same of you," she says.

"For starters, I don't have a vagina."

She sighs. Maybe she's getting tired of my jokes. It's a damn shame, there's plenty more to come. I shrug. "I haven't found anyone."

"Without a criminal record?" she offers.

I open my mouth to argue, but she does have a point. "My taste in women might have something to do with it," I confess. "But I like the type. Not the kind that comes after me with knives and shit," I add quickly. "But the kind who aren't afraid to let loose."

She tilts her head, listening closely. "You mean, women who feel free to express themselves and not fear what others may think?"

"I meant in the bedroom, but I suppose that works, too."

"Have mercy," she says.

"Okay, your turn. How come you're not married with a family and everything?"

It takes her a long time to answer. When she finally does, I could kick my own ass. I didn't mean to ask something that would cause her pain. Except, that's what I end up doing.

She meets me square in the face, shame and sadness darkening her large, pretty eyes. "Because I was supposed to marry Andres. He's the only boyfriend I've ever had."

"Ever?" I ask. There I go again, saying something that maybe I shouldn't. But I don't get it. Allie is smart and nice. She's also gorgeous, which should go without saying. Except women like Allie never believe they're as beautiful as they are.

"Ten years is a long time to commit to someone and simply walk away. Too many years are spent loving and dreaming together." She looks at the decrepit wall. Unlike me, I bet she thinks Dukane and Latifa never made it to the altar. "I'm sorry. I don't expect you to understand."

"You're right. I don't."

She returns her focus to me. I think she expected me to reassure her and to tell her I can relate. If so, she's wrong.

"I can't remember being with a woman more than a handful of weeks. But that's how we O'Briens are." What I say still holds true for my extended family. Not so much for my brothers. Now, it's just me. It was fine when we were young, going from party to bar to party with a good-looking woman attached to our side. But when everybody started settling down before I was ready for it, it started to look pathetic, instead of a young guy sowing his wild oats.

"You seem bothered by it," she says quietly.

I'm not dumb. Neither is Allie.

I don't like where our conversation is headed, so I switch the focus back to her, where it rightfully belongs. "I get that you were with Andres for a long time and having him dump you to marry your sister is all kinds of fucked up. But have you tried to date other men?"

"I have. It took me a long time." She rolls her eyes. "I had trust issues, as you can imagine. When Andres confessed he'd fallen for Valentina, like a fool, I wanted to believe it wouldn't last." Her attention drifts from me and somewhere she shouldn't go. "But like everyone else, he fell hard and kept going."

She tries to swallow down what she's feeling, but pursing her lips is as much as she manages. "I would have given Andres time to sort through his feelings, but when he admitted he had sex with her, I knew he was lost to me."

She shakes her head, squinting her eyes. "I'm sorry. I'm saying too much."

She is. Especially since we just re-met. I don't know Allie well. But someone who tells me as much is she just did, is someone who's had no one else to tell.

"As I was saying," she begins. "I dated a few men, but none of them went past a few dinners. So instead of focusing my energy on dating, I focused on my real estate business."

"I'm going to fix you," I say, cutting her off.

"Pardon?"

"I'm going to make it so Andres cuts off his own balls for letting you go." I lift my palms. "I'm not saying you're going to steal him back. Two wrongs don't make a right. Not to mention, you should sue his ass for wasting ten years of your life."

"I don't think I understand."

"I'm going to fix everything holding you back," I say. "Starting with your clothes and your hair. You're going to be so desirable when I'm done with you, men will be shoving me out of the way just to bask in your hotness."

From what I know of Allie, she's either going to demand I get out of her ride so she can run me over or run away screaming. I don't want her to do either, so I try to make her see I'm only here to help. "I don't mean to be insulting. But it's like you're a caterpillar who's cocooned herself for too damn long."

"A caterpillar?"

At least she's paying attention. "Yeah. Time to stick your head out and sprout the wings. Time to break free."

She glances down, appearing to give my words some thought. When she looks up, she's not exactly smiling. No worries. I know I have her. "You'll be my date to the wedding and the events Valentina has planned?"

"Yup."

"And I'll be yours to your family functions?"

"You got it, baby."

Her voice softens, and while she hesitates, she's starting to like the idea of sprouting those wings. "And you'll help me with my confidence so I can meet someone deserving?"

"I promise," I assure her.

"Very well," she says, nodding. "In exchange, I'll help you with your issues."

"Huh?"

She crinkles her brow. "Seamus, did you ever stop to think that perhaps the reason you're single and childless is because you're doing all the wrong things? Perhaps you could use some direction to remedy whatever faults you possess, and mistakes you've committed, that have kept you from a more fulfilling life?"

"What do you mean? There's nothing to fix." I flex for her, pointing to the mountain of muscle that erupts from my bicep. "Honey, this is perfection. You don't mess with perfection."

She nods thoughtfully. "Very well. We'll work on that, too."

I'm not sure what she means. I let it to go for now and offer her my hand. "So, we have a deal?"

Her hand slips across my skin as she clasps it. "Deal."

"Good." I say the word slowly, noting how soft and warm her skin feels against mine. I shrug it off, thinking I was just cold. "Now, let's get back to the fondling above the sweater rule. . ."

CHAPTER 8

Allie

Seamus picks me up later that week at my townhouse. It's taken several lunch dates and rounds of texting back and forth to get me to this point. I closed on a multimillion-dollar home a few months ago that wasn't as intense as my "Operation Bust Your Ass Out of the Fucking Cocoon," as he calls it.

I answer the door wearing a teal blouse and dark slacks.

"Are you meeting a client?" he asks, his extraordinary blue irises taking me in from my somewhat contained hair to perfectly respectable shoes.

"No," I reply. He follows me into the foyer as I remove my coat from the hall closet. "You told me to free my schedule today." I look down at my clothing thinking perhaps I need a necklace or scarf. "Should I accessorize?"

"Please don't." He makes a face, as he often does, when he feels he said something offensive. For all Seamus is rather abrupt, he's not cruel. "You look nice. Respectable."

"That's exactly what I was going for."

My glee fades when he makes another disappointed face. "Yeah, we have to work on that," he adds.

I'm not certain I know what he means, although we've had several conversations about the way I dress. I've yet to

71

convince him that my clients prefer more professional and less flashy attire. I attempted to compromise by offering to buy shoes with tassels.

I meant it as a joke. That's not how Seamus took it.

"Women should never wear tassels on their shoes. Ever," he told me. "And if you buy that shit, I'll soak them with gasoline, burn them to ash, and put the remains out with holy water. No offense."

I take in all 6 feet and 200 pounds of him. I only know the measurements of his physique because he's told me more than once. Some say it's his favorite topic of conversation. At first, I thought he was simply obnoxious. After a few encounters, I determined he has every right to be confident. Now, I find it strangely endearing. Seamus is who he is and makes no apologies for it. It's something to be admired and something I wish I had.

Today, he's in a long-sleeved navy t-shirt and a dark brown, comfortably worn aviator jacket. His jeans look identical to all the ones he's worn since I've known him, only darker. I only know this because I may have admired his legs once or twice, and perhaps his waistline when he stretches. A woman can't help herself. His "V," the glorious space that hovers between his waistline and groin, practically blinded me with its jaw-dropping perfection.

"Something wrong?" he asked, when he caught me ogling him like I very much wanted to have a lick.

Don't you worry your pretty little head about it, big boy, I wanted to say. "You look cold," I said, instead. No. He looked hot. He always does. Before I could embarrass myself further, I shut my mouth and pretended that I'd forgotten to call a client.

There's no possibility between Seamus and me. I'm not the typical woman he dates or someone he'd stop to glance at.

"Can I be honest with you?" he asks.

I turn around in the middle of fastening the buttons of my dark brown coat. It's cold, considering it's almost April. "I would expect no less," I say, smiling.

My attempt at humor goes over his ridiculously luscious full head of hair. "You're trying on clothes. Don't you have, like, a sweatshirt and sweatpants, maybe some high heels? Like, real high heels? Not the kind of shoes my niece will be sporting as a flower girl."

"I like my shoes," I say. I tug on the pant leg to give him a better look. "They're booties: cute and practical."

He leans a shoulder against the wall as I shut the closet. "The only cute booty you should be showing off is yours."

"I . . ."

Before I can enjoy what I interpret as a compliment, he moves on. "And what the hell did I say about practical, respectable, and demure? You were supposed to be taking notes."

And I did, at our first lunch together and practically every get-together following that. I groan, begrudgingly remembering what should now be our official mantra. "Practical, respectable, and demure won't get me laid." I mutter.

"Won't get you laid by the *right* guy," he clarifies. He holds out his hands in desperation. "Baby, I'm doing this for you. I want you to get the kind of man who doesn't need a little blue pill to get going or help changing his Depends. You want that, too. Don't you?"

"I do." I adjust the sleeves of my long wool coat. "I realize you think I need help in the fashion department, among other things. But, must I point out that sweatpants and high heels don't go together."

"You wear clothes you can slip in and out of easily, and the shoes are shoved into a bag."

"Shoes? As in more than one pair?" I ask.

"Sure. My sisters-in-law—and Wren, who they have to drag cursing and screaming—always bring at least two pairs of shoes when they shop."

"You know a lot about what women do," I point out.

He shrugs. "Not really. I just pay attention."

"I can see that." Nothing seems to slip past Seamus, even in those moments where it seems he's not paying attention.

"You have a sundress, or some shit you pull off easily?"

I glance in the direction of the door. "I do, but it looks like it could snow."

"That's why God invented the coat," he says, tugging on the lapels of my wool coat and coaxing my smile out.

I do a quick change into a spaghetti strap sundress and shove my feet into a pair of kitten heels. "It's freezing," I say, when we rush out to Seamus's F-150.

"No worries. I'll crank the heat. Trust me, you look better already."

He holds open the door for me. I didn't expect his chivalry to continue. If anything, I imagined he'd be too busy dragging his knuckles along the sidewalk, given the comments that shoot out of his mouth. And his texts? They were practically grunts. I was more specific, of course. His words were more to the point and seemingly between long admirable looks at his reflection. But here he is, watching out for me.

He pulls away from my street. I live in the historic part of Philadelphia where parking is a daily struggle, but the beautiful buildings make up for it.

We don't stay in my neighborhood for long. Seamus takes us all the way to Kensington into a neighborhood that deteriorates before my eyes. Trendy little stores and restaurants vanish, replaced by the neon flashing lights of pawn shops and adult toys.

"Oh, hey," Seamus says. "There's a two for one sale on rubber penises. I never knew there was such a thing."

"Rubber penises?" I ask.

"Are you kidding? It's Philly. I meant sales like that. I'll bet they sell out."

An elderly couple hurries into the store. "I bet that, too," I say, not wanting to focus on how giddy they appear.

At the next block, the row homes grow narrower and the graffiti lining the walls more daring and colorful. "I thought we were going to a hair salon," I say, watching a crack dealer at the corner drop several bags of white powder into a young woman's outstretched hands.

"We are," he replies. "I'm taking you to the best stylist in town. Just do me a favor, don't look her directly in the eye, she'll take it as a challenge."

"*What*?"

"Oh, Allie, relax. Shaqwana Lopez-Morales is the best of the best. A little psycho, but a lot of the great artists are. Remember Picasso? Didn't he cut off his ear and mail it to that chick who dumped his ass? I wouldn't let him babysit my nieces. But I'd let him paint me a portrait."

"That was van Gogh and I may have to kill you," I say.

"What's wrong this time?" he asks.

"What do you mean what's wrong this time? You're taking me to someone I can't stare at directly or risk her stabbing me in the eye with scissors."

"Hey. I never said she would stab you. To her credit, if she's going to fight you, she'll throw hands."

"An honorable psycho, that's . . . that's wonderful, Seamus."

Seamus nods, missing the point entirely. "Yeah, you ain't nothing without honor."

He tugs on my long braid playfully. It's something he's done more than once.

As hesitant I was to participate in this arrangement, I confess I enjoy his company.

Seamus didn't remember me. Not from all the times I showed him and his brothers the apartment building they ultimately purchased, nor all the work I did to help them secure a lucrative deal. He didn't remember me from the years we'd spent attending the same church, nor the years I'd spent separating his siblings from fighting with other children.

He remembered Valentina. Everyone remembers Valentina. I get it. But this day was so much harder than the rest.

I was mortified to be so easily forgotten, especially given my history with Seamus and his family. I wanted to dismiss him as a simple, thickheaded brute. Until he remembered my kindness. When it's my turn to die, out of everything, it's how I want others to remember me.

"What are you thinking about?" he asks.

I scan our surroundings. Just as the neighborhood begins to take a turn for the better and resemble an area recovering from the madness surrounding it, Seamus makes a sharp right turn, taking us into the very heart of urban decay.

"That you're a nice man," I say, my thoughts and words vanishing in the air as we pass a group of homeless people warming their hands around a fire from an old metal barrel.

Where is this man taking me?

"Thanks," he says, ignoring my growing panic. "You're pretty decent, too. Hey. You want to hit Gino's for steaks afterward?"

"Um. Yes. That would be lovely."

I don't think he's intentionally trying to ease my discomfort. But it's what he manages to do with his comment and easy demeanor. It reminds me that there is a great deal of sweetness lurking beneath the often oblivious surface.

After we agreed to help each other through our dilemmas, he took me out to an early lunch so we could discuss the details. I didn't expect him to have such a hearty appetite following the dessert tray he consumed. Nevertheless, he ate an entire cheesesteak like a bear preparing for hibernation then chugged down a milkshake as if his very existence depended on it.

It was nice spending time with him. It was also nice receiving his texts, no matter how brief. I hadn't realized how little interaction I had socially until I began replying to texts that had nothing to do with my real estate business.

"So, you ready to lose all those inches?" he asks me. "That's a lot of hair you have going on."

"No," I confess. "But it's something I've contemplated for a long time. I just don't know what I'm going to do with it." I make a motion with my fingers around my entire scalp. "My hair is gigantic. The only way to tame it is by braiding it the way I do."

"Don't sweat it. We'll donate it to someone who needs it, and trust me when I say you're going to love how it looks and what it does for your sex life."

"Sex life?" I ask. "I'm not certain I understand."

He laughs. "Alz, when I'm done with you, men are going to beg you to take them to bed and be sucker-punching each other just to date you."

I should be offended, frightened, something. Instead, something that feels too much like hope fills me. "Are you serious?" I ask. "About men possibly be wanting to date me?"

He frowns. "Why wouldn't I be? You're hot."

"Hot?" I ask, wary that he's having fun at my expense.

"Totally. You just don't know it, on account of all those clothes and hair that have stifled the fire. Kept it from burning. You hear what I'm saying?"

"I guess so," I reply cautiously, my thoughts remaining fixed on Seamus believing me "hot."

"Come on," he says, stealing a glimpse at my face. "Trust me."

"I trust you," I respond.

I do. But as we pull further down the street and a fight breaks out between two teenage girls, trust races off in the distance, laughing at me for being so naïve.

"I remember my first fight," Seamus says rolling to a stop at a light and watching their friends separate them. "It was second grade and Will Peterson stole my Trapper Keeper. He claimed it was his and threw out all my homework. I was so mad. There was a picture of a horse on the cover. I was going through my cowboy phase, so you can imagine what that did to me."

"I can imagine," I agree. My eyes wander over his strapping physique. "I take it you won the fight?"

"Oh, hell no. Will Peterson was as dumb as rocks and had been held back two years. He had like forty pounds on me and totally kicked my ass. But you know what? I got my Trapper Keeper back."

I don't know whether to laugh or feel sorry for him. I'm still contemplating both reactions when a sense of pride fills me. There were plenty of Will Petersons in my life growing up. But I never had the courage to fight for my Trapper Keeper. I attributed the low self-esteem to having grown up in my sister's shadow. It wasn't until I went away to college and gathered a better sense of myself that I began to fight for what I thought I deserved in all avenues in my life. Except when it came to my family.

Seamus rolls to a stop in front of Bare Beauty, *A Salon for the Diva-lushus You*. Hip-hop music blasts from the open doorway and women in barely-there clothes in very thick "fur" coats strut out. It may be a cold day, but there's plenty of heat seeping from Bare Beauty.

"Here," he says, yanking my door open and offering his hand. "Let me help you out." I didn't even notice him come around, too entranced by what resembles hell's version of the *Steel Magnolia's* salon.

"Allie," Seamus says when I don't move. "Shaqwana has a full day and she did me one to get you in. I don't want to be late and piss her off."

I hurry out. I don't want to anger her, either. I'm not sure I want to do anything with her. "Are you certain this is the right place for me?" I ask.

"I thought you trusted me," he says, a smirk forming across his face and giving him a very unfair extra-dose of sex appeal.

"All right," I say, taking his arm and allowing him to help me down. "Let's do this."

"Hi, Seamus."

"Hey, Seamus."

Two women wearing the equivalent amount of material as the scarf around my neck flounce out of Bare Beauty. "Whaddup, ladies?" he says.

He places his arm around me and leads me forward when the "ladies" glare at me like they want to "cut" me.

"You don't know their names, do you?" I whisper as we head inside.

"Nope," he admits. "But I'm not letting them know that. They'll cut you."

I *so* didn't want to be right about that . . .

The hip-hop music blasting from the salon grows that much louder when we step in, the deep bass vibrating the floor at my feet.

Idle chatter cuts through the music and the laughter rings loud and clear. Seamus leans into the reception desk perched directly in front of us, rows of old plastic chairs on either side filled with women flipping through magazines or hanging tight to their children playing on their phones.

"Hey, baby," a pretty young Latina with braids down to her back says. "What you want done?"

"Seamus!" A woman from the rear end of the salon shouts. "It's okay, Yesenia. I got him."

I don't have to guess this is Shaqwana Lopez-Morales. Not with her name affixed to the neon-teal sign atop her station with an arrow pointing to the chair I'm to sit in.

From a distance, Shaqwana seems fabulous, and when I say fabulous, what I really mean is superbly provocative. Seamus leads me forward when it becomes apparent I'm not moving. I haven't felt intimidated by anyone in a very long time, but Shaqwana leaves me speechless.

A short, tight, gray skirt barely covers her epic, global Latina butt cheeks. Matching gray boots skim the lower half of her thighs and a white sweater clings to breasts that were either cosmetically enhanced or unfairly molded by Athena herself to perfection.

Shaqwana's hair is a mane of silky twists defying gravity to expose her round face with equally large brown lips glossed to a blinding sheen. My best guess is she's of

Peruvian descent or possibly Colombian, having had received the best genes her ancestors could bestow.

It seems odd Seamus would know her. This place isn't easy to locate. "This is who cuts your hair?" I ask, barely able to get the words out.

"Oh, hell no," he mutters. "I wouldn't be caught dead getting a cut here."

"*What?*"

He doesn't answer me, too oblivious to see that I'm all but running out of here and flailing. If he notices how quiet the rows of women getting their hair done grow as we pass, he doesn't show it. Some are young enough to be teens, others old enough to be grandmothers. Most are of Latin descent, a large number first generation, speaking in thick Spanish accents.

"Sorry about your grandmother," a woman with a high braided bun tells Seamus as we pass. "Hit me up when you're done mourning."

"You got it," Seamus tells her.

"Oh, God," I squeak. We're almost to Shaqwana. I stumble when I realize she has a lazy eye.

"You're challenging her," Seamus mumbles hanging tight to his grin.

I presume he realizes I've met one of her two eyes. In my defense, I'm not exactly sure where to look.

"This her?" Shaqwana says, motioning to me to sit with an irritated flick of the comb in her hand.

"Yeah, this is Allie," Seamus tells her. "Thanks for fitting us in."

"Yes, thank you. Nice to meet you," I stammer, focusing on her pronounced bosom, because honest to God there is no other safe place to look. "I appreciate your willingness to see me." *And please don't shave my head.*

"What's wrong with her?" Shaqwana asks, looking at me but speaking to Seamus.

"She's just nervous about losing all her hair."

His excuse appears to pacify Shaqwana. For the moment, she doesn't seem too ready to drown me in the nearby sink.

Seamus takes my coat and hangs it on a hook, allowing me to sit in the designated chair of doom. I'm ready to vomit. The only thing squelching my terror-filled angst and keeping me in place is that I trust Seamus. Besides, even with those high-heeled boots she's wearing, I can't outrun Shaqwana. Her thighs may be as thick as my waist, but don't let that fool you. There's a great deal of muscle lurking beneath her tiny skirt.

Shaqwana circles me, very much like a fox would circle an unsuspecting chipmunk just trying to mind her own business, and not scream at the sexy wolf who convinced her that invading Shaqwana's territory was a good idea.

"I see what you mean," Shaqwana says, lifting my braid and twisting it between her fingers. "Shit's thick and healthy, but not doing her any favors."

Shaqwana possesses the reflexes of a ninja. Before I can thank her for what I believe is a compliment, she cuts off my long braid at my shoulders and holds it up by the end.

Like a wave of spiraling serpents, my hair explodes in an eruption of curls around my face.

"Hey, Shaqwana!" a woman three seats down from me yells. "How much you want for that hair?"

"Bitch, this isn't your hair to take," Shaqwana snaps. She leans her mouth *and* scissors close to my neck. "How much you want for it, girl?"

"Don't take less than two hundred," Seamus whispers.

Seamus seems to have abandoned ship and hopped on the Shaqwana Express. "You said we were donating it to a good cause," I remind him.

"You saying that Monique ain't a good cause?" Shaqwana demands. "That woman is raising six kids. How is she going to land a decent man without decent hair?"

I'll admit, I don't have a response for that.

Seamus, of course, has plenty to say. "I say take whatever you can get for your hair and donate it to the Children's Hospital."

His "everyone wins" mentality, while impressive, doesn't diminish the fact I lost at least twelve inches of hair and what remains has taken on a life of its own.

Seamus's hands are a different story. He turns my chair without warning, threading his fingers along my scalp, his eyes never leave mine, his hands gingerly fisting my curls. A sinful smile tugs at the corners of his mouth, hot enough to singe wood and rob my lungs of air. "This is what I'm talking about," he murmurs. "Just enough to grab."

"What are you thinking?" Shaqwana asks him.

"Yes," I stammer. "What are you thinking?"

"Fuckable," Seamus replies.

"Eh?" I squeak, unable to tear my gaze away from his commanding stare.

Seamus releases me slowly, the strands of curls sliding through his fingers as if it's killing him to let go. He coughs, clearing his throat. "I want to give you fuckable hair."

I'm trying to remember how to breathe when Shaqwana starts playing with my hair, fluffing it out and upward. "I can do fuckable."

"What exactly do you mean by fuckable?" I ask, blushing at how delicious the word sounds with Seamus this close.

"What you're going to be when I'm done with you," he murmurs.

Something I very much intend to be a word sweeps through my lips. When I can't make sense of it at all, I take a breath and try again. "I –I–I don't understand."

Seamus may have released me with his hands, but his gaze holds strong, mesmerizing me, stroking me like a warm, invisible caress, and entrancing me so ruthlessly, the world falls away, leaving only him and his dark, rough voice. "Men like hair they can grab. Long enough to ball into a fist when they work a woman from behind or grab hold of when their woman falls to her knees in front of him."

"Uh, huh. You got that right," Shaqwana agrees.

I barely know Seamus. But the way his intensity and allure entrap me, I very much want to be that woman who falls to her knees in front of him.

"If that's what you want, that's what we'll do," I say, unable to recognize the husky tone my voice takes on.

His eyes fly open, and for a split second he seems to remember where he is and who he's with. He coughs into his hand and takes a giant step away, giving me plenty of room.

"Come on, sweetie," Shaqwana says. "Let's get you started. The two of you have given my place enough of a show."

"Mmm-hmm," the older woman beside me agrees. "Lord have mercy, it was getting all filthy up in here."

The women around us erupt in laughter while I pretty much try not to die on the spot.

Seamus's features brighten, a shade of red that likely matches the flush burning through my flesh.

"Hey," he tells Shaqwana, attempting to get back to business. "Do you have anything she can put in her hair to make it shiny and easier to take care of? That's a lot of hair."

"Yeah. I have something. It'll help her curls, too." She lifts my hair, fluffing it out. "But I'll do you both one better. Let's add some color. I have the perfect shade that'll add shine and not fade out."

"Wait," I say to Seamus, snapping out of my stupor. "You didn't mention anything about dying my hair."

Shaqwana slams her hands against her voluptuous hips. "You trying to tell me I don't know what I'm doing?" she demands.

"Yeah," Seamus asks, grinning. Unlike Shaqwana, he appears to be enjoying the moment. "You sayin' we don't know what we're doing?"

I clench my teeth, noting he's baiting me. "Of course not," I say. "Forgive me, Shaqwana, I'm just very nervous about the experience. I don't doubt you in the least, my Latina queen."

There's a reason I'm successful. I know what to say and who to say it to.

Seamus nods, appearing as impressed as Shaqwana. "Then let's get to it, honey," Shaqwana says.

Using her foot and giving me another taste of her ninja skills, Shaqwana pulls a black rolling cart over, the force she uses just enough to allow the cart to stop just in front of her. "I'll be right back. Gotta mix the color."

I watch Shaqwana walk to a small room in the rear of the shop, fighting with everything I have not to look back at Seamus and wonder what it would feel like to fall to my knees in front of him.

CHAPTER 9

Seamus

What the fuck is happening here? Seriously, what the hell am I doing?

Allie is a pretty woman. Sweet face, nice round ass, and nipples that point skyward if I'm not mistaken. Scratch that. You can set a compass by them, I'm sure of it. We have a deal. I help her so she stops looking like the pathetic castaway her family treats her as, *and* so she can land someone decent for once in her life, a nice guy who won't treat her like shit and will actually give her a chance at forever. She helps me on a few dates to shut my family up and that's it.

Do I want to make her over and unleash that sex goddess trapped beneath the persona of an old spinster? Hell to the yes—*for someone else*. Not me.

Yeah, yeah. I think it's about time I find someone without a rap sheet—someone whose name is worth remembering for more than reporting her to the police when she steals all my shit. But Allie isn't it. A few make-believe dates. A little bit of making over. That's all we promised each other. Can't be more than that. Right?

I look over in time to see her gather the towel around her neck when Shaqwana finishes washing her hair. As Allie eases herself back into the chair, she looks scared, nervous, and glances at me like I can somehow save her. See, that's her first problem. I'm no savior.

"Looking good, sweetheart!" I say, trying to reassure her.

Shit. She looks like she got caught in the rain without an umbrella and some asshole in a car splashed water on her as he drove by. There's no rain and no asshole in a car. Still, I want to protect her from any asshole who might even think about splashing her and beat the hell out of him for messing with her. Again, what the *fuck* is wrong with me?

She smiles at me gently. There's too much appreciation in that smile, considering I think I should kick her to the curb. Or at least kick her from any thoughts that involve us in bed. I don't take women like Allie to bed. They get too attached. Case in point, dipshit Andres. It's been years since he broke her heart. She never got past it, which makes me think she's the kind of gal who doesn't easily let go.

As much as I think Allie is dreaming of someone to settle down with, I can't settle down with the first decent person I meet. Especially someone who's still hung up on a man who made her believe she wasn't good enough . . . or maybe not as good as her sister.

I need . . . aw, hell. I don't know who or what I need. But it's not Allie. Just like she sure as hell doesn't need anything more from me than advice. A few dates, I remind myself. A few dates and we say goodbye.

"Seamus," Shaqwana calls. "How much you want off the back?"

Allie's hair is colored and washed. All she needs is the cut and for Shaqwana to style it. We've been here an hour. But already, Shaqwana has done a lot.

"Seamus?" Shaqwana says.

There I go, staring at her again. When the hell did I turn into the creepy bastard up the street? "Just enough to grab," I remind her. "More in the front."

"Inverted bob?" Shaqwana asks. She doesn't wait for me to answer, knowing I have no clue what it's called. "I got you."

Shaqwana moves to the back of Allie's head and grabs a little more than a fistful. It does nothing to ease the deer in the headlights look Allie has going on. My woman is definitely getting fuckable hair. That was the goal, right? To bring her out of that self-imposed spinster sentence she shoved herself into?

"That may be too short," Allie tells her, careful not to make direct eye contact with either of Shaqwana's eyes. "My hair is going to go all over the place."

Shaqwana grins with all the warmth of a horny tiger. "That's what we're going for, *nena*. You want to give your man over here a good idea how it's going to look when he messes it all up for you." She grabs her scissors and Allie's hair starts flying all over the place. "The hair school people would call this a curly, inverted bob. But that's not what we call it all up in here. Is it, ladies?"

All the patrons full-out cackle and the woman opposite Shaqwana's station slaps her leg. "That there is going to get you some tonight."

Allie glances in my direction again, her small features hopeful for better hair and a better look. That's it. She's not hopeful that I'll be the one to give her some. She can't be.

I start to look away, but I can't seem to. Her large brown eyes keep me in place, making me think I'm here for more than I promised.

Maybe I shouldn't have said all those things or touched her like I did. It gave the wrong impression, even though I couldn't help myself. Allie may have an old lady vibe going on, but there's a whole lot of hellcat waiting to scratch her claws down someone's back. I see it and with my help, maybe she'll see it, too.

I turn away when I realize how long I've been staring at Allie. I should say something shitty and be a dick. Maybe start talking to one of the women in the front. But I came here to help Allie, not to help myself. And, well, you'd have to be a real douche to be mean to someone like Allie. As much as she might think I'm perfection wrapped in a ruggedly handsome package, she can't go for a guy like me. I'm supposed to end up with someone else. Except I'm not sure who that someone is.

Shaqwana reaches for some spray, working it into Allie's hair. "You need to buy you some of this."

"I'm not sure I'll know what to do with it," Allie says.

She glances at me, like I know. *I don't know*, I want to tell her. *I don't know what to do with that spray and I don't know why I keep looking at you this way. I just wanted a date. Any date. Then you showed up. Looking all cute and now sexy, and Jesus God, why can't I shut up?*

I reach for my phone, more for something to play with. The hell? It's like I woke up and turned twelve.

"Aw, honey, you don't have to do a thing," Shaqwana tells Allie. "Take a shower, spray it on your damp hair, and go to bed. Let your pillow," she smirks at me. "Or your man, do the rest, while you toss and turn."

I lift my head slowly. Shaqwana shrugs as if she didn't just flat out tell me to bang her like a set a drums at a Van Halen concert. Yeah peeps, I'm that damn old.

"In the morning, twirl the fly-aways with your fingers and add a little spray. Easy," Shaqwana adds. "You'll see."

Except now all I'm seeing is Allie naked in my apartment with Metallica playing in the background. Hey. We all have our fantasies. This one's mine.

Shit. Double Shit. *Damn.* I scroll through my phone like I'm busy working or something and not busy wondering about Allie. Now is not the time to get involved with anyone. Especially someone like Allie. I'll only end up hurting her. That is, if she'll even go for a guy like me at all.

A few dates, I remind myself. That's all I need and nothing more.

"Hey, Seamus," Shaqwana says. "Jesseeka is finishing up her cosmetology license at school. She's real good and needs the hours." She motions at Allie as she dries and fluffs her hair. "What you say about her working Allie up."

I meet Allie's gaze and hold it. Already she looks like a completely different woman. The back of her hair barely skims the nape of her neck while the front fans out from her delicate features, a mane of large, shiny curls showing off and demanding attention all while highlighting Allie's natural beauty.

Beautiful. That's what Allie is. I just hope I can get her to see it.

"She doesn't need anything," I answer Shaqwana, trying to look away from Allie and not exactly managing.

"Jesseeka won't do much," Shaqwana argues. "Just accentuate what your woman's already got."

"Yeah, what she already got," a few women chime in.

Allie glances around, but it's clear she's waiting on me. It's crazy how much she trusts me. She shouldn't. I mean I'm not going to do anything to her. She just, well, maybe shouldn't.

"Fine," I say. "But just her eyes and maybe some gloss to her lips."

Jesseeka, I assume, struts over, her overly drawn eyebrows set way too close to her hairline as far as I'm concerned. "Are you upset?" Allie asks when she approaches.

"Naw. Why do you ask?" Jesseeka says, appearing to frown although her eyebrows stay put.

"Because you went and placed your eyebrows in the damn middle of your forehead, again," Shaqwana tells her. She points to me. "Don't be making Allie look bad in front of her man, especially after I fixed her hair."

Jesseeka waves a hand, trying to appear like she's not afraid of Shaqwana. I know better. She's careful not to look her in either eye. "You know I won't."

As instructed, Jesseeka doesn't do much. What she does is more than enough. She gives Allie smoky eyes, taking them from large to huge and adds light pink gloss to her lips, altering them from full to downright pouty. Again, it's not a lot, but it's enough to transform Allie from innocent to nymph, readying to dive naked into a clear pool of water.

Jesus Christ, how am I going to keep from kissing her?

For the reveal, Shaqwana whips off Allie's cape and whirls her around to face the mirror. Allie blinks back at her reflection, completely floored.

"What do you think, girl?" Shaqwana asks.

Allie's eyes shimmer with the start of tears. It's not until her small fingers play with the edges of her hair and a smile forms that I realize she's happy. "I love it, Shaqwana. Thank you."

The women in the chairs close to us and those who gathered to get a better look at Allie erupt in *woot-woots* and applause. Allie laughs, her cheeks flushing pink, but it's me she looks to when the applause dies down. "Do you like it, Seamus?" she asks.

"Yeah," I reply. Maybe a little too much.

CHAPTER 10

Allie

I do my best to ring Seamus's door and not drop the crazy number of bags I'm carrying. I readjust my hold, again and again, when he doesn't answer.

Seamus texted me that he was home. We were supposed to get together to work out the final kinks of our pseudo relationship before meeting his family, but every spare moment I've had, he's been busy.

I press the doorbell again when he doesn't answer, wondering what's taking him so long. His truck is parked in front.

My eyes widen when I realize he never claimed to be alone. What if he's not answering because he's busy entertaining someone else? Oh, no. No, no, no, no, no. What if he's not answering because he can't leave the naked woman doing back-flips in his bed?

I start to hurry down the brick steps when the door is thrown open.

"*What*?" he yells.

His deep voice and the rage behind it almost has me falling down the last step. "Oh. It's you."

It's only because of the sudden shift in his voice that I even dare to turn around. I wouldn't call it excitement that I hear, nor exquisite joy, at my arrival. This was a mistake and now I'm stuck.

"Yes. Just me."

Seamus edges to the end of the small porch. With the safety glasses perched on top of his head, his ripped white T-shirt, and a pair of old dirty jeans, the hems brushing over a pair of soiled work boots, he looks like the primal God of Carpentry. If there was a God of carpentry. Oh, please, let there be a God of Carpentry.

He tugs off his soiled work gloves and shoves them into his back pocket, the mild flex of muscle bulging his bicep and the twist of his waist giving me a very nice view of his abs when the shredded T-shirt rides up.

If he's trying not to singe the black bra I'm wearing with his hotness, he doesn't succeed. I can practically smell the lace burning.

The warming spring breeze sends a curl to bat gently against my cheek. I'm still not used to the short length. That doesn't mean I don't absolutely love it. I tuck the strand nervously behind my ear, the motion causing Seamus to stiffen, although I'm not certain why.

I adjust the paper bags in my hands, realizing it's going to be up to me to speak. "You mentioned you were finishing a project." My voice softens. "And that you were hungry." He leans back on his heels, listening closely and I suppose waiting for me to stop sounding like a babbling idiot. "We never managed a decent lunch the day we went shopping and I thought—" I clear my throat, trying to shake my nervousness. "I just wanted to make sure you had something to eat."

"Yeah?"

"Yes," I agree

He stares at me for a long moment. Perhaps this truly is a bad time and I'm keeping him from his work, being more of an inconvenience than the help I intend.

"We also haven't spoken much about your family. I'm supposed to meet them Sunday."

He watches me, saying nothing. "I know," he says.

When he bows his head, I'm certain he'll tell me he needs to work and doesn't have time. "Come in," he says, sparing me from offering to leave.

He lifts the two larger bags with one hand as I step forward, using his free hand to open the door for me. Seamus doesn't live in a traditional house. He lives in what could only be described as a trendy industrial park just outside of Philly. From what he told me, the entire structure was once used to store books by a major New York publishing house.

Since the surge of eBooks, there was less need for the space and the publisher opted for a smaller building someplace less expensive. "The park refused to go down without a fight," as per Seamus. The owner hired him and his brother Angus to convert the large rows of opened structures into smaller units. There's a yoga studio just to the right, a larger gymnastics school when you first enter the complex, in addition to a UFC gym, an art studio, and even a Montessori school.

I step into Seamus's workshop. The raw smell of wood and sawdust is potent, matched only by of the aroma of machine oil and the deep tang of stain. I don't mind the scents. They remind me of Seamus and fill me with a sense of peace.

"Did anyone ever tell you that you have a contagious smile?" he asks.

I didn't realize I was smiling, I look up at him. "No," I confess, my skin warming.

He swipes at his face. "Jesus," he mutters.

I glance down at the teal silk shirt I'm wearing. The plunging neckline is low, but falls in a way that's respectable, and the hem cinches against the waistband of my dark slacks. He hand-selected this ensemble himself. I thought he liked it.

"Is something wrong?" I ask, smoothing out the fabric, nervously when I realize he isn't moving.

"No, just busy," he says. He rubs his eyes. "Let's go upstairs."

"Yes," I agree, embarrassed. "Let's get you settled."

The heels of my ankle length boots tap against his battered and sawdust-covered wood floors. Like the other businesses, there's space for offices on the second level. Instead of an office, Seamus converted his space into an apartment.

Considering how dusty the floor is, the windows that run along the entire second floor are surprisingly clean and transparent, giving the illusion of a large open loft. If not for the sunlight reflecting against the glass, I wouldn't see it. At least, not right away.

I follow him up a beautiful and freshly stained staircase. The railings were cleverly made from pipes, giving the space a fresh, modern feel and luring the eye from the chaos below.

I take in the sprawling space that makes up his workshop. The large kaleidoscope front window, each rectangular pane varying in size and tints of green, purple, and blue and carefully framed in dark wood paints his foyer in a rainbow of color, while the clear rectangular window running above it sends long beams of sunlight across piles of freshly cut lumber, two large machines at the center, and a multitude of tools discarded on the dusty floor,

"Did you make that?" I ask, motioning toward the window.

I'd meant to ask him the first time I'd stopped by, but Seamus was shirtless and, well, I believe that's explanation enough. He tugged on a pullover, grabbed his keys, and took us out to a nearby diner before I could finish rolling my lolling tongue back into my mouth enough to ask.

He stops, taking it in as if he's never had the time before. "Yeah. I'd just bought a glass cutter and was playing around." He rolls his shoulder. "It was hard to shape the smaller rectangles, but once I got going it was a little hard to stop. Next thing I know, I had all these pieces. I was moving in here, thought I could make something cool with it, and, there you go. It's a good way to advertise some of the things I can do when clients stop in, and it's another piece to add to my website portfolio."

"It's beautiful," I say.

"And practical," he adds, his voice quieting. "Gives me privacy and lets light in." His head drops slightly. "Sorry. I'm rambling and you're just standing there."

I start to tell him that I don't mind, but then he hops up the stairs.

Although he seems rushed, I trail behind him. I should have warned him I was stopping in. But he's been so distant since our day at the salon and our shopping excursion, I was worried he'd tell me no.

The salon experience was odd. That's the only way I can describe it. I thought he liked my new hair, but he kept jerking his head away from me as if he was forgetting to do something. What I thought would be a nice quiet lunch turned into fast food along the way to Macy's. That was an experience. He kept grabbing clothes, shoving them into my arms without bothering to glance in my direction.

If he didn't like something when I stepped out of the dressing room, he told me no right away. His "yes's" were only long enough to take a good look at me before quickly returning his focus to his phone. A few times, when I stepped out, he'd pinch the bridge of his nose as if my ensemble pained him, only to tell me, "Yup. That's the one."

At first, I was delighted, thinking he really liked what I wore. But each time I'd put on something completely out of my comfort zone, instead of reassuring me, he'd storm away, swearing and muttering under his breath. I didn't know what to think, especially when he dropped me off. He stayed long enough to help me carry in my new wardrobe and then ran from my house as if he was on fire.

He stops at the top of the steps when I linger, glancing up at the ceiling. "Do you need help?" he asks.

It doesn't take a genius to guess he's hoping I say no. What is wrong with him? "I'm all right," I say. "Just getting used to the heels."

It's not just these heels. It's all the shoes Seamus picked out. They were all cute, I'll admit, but none gave me fewer than two inches of height. "My sister always says fashion hurts," he told me, pointing. "You need to own that shit."

It's what he said before quickly returning his full attention to his phone. Again.

I reach the landing. His loft is misleading from the first level. Anyone would naturally presume it's small with little to offer. Instead, the large open area takes up about 2,000 square feet. The steps immediately lead to an ultra-modern and very male kitchen. The combination of white cabinets and quartz countertops are practically blinding and the chrome appliances the only accents.

The living room to the left is only slightly different. An immense midnight blue modular sectional arches around the largest flat-screen I've ever seen in a private home, the white fluffy area rug in the center the only buffer against the gray and chestnut modern wood floors.

From where I stand, I can see his bedroom and the massive walk-in closet. A king-sized bed with rich brown, cushioned leather headboard rests against a stone wall panel of grey, beige, and earth tones. The linens on his bed vary from light to dark brown, the color scheme broken up by a few white pillows among the sea of multi-toned browns.

This is a bed one can only sink into, one to spend long, lazy mornings doing absolutely nothing.

Or several nights having crazy amounts of sex.

I'm not exaggerating. This is not a bed *just* to sleep in. Not with the headboard like that. I don't want to think about all the women that headboard protected from the wrath of Seamus's baby-making hips, or just why one man needs that many pillows. For positioning her? Him? Them?

I turn away to give my libido a chance to cool and my evidently lonely lady parts a good mental slap.

I pause when I realize the bed and all its blessed body contouring pillows are not the only eye-catching pieces within the vicinity.

Between his kitchen and bathroom stands a large statue, intricately carved from wood. It's massive. The couple it depicts are life-size. I'm not certain why I didn't initially see it, likely because the smooth and perfectly sanded wood blends in with the decorative color schemes.

Like a hypnotic call, the statue lures me forward. The granite slab it's secured to is a meld of curves, abstract like the work of art it holds in place. I pause before the ever-still couple. The man is about Seamus's height, the woman shorter, but many inches taller than me.

I don't understand a great deal about art. But the significance of this piece is clear, and the closeness this couple shares so intimate, I feel like I'm somehow intruding, a voyeur peering into a deeply personal moment between lovers who've been apart for too long.

Slowly, I circle the piece, noting the natural imperfections that somehow make the subjects more real, the sensuality and passion they emit akin to corporeal beings.

"Wow," I whisper. I drift closer, the pull of its eroticism and beauty is physical, an embrace I can't break free from. "It's stunning."

Seamus ambles to my side, walking slowly, his steps almost silent.

"You like it?" he asks.

Seamus doesn't strike me as insecure. In fact, I believe he swaggered from his mother's womb on his terms, rather than waiting to be forced out. "Shy," "mousy," "skittish"… these concepts and words are completely unfamiliar to him. They're simply not a part of this confident and strong individual's vocabulary—not when he's this attractive and flexes as much as he does.

So, when his voice takes on an underlying hint of doubt and uncertainty, it takes me aback.

"I mean it," he says. "I need you to tell me if it sucks."

My face meets his. He wants me to like this masterpiece and perhaps needs me to, as well.

I wish I could explain how touched I am that he values my opinion to describe what a perfect meld of lust and desire this couple evokes. I wish I could share what it and his presence are doing to me, and how his ability to manipulate wood tapped into long forgotten needs and abandoned temptations.

"It's *incredible*," I reply, my words mere gasps.

"Incredible?" he questions, disbelief lowering his tone.

I nod. "This isn't merely a block of wood brought to life by your hands and talent."

"It's not?" he asks.

"No," I say barely breathing. "It's ardor and fervor so raw I can taste it, a lucid and provocative invitation to sin."

"Ah. Do you know what it is?" he asks slowly.

I swallow hard, taking in how possessively the male figure shields and claims the woman. They're naked. Nothing to hide what they're doing, or feeling, or how badly they want each other.

I look at Seamus, unusually breathless and unable to shy away from what this statue epitomizes. "It's a man and woman, making love while standing."

A shade of red, as brilliant as lava spilling from an active volcano, overtakes Seamus's face and his jaw audibly pops open.

It's then I know I've made a huge mistake.

"Holy shit, Allie. *That's my sister*!"

"Wha-what?"

"And Evan!" Seamus yells. He walks away, digging his hands through his hair. He slaps them down against his sides and veers back to me, his skin now almost white. "They were dancing at my cousin Colleen's wedding a few months back. They looked nice. I took a picture and thought I'd recreate it as a wedding gift." He makes a face, glancing at the statue. "Now all I want to do is set it on fire."

"Oh, *God*," I say. I shake out my hands, because what else can I do that doesn't involve running and hiding?

He points to it. "That wood came from a tree in my Grammie's—God rest her soul—backyard."

"I'm sorry!"

"I swung from that tree . . ."

"I didn't mean to," I insist.

"On a swing Pop-Pop made us."

Of course he did.

"Ignoring the pain from his arthritic fingers."

"I'm *really* sorry."

His voice grows quiet, distant. "I don't remember Pop-Pop . . . I was too little when he died." His pained expression wanders all over the statue. "The tree fell over during that blizzard in January. I thought it was a nice way to keep the memory of Grammie and Pop-Pop alive."

"It's a beautiful way to honor them," I say, bouncing in place with nervous energy. "Sweet—lovely—darling."

"I believe your words were 'lucid' and 'sinful'—and before you explain, I know what they mean."

"I-I-I know you do," I say, speaking fast and tripping over my words. "I didn't know that was your sister, or Evan, or made from your dead grandmother's tree."

"And Pop-Pop," he adds. "Don't you forget Pop-Pop—God rest his soul."

We both cross ourselves like good Catholics, not that it absolves me in any way.

Seamus takes another long glance at his *magnum opus*. He gags a few times and makes batting motions with his hands as if trying to push all the awful images of his sister getting it on from his mind. "I could've gone my whole life without hearing that," he says, shuddering. "Thanks for the visual."

"Sorry?" I offer again. As if that helps. Forget that I epically mistook a sweet gesture meant for his sister and dumped it straight into a vat of smut. Why didn't I just tell him I was lonely and that my lady parts had never seen any action beyond two or three decent thrusts?

It's fair to say Andres cared as much about pleasing me as he did about tying his shoes.

Seamus strolls into the kitchen shaking and shuddering and I imagine doing his best not to hurl.

"I'm normally not like this," I begin.

He swivels his head. "You mean horny?"

Kill me, Jesus. Yes, that, too.

"Dirty minded?" he suggests when I take too long to answer.

"No!" I say.

"Kinky?"

"Seamus!"

"Pornographically inclined?" he presumes.

By now, his disgust has disappeared and he's enjoying torturing me. When he laughs at my reddening face, I lift a pillow from the couch and fling it at him. It lands near the clear glass partition and nowhere close to him.

"What about athletically challenged?" he suggests.

By now he's holding his sides, the glee stirred by my asinine behavior sparkling in his blue eyes and making him unreasonably alluring.

Must he be so attractive while I stand here dying a humiliating death?

"You're not funny," I tell him.

"Sure I am." He points. "And don't forget good looking."

I drop my head, causing my wild curls to spill forward. I push them away slowly, allowing my hand to keep going and glide down my neck. I peer up at Seamus cautiously. *No. I can't forget.*

"What?" he asks.

I wonder briefly if I spoke aloud. "What?" I ask, very much aware I asked the same question.

He turns around, his spine rigid as he grips the edges of the counter. Perhaps I shouldn't be surprised. I made him uncomfortable. He's probably rethinking our agreement.

"You got me a lot of food," he says. "We should get cracking if we want to make a dent in it."

I can't be certain if he means to be polite or if he genuinely wants me to join him.

Seamus keeps his back to me as he unpacks the first of several paper bags. He removes the first container, a round one that contains salmon, yellow rice, and green beans. As he moves to the next, a rectangular container stuffed to the brim with Cypriot grain salad. He frowns and lifts the dish.

My blush remains very much in place. "This is a lot of food," he says. "What are you trying to do to me?"

His question seems odd. "I'm not trying to do anything to you," I reply, my shrill voice alerting him that I'm lying. It's such a dastardly lie, I should just strike myself down and save God the trouble.

There are many things I want to do to Seamus. He drips sex appeal like honey, honey pouring down his very naked sculpted body. Any heterosexual woman alive would want a piece of him.

I slap my hand over my eyes.

"Is something wrong?" he asks.

No. I'm just picturing you wearing a tool belt, a smile, and nothing else. Damn that sensual statue. "Sorry. I have a headache," I say. I don't bother to mention my out of control hormones and, good *Lord* he would look so good in that tool belt.

"More reason for you to eat," he says, oblivious to my ovaries shaking like maracas.

The next paper bag scrunches loudly as he pushes his large hands through it, tearing it down the rim with the force he uses. "Alz, you didn't bring me lunch. You bought a week's worth of groceries."

I step forward. It beats standing and melting from all the ardor burning through my veins. "I wouldn't call them groceries," I say.

"Then what would you call them?" he asks, pulling a large bottle of organic carrot juice from another bag.

"Perfectly prepared and healthy meals you simply have to reheat or enjoy." I try to jump onto the counter, don't quite make it, and end up smacking my ass against the hard edge. I stretch out my hands, sliding them across the slick quartz and attempting to bite back the pain.

Ow.

Seamus wanders over, lifts me with as much effort as he did the container, and plops me on the counter. The motion is quick, but not the way his hands withdraw from my hips. I can't breathe, his fingers dragging along my thighs.

"I've got barstools. Lots of them if it's easier for you," he murmurs.

"No. I'm good," I whisper, melting into his warm stare. I am good, but only in his arms.

He looks away, his hands releasing me and returning to the food. The way he casually dismisses me is akin to the way my family treats me. I hate it. Mostly, I hate that he'll never see me as more than a convenient date.

"Why did you bring all this food?" he asks.

I didn't know my chin had lowered until I glance up. "Pardon?" I heard him, I just don't understand the question.

"You told me you were on deadline and that you don't eat when you have projects due," I reply before he can ask again. "I know how committed you are to your work and that you always promise your clients to deliver on time when they hire you." I fold my hands on my lap when it occurs to me I'm rambling. "That shouldn't mean you should suffer."

"Suffer?" he asks. "I wouldn't exactly call it suffering." He takes a good look at me and smiles. "Let me get this straight. You've never skipped a meal to make sure your clients have everything they need? Never worked through lunch? Maybe dinner? You've always eaten and been okay?"

"That's not what I'm saying," I reply, my own grin fixed in place. "But I can tell you, I wish I had someone to bring me food. Sometimes I've been so hungry, I could have used a snack, so maybe I could have worked longer and completed my task a bit sooner." I wonder briefly if I'm treating him like a child. But his smile and the gratitude I sense beyond it tells me perhaps this is something he needed.

"I suppose what I'm trying to say is, it would've been nice if someone remembered me. Or at least remembered enough to bring me a meal."

"You were trying to take care of me," he says, his lips widening into a bigger smile. "You were trying to make sure I would be okay."

"Yes," I admit.

"Good," he says. "Nice to have an Allie around to watch my back."

I nibble on my bottom lip. It's not something I'm in the habit of doing, but Seamus brings out my shyness better than anyone.

"You know what?" he asks, watching me closely. "The takeout you brought, in addition to all these meals, they're too much for just me. Sit with me. Make sure I eat them." He winks. "Make sure I stay okay."

I'm not hungry and I have contracts to review piled on my desk. But I think for once my work can wait. For once, I want to be that woman in the company of a gorgeous man, sharing a meal and the happiness his presence brings.

I expect Seamus to turn on his mammoth television. Instead we sit at his elevated counter, twisting to face each other as we eat and speak about everything from the stained glass doors he's installing later tonight, to the house I listed earlier that morning. We talk about sports and memories we share from church functions, and he tells me plenty of stories about his family, making me laugh.

When the soup he poured and the half sandwich on my plate is finished, I carefully wipe my mouth. I don't really realize how much I've missed his company, or how much I laugh in his presence until this moment. But maybe I did and perhaps it's why I was so compelled to see him.

I gather my plate. "I should go," I say.

Seamus follows me, lifting his plate and some of the leftover garbage. "Yeah, I need to finish this headboard before I head out to install the doors."

I rinse our plates while he finishes tidying up the kitchen, using care as I place them into the dishwasher.

I can't stop smiling. Seamus did most of the talking and I did the majority of the laughing. The conversation is brief yet gives me a better understanding of who this man is. I'm glad to know Seamus, and perhaps a little proud, as well.

Although he seems rushed, he takes his time, placing a hand on my lower back as I start to walk down. "You don't trust me to maneuver the steps on my own?" I tease.

"Not even a little bit," he says, laughing.

"Oh, shit," he says, glancing at the iron clock on the wall.

"What's wrong?"

"I forgot Mandy's coming over."

My steps slow and I tuck my hair behind my ear, although it's not in the way. "Oh. Who's Mandy?"

"She runs the yoga studio next-door and says she needs help redesigning it. The place is brand new. I'm not sure what she needs."

My shoulders sag. I'll bet I know what she needs. One hot carpenter.

The doorbell rings as we reach the ground floor. "Hey. That must be her. Come on, I'll introduce you."

He takes my hand. He's not rushing me, not with how carefully he leads me forward, and it's not until we reach the door and he swings it open that he releases me.

I'm so happy we spent such a lovely afternoon. I'm not so happy when I see who's waiting rather enthusiastically for him at his doorstep.

A woman, close to Seamus's height, stands with one leg firmly fixed on the floor, the other wrapped around her neck.

"Oh, hi," she says. She slowly lowers her foot from where the heel rests against her breast, giving a glimpse of how flexible *and* graceful she is.

She giggles. "I was just getting a good stretch in while I waited for you, cutie."

More like she was giving Seamus a good view of her body parts and all the limber things she can do with them.

Seamus isn't my boyfriend. We haven't slept together. We haven't kissed. We've barely touched each other. But, my goodness, I'm standing right here!

"Hey, Mandy," Seamus says. He angles his body so I can slip through and I presume leave. "This is Allie."

Mandy giggles again, bringing her long French braided hair to the front of her voluptuous breasts to play with. It's the same way I used to wear my hair. But my hair never looked like hers and I certainly don't look like Mandy. "I'm sorry," she says. "I didn't notice you."

"I'll bet," I say, smiling and doing my best to keep the bite from my tone. "Perhaps your foot was in the way?"

I don't mean to sound so harsh. But Mandy won't be someone who ignores me as easily as my family does. Not while I'm standing beside Seamus.

"Could be," Mandy chimes, her eyes narrowed as she smiles. "I am rather flexible and sometimes I can't help but show it off."

Oh, yes, she knows I'm onto her. Fine, just so she understands, I'm making my own shameless claim. I glance up at Seamus adoringly, something that comes easy, my hand skimming up his arm. "Thank you for lunch," I say.

He smirks, watching my hand. "Shouldn't I be thanking you?" he asks.

I shrug with one shoulder, lowering my lashes. Flirting isn't a superpower I possess, nor do I usually find it necessary. Except today. "It was my pleasure."

Perhaps I'm being unreasonable. But she started it. I should be ordering myself to my room without supper, seeing I'm suddenly twelve again.

"You know what?" Seamus asks, his light irises glinting with excitement. "Mandy has some kind of special going on for new members. A week of free classes. Maybe you should try Mandy out?"

No, I shouldn't try Mandy out. Based on her growing scowl, I should kick her down the stairs like she very much deserves.

Now would be a good time to remind myself that I'm a grown woman and a professional, and that although I was raised in a rough neighborhood, I'm not the type of woman to rough someone up. Yet, the more I stare at Mandy and her tight little spandex-clad body, the more I respect those women who would throw down.

"I don't think that's something I'd enjoy," I respond. I'm no longer smiling, and neither is Mandy.

"That's all right, sweetie," Mandy says. "I'm not sure you could keep up."

I laugh. "You're right, Sandy. I'm too busy running a real estate company. I don't have the time for that kind of commitment." I sigh and glance leisurely at Seamus. "I suppose I'll have to find a different way to get my workout in."

Seamus is oblivious that Mandy and I are all but clawing each other's eyes out, but thankfully plays along. "Killian's offering kickboxing classes for two weeks if you're interested," he says. "And he's open much later than Mandy. If you want, I'll hook you up."

"That sounds wonderful," I say, ignoring the images of me unconscious and bleeding all over Killian's gym floor. "Perhaps we can talk to him about it Sunday at brunch when we see your family."

The comment is directed at Mandy although I'm speaking to Seamus. He throws his arm around me as if remembering brunch will be our first appearance as a couple to his family. "Sounds good," he says.

He walks me out to my car and opens the door for me. "Thanks for the food and everything. How about I give you a few bills for it?"

"No," I reply softly. "You paid for my trip to the salon when you didn't have to. Bringing you a meal was the least I could do."

He grins, tugging on the end of one of my long curls. "It looks nice he says."

He bends and kisses me on the cheek. I'm not certain if the display of affection is meant for my sake or Mandy's. But I take it. Wishing that kiss could be so much more.

CHAPTER 11

Seamus

"Are you nervous?" Allie asks me.

"No. Why?" I ask.

"You keep cracking your knuckles," she points out. "I've noticed it's something you do when you're nervous or about to punch someone."

"That asshole got too close," I say reminding her, because he damn well had.

I took Allie out to grab a bite the other day. Except the place we hit was filled with too many suits that had their fill of happy hour drink prices. One guy reached for Allie's ass as she walked by. He would have grabbed it if I hadn't hauled her out of the way. He thought better of it when I, yeah, cracked my knuckles and loomed over him. The hell? I'd taken her to a nicer place to thank her for bringing me all that food. Not to be groped by some dick who had too much to drink.

That's what I told myself, anyway.

Before she showed up at my place the other day, I'd been blowing her off by not calling or texting, so she wouldn't blow me off, if that makes sense. All right. I'll admit it doesn't. But me and Alz are people who just don't belong.

She's books. I'm a jackhammer. She's brains and I'm damn good-looking. She's sweet and I'm sexy.

She's also fucking beautiful, but I can't really go there.

We're supposed to be dating for show. I need to make sure we can get through these next few months. I don't want to date for real and screw-up our relationship.

"Our relationship?" Christ, wasn't this supposed to be just a few dates?

Allie laughs. "You also do it when you're lying."

"Do what?" I ask, paying more attention to how good she looks than our conversation.

"Crack your knuckles," she reminds me.

"You saying I lie to you?"

Her smirk is the only thing hiding a glimpse of her pearly whites. "I think it's fair to say you enjoy exaggerating the truth."

"Maybe a little," I agree. I frown when she rubs her hands together. "Are *you* nervous?"

"Yes."

There is no hesitation in that yes. Can't blame her. When Curran and Tess asked me to bring my new girlfriend to brunch, I couldn't say no, not like I had the last few times my family asked to meet her. Like me, Allie's not sure we can pull this off. My family knows me like I know them, in a way that shouldn't be natural.

"Are you done with your run?" Curran will ask, just as I'm finishing my run.

"You're not taking Susie Dwyer back to your place?" Finnie texted, that time I was unlocking the door to my apartment and encouraging Susie inside.

See? They're all a bunch of freaks who can read me like a book.

Unlike me, Allie isn't much of a liar. I don't think she has it in her. I take a long glance at her. At least we have her new look down.

In the killer coral dress she's wearing, she's sexy enough to be a believable girlfriend, but not so slutty that they'll question the morals she waves like a flag. Her hair? What can I say? She's followed Shaqwana's advice to shower and let the spray and her bed do the rest.

Allie looks hot. My entire hand will catch fire if I touch her. Don't get me wrong, that hotness was always there, just buried beneath a lot of hair and clothing. Hair and clothing that hid the beautiful and elegant professional and made her look more like a sister wife of some messed up cult—

Her phone buzzes, again, again, and again, screwing with my train of thought.

She turns it off after a quick look at the screen.

"Is that your Mom?"

Allie sighs. "And my aunts, and . . . Valentina."

"Why?"

"I'm supposed to be at a fitting for the bridesmaid's dress. I . . . I didn't want to be a part of it."

I huff. "No shit."

"I told them I'd find a different time to be fitted and that I had plans." She wrings her hands. "But they didn't believe me."

"That you had plans?" I ask.

"Yes," she says, although she doesn't seem to want to admit it.

"Why?"

She seems sad, but she still finds her smile. "Because if you hadn't invited me to join you, they would be right." She fiddles with her dress, trying to tug it down. "I think this is too short."

Allie is trying to change the subject. I let her, knowing she's embarrassed. "What do you mean? It's almost down to your knees."

"No, it's at the very top of my knees," she argues.

I laugh and accelerate up an incline. Curran and Tess bought a nice plot of land in the burbs. A lot of the houses are still in the process of being built, the extra sections of underdeveloped land sprawling with oaks at least a hundred years old.

"Would you prefer it at the top of your ankles?" I ask when she gives the hem another tug.

When she doesn't answer, I think I'm right. "Allie, you're a real estate goddess, not some pilgrim. Surrender your butter churn already, whip off the bonnet, and have a little fun."

"You're not making me feel better. I told you, I'm nervous."

"Ah, don't be. It'll be fine." I crack my knuckles at an intersection. She eyes me like she's onto me, so I make it all about her. "My family is a good warm-up before we have dinner with Valentina and dickless. No offense, but we weren't exactly what you'd call believable that first time they saw us."

I crack my knuckles again when we reach the next intersection. For all the bucks buyers are laying out for these houses, you'd think they'd install a damn traffic light.

"For someone who claims he isn't nervous, you're certainly not playing the part."

I shrug, trying to shake off her reasoning. "There's only one part we have to play and that's you and me being crazy about each other. So be crazy about me. If I screw up, you can spank me with your butter churn later."

She swivels abruptly away, as if bothered by the idea of seeing me naked. See, that's what I mean. We're different.

Allie fiddles with the strap of her seatbelt. "Tell me, how exactly do I appear crazy about you without being over-the-top?"

"You don't have to be over the top," I explain. "But the occasional fondling of the package might help." She looks at me. "What's the problem? Can't the pilgrim take a joke?"

"Seamus, you're not hearing me. I'm scared. Your family has the reputation of—"

"They're not so bad," I insist. "That fire was a total accident. Besides, the building needed to come down anyway."

"What are you talking about?"

Oops. "Nothing. What were you talking about?"

She blinks at me, like she's about to leap from my truck and flag down the nearest cop. Nah. That can't be right.

"I was saying your family has a reputation for being passionate, but good-hearted, people," she says slowly.

"Oh, yeah. You're right about that one."

I hang a right down Curran and Tess's long driveway, parking between the neat rows of F-150s. It's their turn to host Sunday brunch and my turn to eat everything I can to keep from talking more than I have to.

As nervous as Allie seems, I'm ready to turn around and claim food-poisoning. Except my absence and lame excuse will only convince my family I'm lying in bed hungover, while the chick I spent the night with is sneaking out with my credit cards shoved into the cups of her double-Ds.

Allie is the best fake girlfriend option I have, but even if she wasn't, I probably would've asked her anyway. Her affinity for dressing to seduce the nearest Quaker aside, she's nice. She laughs at all my jokes without thinking I'm a complete dumbass and brings me food to make sure I'll be all right. Shit, if those two things alone don't say a lot about her, I don't know what does.

I slide out and walk to passenger side, hauling the door open and offering her my hand. She gives her skirt another tug and allows me to help her down. "Thank you," she says. "That was very gallant of you."

I nod, agreeing. "Boyfriends are supposed to do that."

"Are they?" she asks. "What else do you plan to do as my boyfriend?"

"Rip you off my body like Velcro as much as possible. Don't look at me that way," I say when she does. "There has to be believability." I shrug. "I may or may not have ripped a few girls off me in front of my Ma. But let's try not to do that. She doesn't like it, and I think she still carries a knife in the waistband of her underwear. Ready to go?"

Allie doesn't move.

"It's just a little knife," I assure her.

"Oh, God."

"I mean, it's not like she needs it," I say, trying to make her feel better. "She's Irish. She could probably kill you with her bare hands."

Look at that, now she's glaring. "Seamus, you are the worst motivational speaker ever."

"I don't know about that," I begin.

"Are you not listening? I want to make a good impression. I don't want to upset anyone, let alone be stabbed."

"It was just that one time, and no offense, that guy deserved it for trying to steal Ma's purse."

Wow. I can actually see the color drain from her face. "I guess we should head inside," I say.

"I guess so," she says, not meaning one word. She squares her shoulders. "Just do me a favor. Whatever happens, don't leave me alone with your family. I'm not certain I can pull this off without you beside me."

I pull the egg casserole she made from the back and shut the doors, leading her toward the wrap-around porch with my hand. "I think I can do that. At least for the first two minutes we're there."

"For the first two minutes?" she shrieks, stopping at the bottom of the steps. "What's that supposed to mean?"

"We're kind of old fashioned, at least when it comes to meals. The womenfolk usually gather in the kitchen getting all the food ready. Except for Wren. She usually hangs with us. She's good at serving the food and setting the table. But that, and helping me and the boys clean up after, are the only things we let her do. She tried to cook once. But she fucked up the potato pancakes so bad it's like our insides melted and we were sick for a week. So, if she tries to offer you anything she's claimed to have made, don't take it. She needs to leave the cooking to Evan. The food he makes is good and our insides haven't fallen out yet." I slap her ass when we reach the front door. "Ready gorgeous?"

She rubs her butt. "After that gentle caress of encouragement, how can I not be?"

"Hey, ballers do it all the time," I say. "I wouldn't do it if I didn't like you or if you didn't look so hot in that dress."

"Ah, thank you?" she replies.

"Anytime," I assure her.

She watches me warily and reaches for the crook of my arm at the same time I try to hold her hand. We end up slapping at each other, trying to do what the other one wants and laughing as we try to figure it out.

The door flies open and out steps Curran, his baby girl chewing on her fist as she lays against him. I snag Allie's hand in mine as his stare bounces from her, to me, and back to her again.

"Hi," Curran says.

"What's up?" I lift my hand to wave, remembering too late I should be using it to hold Allie's. "This is Allie. You remember her? She taught you all about Saint Christopher right after she broke up the fight you had with little Stephen Dormer when he tore your picture of the Holy Mother."

"Allie Mendes?" Curran asks, glancing back at me. "*You're* here with *Allie Mendes*?"

Allie offers a little wave. "How are you, Curran? I never told you this, but your paint by numbers rendition of the baby Jesus was the best I've ever seen."

"No, shit," Curran says, beaming.

Whatever doubt Curran has dissolves at the paint by numbers reference. I remember that painting. He gave Jesus some kind of green blanket the color of puke. We crossed ourselves when we first saw it, insisting no way did Jesus deserve a puke colored blanket. But Curran thought it helped the image of Jesus to pop. "You don't want Jesus to pop?" he asked the rest of us. I'll admit, none of us could deny him that one.

He grins and looks back at me. "You're seeing Allie Mendes," he repeats.

By now, he's sounding impressed. "Sure am," I say, lifting her hand as proof. "Isn't that right, sweet cheeks?"

Allie's smile falters at the reference. I'm guessing that's not a nickname on her approved list. Like the champ she is, the corners of her mouth lift. "That's right, Teddy Bear," she says, looking up at me. "I'm all yours."

Curran cracks up. I can't be sure if it's because of the look on my face when Allie calls me her Teddy Bear, or because I'm just standing there. Of all the things she could've called me, stud muffin, hotness, sex god, Teddy Bear doesn't fit my very awesome package.

"Hey," Curran hollers behind him. "Seamus is here. With his girlfriend."

"Is she trying to steal your car?" Finnie asks, confused.

"It was one time!" I yell. Christ. You smile at a pretty girl and things are going great. Next thing you know, you're naked in the woods, tied to a tree, watching that pretty girl drive off with your truck.

Curran shakes with laughter, matching Allie and all the giggles she's trying to hold in. Sweet. We can do this. All she has to do is keep laughing and being cute and my family will believe we're together.

"Come on," I mutter. "Let's get it over with."

We're a little late. That's all my fault and maybe Allie's, too. She was so worried about how to dress, she tried on close to seventeen outfits. After the sixth, I helped myself to breakfast, because I was getting hungry and thought it was better to shove food in my mouth than say something stupid like, "Hey, you're smoking. Can I see your bra and panties without all the titillating clothes getting in the way?"

I think that might have been inappropriate, but maybe it's just me.

Allie hangs tight to my hand. I think she's worried about falling, since she's still not used to the high heels I told her looked hot. She probably also feels guilt about lying, especially if she thinks so highly of my crazy family. Maybe her guilt makes me feel a little guilty, too. I remind myself this is for both of us, and may help us get to know each other better.

I don't want to admit it, but I really like what I see. I don't just mean how her dress cups her ass or how the color brings out her olive skin tone and those eyes, too. I'm not even talking about how her pouty mouth looks fuller with that gloss she's wearing. Allie is a good person with a sweet personality. Maybe God sent her to me, instead of the other way around as I claimed.

"Are you certain I look all right?" Allie asks me, keeping her voice quiet.

"Nope," I answer.

She pauses before turning the corner into the family room. "I don't?"

My gaze fixes to her panicked expression. "No. You look beautiful."

Shock swirls through her pretty eyes. She doesn't believe me. But she should.

"Aw. Isn't that cute?" Curran says bringing me back to the moment.

What I said was good for show. But that's not why I said it. Allie is beautiful. She just needs to believe it.

We follow Curran through the foyer and into his large family room. He holds out his hand, getting everyone's attention. "Youz are going to fall over when you see who Seamus brought."

"Aw, shit," Wren says already psyching herself up for the worst.

Curran steps back, unveiling Allie directly behind him like a human curtain. All at once time stops, everyone freezing in place like I'm hefting the Ten Commandments on my shoulders, instead of holding Allie on one arm.

Tess is the first to move, inching slowly, little Fiona glued to her hip and a tray of monkey bread in her hands. Awesome, that's my favorite.

I head straight for the monkey bread, until I realize I'm still attached by Allie's vice grip on my hand. I'm reminded everyone still hasn't moved. I understand Fiona's shyness. She's little and is probably wondering what a stranger is doing in her house. Especially when the stranger is holding her favorite uncle's hand. I can respect that.

Everyone else doesn't have that excuse. They're staring, waiting for my next move. The only sound is coming from the television as the Phils take the field.

Ma crosses her arms over her chest like I'm up to something. That's when I forget about having my first bite of monkey bread. She knows. Everything. At least, that's my guess.

Allie is dressed like someone I would date, except not dressed like someone I would date, if that makes sense. She's arousing. Someone I'd take to bed, yet something about her gives the impression she doesn't go to bed with just anyone.

I'm starting to doubt whether I can pull this off. Wren doesn't help. She sits up from where she's perched on Evan's lap. "Allie Mendes," she says, barely believing it. She looks at me *"You're* dating Allie Mendes."

It takes some doing, but I release Allie's death grip on my hand and drape an arm around her shoulders. "Yup," I say. Short and simple. That's how I need to do things. The more I talk, the more my mouth will get us in trouble.

"Allie Mendes," Wren repeats, unable to believe it. "But she's . . . *nice*."

"Why does that shock you?" I ask.

Wren gives me a look. The same look everyone else does. "Never mind," I mutter.

This is where Allie's choice of dress works to her advantage. She doesn't notice everyone scanning her bare arms for tattoos. But I do.

"Is something wrong?" Tess asks.

"No," Sofia says, "everything is wonderful."

Tess sighs, likely thanking God Curran won't have to frisk her for weapons.

Sofia doesn't talk much, but what she says in her gentle voice always seems to ease the tension. She slips away from Killian. It's the first time I can really see her baby bump. I almost tell her how cute she looks carrying my little brother's baby, but her tender voice beats me to the punch.

"It's so nice to see, Allie," she says. "It's been a long time, but I really appreciate all the help you gave us in preparation for our wedding."

Allie smiles, appearing relieved to interact with someone who's almost as quiet as she is.

"You're very sweet," Allie tells Sofia. "But I didn't do much. I merely referred you to a florist."

"A wonderful florist," Sofia says. "And the most lovely woman to sing at our wedding."

Sofia turns to Killian as he reaches her. "You remember how Allie saw to all the church details, don't you?"

Killian is another one who doesn't talk much, leaving all the loudmouth bickering to the rest of us. Like me, he's not great at remembering people he's met in passing. But he remembers Allie and it's not just to placate Sofia. "You recommended that violinist," he agrees. "I didn't think we needed one, but she played the best version of *Ave Maria* I'd ever heard."

"I remember that, too," I say, surprising myself. "Hey, Alz. How were you still volunteering at the church with your business running like it was?"

As if on cue, and to add to all the good vibes Allie has going on, she blushes. "Mrs. Rodriguez normally handled all the wedding preparations. When she broke her ankle, Father Flanagan asked me to help." She looks at my brother and Sofia. "It just happened to be during the time you were getting married."

Killian reaches out to lift the casserole Allie made out of my hands, as well as Tess's monkey bread, placing it on the buffet table near the fireplace.

Sol speaks up, glancing around. "Seamus brought someone nice home? What does this mean, exactly?"

Sol is getting her doctorate in psychology and is one of the smartest people I know. She doesn't sound as smart now. In her defense, she seems as dumbstruck as the rest of my family.

Finn laughs, taking a bite out of the muffin Sol is holding and speaking as he chews. "It means you don't have to hide all the booze like the last time."

Sol covers her heart, appearing relieved. I feel bad for her. It took her an hour to scrub down that bathroom. I feel bad for me, too. Drunk or not, the last date I brought to brunch chased me three damn blocks. I had to hide behind a dumpster to escape that crazy bitch.

Wren clasps Evan's shoulder like this is the greatest day ever. "Allie used to teach Sunday school," she explains, loud enough for the rest of to hear. "She still volunteers at the church, owns a killer real estate business, and might possibly still be a virgin." She scowls at me. "Possibly."

Allie's voice trails as she finishes congratulating Sofia and Killian on her pregnancy.

Me being me, I become defensive. "I'll have you know I didn't pluck the cherry off this tree."

"Seamus," Allie warns, stealing a glance in my mother's direction.

"It's okay. I've got you," I promise.

"Oh, yeah," Wren says, like she's remembering. "It was Andres what's his face? The guy with the Velcro shoes."

"The special needs guy?" Curran asks.

"Yeah, that's the one," Wren says.

"It was real nice of you to help him out like that," Finnie says, even though he doesn't seem to really mean it. "I don't think many women, or men, would have put up with all that *Dungeons and Dragons* shit. Hey, who wants to bet he would've banged that green chick from *Star Trek* if he could?"

I point at him. "That's what I was thinking."

"What green chick?" Wren asks.

"The one with the octopus arms," Angus says, chiming in and sounding way too curious for his own damn good.

Finnie grimaces. "She had octopus arms? I'm not a racist or anything. But if a woman has tentacles, there has to be something wrong with her—"

"Finn!" Sol shrieks. "Your mother is right there."

"I hear ya," Finnie says. "Hey, Ma. Don't you think a woman with tentacles must have some messed up lady parts?"

Ma looks at Finnie. Finnie takes her barely-there response as a resounding, yes. "See," Finnie says to Sol, all proud-like. "Told you."

"Your ex-boyfriend was into some kinky shit," Curran agrees, grimacing.

Allie stumbles into me. I catch her and keep her on her feet. "Something wrong?" I ask.

"You mean besides everyone here thinking Allie lost her virginity to some guy in Velcro shoes who fantasizes about having sex with Octopussy?" Killian asks, unable to beat down his smirk. "Probably."

Sofia gasps, blushing in a show of solidarity for Allie, whose face is roughly the color of a stop sign. "*Killian*," she whispers.

Finnie raises his hand. "Just one question and I'll let it go. Did he take the Velcro shoes off during the act?"

Sol covers her face with her hand and groans. "What?" Finnie asks. "I think it's a fair question."

"Bastard owes me a pack of gum," Angus mumbles.

"Sorry we're late," Declan and Melissa stop dead in the archway, their arms filled with baked goods.

"Allie Mendes?" Declan asks. He analyzes the way I'm holding her. Shouldn't surprise me. As the current District Attorney, Declan dismantles everything piece by piece. "What are you doing here?"

Tess, Wren, Sofia, and Sol rush forward, giving Declan and Melissa kisses and lifting the bakery boxes from their grasps.

No one is kissing me or Allie yet. I kind of take offense to it. Yeah, yeah, they're all in shock and shit. But come on. I showed up with the best woman I could find, like, ever. Maybe even on the entire planet. Cut me some slack here.

"What do you mean, what is she doing here?" I ask Declan. "She's here with me. She's my girlfriend."

I almost trip over the word "girlfriend." Almost. Melissa doesn't seem to understand what's happening and she can't read our lips with our backs to her. Curran passes the baby to Sofia so he can catch Melissa up in sign language, his hands moving fast.

Thank God Curran only shares the good parts.

Declan holds his palms up, trying to stop Curran or at least get him to slow down. He's just learning sign language and can't keep up with how fast Curran is signing. "Curran, wait. I'm lost. All I got was something about a green woman with octopi vagina." He glances at Melissa. "That can't be right."

"Yeah, it is," Curran replies, like Declan is the stupid one.

Melissa places her hand gently on Allie's shoulder. Melissa is tall and very voluptuous, her figure dwarfing Allie's petite body. "If Allie wants to have consensual relations, it shouldn't matter whether her partner wears Velcro shoes—"

"Yes, it should," me and my brothers collectively mutter.

"Real men take that shit off," Wren says.

"Hell, yeah. Damn straight," my boys and me agree.

Wren dances her eyebrows at Evan. "Or wear nothing at all."

She had to go and spoil it.

"What the hell?"

"Seriously?"

"God, Wren."

The women and Evan, unless you count Evan's chuckle, have been tight-lipped. But it's like all at once, they have to save Allie.

Tess slips in to put her arm around Allie, knocking mine out of the way and trying to shield her from the rest of us. I don't know what Tess's problem is. We're just having a little fun.

"Don't you worry," Tess tells Allie. "We've all been there and somehow made it out unscathed."

"What that's supposed to mean?" I ask.

Tess adjusts her tiny black glasses. That's how I know we're all in trouble. That's when I know we've gone too far. "It is absolutely unconscionable how this poor woman has been treated," she tells me. "Look at her. She didn't take two steps into my house before you accused her of losing her virginity to a man suffering from severe mental retardation and tasteless fashion."

Finnie raises his hand. "I'm sorry, Tess. You lost me after unconscious."

"She means youz are all a bunch of animals," Molly, Angus' fiancée answers for her, her high-pitched Edith Bunker voice sharp enough to cut glass and her red hair practically on fire. "It's like any time any of youz bring someone decent home, youz jump on her like a pride of hungry jackals on an unsuspecting flamingo."

"You trying to call us flamingoes?" Angus asks, his face turning beet red with anger.

"No, leopards, dumbass," Finnie fires back.

"Jesus," Tess says, like she can hardly believe she's stuck around this long.

"We're not trying to make her feel bad." Curran signs as he speaks, seeing Melissa isn't all the way caught up. "Believe it or not, it's a compliment. Allie goes to church and volunteers at orphanages and leper colonies. Helping out that nerd with the Fraggle Rock looking hair pop his cherry and fasten his Velcro shoes is just one more thing she's done out of the goodness of her heart."

Allie makes one of her famous squeaky noises. I snag her carefully away from Tess and lead her to Ma. No one is going to say anything to Allie with Ma right beside her. Besides, Ma will be the biggest test yet.

Time to get down to business.

CHAPTER 12

Allie

This is a complete disaster. I've always known the O'Briens as a lively and eccentric bunch, but I have never known them like this. Once free of Tess's protective hold I feel doomed, like a convicted felon ready to be stoned.

I glance back at Tess and Sofia, silently pleading with them to rescue me. They offer encouraging smiles, Tess's toddler reaching to Curran to hold her. Curran scoops her with his free arm. His opposite hand strokes Tess's backside as he speaks to Declan and his fiancée Melissa.

I'm literally on my own because, goodness knows, Seamus has been absolutely no help. "You having a good time?" he asks me.

Now is not a good time to kick him in the groin, I remind myself. I simply look at him silently, at a complete loss of words. How do I explain that no, I'm not having a good time. In fact, I've died and gone to Hades. But I can't hear why I'm condemned to eternal damnation. You see, the O'Briens are in Hades with me, yelling at Oedipus that he's poking his eyes out all wrong, and calling him a dumbass for marrying his mother.

Five minutes. How is it possible that I've only been here *five minutes*? And now I'm to meet Seamus's mother.

Seamus often jokes that his mother is the midget of the family. In all actuality, she's close to my size. But when your smallest sibling is Wren at about 5 feet 8 inches, I suppose it's fair to classify anyone smaller into little person status.

What makes her appear tiny is her thin and delicate figure. There's barely a wrinkle on her fair skin and while she's petite, the stern gaze she pelts me with squashes any misconceptions that I could take her in a fight. This woman would snap my neck like a taco shell before I could finish screaming.

"Don't panic," Seamus says through his teeth. "You're totally panicking. Ma is like a hornet. She'll smell fear and sting your ass."

I return his smile, speaking through my teeth. "If this is your idea of cheering me on, I'm going to rip off your pom-poms and throw them at you."

"You can't do that. I'm you're ride home. Besides, the pom-poms are good for covering unmentionables, and if anyone asks, can I brag that you've used some to cover yours?"

"Of course. Why not?" I spit out. "We've gone this far."

"Thanks. You're a real doll," he tells me proudly.

The room closes in and all eyes fall upon me. This must be what it's like to walk down the corridor of an ancient insane asylum, right before the door shuts tight behind you and the shock therapy begins.

My throat tightens and my breathing quickens. I shouldn't be so afraid. She's one woman. One.

A soft, light blue cardigan that matches her eyes, wraps around the bodice of her denim dress. Brown Ugg boots, cover her feet. As long as I've known her, Mrs. O'Brien has never worn pants or jeans. She's not a woman who fusses over fashion, nor does she fret about how others may see her. After a lifetime of being judged and talked about in whispers, she doesn't care and perhaps she never did.

Simply speaking, she's a woman comfortable in her own skin who dresses for comfort in return.

"Hey, Ma," Seamus says. He practically bends in half to kiss her cheek. "I'd like you to meet my girlfriend, Allie. She goes to church and everything."

This is how he introduces me to his mother. Perhaps I should be grateful he didn't bring up the green woman with tentacles Andres supposedly pleasured himself with.

"Hello, Mrs. O'Brien. I don't know if you remember me." I offer her my hand. "It's nice to see you again." She doesn't take my hand, keeping her arms crossed over her small chest. I try not to take offense, grateful instead that she didn't rip my limb off at the shoulder and smack me across the face with it.

"It's okay, Ma!" Finn yells from his position on the couch. Sol remains on his lap. I now presume to keep him put and out of trouble. "It's not Allie's fault she had sex with a loser. The important thing is she's having sex with Seamus now. Isn't that right, Seamus?"

"That's right," Seamus agrees, proudly.

"Jesus," Sol says, her hands returning to cover her face.

"What?" Finn asks. "We're all adults here."

"No, we're not," Tess snaps, motioning to her daughters.

"Tess, Fiona doesn't know what we're talking about," Curran says, coming to his brother's defense. "Remember the time she caught us going at it? All she cared about was me putting you down long enough to get her a cookie."

"Curran!" Tess says, blushing, although she doesn't strike me as someone who blushes.

"Where are you going?" Curran asks, chasing her into the kitchen. "I gave her the cookie."

"Animals," Molly mutters. "Just a bunch of animals."

As my skin returns to a somewhat less dangerous temperature, I wrestle with what to say to connect with Mrs. O'Brien. Perhaps I should ask her about the upcoming church social, the one to raise money for that family who lost their home to a fire. I change my mind, not wanting to appear disingenuous. My office is contributing to the event, but I want her to like me for me. Not necessarily the things I've done.

"I know you," Mrs. O'Brien says before I manage to speak. "You took care of my children. Every Sunday before mass."

I swallow back the sigh of relief that wants to escape. She does remember me. "Yes, Mrs. O'Brien. I taught your youngest children Sunday school."

A small sad smile appears on her face. It's my first glimpse of the mother behind the impenetrable matriarch. "You helped my Killian when those boys attacked him in the bathroom."

I don't mean to appear as surprised as I am, but I had forgotten the moment until now. Killian used to be a small, almost frail child, not the Goliath he is now. I remember that day. He'd raised his hand following the Lord's Prayer and asked politely to use the restroom. Two other boys hadn't shown up for class. They walked in shortly after Killian's departure, their shirts ripped and stained with drops of blood.

I knew right away what had happened and ran to the boy's bathroom. I found Killian crying in one of the stalls. His tears embarrassed him and he wouldn't initially show me his face. I stayed on the floor with him, until he regained his composure and allowed me to clean up his bloody nose.

When I returned to the classroom, I made the boys who hurt Killian apologize and rewrite the Hail Mary a hundred times in their copy books. Killian was very young, no more than eight. He probably doesn't remember me helping him, but his mother does and that means more to me than she'll ever know.

"Yes, ma'am," I say. "That was me."

"I never had the chance to thank you like I wanted to," she tells me. "But thank you for looking after me son."

I nod, her kindness and love for her children choking me up. She looks up at Seamus and then back to me. "We have a few things to finish in the kitchen before we can eat. Would you like to help us put out the food?"

My chest warms and I almost can't speak. "It would be my honor, Mrs. O'Brien."

CHAPTER 13

Seamus

"You seem upset."

"Now, why would I be upset?" Allie asks.

"Because I was late," I remind her.

She flips open the tiny little black purse she's carrying, groaning when she checks a text on her phone.

"Mamacita?" I ask.

She scrolls though her texts. "And my aunts. All five of them."

"Again?" I ask. "What do they want this time?" Christ, we can't go anywhere without them hounding her.

"My mother wanted to make sure we were on our way and wouldn't be late." She sighs. "And my aunts wanted me to call my mother to tell her we are on our way, so she wouldn't worry. After all, she has enough to worry about."

"Boy, they're going to be pissed when they find out we are late. Feel free to blame it on me, since it's my fault."

"You weren't late," she says, turning off her phone.

"Yeah, I was," I reply. "I was dead tired after my run and took a longer nap than I intended. I was supposed to be at your place by six-thirty. I didn't get there till almost seven. Considering we have dinner reservations, that's pretty damn late."

She tosses me a knowing glance like I don't know what I'm supposed to know. "Seamus, you run seven miles every Friday after you close your shop. After that, you take a hot shower to relax your muscles and end up face down on the couch. You usually snap awake, remembering you have to be somewhere."

"I do?" I ask.

"Mm-hmm."

Damn. She's right, I do.

"It takes you fifteen minutes to get dressed and fluff your hair—"

"I don't fluff my hair," I fire back. "I style it." She tosses me another know-it-all look. "All right, a little fluff, but not much more than that. I am a real man, you know."

"Yes. I know. You mentioned it once or twice." She continues. "It takes you another ten to get to my place so, in all actuality, you were five minutes early, because I really needed you at my house no later than seven."

I flick on my turn signal to make a left at the light. "You saying you have to lie to me in order for me to be somewhere on time?"

Allie pulls down my visor and flips open the mirror, coating her spectacularly full lips with a light pink gloss. I didn't pick out the shade for her. But damn, I would have if I'd seen it. She looks amazing.

She rubs her lips together. "I'm saying that maybe I know you and your routine better than you think," she says. Her smile is the biggest yet, gleaming and as bright as her gloss.

Considering how much time we've spent together, maybe she does know me by now. It's weird. After she met my family, it's like they couldn't get enough of us. We were invited to Angus and Molly's for dinner that Friday following brunch. The next week, we were out with Killian, Sofia, Finnie and Sol, as guests of honor for the MMA match-up Killian and Finnie were hosting. The topper was last night. As a gift to his groomsmen, Evan bought us box seats to the Phil's game. We lost our minds when the Phils won, everyone jumping and hugging each other. For the first time, I wasn't just high-fiving my brothers, I had my own woman to hug.

To prepare for each "date," we've shared a few meals at my place or hers, talking and cooking, and getting to know each other so we seem like a real couple rather than pretending to be one. Allie is a great gal. Do I still want her? Hell to the yes, especially the more I get to know her. It's not just because she's hot, it's because of everything she is. Everything that probably doesn't need a guy like me.

"Are you all right?" she asks.

"Yeah. Just getting hungry," I mutter.

There's mist in the air tonight, enough to see droplets spinning along the broad funnels of my truck lights and make me set my wipers. The blades glide across my windshield every few seconds. Every time I start to think I should set them faster, they wipe the glass and clear the way.

"Okay," I say. "So you're not mad about me being late, because I was a little early. Are you mad about the toast I made at the Phils game?"

Allie clears her throat, feigning annoyance she doesn't quite manage. "You mean the one about virgins in Velcro shoes never hitting a homer like that?" Her voice drops to imitate mine, "To whores and homers. Yeah!"

"I was just glad to have you there with me and wanted to make the moment all about you."

"Are you implying I should be honored?"

"Yep." I point at her. "You're welcome."

We crack up.

"It was a show of support for you, and to let you know you're better off without Andres and all the nerd vibe he had going on," I explain. "You don't need nerds. You need hot guys like me in your life."

"Is that right? Seamus, don't you know it's the nerds, not the meek, who will inherit the earth?"

"Not my earth," I disagree. "We need less pocket-protectors, fewer Doctor Whos, and more high-tech devices that emit fewer harmful gasses and doctors to cure cancers and all those diseases killing kids and destroying families."

She blinks at me, stunned. "What?" I ask. "I read stuff."

"Seamus, you do realize those same engineers developing high-tech devices and researchers creating breakthrough medications are likely nerds themselves?"

"Nerds who deserve to get laid," I say. I shudder. "Unlike Andres. All he did was create something to blow more things up. You noticed that, didn't you? That machine or whatever only helped him and his bank account."

"I did notice that," she says. Her voice quiets, but then she smiles. "But have you noticed how much you enjoy the company of nerds?"

"Oh, Finnie's always liked to read urban fantasy. I even stood in line for an hour behind a couple dressed in chainmail to get an autographed copy of Jim Butcher's book for his birthday. But Finnie and Jim know eight million ways to kill someone, so that makes up for it."

Allie laughs, the sweet way it rings drawing my focus back to her. "I meant me. You're entertaining the company of a nerd in sheep's clothing and you don't even know it."

"No. I'm entertaining the company of a sexy woman who will soon have her arm around an equally sexy guy. That's me," I add. "In case you were wondering."

"I wasn't wondering," she says, her voice fading.

The fact that she agrees I'm sexy gives me pause. Don't get me wrong, it's not that I don't know I'm sexy. Are you kidding? Those grays hairs on my chest practically bow to me, happy to lay across my chiseled torso. It's more like I'm not convinced my kind of sexy is the kind Allie would like, or need.

Did I catch her checking me out that first time at the bakery? Sure. Most women do. But women like Allie require a special kind of attraction to keep and hold their interest. That kind requires a degree, a medical license, or at the very least a doctorate. I'm not saying she's a snob. I'm saying someone like Allie needs someone that's not me. Someone she won't grow tired of just talking sports and busting balls.

Yeah. A woman like Allie needs something more.

My gaze travels in her direction. I can't see much of her now. She's looking outside the passenger-side window. But I see enough to know she's smiling, and that's good enough for me.

My F-150 barrels down the street, mowing through a recently patched pothole and making it my bitch. The city workers had done a poor job sealing it. With all this traffic and all these potholes, I suppose they can only do so much.

My focus is back on Allie. I'm not sure if she realizes how often I look at her. If she does, she gives nothing away. I knew she wasn't really mad at the whole toast thing. I saw her laughing. It made me laugh, too. I love drawing her smile and hearing her laugh with her whole heart.

She's not dressed like she was the other day at the game. There, she wore jeans and the pink Phils shirt I bought her. She looked cute, playful, and plenty beautiful.

Tonight, she's in the little black dress I picked out for her the day we went shopping. The halter top reveals a peek at the swell of her breasts. The waistband cinches her tiny waist and the skirt fans out to emphasize the perfection that is her ass.

She wasn't sure about the dress. She wasn't sure about anything I picked out. Some things didn't work out. I didn't expect everything to. I'm no expert on clothes. What I know is women's bodies and what makes their goods look even better.

To my family, her new clothes proved she's someone I could be interested in. To her coworkers and clients, her new business wardrobe spotlighted a successful, competent, and, more importantly, confident woman you'd be stupid not to trust.

"Did I tell you I picked up twenty-three clients this week?"

"Yeah," I say. "You mentioned it."

"That's a new record," she adds, beaming. "I'm promoting all three of my assistants and dividing the listings to place them on the market sooner rather than later. If this keeps up, I'll have to hire more staff."

"It'll keep up," I say, remembering how great she looked in that black and white Marc Jacobs dress she wore to my niece's Christening last Sunday. "I say we go out and celebrate."

"Just you and me?" she asks.

It's been just us for a lot of things, but the enthusiasm in her voice and the blush that no doubt follows, makes me think that maybe, just maybe, I may not need that doctorate.

Tonight, the way she's dressed and carries herself, *man*. She'll never tell her bitchy sister or her loser ex-boyfriend to fuck off, but she doesn't have to. That dress and everything that makes Allie, Allie, will do it for her.

"Yeah," I say. "Just you and me."

I haven't missed the way she's avoided seeing her family and I've overheard enough calls from Valentina, Mamacita Mendes, and all her aunts to see why she avoids talking to them as much as she does. They either think they deserve to treat her that badly, or they're not smart enough to know what it does to her. Allie didn't become the designated spinster on her own. She didn't turn complicit overnight. Nope. That crap has been a lifetime in the making.

I slam on the brakes when the car in front of me stops short. More instinct, than anything, my hand whips out to cup her shoulder. At least I think it's her shoulder, until I give a squeeze and realize it's too bouncy and perky to be bone.

My gaze shifts in her direction. "Ah, sorry?"

She glances down to where I'm cupping her breast. Not to brag, but I don't think I could've aimed better if I'd planned. I'm so impressed by my move, and how perfectly her breast conforms to my palm, it takes me a moment to realize I'm still trying to protect her from going through the windshield.

Seatbelts be damned. I just saved her life.

I think I could've been a lot smoother about removing my hand. Maybe give her a little wink and thank her for the opportunity. Instead I yank my hand back like I had it on the stove and she cranked up the heat.

It's not an awkward movement. It's all about me respecting Allie. I would never purposely cop a feel unless she begged me for it.

Okay, maybe she doesn't have to *beg*.

We're staring at each other now. Her, dumbfounded beyond belief, and me, thinking maybe I should have moved my hand away quicker. It takes the douche in the Mercedes behind me blasting on his horn to realize traffic has resumed full speed ahead.

"I was trying to keep you safe," I explain a little too late. "You could have flown through the glass and landed on the street bleeding with your organs hanging out and shit."

It's probably impossible to sound lamer than I feel. But I have mad skills and manage just fine.

"I'm wearing my seatbelt," she reminds me.

"Seatbelts don't always work," I say, like I'm some kind of expert. "The locking mechanism fails if not properly engaged." I'm tempted to make up a percentage of faulty seatbelt related deaths, but I think I sound enough like a dumbass.

Allie adjusts herself in her seat and fiddles with the strap. She's probably thinking the jaws of life are going to have to extract her from this deathtrap known as my vehicle before the night ends. "I thought you said that Wren sold you and your brothers on this truck based on its impeccable safety record and reputation?"

I really should learn to keep my trap shut. "Sure. But just because something seems great doesn't mean that crazy shit can't happen. I don't want any of that crazy shit to happen to you. So, if that means accidentally grabbing your breasts and fondling now and then to save your life, damn it, I'm going to do it."

My stupid comments make her laugh like I intended, assuring me that at least for now, I won't end up on some perv list.

In the quiet that follows, it occurs to me I'm still smiling. It's an easy thing to do around Allie. In general, I'm an easy-going kind of guy and my grins come quick. Except, around Allie, those grins are different, probably since she's different, too.

Allie isn't loud and obnoxious like me and my family. She's not as quiet as Sofia or as assertive as Tess. She's not the plus-size supermodel Melissa easily could be, or someone who bounces into a room and immediately makes friends with everyone like Sol. She's simply Allie. Someone you automatically know is a good person and will always do right by the world.

"What do you think will happen tonight?" she asks, pulling me from the thoughts and feelings that come when I think about her, and my preoccupation with when, exactly, those thoughts and feelings began. Was it when Shaqwana cut her long hair and brought out the woman beneath that all-too conservative exterior, when I saw the way she held my niece, or was it the way she touched me at the bakery—the way she always touches me, a little shy and reserved, giving me another hint of her gentle nature.

"Seamus?" she asks.

I grin. "Depends. Is good ol' 'I'm too cool to wear shoes with laces' Andy buying?"

For some reason, my remark makes her nervous. "Valentina mentioned that he would," she answers cautiously.

She thinks I'm up to no good. She's right. "In that case, I say we order the most expensive items on the menu, and take a few extras for leftovers. Why are you looking at me like that? It's the least the little prick can do after all that gum I gave him." I shrug. "It all evens out. The price of gum isn't what it used to be."

"Oh, goodness," she says. She seems mortified, but then she starts laughing.

"Very well," she says. "Order whatever you'd like. But what I was referring to is what if they're expecting an exchange of affection?"

"You mean if he tries to stick his tongue down her throat during dessert or something?" I grimace, trying not to gag. "I guess I'll look away. I don't want to see that shit."

"You would be offended by them kissing?" she asks.

"Wouldn't you be? I just picture this short, stubby tongue, grazing her teeth since it's as far as it will go." I cut myself off, making this choking sound as my stomach churns. "Damn. Why did you have to go there?"

Allie gasps. "What do you mean why did I have to go there? You're the one who asked and answered a question I in no way suggested." She quivers, as if trying not to get sick herself. "And while we're on the topic, thank you for your rather graphic description. I could have done without the visual."

"It couldn't have been as bad as that visual you gave me. That statue I made of Wren and Evan dancing was supposed to be innocent," I remind her. "Now I have to keep it covered or risk having nightmares."

"I told you I'm sorry," she squeaks. "How many times can I apologize for such an erroneous interpretation?"

"Not enough," I say remembering that day. I point at her. "And about Andy's tongue, you only have yourself to blame."

"How is that my fault?" she asks, waving her hands.

Man, she's cute when she's animated. "You know how my mind wanders all over the place. You know I wouldn't just stop. Now, I'm picturing all his other disturbingly stubby parts grabbing at her while she smiles and pretends to like it. Ugh. Did you really have to go there?"

The traffic is getting bad. Lots of assholes out, and even more young idiots who shouldn't be driving reminding me to keep my eyes on the road. I let the faster drivers with the death wishes pass me, and angle around all the geriatric population coming home from the blue-plate specials featured in town. My mind needs to stay sharp, except visions of freakishly shaped little body parts wandering around man-made bouncy ones dance through my head.

I don't realize Allie is laughing until I glance in her direction. She isn't making a sound. It's one of those silent laughs that hurt. Yup. Here she is, clutching her belly, her head thrown back, and little puffs of air releasing in tiny spurts. Then it happens. She can't take it anymore. The sweet sounds of her hysterics fill my cabin like the laughter of angels who just placed a whoopee cushion on St. Peter's chair. I don't know if angels are allowed to pull practical jokes. But if they did, their laughter would sound like Allie's.

"Fine. Crack up," I tell her. "But there's some shit you can't unsee. Minute fingers making grabby motions are in my top ten, second only to bearded women with equally bearded penises."

"You didn't even see it!" she counters.

"I did so. But we were in Tijuana and it was a total accident."

Allie is officially hunched over, curling into her stomach as if her insides will spill out if she lets go. "I meant the grabby little fingers," she says. At least, that's as much as I make out through her bursts of giggles.

"It doesn't matter." I tap my temple. "It's all up here. Jesus, how did you put up with that all those years?"

I shouldn't have gone there, knowing what that dickhead did and how her family responded. What happened still hurts her. She didn't just lose a man who claimed to love her, she lost her family the day they took his and Valentina's side.

Instead of growing sad like I expect, she says something I don't. "I'm not sure."

"Neither am I," I say, knowing she's always deserved better.

A smirk forms around her cute face. If I were to ask her how she thinks she looks when she smirks, she'd probably assume she looks silly, not alluringly naughty.

"Can I ask you something?" she asks.

"You know you can ask me anything," I say.

Although she doesn't say anything right away. "How do you know Andres has stubby body parts?"

"Men know these things," I answer truthfully.

She nods as if she picked up on something obvious. "You mean the locker room."

I stop at a light. Considering the weather, everyone in Philly seems to be out tonight. "What do you mean the locker room?" I ask, swiveling so I can better see her. "I never dressed anywhere near him. Even if I had, I wouldn't be looking. Guys don't look. We have what you call above the waist precision focus."

"All right then. So how do you know he wasn't . . ." Her gaze drops to my lap. I think she catches herself and jerks her head up. "Gifted," she stammers.

"Not all of us can be," I admit. Hey, she was probably wondering, might as well put her worries to rest.

"Um . . ."

Is it hot in here? No, it's just Allie's blush.

I let her off the hook. Well, somewhat. "So, let me ask you this. If you weren't talking about Andres and his lack of suitable body parts, what were you talking about?"

Allie fusses with her skirt as if trying to straighten it. "I was talking about displays of affection between us."

"Us?" I say, accelerating forward. I know what she means, I just think she needs to be the one to say it.

"Yes. I think my family may question our relationship if we're not affectionate to some degree." She plays with her hands. "It was different with your family. There I could sit on your lap, we could embrace, and that was enough. A restaurant isn't the type of atmosphere that allows those types of exchanges."

"No. It's not," I agree, liking how this sounds. I also love how flustered she's getting. Damn. I would love to be the man for her. "Don't worry. I'll hold your hand. I may even pull out your chair. But only if you're good."

She giggles. "So, all those times you've pulled out my chair for me, and all the doors you've opened to allow me through, have only been because I've been good?"

"Yeah. You should see what I'll do if you're naughty."

At once her humor dies and my temperature spikes. Did I really just go there? My foot slides off the gas when she bites down on the little freckle on her bottom lip. I quickly work to regain control. Forget the pseudo-malfunctioning seatbelts. I'm going to get us killed if I don't pay attention.

Allie is a little distracting. Who the hell am I fooling? Allie is making it almost impossible to drive. "You were really into character at the game," she says. "The way you stroked my back and played with my hair was a sweet way to remind your family we're together."

"I was imitating, Killian and Sofia," I admit, not that I minded. "And at times, Wren and Evan. But I didn't hang tight to your ass. It's something Finnie does with Sol. I didn't think you'd like it, seeing how the first, and the second time I did it, you seemed ready to kill me."

"It's not that I didn't like it. You caught me off guard and I wasn't expecting it."

She stops herself. I think it's because she revealed more than she wanted to. But then, it's like the misery that surges suddenly punches her in the gut. I don't tell her that after a few passes of copying my sibs, my motions became as easy as breathing. Based on how sad she seems, I think I already said too much.

"What's wrong?" I ask, hating how miserable she appears.

"I'm sorry. I didn't think you were emulating anyone." She sighs, her chin dropping. "I thought you were embracing and enjoying our time together."

Holy shit. She wanted me to mean it. I'll admit, at first, it was awkward and I was sure my family would call me on it. But each time my knuckles swept along her spine, she settled against me, and everything felt natural.

I never would have guessed it actually meant something to her, and I sure as hell didn't mean to hurt her.

"Don't worry," she says. "I don't expect you to do anything if it makes you feel uncomfortable."

The hotel comes into view and so does all its glory. Marble steps leading up to an extravagant entrance are cloaked with red carpet, welcoming anyone with enough bills to pay for their two-grand-a-night suites.

I pull in behind a Porsche, watching one of a team of valets hurry toward me. I set my truck in park and catch

Allie's stare. "Don't worry about me," I murmur. "I won't do anything that makes me uncomfortable."

I slide out of my truck and toss my keys to the valet. He's a young kid with decent reflexes. Without missing a beat, he catches the keys and hands me a ticket. I march to Allie's side, and as if we've done it a thousand times, she easily slips her arm through mine.

"What if Valentina and Andres are expecting more than just handholding?" she asks, eyeing the stone steps ahead instead of me.

"Like I said, I won't do anything that makes me uncomfortable."

CHAPTER 14

Seamus

We walk through a foyer of black granite and steel and head straight to the elevators. I'm not one for glitz and glamour. I prefer sitting at a dive bar, eating wings, and shooting the shit. That doesn't mean I can't handle what's coming.

Money doesn't intimidate me. Neither do assholes who think they're better 'cause they have it. I'm hoping Allie feels the same way. But I can sense her nervousness as easily as I feel the wool of her black cape rub against my arm.

Ordinarily, I'd keep yapping like a dog on steroids. But I'm not too dense to know she needs a moment. I let her have it, keeping her arm hooked through mine, reminding her she's not in this alone.

I hit the button to the 50th floor, holding the door open to allow an elderly couple through. The man nods his thanks, adjusting his position so he and his wife face straight ahead.

"It's a little cold tonight," Allie says.

I watch the numbers change on the screen as we jet upward. I thought we were long past idle chitchat and remind her with my next comment. "Don't worry, baby. I'll keep you warm."

Her eyes round as the woman standing in front of us turns back to glance at us briefly. The man turns too, offering me an encouraging wink.

I whisper into Allie's ear. "Just getting into character. What do you think?" My lips hover close enough to brush against her skin. "Should I kick it up a notch?"

"No," she stammers. "This is good."

I ease away from Allie, noting how tense she appears, and how she didn't seem to welcome my lips so close to her skin. I barely touched her. But if she thinks I'll keep my hands to myself in front of Valentina and Andres, she's dead wrong. I owe it to Allie to show them all she can have anyone she wants.

The elevator door opens with a *ding*. Allie keeps me in place, giving the elderly couple as much distance as the small space between the elevator and the restaurant allows.

My gaze takes in the area. Between the foyer and the combined floors, there's enough marble and steel to build a castle and a few villages. Unlike the ancient look of a castle, the entire building screams ultra-modern and would be happy to tell any would-be castle to fuck off.

We walk casually forward. There's only a yard or so keeping us from the hostess desk. But the acoustics are enough to send the wave of murmurs from inside to greet us. Okay. Maybe not greet us.

There's a coolness in the air and a heavy sense of entitlement. I've felt it when I've dined at so-called exclusive places. I guess that's why I prefer local pubs and neighborhood restaurants. The people there are out to be out and have a good time. The owners are decent, they know you by name and want to run a nice place. Restaurants like this one are all about their reputations and need to maintain a high-level clientele.

The elderly couple is greeted by a tall woman with a bun on top of her head. We've given them enough time to give their names and be escorted to their seats.

"Welcome to Savate's Steakhouse," the second hostess says when she sees us. "Do you have reservations?"

Like Allie, the hostess is in a tiny black dress. But Allie looks better and definitely acts better. "I'm afraid our dining area is otherwise filled for the evening."

Allie smiles at the snub, which is a lot better than how I take it. The hostess can probably guess I'm not a member of any country club.

"Party of four under Valentina Mendes," Allie adds coolly.

The woman lights up. "Oh, yes," she says, letting us know she recognized Valentina and how honored she was to be in her presence. "Your party is ready for you. May I take your coat?"

"Yeah. You could," I say. I chose not to wear a coat, unless you count the jacket of my Dior suit. Don't be surprised. I can be classy, and Evan was a real pal to lend it to me.

In one smooth move, I slip Allie's cape from her shoulders.

"Ah, I'd rather keep it on," she says.

The dark environment casts a shadow along her irises, adding to her allure. Good for her. Not so good for me. Jesus, it's getting harder for me to stay in the friend zone, where I'm pretty sure she expects me to stay.

"Why?" I ask. I already know the answer. She's having second thoughts about whether we can pull this off and feeling insecure, rather than owning how fantastic she looks.

"I get cold in these restaurants," she says, the slight quiver in her tone alerting me she's going downhill real fast.

"Then you leave me no choice," I say as if it's killing me. My arm wraps around her shoulders and I kiss her temple. "I'll have to hold you close all night long."

"Um," Allie says.

"Oh," the hostess responds.

She's a young woman and can probably recite Twilight by heart. She clutches her chest, gushing at the same time terror grips Allie's features.

It shouldn't make me laugh, but it does. "Come on, gorgeous. I've got you."

The dining area is dark and gloomy. "Ambiance," that's what they call it. I'm tempted to turn my flashlight feature on my phone on, just to make a point. But I remind myself I'm here for Allie, not for a laugh and not to embarrass her.

Through the gentle *clinks* of knives and forks tapping against oversized plates, conversation that sounds too forced to be genuine, and laughter to mocking to be sweet, we make our way around the tables.

The hostess turns around. "I shouldn't tell you this, but Miss Valentina has been my hero for years. When I was thirteen, I'd make my mother buy all the magazines with her face on it and spend hours matching my makeup to hers." She stops suddenly. "Do you know her? Personally?"

"Valentina is my sister," Allie explains.

The hostess's gaze traveled down Allie's body, returning to stop on her face. "I never would have guessed," she says.

Allie bristles against me. It takes all I have not to let this airhead have it. "Yeah, Allie is beautiful and sweet, incapable of stabbing someone in the back or stepping on someone just to claw her way to the top," I say. "Unlike Valentina, who probably tried to use her celebrity status to get a free meal. Am I right?"

The hostess with the most-est quiets, letting me know that, yeah, Valentina probably already had her parking taken care of too. "You're very pretty, too," she tells Allie as an afterthought. "This way, please."

I'm betting this broad would have begged Allie to ask the great and powerful Valentina for an autograph or maybe a picture. Not anymore. I shut her down and let her know she shouldn't bother trying. What the hell? Is this what Allie puts up with on a regular basis? I shake my head, remembering how I told her Valentina was hot that day we met at the bakery. If this is a regular day for Allie in Valentina's presence, I'm just as guilty. But that shit ends tonight.

I spot Andres and Valentina sprawled out along a large cushy leather booth. Andres's puny eyes enlarge when he sees us. Or should I say, when he sees Allie.

He catches himself half a second too late, his attention returning to his phone. Valentina is dressed in her signature red, eye-catching wardrobe. I don't like her, that doesn't mean I'm not blind. She looks gorgeous, the neckline falling to her waist. She has more to show than Allie. But that glitz and glamour is very much like this restaurant, overpriced, overdone, and full of itself.

Valentina continues to scroll through the wine list, making a show of flipping through the pages. That's when I know she knows we're here, and is working hard not to see us. For a loving couple on their way to the altar, there's not much love going on.

Once we reach the table, not a moment before, Valentina looks up. "Oh, there you are," she says. She scoots out, her motions graceful as she stands. The shoes she's wearing drop her just a few inches from my height, forcing her to crouch to kiss Allie's cheek.

"How are you, Valentina?" Allie asks.

"Splendid," Valentina replies. She laughs a little. "And to be honest, hungry."

Valentina doesn't bother to tell Allie how nice she looks or comment on her hair. Allie told me she hasn't seen Valentina since that day in the bakery. Allie has literally transformed herself into a different woman. Either Valentina is too enraptured with herself to notice, or she flat out refuses to share the spotlight with someone she doesn't feel deserves it. Maybe it's a little bit of both. Either way it's enough to piss me off.

"Seamus," Valentina says, lifting up on her toes to kiss my cheek. I pat her on the back. That's as good as it's going to get. I'm not kissing her.

Her lips linger a fraction of a moment longer than they did with her own blood. She's losing points real fast. Damn. Whatever made me think she was anything special?

I step away when Andres approaches Allie, reaching for her waist. I'm not trying to act possessive. I just am.

"Hi, Allie," he says, scowling at the way my arm keeps Allie against me.

"Hi, Andres," Allie replies. She eases away from me, following Valentina back into the booth. I think she's annoyed until she reaches for my hand, encouraging me to follow.

Andres purses his lips, watching her before looking rather accusingly back at me. He tilts his chin. "Seamus," he says.

I nod. Dipshit.

I don't realize the hostess is still there until she hands us our menus. A waiter shuffles over, introducing himself as "Don," rattling off the specials, and offering to get us our drinks.

"A bottle of Rudd Samantha's Cabernet Sauvignon to start would be delightful," Valentina says. She smiles. "You like wine, don't you?" she asks Allie.

"Guinness Nitro or a Blonde if you have it," I say, noting how Valentina wasn't really giving Allie a choice.

"Bottle or draft, sir?" Don asks.

"Bottle," I slip my arm around Allie, my protectiveness kicking up a notch. "What about you, Alz? You liked that Old Fashioned you had at the game."

Allie's smile is more grateful than it needs to be. "That sounds perfect. Thank you."

"An Old Fashioned for the lady, please," I tell Don.

"And for you, sir?" Don asks Andres.

"I'll have the wine," he says, annoyance in his voice.

My guess is maybe he has more balls than I give him credit for. He's pissed to have Valentina order for him. But then I see the way he's watching me hold Allie. I do the right thing and hold her closer. "You still cold, babe?" I whisper against her crown, my gaze never leaving Andres.

Allie quivers against me. "No. I feel good," she says, the tremble in her voice matching the shudder that follows.

Valentina carries on, speaking about the wedding and who will be there. She doesn't just rattle off big name celebs like I expect. Instead, she talks about the wonderful friendships she's developed with these big shots.

"Oh, the stories. The stories." Her words, her fake modesty, not mine.

I'm bored before I finish my salad, wishing we'd stayed in for pizza and beers at my place. So, I do the only thing I can do: run my fingers up Allie's leg.

Her spoon lowers cautiously as she straightens when my fingertips give the first, slow, lazy circle of her knee. I don't think anyone's noticed I've switched my fork to my left hand, just like I think no one will care if I have a little more fun.

Being the good Catholic I am, I began outlining the Michelangelo's Sistine Chapel against Allie's skin, moving a few centimeters higher. Now, I don't really know what the Sistine Chapel looks like. Never seen it aside from a few pictures I Googled once. But, you know, Michelangelo seemed like a decent guy and I think he'd appreciate the effort.

Allie tries to swallow back one of her famous squeaky noise. But something like "urpee" comes out and overpowers her skin with a coat of red. Her hand slaps over my knee as I wander just a little higher. I'm dying to see what other fun sounds she can make and give her thigh a not-so gentle squeeze.

Allie bangs her knee against the table with how hard she jolts. "Sorry, sweetie," I say, chuckling against her ear.

Another squeak, this time, more like a gasp. It's only then Valentina clues in that we're having fun without her and that, no, I don't care how many Oscar parties she's attended. Andres, though . . . I try to tone down my smirk. It doesn't work. Smirks are like wolves. You have to let them loose to run free.

"You do realize you're in public," he snaps.

For a guy with his own gorgeous babe, he seems rather tense. I smile. "What can I say? Can't keep my hands off my woman." I stop smiling, my hand gliding across Allie's small shoulders. "You know what I mean. Don't you?" I scan the space separating him and his beloved. Valentina is closer to Allie than she is to him. "I guess you don't," I point out.

Valentina shakes her head and scoots over to Andres. She kisses his temple. "I'm sorry, darling," she says. "I just haven't seen Allie in so long." She sighs, appearing sad, but I know better. "When you've been together as long as we have, you start to fall into a comfortable existence where you don't rely on touch as much as you do on the confidence and peace of having your lover beside you."

"You sayin' we're not confident or peaceful?" I ask. I keep my voice casual. Allie doesn't, speaking over my words as if Valentina's were all she heard.

"How long have you been together?" she asks.

"Seven years," Valentina says, her voice full of admiration when Andres clutches her hand. "Seven wonderful years."

Seven without Allie knowing or anyone bothering to tell her. Allie takes a few breaths, then a few more. Allie has never mattered to Valentina. If she didn't know it before, she knows it now.

Allie shrinks inward. She's still as close to me physically as she was when I was teasing her skin. But she's not the same woman I was laughing with in my truck, or the woman who should be owning how incredible she looks. She's the little sister, her speech and confidence dimmed by the way Valentina's shadow continues to hide her from the world.

It takes all I have not to drag Allie out of here. Fuck you, Valentina. Fuck you, Andres. Fuck you for hurting my woman.

I'm full, more from Valentina's awesomeness than my puny steak by the time Don returns with a rolling cart stacked with desserts.

Allie opts for another drink instead. Can't blame her. I can barely stomach another Stella McCartney runway retelling. Christ Almighty, when is this night going to end?

"What time will you be at Tía Blanca's?" Valentina asks, waving away the dessert tray and taking the last sip of her wine.

Allie looks at her like she's forgotten she's there. "I'm not going to Tía Blanca's," Allie replies.

"What's at Tía Blanca's?" I ask.

Valentina acts like I should already know. "It's a family tradition going back generations. The women make centerpieces for the brunch the day after the wedding. Silk flowers, silk ribbons, and more colorful vases than you ever thought possible." She laughs like she's embarrassed. I know better. "The flowers represent the bride's fertility, or the petals plucked on the wedding night. The ribbons symbolize the groom's virility. Didn't Allie tell you?"

Valentina lifts her glass to take another sip, forgetting for a moment not a drop remains. "No, she didn't," I answer.

"Because I won't be a part of it," Allie says, for the first time giving Valentina a taste of the anger she's held back. "I purchased the supplies like Mom asked. That's more than enough."

"They made you buy her that shit?" I ask, unable to hold back. "I'm surprised they didn't ask you to video them fucking."

Allie rights herself, responding to Valentina, seeing I'm not doing her any favors. "Mom and the Tías have everything they need."

"Except you," Valentina asks, only just recovering from my sex-tape jab. "You should be there."

"Are you kidding me?" Allie demands. "I'll hold your flowers. I'll fluff your veil, but no way will I celebrate you consummating your union." Her eyes narrow at Andres. "I believe that ship already left the dock."

"And crashed into a fucking ugly tug boat," I add, lifting my beer to toast Andres.

"You *dick*," Andres spits out.

I roll my eyes. Like no one's ever called me *that* before.

Valentina ignores us, but then again, she's not done scraping her claws. "Oh, that's right. I understand," she agrees sadly.

They're only a handful of words, but mean so much more.

Poor, *miserable*, lonely Allie.

She still hurts.

Still feels.

Still envies.

She'll probably die alone.

I'm ready to overturn the damn table and take Allie away from this shit. But that won't earn Allie respect.

"Good," I say, my eyes fixing on Allie's. I cup her jaw, stroking the soft skin. "We have too much to do and not enough time to do it."

I don't think about what could happen. It just does. As easy as I press against her, I welcome Allie's lips against mine. She starts to say something, but my lips dissolve against hers, fading her words into soft, sweet air.

There's no sound now. No clinking of knives and forks idly against bleached white plates, no murmurs or forced laughter drifting around and fighting to sound real. No one's here. Just us.

It's a long kiss, slow.

No urgency behind it.

No rush to break away before we're caught.

No worry that it will end too soon. No fear that it's wrong.

It's just one hell of a good first kiss.

I don't pull away until it ends. Until we both need to breathe and our skin to cool.

With a sigh, I reach for my wallet and drop down five Benjamins. It's enough for Allie and me and a thirty percent tip. No way am I letting Andres pay for us. He's done enough.

"Night," I say, with a half-assed salute. "It's been real."

I reach for Allie's hand, scared shitless she won't take it. She does, neither of us stopping to look at either Andres or Valentina. That doesn't mean I don't feel what they're pegging us with. Shock is one of the prominent feels, but it's the anger that swallows the shock and spits it onto the floor that I feel the most. I'm not sure if it comes from Andres or Valentina, and don't care enough to do anything except take Allie away from this place.

I place her cape around her shoulders and gather her to me as we wait for the elevator. If that's not possessive or psycho enough, I hold her against me as we wait for my truck. It's an overwhelming need to defend her from the verbal assaults she's spent a lifetime taking.

It's a long, silent drive back to her place, the echo of my footsteps as I walk her to the door as loud as my beating heart.

Allie doesn't invite me in. I don't expect her to, not with how sad she appears.

"Thank you. For everything," she says, her voice fading in the breeze.

I nod, for the first time in my life having too much to say and unable to say it. At this point, I'm content with a, "Fuck 'em. You don't need them."

Her eyes shimmer, not with humor or happiness, but with something that makes me want to tear someone apart. "She's still my sister, Seamus," she says.

"I know," I reply.

CHAPTER 15

Seamus

"Wow, Evie. This is quite a spread you have here."

I lift one prawn from what looks like fifty from a tray covered with that fancy lettuce. The moment all the seafood goodness hits my belly I reach for another, only to have Evie and her two mini versions shove their way in front of me and spread their arms out, blocking my brothers and me from the sprawling buffet. Evie's smallest daughter looks from Evie to her big sister, making sure she's assuming the proper form to keep us ravenous men off the goods.

"Why don't we hold off on eating and go outside?" Evie suggests, smiling.

"We should never hold off on eating when there's food," Finn says, speaking up. "It's a sin."

"Yeah, a sin," my brothers and me chime in.

Evie keeps her smile like a good hostess and calls for backup, like a woman who's shared enough meals with us. "Mateo, honey," she yells to her husband. "Could you kindly escort your friends outside?"

Mateo stomps into the large dining room, shadowed closely by his son. Mateo crosses his arms. So does the kid. "Leave the food the fuck alone and get your asses outside. We're on a schedule."

"Yeah, schedule," his mini-me agrees.

Mateo's voice means business and something else I can't place a finger on. Allie, like the rest of our women, falls into the role of ushering the menfolk out. Her arms wrap around mine, encouraging me forward.

"Our hosts asked us politely to step outside," she says, when I don't initially move.

I watch the way her arms hold me. This is the first time Allie's touched me since dinner with Valentina the Mighty and Andres the Asshole. It's also the first time I've seen her in a week. I can blame it on our schedules. We've both been slammed. But I'm also wondering if I should blame it on that kiss.

Don't get me wrong. It was a once in a lifetime kiss that women dream of and men want more of. I told Allie I wouldn't do anything that made me uncomfortable and I didn't. But I'm not sure if the same went for her. She didn't have to kiss me like she did. That's what I told myself. Except the more time that's passed, the more I'm no longer sure.

"I wouldn't exactly call that polite," I counter, walking slowly forward and allowing her to lead me outside. Hey, hungry as hell or not, no one can accuse me of not having manners.

We step onto the stone terrace that Angus and me helped Mateo build when they first bought their place. Finn crashes right into my back when I stop short.

"The hell, Seamus?" Finnie says. "You could have crushed Sol."

"Sorry," I say, glancing back to see if she's okay.

"It's okay," Sol laughs. Her smile fades and Finn frowns when they catch sight of my face.

"What's wrong?" Finnie asks.

I step aside so they can see what I'm seeing. Mateo and Evie's place is an entertainer's dream. Beautiful pool with a waterfall and Jacuzzi built in, a fire pit and bar area, and artistic landscape that would shame most royal gardens. But this afternoon, it's become something more.

What has to be thousands of clear Christmas lights and streamers of white silk fabric woven through tall wrought iron posts create an arc, transforming the yard into a fantasy world.

To our right, a small collection of chairs separated by an aisle lead to a gazebo, brightly decorated with more lights and sprays of white flowers.

My first guess is that Teo and Evie are renewing their vows. They're one of those couples who will always be in love no matter how old they get. I turn to Teo and Evie, grinning, pausing when I realize they're dressed more like guests in their own home, not a bride and groom about to get re-hitched.

Teo places his arm around Evie and hoists his youngest daughter on his hip. They return my smile, but there's something else there, a sadness I don't expect. I can't put a finger on what's happening until Declan steps onto the terrace dressed in a slick, black suit. His expression mimics Teo's; strong, happy, and a little sad, too.

"Hi," Declan says. He looks around, taking each of us in. Declan isn't like the rest of us. He's what you call polished and one of those men you always knew could be president. We used to joke that Ma swapped him out for a Kennedy at the hospital. A born politician and leader, and the youngest Distract Attorney in American history, we always knew Declan would change the world. You'll never see Deck sweat. You won't see him panic. But for once, my supposedly dashing brother with the blond wavy hair and stately appeal, struggles to find his words. We quiet, all of us, even the little ones who aren't so young they don't know he has something important to say.

"We're not certain how much time Miles has," Declan begins. He smiles, the way all men do when they have to share bad news along with the good. "Because of his illness, but mostly because I love her, Melissa and I are getting married today."

If Declan had only shared the news about marrying Melissa, we'd lose our shit. Out of everything Declan has done, nothing compares to the happiness Mel brings him. Except this thing with Deck and Melissa was never normal from the start. It was filled with a lot of love, sure, but enough sadness to dull our smiles.

Like an obedient group, instead of a loud and insane one, we part, allowing Declan through when he walks toward Ma. He pauses briefly when he reaches her, taking her hands in his.

I always pictured Ma as this giant being, one who could take on Godzilla if he ever had the balls to mess with our family. For the first time, I see how small and delicate she really is, and what a lifetime of hard work and raising seven kids did to her.

"I'm sorry for not getting married in the church," Declan tells her softly. "If Miles makes it through, I promise you we will."

Ma lifts her hand and places it on Declan's cheek. "God will understand and so do I, dear boy."

Their moment is brief, but enough to fill our hearts.

Declan bends to kiss Ma's cheek, "Thank you, Mama," he says, releasing her carefully. Almost as slowly as my next breath comes, he turns to Curran.

"Will you stand at the altar as my best man?" Declan asks him.

Curran doesn't answer, staring back in shock.

"Are you sure?" Curran asks.

"If you're not available, I could   always ask Wren."

We bust out laughing, even Wren, as she flips Declan off behind Ma's back.

The small smile Declan manages quickly fades. "I have many good men to choose from," he says, his gaze stopping on each of us, exchanging words that go unsaid like only brothers can. "Today, I choose you."

Curran nods, shaking Deck's hand firmly and clapping him on the shoulder. We watch, none of us able to move until Evie whispers something to Tess that widen her eyes.

"Stay with Aunties Sofia and Sol," Tess tells her girls.

As Tess and Evie take off into the house, Sofia and Sol reach for my nieces before they can fuss.

Slowly, in what feels more like a funeral procession than a promise of "I do," we walk down the stone steps. I don't realize I'm the one leading Allie or how close I'm holding her until we reach the yard, my steps heavy as we trickle to our seats.

I sit when Allie does, watching as Teo escorts two violinists and a cellist to the gazebo. The moment the trio settles, they begin to play the *Ave Maria*. I don't know what I should feel, pride, happiness, maybe misery? Deck and Melissa aren't racing down the aisle because he knocked her up or because they're so in love they can't wait. They're rushing because Mel's father could be dying, and they want him there to see his little girl marry the one man who'll be able to take of her when he's gone.

I feel numb. Maybe Allie can guess and gives my hand a squeeze. I'm not sure how her hand ends up in mine. It just appears, right where it should be.

Wren and Evan are sitting in front of us. She looks around, taking in how elegant, yet subtle, the decorations look. "How long did it take you to put all this together?" Wren asks Evie when she and Teo sit beside them.

"Two days," Evie replies. "But I had a great deal of help. Do you like it?"

Wren sighs, using her fingertips to wipe the corner of her eyes. "It's perfect, Ev."

Evie smiles, blinking and releasing a few tears of her own. I look away for a sec and let out a breath. Man. How am I going to get through the ceremony without looking like a blubbering fool?

"I wanted to do something nice for them," Evie admits her voice breaking.

Teo drapes his arm around Evie. "We owe him," he says, stroking his baby girl's hair away from her brow before he sneaks a glance toward the house.

Allie and I turn in the direction Teo's attention drifts to. She doesn't know Teo's family or anything about what they've been through. She quietly observes the interaction between Teo's sister, Lety, her husband, Brody, and Melissa's father, Miles.

Miles is sitting quietly on the patio leading out from Teo's full-finished basement. Lety is doing that smile thing women do, when they're trying to be brave and can't quite manage. She laughs at something Miles says, not that it stops the tears spilling from her eyes. She bends and kisses his cheek, wiping her eyes as Brody shakes his hand.

Brody leads Lety forward, his hand pressed against her lower back. It's the first time I've seen her since learning she's pregnant with twins. It's also the first time I see Brody without some semblance of laughter ready to erupt deep from his chest.

I nudge her a little as she passes. She grins at me and ruffles my hair, something I used to do to her when she was just a little kid with a big attitude. Given the atmosphere, I don't think it will be the last time we'll smile, or maybe even cry. But life is like that, sometimes giving you one hell of a blow one minute then making you laugh through the pain the next.

"Are you all right?" Allie asks.

I lift her chin and kiss her lips. I can't help myself, just like I couldn't help myself the other night. I want to feel close to her, I guess. There's a good number of us around, but everyone has someone, even Ma, who's surrounded by her small herd of grandchildren. If it wasn't for Allie, I'd be all alone.

Finn called me old. Maybe I am compared to him. But God willing, I have decades left. That doesn't seem to be the case for Miles.

Miles was a big guy when I first met him, tall with a decent gut that used to hang over his belt. Now all the pudge he had is just loose skin, dangling from a frame that no longer stands as tall or gives a hint of strength hidden beneath. I don't tell Allie. But it's like everything I'm feeling, she understands. She wipes a tear and smiles softly, leaning into me when I sling an arm around her.

From the gazebo, the trio switches from the *Ave Maria* to a classic melody I don't recognize, but one that fits the mood, beautiful and bittersweet. We stand, almost as one, including the little kids. From the direction of a small garden, Tess appears in what looks like one of Evie's dresses, given the short length of the skirt. Damn. Curran was right, she is all legs.

Tess clutches a spray of wildflowers against the waist of her dark-orange sleeveless dress. She walks forward, smiling softly, that smile widening when Curran gives her a wink.

Melissa must have selected Tess as her matron of honor. I'm not surprised. They're pretty tight. But Tess walking down the aisle makes this moment more real, adding another layer of emotion I'm not ready to feel.

I'm not going to let Allie see me cry. No fucking way. But when Melissa steps through an archway of white flowers, dressed in a simple white gown that captures her beauty and curves as if made for her, as Miles uses all the strength he has left to stand, I can't stop the sting across my eyes.

Miles is one of the strongest men I've ever met. He's Declan's mentor and a political icon. Today, he's just a father with a full and happy heart.

Miles takes a cautious step forward, leaning heavily on a cane. The chemo the docs used have reduced him to a shell of what he once was. Still, he smiles like all good men do when it's time for their daughters to become wives. There are no tears in his eyes. None that I can see. I suppose my family and I have enough.

Sofia, Sol, Lety, and Evie openly weep. Their men hold them closer, comforting them as well as themselves. Allie is crying, too. I clutch her tighter, reminding her I'm here for her and that I'm glad she's with me.

I'm barely keeping it together. We O'Briens have tough exteriors, but seeing Melissa with Miles rips us apart.

You don't have to know Miles to see how he's suffered, or be close to the family to feel the love he has for his little girl. It's just there, awful and awesome and mind-blowing all at once.

I give Allie a squeeze, wondering how I'm going to smile at all. But when I see Melissa's face when she reaches Declan, that smile isn't as hard as I thought. We don't know what the future holds for Miles. But this isn't a funeral. It's a fucking wedding.

There's not much to her flowers, just a few brightly colored roses. There's also not much to her hair. Just a neat bun at the base of her neck, held by a silver pin. That's all she needs to make one perfect bride and Declan knows it.

"Hi," Declan says, grinning.

"Hi, Declan," Melissa says, her voice so soft I barely hear it.

I hold Allie against me. It's nothing I think I should do. It's just natural.

Declan . . . I don't want to say he's a tight-ass, at least not on his wedding day. But out of all of us, he has always been the most serious. I've seen him at his best, when our father died and he stepped up, throwing himself into his education so he'd be able to give us a good life. I've seen him at his worst, when he thought he failed a victim he was representing, then did his damnedest to make that right. But today, I see him in a way I never have.

Declan straightens to his full height, his blond hair freakishly perfect like always, the strength he carries squaring his shoulders. But it's the softness in his gaze when he looks at Melissa . . . now, that's something I've never seen. For the first time ever, I see my brother as the man he's become.

I swipe my eyes. This is the first, of now, four weddings I have to attend. How the hell am I going to get through them all?

"You're going to be okay," Allie says, like she can read my mind.

Her voice shakes as she speaks, but there's her smile and I suppose it's enough.

I return her grin. "Yeah. We'll be fine," I assure her.

Miles kisses Melissa's cheek. "I love you, Daddy," she says, nut-punching what's left of my heart. Miles nods. It's not until he shuffles to his seat beside Mae, that I realize how much the brief walk affected his battered body. The strong stance he held abandons him. He rests his back against the chair, allowing it to bear his weight.

I turn back to the bride and groom, sad for Miles, but happy as anything for Deck and Mel. The Justice of the Peace who materialized out of nowhere takes a step back, allowing Father Flanagan forward. I hadn't seen him and I didn't expect to. But Teo and Evie must have handled it all.

Father Flanagan stares out into the small audience. "To all who have come to share this union, may the Lord bless you now and always." He addresses Melissa and Declan. "And to you Melissa and Declan, may the Lord bless your union, your children, and your future as husband-and-wife." He blesses Declan and Melissa with holy water and the sign of the cross. It's not much, but something that will mean everything to Ma. Father Flanagan steps away, allowing the Justice of the Peace forward.

The ceremony is brief, but the words shared mean just as much. We're all smiling, doing a real good job keeping it together until Declan signs the last of his vows.

"Your father loved you first," Declan says, motioning with his hands as he says each word. "Like him, I promise to love you forever."

"*Fuck*," I mutter, pinching the bridge of my nose.

In my defense, I'm not the only one of my brothers who dropped the "F" bomb. Even Curran, standing at the damn altar, let it rip. The women are all bawling except for Ma, who couldn't be prouder, and Wren, who only releases a tear and one big smile.

"Sorry," I whisper to Allie as Declan and Melissa walk past us as husband and wife. "I really thought we were coming here just to eat."

By this point, Allie is wearing most of her mascara on her cheeks. She dabs her eyes with a tissue. "Don't be sorry. This is good practice and . . ."

She loses it all over again when Miles walks down the aisle leaning heavily on Mae. "I don't think I can watch the father daughter dance," she says.

"Same," I agree. "I have an idea. Let's sneak away to the bathroom and pretend to have sex."

Allie's expression splits between laughing and a dark desire to smack me upside the head. I don't see a problem. Personally, I think it's a brilliant plan.

"What?" I ask.

My family is already making their way to the terrace where a DJ is setting up the music. "There's something very wrong with you," Allie finally says.

"I'm not saying we have to be loud or anything," I assure her. "We just have to make sure somebody catches us going in and coming out. They'll assume the rest."

"We're guests in someone's home," Allie reminds me, speaking slowly as if I'm missing something obvious.

"Oh, don't worry about it. Evie is already knocked up with their fourth kid. If anyone understands we need a moment, it's Teo."

Allie holds out her hands, the strap of her small purse slipping to the crook of her elbow. "Just so I'm clear, you want to sneak away during the father daughter dance, taking place in someone's home, to pretend to have sex with *me* in a *bathroom*, so you don't cry in front of your brothers while watching something beautiful?"

"It sounds dirty when you put it that way."

"How else would you like me to put it, Seamus?"

I lead her forward when I realize we're the only ones trailing behind. "If it makes you feel better, people make sweet love in the bathroom all the time."

Allie gasps. "They do not."

"Maybe they should," I say, growing defensive. "I bet you most marriages wouldn't end in divorce if there was more sex in the bathroom."

Finnie turns around and bumps my fist. "Hell yeah, to sex in the bathroom. Sol and I will take the upstairs."

"*Finn*," Sol hisses, doing her best to cover my niece's ears. "We're in my cousin's house."

"He'll understand," Finn replies, like Sol is the crazy one. Hell, maybe she is.

"Told you," I mutter to Allie.

All right, all right, I sound like a flaming idiot. I get it. But when Allie shoots me a smirk followed by a laugh, it's all worth it. "Keep your hands to yourself during the father daughter dance and no one will get hurt."

"I'm not making any promises," I tell her, grinning.

I offer her my arm, her smile fading when her phone buzzes and she checks the screen.

I roll my eyes when one text follows the next. "Let me guess, you're late for Valentina's fertility dance rehearsal."

Her gaze drops as she fumbles to place her phone back into her purse. "It's Andres. He says he wants to see me."

CHAPTER 16

Allie

"Why are you avoiding your sister?" Mom asks.

A better question would be, why does Valentina feel the need to rub this wedding in? I was hoping the wedding would keep her and Mom so busy they'd leave me alone. Instead, the incessant calls from my mother and aunts have multiplied. Throw in Valentina's constant texts and pics in her dress, picking out flowers, or images from her various glamorous luncheons with her model-esque friends, I'm ready to toss my phone in the Delaware.

"Mom, my final fitting was Tuesday and I pick up the dress this week. What can Valentina possibly need from me?"

"Your support. We never see you. You're always working or with *that man*."

"His name is Seamus and I have to go."

"To be with him?" she snaps.

I look up at the stained-glass window that adorns the front of his shop. "Yes," I say.

"Do you love him?" she asks, her tone prickly.

I do. But I don't tell her that and I'm definitely not ready to tell him. "I have to go, Mom," I say and disconnect.

I've only really known Seamus a few weeks. But if this isn't love, I doubt I'll ever feel it. I miss him all the time and I haven't seen him in a while, which is why I drove to his place today.

I knock on the door, hurrying to adjust my breasts beneath my bra when I hear Seamus's heavy footsteps approach. It's not that I want my breasts to look good in this white T-shirt. It's just that the lingerie I'm wearing makes it challenging to keep the girls from pointing skyward.

"Who the hell is it?" he barks from behind the door. "I'm not buying anything or changing my religion. And if you're from the Girl Scouts, I never got my fucking Samoas."

I'm already laughing and I'm not even through the door. It's wonderful to hear his voice and even better to be around him, I only hope he feels the same. "It's Allie, Seamus."

He swings open the door, grimacing. At first, I think he's still upset with me. Andres' text pushed an unexpected wedge between us. I tried to ignore the feelings of being abandoned it stirred, along with all the insecurities I thought were long behind me. But his message dampened the already sober atmosphere of Declan and Melissa's wedding.

While I didn't respond to Andres' text or the next few that followed, I reverted to the role I adopted when we broke up. I dove into my work like nothing else mattered, except there was someone who obviously did.

"I'm sorry I haven't called," I say to Seamus.

He doesn't reply, watching me closely.

"And I'm sorry I wasn't able to make lunch the other day." I glance up, wishing I could express how much I've missed him these past two weeks. "And that I had to cancel our dinner plans."

I sigh when he says nothing. It wasn't my intention to ignore him. I did have to work and so did he. But I was hoping he'd miss me, and maybe make the effort to see me. "I'm really sorry, Seamus."

"It's okay," he says, smiling. It's not his typically wide 'you're not going to believe what happened to me' smile. But it's there, casting a glimmer on perfectly conceived irises and an extraordinarily rugged exterior. Okay, perhaps I did want to look nice for him and I'm really hoping I do in the jeans and cute heels I selected.

He leans against the door frame. "Why didn't you just use your key?"

I gnaw at my lip, remembering how he passed me his spare key following Declan's ceremony. "I thought that was for show. I didn't want to assume I could walk into your home without asking." I also didn't want to assume he'd be alone. Not with yoga girl next door, or the postal carrier who's wearing less and less each time she brings a package to the door.

"I wouldn't have given it to you if I hadn't expected you to use it." He throws open the door. "Come in."

Seamus locks the door as I slip out of my stylish olive Anorak jacket, another sweet item he helped pick out. He reaches for it and hangs it in the closet. As usual, the fresh scent of wood and oil reach my nose, but instead of the array of tools and pieces of lumbar scattered about, everything lays in neat piles. He hasn't been working and I'm wondering why.

He shuffles up the stairs, his movements off. I hurry after him, the sound of my steps echoing in the large space.

"Are you all right?" I ask, watching him lean against the counter with his arms spread.

Again, he grimaces, turning his neck from side to side. "I hurt my back last night."

I reach into his fridge and pull out a water bottle, putting it in front of him before searching his freezer for a bag of peas or something frozen I can place on his back. "On the boat?" I ask.

"Yup."

His smirk causes his eyes to twinkle. I do believe Seamus O'Brien might be a little bit sexy. I say just a little bit, because I'm trying to be nice. I shut the door to the freezer when all I find is ice cream, wondering when I turned into such a liar. Seamus is the sexiest man I've ever met.

"Did you catch a big fish? A shark or something?"

"No. It was the damn stripper pole."

I stop in front of him. "I thought you were taking Finn deep sea fishing for his bachelor party?" I don't mean to sound disappointed, but I am. "Don't you think Sol might be upset when she learns Finn lied to her?"

Yes, let's make this all about Sol, so I don't look like the jealous one.

Seamus almost chokes on his water. Yet it's the pained scrunch of his face that makes me realize how sore he actually is. Poor thong-chasing slut.

"We did go fishing, babe," he says.

"With strippers?" I ask. I nod thoughtfully. "I hear their casting abilities are superb."

Seamus cracks up, the way he throws his head back causing him to groan. He rolls his shoulders. "There weren't any strippers," he says, rubbing his neck. "Just the poles."

I fold my hands in front of me, waiting for him to elaborate. He doesn't respond, taking me in as if he's expecting some kind of reaction.

"Are you jealous?"

"No," I reply a little too fast.

"You sure?" He smirks. "You seem ready to belt me."

"Why would I do that?" I ask sweetly. I don't want to be the jealous type. I think it's petty and unnecessary and good God, what kind of boat has stripper poles?

He laughs, appearing to enjoy himself. "Fine," I say. "I give up. What happened to the ladies with the merrily swinging tassels dancing on the poles?"

"Well, since you asked, I'll tell you." He points at me. "But only because you asked, since a gentleman never tells."

"I'll be sure to inform the gentleman next time I see one."

Again, Seamus cracks up. Well, aren't we just having a lovely good time? "You're having fun, aren't you?"

"I am. But I'll let you off the hook." He plants his hands back on the counter and leans toward me, causing his light blue shirt to stretch across his biceps, not that I really notice. "Angus hasn't done shit for any of the weddings. Not Deck's. Not Wren's. Not Finnie's," Seamus begins. "Granted, we've tried to give him as little as possible. Last night was a prime example of why he's better off complaining no one trusts him or blowing us off, because he's supposedly busy. Are you ready for this?"

By now I'm smiling, too, ignoring the jealousy that remains, because God knows I don't stand a chance against Seamus's gorgeous face. "You have me at the edge of my seat," I respond.

He falls into his best impression of Angus, his voice almost too deep to be human. "Don't youz worry," he says. "I hooked Finnie up good. Picture this. Luxury fishing boat. All the food we can eat and the best fishing the Atlantic Ocean has to offer. All for only four-fifty a pop."

He switches his expression and glances around, appearing confused and altering his voice to mimic Curran's. "Four-fifty a pop? Just because you plan the party doesn't mean the rest of us have to pay for your ass."

Once more Angus makes an appearance through Seamus's expression and tone. "Fine," he says, throwing out his hands. "Three-fifty a pop."

Seamus takes on Killian next, standing on top of his chair to mirror Killian's immense size. "Are you kidding me? What the hell was the extra hundred dollars paying for? Your mortgage?"

Seamus jumps off the chair, his expression agonized as he spreads out his arms. "Silence. Only silence, followed by the rest of us calling him an asshole."

As much as he's making me laugh, I can see what this riveting retelling of the bachelor party is costing him. I walk around the counter and rub his shoulders.

He tenses, then slowly relaxes. "Damn, that feels good."

I'm not doing much, but he seems to like it. "How was the boat?" I ask, sparing him the trouble of having to continue with his performance.

He takes a few pulls of his water. "The best thing I can tell you about that piece of shit is that we'll be fine after another two tetanus shots. It was nothing but rust on rust with a motor. I think if we had a nicer boat, the trip would've been smoother and Finn and Killian wouldn't have puked as much as they did."

"Oh," I say.

"Tell me about it," he says. "I don't know what the fuck their women feed them, but it went all over the upper deck—next to where the food Angus supposedly ordered was supposed to go." He shudders. "But they weren't the only ones. Everyone was hurling off the side of the boat except for me. I was always the only one who could handle those dizzy rides at Six Flags. By the time we made it out to our chosen destination, everybody was lying on their sides begging to die. It was just me and the stripper pole left to save the party."

"I apologize," I say, scratching his back lightly. "But what exactly was a stripper pole doing on a boat?"

He glances at the way I'm gingerly touching him. "I told you," he says. "We made the mistake of letting Angus book the trip. Everyone is looking and feeling like shit so I try to get a laugh out of them. I think I managed one and a half swings around the pole before the boat tipped to the side and I went flying. I hit a couple of metal cages. There was rotting meat in at least one."

"Why were there metal cages and rotting meat on a boat?"

"Because when the captain isn't hosting these awesome fishing excursions, he illegally transports exotic animals. Tiger cubs and lions if you can believe it. That was another thing that pissed Curran and Declan off. Not only did they puke themselves into oblivion, they had to report the captain, *and* arrange to have him arrested once we docked."

I gasp. "Oh, goodness."

"That's a nice way of putting it. The whole thing sucked. We had to play like we were having a good time so the captain wouldn't suspect he was in trouble and toss our asses overboard."

"That sounds absolutely awful."

"Oh, it totally sucked balls." He takes a breath when I hit a tender spot. "Evan came to the rescue, once he stopped puking, I mean," he adds. "He's taking us to the World Series for his bachelor party. Box seats, VIP passes, the whole shebang." He motions to the phone, although it seems to hurt him. "I just got the text from him and the one from Wren ripping Angus apart."

Seamus curls forward, every part of him appearing battered and bruised. "You're not doing so well, are you?"

"I've had better pole dancing experiences," he admits.

I pat his back. "I'm sure you have, big guy. How about I give you a massage. A real one?"

He raises his eyebrows. "You'd do that for me, Curvy Sue?"

"You bet all those singles you earned in your G-string."

"How did you know I was in a G-string?" he asks.

"I would expect nothing else," I say, lightly pushing him toward his bedroom.

He glances at me over his shoulder. I shouldn't love it as much as I do. The kisses he's given me meant the world to me. I wish they meant more to him than just a show. Seamus is so cute. His personality. His face. Even the wall of muscles that tighten so firmly against my palms.

"Just lay on your bed and allow me to work my magic."

"I can't wait," he murmurs.

I try not to focus on the deep thrum that lingers over each word he utters. "You have any medicated cream for muscle aches?" I ask, grateful that for once my voice doesn't crack from the weight of his hotness.

"Tiger Balm," he says. My hand slip away from him as he shuffles into his bathroom. "It's the greatest stuff ever. Killian and Finnie use it all the time after their workouts."

The opening and closing of several drawers are followed by his quick return.

I edge toward the bed. His stance seems off. "You really did a number on your back, didn't you?" My words stick to my throat when he strips out of his shirt and exposes everything nature blessed him with. Holy . . . Seamus isn't attractive. He's perfection dripping in sex and freakish manliness.

And now I'm supposed to touch him!

"Do you like what you see?" he asks.

If that's not bad enough, he winks. *Winks.* My heart cartwheels and then slams to a halt. I clutch my chest, lucky to be alive.

"Allie?"

It's not just that he says my name. It's how he says it. As if he's unsure what I may do next. Of course, because I haven't completely embarrassed myself enough, I'm pointing, actually *pointing,* at him.

I'm going to orgasm where I stand. I swear I am. "You have a bruise," I stammer. I motion to a dark spot along his side, ignoring the fact that it's nowhere close to where I was pointing. "Right there," I add when he stares at me.

He lifts his left arm and looks down. "You're right. Shit." He turns around slowly with his arms out. "How does the rest of me look?"

Um. Fan-fucking-tastic? Seamus is inhuman. A life-sized sculpture of a superhero without a cape, shield, or anything else that might block his magnificence.

The best I can say about my behavior is that I don't outwardly faint. My heart races ahead, scorching my insides with blood-sizzling desire. I volunteered to touch him and his muscles and tendons and silky, flawless skin—

I slap my hands over my eyes. How am I going to keep from straddling him? I'm his friend, dammit. He made it more than clear following that dinner with Valentina and Andres. He didn't ask to spend the night, or even to spend a few hours when he took me home. He simply walked away as if the kiss had meant nothing.

"What are you thinking?" Seamus asks, his deep voice unfairly husky.

I drop my hands away. "That you really did a number on yourself, mister."

There are moments when I wish I could really slap myself. This is one of those moments.

"Oh." He tosses his shirt on the bed, crumpling his forehead. He must be in complete torment. Thank the good Lord he has me and all my asinine comments to help him.

I wish I could be better. That I can somehow save us from a life of loneliness. But I'm not Valentina, the woman he couldn't forget and always found attractive.

"Where do you want me?" he asks.

"In bed," I reply honestly.

He pauses briefly then spreads across his dark chocolate comforter, his stomach on the mattress and his bulging arms crossing in front of him.

Each word spills from my lips before I realize my sadly deprived nether regions have taken over my mind. "Would you mind if I straddled you?"

"No," he replies before I can finish.

His response is enticing, daring, and nothing I expected. Perhaps because there's nothing to expect. Seamus would never be interested in a woman like me. He doesn't want to settle down, or anything more than a good night and a goodbye. Why should he? Our agreement didn't include any real feelings, even though that's what I've come to have.

I inch forward, resolving to treat him as the friend he's been to me. I won't ruin what we have by forcing something that isn't there.

I lift the tin lying directly beside him, opening the lid with a brief *ping*. "I hope you have time," I say. "It's going to take me a while to work all your muscles."

My frustration punches my comment. I shouldn't be angry at him, and I'm not. Perhaps I'm just angry at myself.

Seamus drops his forehead against his arms. "Do what you want," he says. "I've got time."

He sounds angry, too. I can't blame him. I sound like a raging idiot.

I slip out of my shoes and straddle his back, my knees falling on either side of his waist. I drop my hand, the tension between us increasing with every breath I take. I don't want to touch him merely to relieve his pain. I want to touch him like a lover, someone who means more to him than the woman he jokes with.

Time passes. Too much for the both of us. "Look," he says. "If you don't want to do this, you don't have to. It's not like I expect anything from you."

"I know you don't," I reply. This time, instead of exasperation, another emotion pokes through, one of longing and more disappointment than I dare to admit.

With shaky fingers, I dip into the balm. The scent of eucalyptus, and what might be cannabis, drift into the air, strong yet oddly soothing. I welcome the aroma, allowing it to relax me.

My fingers trace down Seamus's spine, dissolving the ointment into a thin liquid. His shoulder blades quiver. "Are you cold?" I ask, speaking quietly.

"No," he replies.

"Are you certain?" I rub my hands along his shoulders in small circles and widen them slowly, digging into the thick and dense musculature that makes up his back. The balm alternates between warming and cooling. Again, he trembles. "Would you like me to turn on the heat?"

"I'm fine," he says, his voice tighter.

"Okay . . ." I adjust my hips, focusing on how his skin just barely moves beneath my splaying fingers. "If you change your mind, just let me know."

He doesn't respond, unless you count the primal groan breaking through his chest.

"Am I being too rough?" I ask.

"No. Don't. *Stop*." He clears his throat, but not all the rasp behind it. "You're fucking amazing."

Oh, that's so sweet. "I'm glad you like it," I say, unable to stop my smile. Seamus has done so much for me, the least I can do is relieve his pain. Even though I wish this was more than a therapeutic session.

I want to make him feel good in ways he can't possibly imagine. I want to take him deep with each pass of my naked hips and feel his bare skin glide against mine. It's how I picture us every night since he kissed me. It's sweet, sexy, becoming rough and wild when he flips me onto my knees.

I adjust my position, wiggling down until I'm almost to his thighs. His breath hitches. "I'm so sorry. Did I hurt you?" He shakes his head, appearing out of it. "I need to get lower so I can reach the muscles along your waist."

He grunts, but otherwise doesn't reply.

I'm starting to wonder if I'm doing more harm than good. "Seamus . . . are you all right with me on top of you?"

At least from this position he can't see me blush.

"Totally," he says, his voice oddly terse.

I start to lift off him, worried he's just being nice. "*No,*" he warns. "Don't you dare move now."

I settle back on top of him. "All right. If you insist," I say. He seems *uncomfortable,* if that makes any sense. Still, if this is what he wants . . .

My fingers work him from his waist, to both sides of his spine, and back down, repeating the motion and using the weight of my upper body to soothe the tightness I feel.

Seamus grows abruptly still when I reach for more balm. "Did something snap?"

"No."

My goodness, he sounds grumpy. I dig my hands and fingers deeper into his skin. "Don't be surprised if you hear a crack, I'm working you pretty well."

"Got that right," he mutters, the rigid planes of his back twitching.

I pause in the middle of working his shoulders. Grumpy isn't the right word here. Neither is tense. He sounds turned on. No. That can't be right. All I'm doing is rubbing his back.

I resume my work, flexing and extending my fingers into his shoulders hard enough to make them ache and him moan.

"Allie," he says in a grunt. "What the *fuck* are you doing to me?"

"It sounds ridiculous, I know. But therapeutic massage is often quite strenuous. You'll feel better when I'm done. I promise."

"Therapeutic massage?" he asks. "Is that what you're doing?"

"Well, yes," I reply. "Based on your stance, you don't need a relaxing massage or hot stones. You needed some roughening up to exhaust the muscles so they naturally relax."

I sigh when he doesn't reply. I'm trying to make him feel good, but I'm not certain it's working.

"You seem to know a lot about this sort of thing."

I shift position and start on his arms. "A little more than the average person, but not as much as a professional masseuse," I admit.

"What does that mean exactly?"

"I took massage as an elective in college, believing it was an easy way to earn an 'A.'" I laugh a little. "I had no idea I'd have to study anatomy." I toss my head back to remove some of the hair gathered around my face. "But I was committed to doing well, and learned a great deal more than I'd planned."

"You don't strike me as a science person."

I shake my head, although he can't see me. "I'm not. It was the last class I needed to graduate, and was so stressed because of it. I struggled with understanding the human body and the science of massage. What helped me was that the physical piece of it came naturally."

He pushes up enough to turn his head. "So, why'd you stay with it? You could have dropped the class when you saw the syllabus and switched to something you didn't have to be so stressed about passing."

I play with his hands, noting how massive they are compared to mine. He watches me, his eyes glazing over with something I don't quite recognize. "I wanted to be good at massage. I thought it would help me please Andres."

"*What*?"

As hilarious as my intentions sound now, they're not even worth a giggle. "In many ways I'm a traditional Latina and traditional Latinas please their men in every way possible. I thought if I learned to touch Andres better, he'd stay a happy and contented husband." I try to laugh. "It sounds stupid, doesn't it?"

Seamus frowns. "The only stupid thing here is Andres. Allie, I don't get how that loser broke your heart. I mean, I do, but I don't. You wasted your time."

I return to Seamus's back so I don't have to face him, dragging my fingernails in a backward motion. "You're right. But I didn't know it at the time."

Seamus makes a funky movement with his toes. I wish I could relish the effect I have, but all I can think about are his words, and how little he can relate to my situation with Andres.

"This may be hard for you to understand," I say, my tone barely audible. "But it wasn't just me believing I loved Andres. It was me believing I'd never have a chance to love anyone else."

"Why? That's insane."

I stop for a moment, staring across the mountains of silky flesh beneath rock hard strength. "Seamus, you had your choice of pretty girls from the moment you began to notice them. I only ever had Andres, who I believed was my friend."

When the only thing that comes is silence, I think I more than proved my point.

"I'm going to ask you something that's completely out of line," he says, halting me when I try to lift off him.

"It won't be the first time," I remind him.

He can't see me smiling, but his laugh makes me thinks he knows I am. "All right. I'll give you that one." He waits and asks, "Have you ever slept with anybody besides him?"

"Yes."

My lack of hesitation seems to give him pause. For a moment, all that exists is air between us. "Okay . . . give me a number."

"You want specifics?"

"Why not?" He pauses. "We're friends, aren't we?"

Although I've dreamt of more, yes, I suppose we are.

"Four," I confess. "One almost immediately following Andres. The others about every two years." I resume my massage. "The first time was because I needed to feel desirable. He was a good kisser and that's about it."

"And the others?" he asks, sounding perturbed. "Were they good kissers, too?"

I lean forward slowly, using my weight to dig the heels of my palms. "They weren't much of anything. We went out a few times and not much more afterward."

"After you had sex, you mean?"

"Yes," I admit.

He huffs. "Did the shitheads at least call you?" he asks.

Wow. Now he sounds angry.

"I didn't feel like I was going anywhere with anyone. They were wasting my time and I was done with that nonsense following Andres." I shrug. "So, instead of committing to a man, I committed to becoming successful. I suppose a lot of good came out of it."

"But did they call?" he asks as if my explanation wasn't enough. "Or were they assholes who used you until they got what they wanted?"

I throw my leg to the side as if dismounting from a horse, not a man with enough sex appeal to bring an equestrian down.

Seamus snags my wrist. "Wait, where are you going?"

"I'm moving on to your legs," I respond.

"Do you want me to take my pants off?"

"Please don't," I say a little too quickly.

He releases his hold like I slapped him. "All right."

"I'm sorry, I didn't mean—"

"I knew what you meant, Alz," he says.

Throughout our time, his voice has conveyed a great deal of emotion: anger, annoyance, resentment, but this time there's a sense of sadness to it that practically splits my heart. "Just answer the question. Did the dickheads call you or not?"

I lower my hand to his thigh, although at this point I'm not certain he wants me touching him. When he doesn't object, I begin to work the muscles of his legs. I finally answer. "They called, but I told them I didn't think we'd make a good match."

"All righty then," he says, appearing satisfied.

"Why did you want to know?" I clarify my response before he can explain. "It seems like you're happy they called me. But from what you've told me, you don't call back the women you sleep with. Ever."

"That's different," he answers.

"Why?" I ask. "Those women are no different than me and what I wanted, someone who would change their lives forever."

"You don't know the women I've slept with. And, no offense, you're romanticizing something that isn't there. The only men capable of changing their lives are their probation officers when they catch them doing shit they're not supposed to."

I sit back on my heels, reaching for his calves. "That's not fair, Seamus. They all can't be that bad, and like I mentioned, they're looking for someone to love."

"No, they're looking for sex and that's what I give them."

"Why?" I ask.

"Because I want it, too, and I'm damn good at it."

I shake my head. "That's not what I mean. If these women are so terrible, why not look for someone who isn't so terrible, who hasn't served a prison term or stabbed her last boyfriend?" He jerks, making me think I'm being too aggressive. "When we were discussing books the other week, you mention *The Good Earth* and how you empathized with that poor Asian woman who was stuck with that horrible creature of a man."

"You're assuming I look for women with a rap sheet." He turns enough to show me he's frowning. "And that I'm that horrible creature of a man."

"That's not exactly what I mean. But Seamus, you have to take responsibility for the type of woman you sleep with and are attracted to."

He pushes up on his elbow and flips onto his back, fiddling with the pillows until he gets them just right. "It's not that I'm attracted to them." He holds out a hand. "Scratch that. There's some attraction there." I look at him. "Okay. A lot of attraction. But the places I go tend to be, ah, what's a good word?"

"Seedy?" I guess.

He points at me. "But with good food and you know it."

I cover my mouth, albeit briefly. "How do you make me laugh, even though I have every right to be angry at you?"

"It's a gift?" he offers.

For a moment I stare at him, embarrassed that I'm not trying to hide it. He smiles, making me think it's okay to stare. "Like I was saying, I don't hang out in the classiest joints this city has to offer. Are the patrons a little hardcore?" He shrugs. "Probably. But you're wrong if you think I go looking for a woman who'll steal my keys and take off with my microwave."

I don't even want to know how that happened. "Then how do you end up with the women that you do?"

Seamus doesn't hesitate, but it's like his explanation comes to him all at once. "I don't necessarily look for dangerous women. But I think I give off that dangerous, willing to try anything, let's go crazy, kind of vibe. In the end, I'm usually the one in danger, with some psycho trying to slice me into confetti or booking the next flight to Singapore with my credit cards. I don't plan it that way, but that's how it always ends up. After years of going through it, I should be used to it. But I'm not."

"So why not try someone better?" I ask. "Perhaps allow someone you trust to introduce you to someone a little more stable."

"You have anyone in mind?" he asks.

"Absolutely not," I snap. I can't believe he hasn't guessed I want him all to myself. But I don't give off that dangerous vibe that seems to attract him. I'm just me.

My attention drifts to the framed picture of Seamus with his family he keeps on his dresser. They're all in bathing suits and Santa hats, straddling an immense promotional bottle of Guinness they dressed up like Rudolph. That must be the Christmas photo they sent last year. As much as I don't like the direction our conversation has strayed in, I wish I would have known him well enough then to have received a card.

I cross my legs, returning my focus to this man I've fallen so hard for. "What's stopped you from meeting a nice woman?"

"I've met my share," he says. "But these so-called nice girls were never interested in me. 'Dumbass' one of them called me. 'I'm hoping to marry a doctor,' another one said. I was told they were nice. But that niceness didn't last when they found out I was 'just a carpenter.'"

"Are you serious?" I ask.

"Why would I lie to my girl?"

His term of endearment hits me harder than it should. This time, he's the one looking away.

"Do I sleep with women who may not be as classy or educated as the so-called nice ones?" he asks, waiting for me to react. "Yeah. But at least they think I'm good enough."

"I understand." I move closer to Seamus. "Never mind. I don't. You're very attractive."

"Good looks and a winning personality only get you so far, babe," he says. I think he means to joke, but the humor doesn't quite reach his eyes.

"I don't just mean your looks, Seamus," I reply, wishing I wasn't so scared to say what I do. "I mean you."

I think I'm going too far, taking our friendship somewhere it may not return from. Even so, I allow the words to come. "I don't always agree with what you say or how you say it. That doesn't mean I don't sense your heart behind every word."

I try to smile when he doesn't respond, reverting to one of the last things he said. "I suppose the women you choose to spend your time with appreciate your honesty." I make a face. "That is, until you use your dead grandmother as an excuse for not calling them."

"Don't bring Grammie—God rest her soul—into this. In all fairness, Pop-Pop would understand."

Again, that humor he's going for fails to light that face I constantly dream about. "My point is, at least you don't promise these women anything past the time you spend with them."

"You're right. I don't," he agrees.

"Then I suppose I can't blame you for seeking the women you do. They're as honest with you as you need them to be."

He nods thoughtfully. "There have been a few married ones, and some who may or may not have warrants out for their arrest. But yeah, they accept me for the carpenter I am instead of dropping me flat for a doctor they may never meet."

I ask my next question, but I'm already afraid to know. "Have you ever wanted to spend more than one night with a woman?"

The way he takes me in robs the universe of time and all celestial beings. No one else exists. It's simply us.

"Just once," he rumbles.

CHAPTER 17

Seamus

I should be used to the way Allie's eyes go wide when I say shit without giving it some thought . . . and maybe when I say shit after giving it some thought. I'm not used it, though. It's like everything that happens between us is always a new experience even though at times it's like we've known each other forever, instead of a handful of weeks.

Her light eyes are blinking back at me. What I said knocked her on her ass. What she doesn't know is that I gave myself a good slap on the ass cheek, too.

I just asked Allie to sleep with me. Scratch that. I told Allie how much I want to sleep with her—to make love to her—whatever women call it to make it sound amazing and not like the one-night hookups I'm used to.

All right. I didn't *ask* her, ask her. I told her how I feel. I want to spend the night with her, getting to know her body and touching her like I've wanted since the first night we kissed.

I was hard as a steel pole when she rubbed my back, each squeeze making me hers. That's not entirely true. I've been Allie's for a while now. I look for her to call when I think she should be home, just to make sure she's safe and that no one fucks with her. Except her family is constantly fucking with her.

Her mother texts when we're together, and her sister, then her aunts, all trying to make her feel guilty for not doing more for Valentina. But it was Andres' text that made me want to find him and snap his scrawny neck. He's not hers anymore. She's mine. I try not to roll my eyes, at least that's what I tell myself.

Am I putting on the moves, sweeping her into my arms, and shoving my tongue down her throat? No. I can't do that to someone like Allie. So, I'm putting it all out there. Except she's not coming, and I'm not sure she wants to.

"What do you think about what I just said?"

"I think you're being honest?" she replies as if she's asking a question instead of answering mine.

The hell? That was a lot for a ball-buster like me.

I drop my head and rub my eyes, feeling tired and more frustrated than I want to be. "I think something is holding you back and I think it's your douchebag ex-boyfriend and your overbearing family."

Allie's mouth slowly falls open. "Where is this coming from?"

I grab hold of her tiny body and tuck her against me, grateful to God my giant erection has called it quits, and that the blue balls aren't as painful as I thought they'd be.

"Here's the deal. As much as I want to believe you moved on from dickweed Andres, I'm not sure you have. He burned you bad, and Valentina was more than happy to pour the gasoline."

Allie quiets. I know I'm hurting her and pointing out the obvious, and it kills me, but she needs to hear what I have to say. "You want my advice?" I don't wait for her to answer. "I think you need to take Andres up on his offer to meet him."

"Valentina and my family won't approve."

"It's not about them." Her expression is so sad I want to kick my own ass for upsetting her. "It's about what this shithead did to you, and how he and your sister got away with all of it."

Allie's gaze grows distant. I know she doesn't want to talk about it, but she tries. "You want to me to confront the past instead of hiding from it and pretending it no longer matters," she reasons.

I nod. "That sounds good. Mostly I think you should tell Andres to fuck off."

Allie tenses against me. "She's my sister," she replies. It's the same thing she said the night we had dinner with those assholes. Like it's supposed to excuse everything Valentina has done.

"Alz," I say. "I love my family. I'd give my life for any one of them without thinking twice. But not all people have the kind of family I do, the kind that would give up their lives right back. And some people aren't *just* poison. They pour it down your throat, happy to let you die in their place."

I wrap my arms loosely around her tiny waist when she tries to lift off me. I don't want her to leave and hold her just enough to know, but not so hard she can't break away. The truth hurts and because it does, I pull her in to me when she starts to cry.

I cup her face, stroking her cheek lightly with my thumb as I kiss away her tears. "I know you're right," she says, her voice shaking. "But they're all I have."

"No," I tell her quietly. "You have me."

It's true, even if I don't get to have her the way that I want.

"Seamus," she says, her voice breaking.

Allie buries her face in my shoulder. I want to take the words back, so the next tear doesn't fall and the one after that doesn't follow. But these tears are the kind of tears that tell me she's listening to what needs to be heard.

"I only ever wanted to do the right thing, to be a good daughter, sister, and friend. Somewhere along the line, everything changed. Instead of being appreciated, I became less than I was, even though all I ever tried to do was help."

"I know, baby," I tell her. "But all they did was help themselves to you."

What I say isn't pretty. It's not gentle or even remotely kind. But she needs to hear it and it needs to come from me. Her staff. They're good people. They help Allie and work hard. Even though she's a great boss, she's still in charge. None of them would ever tell her what she needs to hear the way I'm saying it.

She places her hand on my chest. I cover it with my palm, wondering if she can feel how hard my heart beats for her.

"I'm never going to come out of this looking good," Allie whispers. "I'm not the favorite, and I've let my role as the passive and obedient daughter go too far."

"That's probably true." Her eyes are wet with tears, casting them with a shimmer of sadness. I hate how she's feeling, but if you ask me, I don't think I've ever seen a more beautiful woman.

Allie has the kind of face that's hard to forget, and a body you want to stare at longer than is considered polite. But I don't want to focus on the exterior the world can see. I want to focus on the interior, the part not enough people take the time to know.

I see it. Allie is everything, strong and sweet, loving and so full of life. If her family could see her, *really* see her, they'd treat her like the perfect daughter Valentina pretends to be.

"You're not making me feel better about this," she says quietly.

"Does this mean you're going to do it?" I ask. "Demand respect from your family and give Andres and Valentina the 'fuck yous" they deserve?"

"I want to. I'm just not certain I can get away with it."

"You probably won't," I say, not wanting to lie to her. "That doesn't mean it doesn't need to be said."

She stills when I wipe the tear on her cheek that's lingered too long. "You'd never allow yourself to be treated this way," she says.

"You're right," I agree. "I wouldn't."

She sits up slightly. "And your family would never treat you this way. But if they did, would you say what you had to and risk losing them forever?"

I don't move. Those bad memories Allie has of her family, the ones she tries to bury? I have a few I've shoveled dirt on myself.

Allie's slender fingers sweep across my jawline. "Hey," she says. "Are you okay?"

I clasp her hand gently, keeping her from stroking my skin. It's not that I don't appreciate her kindness. It's that right now, I don't think I deserve it.

She draws her hand away. "I'm sorry," she says. "I didn't mean to make you uncomfortable."

"It's not you," I begin. I'm not sure what I look like, but it can't be good.

"Sweetie, what is it?" she asks.

My emotions take over, causing my frown to deepen. "Can I tell you something? Something I never told anyone?"

Allie angles her body against the pillows so her face rests a few inches from mine. Worry and fear etch her brow, as well as impending sadness. "You can tell me anything." She pauses. "As long as it doesn't hurt you to say it."

"I can't promise you that," I say, remembering and feeling everything that happened that day. "But I still want to tell you. Will you let me?"

She curls her fingers around my hand. "I'll let you do anything."

My chest tightens, making it hard to breathe. I know what she means, but maybe I need her to mean more. I lose my train of thought, wanting to kiss her and feel close to her. But then I remember this moment isn't about us. It's about her and what she needs to understand.

"Like everyone else from the old neighborhood, I guess you know my father died in his mistress's bed."

Allie barely blinks. Yeah. She knew. "Well, there are couple things you probably don't know. Like how the rest of us knew, including our Ma."

Allie watches me carefully, waiting for me to continue. She doesn't have to wait long. "We'd hear Ma crying at night over the man she loved enough to have seven children with. The same man who didn't love her back. One day, I had enough of my father's bullshit and showed up at his lady friend's door."

Allie falls perfectly still, except for her trembling voice. "Were you looking to speak to her?"

I laugh without meaning it. Nothing in my childhood has ever screamed Disney special. "If you think I went to her house to cry and beg her not to break up our happy family, you're wrong."

"That's not what I was thinking," Allie says softly.

The gentleness in her tone softens mine, but not by much. "Yeah, well, yeah."

I need a moment. Maybe more than that. Allie gives it to me, her hand sweeping over mine her only movement. "I was twelve. Finnie was just born. His birth, like, did something to me. Wren was only about eighteen months older. Still a baby herself. And there was our papa, spending his afternoons with someone who wasn't our ma."

My thoughts travel back to our small kitchen, to the hardwood floors where Ma had given birth to Finnie. Except for the day Finnie was born, those floors were always clean enough to eat on 'cause Ma believed a good home consisted of clean floors.

"Ma would take Finnie to work with her," I tell Allie. "She made some kind of sling from an old sheet, so she could feed Finnie and keep him against her skin."

I don't realize how quietly I'm speaking until I see how closely Allie is listening. "The only time Finnie ever left her was when he needed changing or when it was time to put him to bed for the night. That was a good thing. She needed him more than I think he needed her."

"Why?" she asks carefully.

I want to smile, because of all the good Ma's closeness to Finnie brought. But I can't, because of why she needed that closeness. "Finnie was a reminder that she had a lot to live for. Even though her life was falling apart."

I take a few slow breaths when I realize how fast I'm breathing. "I don't think Ma closed the dry-cleaning business for more than a couple of days. She came home from the hospital with Finnie strapped to her chest and left for work the next day. She'd come home the same way, tired and hungry, even though she never once complained."

Allie smiles, her voice full of compassion. I suddenly stop speaking. "Your mother is an amazing woman," she says.

"She is," I agree. "She's had to be."

I turn Allie's hand around so I'm the one holding her. As if I'm some kind of boat, she becomes my anchor, giving me stability so I can say what comes next. "It was all so fucked up," I say, unable to keep my anger from my tone.

"I'm twelve," I repeat. "Angus is fourteen. Declan is thirteen, but a little guy back then. I remember being taller than him and people thinking I was older. Anyway, there we are, making dinner, washing the floors so they stay clean like Ma deserves, and raising Curran, Killian, Wren, and even Finnie when Ma finally collapses from exhaustion in her favorite chair."

"*Seamus,*" Allie says.

It's one of the worst ways she could have said my name, too full of everything I'm feeling and a reminder of how hard my life was then. I didn't realize how much of us went into those years that passed. I do now, and Christ does it kick me in the gut.

I swipe at my face. "It was our normal way of living, I suppose. Curran, Killian, and Wren didn't seem to notice all the other mothers carting their kids to the park, or walking down the street with them. They just noticed us, holding their hands and giving them Irish soda bread dipped in peanut butter for a snack when they got hungry. But we noticed. Me, Angus, and Declan, we saw enough for all of them."

I scoot up in bed, taking Allie with me. She's gone this far with me. I'm not letting her go now, or shutting my trap, even though there's a part of me that wants to.

"Angus never said anything to us. But I remember how mad he'd get when Papa would show up after work to freshen up before heading to his girlfriend's place. Declan always kept a poker face. I don't think he cared even then what people thought of him. I think that's why he could approach Papa when the rest of us didn't dare to. He'd ask Papa for a few dollars, just to have something in our pockets in case the little ones wanted ice cream. Three dollars here, ten there, sometimes even twenty if we were running really low on food. He—"

Son of a bitch. This is harder than I ever would have guessed.

"Declan never asked for much," I say, biting out the words. "He knew what would happen if he did."

Again, it's like I have to stop speaking.

The breath she takes to gather her courage is as quiet as a whisper, but not so silent I don't hear it. "What would happen if Declan asked for too much money?" she asks.

"Funny you should say that," I reply, revving myself up for the so-called climax of the story. "This is the part where things get interesting and where you come in."

"Me?" she questions.

"Oh, yeah," I say, knowing I'm at the point of no return. "Papa was in a rush that day. He just finished a long stretch of shifts at the post office. Whatever Calla—that was her name—had promised him after work must've been good. He ran upstairs, not bothering to say hello to us, and showered. He comes back down wearing his best white T-shirt Ma ironed for him and smelling like too many splashes of Old Spice. Declan steps in front of Papa before he could run out the door. 'Wren needs girl clothes. She can't keep wearing our old stuff,' he told Papa."

Allie looks scared and maybe she should be. That same fear pokes at me, making me want to give up and stop. But that's not fair to her and I don't think it's fair to me, either. "Angus saw the strike coming before I did, and maybe Declan, too. There was Declan, all four feet of him, his chin lifted in defiance."

Allie covers her mouth with her hand. "He hit little Declan?"

I shake my head, my eyes burning. "No. He hit big, fat, stupid Angus. Did you know that's what most of the kids in our neighborhood called him? They didn't know Angus was tougher than hell. Know how he got that way? Because as many smacks Papa tried to give us, he never touched us when Angus was around."

Allie's nose reddens and her tears falls in a silence that encases us like a mother's womb.

"As big as Angus was, even then, he went flying into a wall and almost took Curran with him. He managed to catch himself before he landed on Curran. If Papa felt bad, it was only for a moment. Then it's like he remembered where he had to be and took off."

I rub my face harder than I intend. "I don't think Papa shut the door. I shut it for him. Locked it, too. I tried to shove furniture against it so I could keep him out and protect us."

"Oh, my God."

Why does she have to sound so sweet, especially when my voice is as rough as it is? "I was scared, Allie. I would have held that door closed with my body if that's what it took."

Her slender arms wrap around me, her shoulders quivering as she releases her grief for me and my family. I wipe my eyes with the back of my hand. "We were used to Papa's temper. No one ever cried. Usually no one did much of anything. But we did then. Curran and Killian started crying first. Then Declan. They sat around Angus who was sitting on the floor, his blank expression looking toward our living room. Wren hovered over him, patting his back. I don't think she fully understood what happened, but she seemed to know it happened because her brothers were trying to help her. She didn't cry. I don't think she ever did when it came to Papa. She hated him from the start, and was smart enough to know he wasn't worth her tears."

"I'm sorry," Allie says. "Had I known . . ." She sighs. "I would have been there for you, so you didn't feel so alone."

Alone is exactly how I felt. Allie nailed it without me having to tell her. "I should have been there with the rest of my siblings, gathered around Angus and showing a united front. But I couldn't."

"Why, love?"

Damn, she's killing me. "Like you said, I was all alone. Alone because I wasn't who stepped in front of Declan to take that hit, because I wasn't the one who dared approach our father, and because I didn't do shit to protect our mother."

"You were only twelve," Allie reminds me.

"And Angus was only fourteen and taking blows for us he never should've had to," I point out.

I don't consider myself a bitter bastard, but I sound like one. "It would be one of the worst days of my life if there wasn't more to it," I admit. "I couldn't take it anymore. All that cleaning and cooking and care we were giving just for my father to treat us like we were nothing but little snots keeping him from getting what he needed. It wasn't right."

"No, it wasn't," Allie agrees. The understanding in her voice is something wild. She's not judging my father. She's supporting me. I don't know anyone who could do that without sounding judgmental. But she manages just fine.

"Want to hear the funny part?" I ask. "Okay. Maybe it's not so funny. But in Papa's eyes, he was a provider. He gave us a house, gave us life, so, it's like he had a free pass to do whatever he wanted. But we wanted more. We wanted a father who came to our stupid school pageants. Who'd yell at the ref for making a bad call at one of our games. Someone who'd teach us to throw a ball or ride a bike. But we never got it."

"But it didn't keep you from wanting it," Allie adds.

The warmth in her gaze hits me like a soft mist, brushing against me so I know it's there and somehow solidifying and shielding me.

Except nothing can protect me from those memories.

"No," I agree. "But there's more. I wanted him *to want* to be there and for him to see us as more than seven little burdens he was obliged to feed. I wanted him to stop treating us like shit. Damn it, Allie, I wanted it all. For poor Ma to stop scraping and saving just to take us to that one ballgame a year. The one where we knew better than to ask for more than a soda and some popcorn, knowing how long she had to work just to give us that much. I wanted Papa to sit next to our Ma—who didn't miss one pageant or game, who'd show up after working herself to the bone with a baby attached to her hip, so she could cheer us to victory or hug us when we'd lost."

Allie . . . smiles and that smile hits me hard. "I used to volunteer at the concession stand when you played baseball, Seamus. I remember watching your mother cheer you on. But where you saw a woman burdened with the world, alone, and tired from a long day's work, I saw a mother so in love with her children, she was happy and proud to watch them play."

The lump that I was beating down hardens. But instead of the sour taste of fury, all I sense is the peace Allie offers me. "Thank you," I say. "I needed to hear that."

My focus drops to our hands. Allie is so little compared to me, but the strength contained in her small body is fierce, giving me what I need to continue the story.

"That day that my father hit Angus was the last straw for me. I waited until I was sure Angus could get up before shoving the furniture I had pushed against the door aside. Declan asked me where I was going. I didn't answer, but I think he knew. He was always smart like that."

The silence that surrounded us when I first began my story becomes something more. Like all the ghosts from my past have appeared, deadening the air and making it hard to breathe.

"I knew where Calla lived. We all did. A few times as kids we threatened to mess up her house. Spray paint 'slut' across her door. We thought of mean things. Angry things that reflected the rage we collectively built. But when it came down to it, we weren't mean kids. We were just kids who hurt for each other and for our mother."

Allie clutches my hand as if afraid what will happen to me if she lets go. "Calla was a bitch for knowingly banging a married man with seven kids," I say. "But even though we never said it, our father was a bigger bitch. He's the one who went back on his vows, lying to our mother, even though he knew she no longer believed his lies."

Allie pushes up to better see me and I suppose to better protect me against what comes. I'm not so sure she's going to be enough.

"I stormed to Calla's house, all ninety pounds of me ready to throw down. When I finally reached her front door, I could barely knock I was shaking so hard. My father answered the door without a shirt on. I could have been a neighbor, another lover, even a priest. He didn't care. He was going to do what he wanted."

"Was he expecting you?" Allie asks tenderly, her fingers cupping the fists my hands have become.

I think I might laugh when I remember the look on my father's face, but any genuine humor I feel is smothered by the darkness of that day. "I was the last person he expected to see."

Allie hitches her breath. She knows what's coming and that it doesn't end well for me. She thinks I get hurt. That I bleed. That I cry.

She's right on all counts.

"You're a whore," I told my father. "You hurt Angus when he tried to protect Declan. All because Declan asked you for clothes for our little sister." I rub my eyes. "Believe it or not, I rehearsed everything I was going to tell him on the walk over. But when I saw him standing there shirtless, everything I planned didn't come out the way I intended."

Allie sits up, scanning my features as if trying to figure out the rest of the story so she can spare me from telling it. But I have to say it. I have to slice the wrists of my soul and finish bleeding out. Maybe she knows that. She sure as hell doesn't try to stop me.

My arm bands around Allie's back, trying to somehow help her through it, the way she helped me. "The first smack was the one I really felt," I admit. "It sent me flying like it did Angus. I managed to brace myself and not fall off the front porch." My mind wanders and I almost check out. "The second didn't hurt as bad, and by the fifth, I was completely numb."

This moment is all about me and the not-so-sweet fairytale that was my childhood. The pain across Allie's features temporarily steal the spotlight I inadvertently placed on myself. God help me. Even in all her misery, Allie is beautiful.

"I fought my father, Allie. I raised my hands and let my fists speak for me." I curse under my breath. "I'd been in fights before. I had to be, growing up in the neighborhood I did, it was the only way to hang onto the few toys we had, and to protect my family. But there's something really fucked up about hitting your own father."

Allie covers her mouth, choking back a sob.

My head feels heavy. My arms do, too. Maybe hands have memory. It makes sense. I remember the pain that reached down to my bones each time my fists connected with my father. "I didn't spare him from my rage. I didn't think I needed to. It felt like no matter what, I couldn't stop."

"Why?" she asks.

My mouth continues to move, but it takes a moment for the words come out. "As crazy as it sounds, if I had stopped, I'd be letting my family down. He'd get away with hitting Angus, with making my brothers cry, and treating Ma like she was nothing. It would be his 'get out of jail free card' for all those games he missed, and every smile he flashed when he led my mother into church, pretending to be something he wasn't. Even though everyone knew exactly what he was. So, I couldn't stop, even when my muscles were screaming at me to quit." I groan, wishing all this shit didn't still hurt. "But when it came down to it, I was a little kid and he was a very big man."

Allie brushes my tears away with the tip of her fingers. She didn't expect me to win the fight and she was right.

"It took Calla, that woman who helped break my mother's heart, to make him to stop. 'That's enough,' she said. 'You're going to kill him.' She had a strong Philly accent. I could hear it even over her shrieking. I was this mess of flying limbs, making it hard for him to pin me down. As tired as I was, I fought to keep going. Finally, he grabbed me by the hair and twisted my arm, slamming me onto the porch."

Allie is covering her mouth again, keeping all those cries that want to release from breaking free.

"Memories are a funny thing," I say. "You don't always remember the things you need to, but you never forget the things you should. I remember that front porch. It was a shitty little thing made from wood. Years of brutal winters had warped it, rotting it from the outside in, and staining it black."

The rot. The smell of old, wet wood. The shock emanating from my father and the blood spilling out of my mouth. I breathed it all in. This part I don't share with Allie. But it's a part that still hurts.

"I couldn't move once he had me down and I wasn't sure what he'd do next," I admit. "But then he lifted off me and I was sure I'd get up and start swinging again. But for a long time, I couldn't get my body to move. 'Go home,' he said, then shut the door."

"Did you leave?" Allie asks.

I don't answer with a yes or a no. I answer with the memory. "The sun had gone down during the time we'd fought, and my breath was visible in the cold night air when I finally stood. I don't remember the walk home, but I remember Ma's face when she answered the door."

Seconds go by and then minutes. It takes Allie asking *the* question for me to speak again. "What happened when your mother saw you?" she asks.

"She, ah, cleaned up my cuts and put ice on my face. Then she drew me a warm bath and got me my favorite pajamas. They were Spiderman pajamas—flannel, all warm and soft no matter how many times she washed them." I say, recalling the dark red and blue pattern.

"Ma bought them brand-new," I continue. "She knew how much I liked Spiderman. When she finished combing my hair, she tucked me into bed and kissed me good night."

The next thing I have to tell Allie would make some people smile. I don't smile. I just take the moment to remember Ma, and everything she's done for us. "My father came home a little later. He sat down to dinner as he did every night. And just like Ma did every night, she placed his warm dinner in front of him. It was a routine they both had. Except this time, things were a little different. I don't think he'd taken his first bite before Ma nailed him in the face with a cast-iron skillet."

Allie gasps, her eyes so wide I think she might pass out.

For a brief moment in time, I'm no longer me. I'm that little boy in his pajamas, waking up to screaming and swearing. "Ma didn't stop with one swing," I tell Allie, giving Ma all the credit she deserves. "She let Papa have it."

I stroke Allie's arm. "At first I thought she was finally done pretending she didn't know where he went every afternoon. But when I found my father on the floor, his nose caved in and his hands up, I realized what made her sling that skillet. 'You may have put these children inside of me,' she told him. 'But that doesn't make you their father. You don't touch my babies, ever. You haven't earned that right. And if you ever lay your hands on them again, I'll kill you in your sleep, you bastard.'"

"Oh," Allie says. She doesn't say anything more than that, but I think it pretty much sums it up.

"He never got near us again," I say. "There were no hugs, but there never were to start with. He went from treating us like we were nothing, to pretending we weren't there. It wasn't much of an improvement, but it kept us safe."

"Your mother kept you safe," Allie clarifies gently.

I smile, tasting the pride I have for my mother, as well as the bitterness reserved for my father.

"Seamus," Allie begins. "The affair didn't stop, but I think you know that."

"Alz, it didn't even pause. The next day, he was back with his mistress. Ma may have had the strength to protect us, but she didn't have it in her to stop him from cheating. It took me a while, but I think I finally understood why."

"Why?" she questions when I don't explain.

"My father was a lot like that busted up porch. In need of repair, but not loved enough to be fixed. Ma didn't love him enough to beg him to stay. Calla didn't love him enough to beg him not to leave. He only got enough to keep standing, until the day came when he didn't get back up."

Allie leans in and kisses me, her lips sealing over mine. I take the kiss and own it, making it mine, making it ours.

It's not an outrageously deep kiss, nor is lustful. It's full of love and meant to heal and that's exactly what it does. She pulls away, her soft gaze mesmerizing me.

"I'm sorry," she says. "For your pain, for what you endured, and everything your family did to protect you."

"Thank you," I tell her. "Look, I don't know if you know this, but when my father died, he left my mother his military and post office pensions, as well as his life insurance. He wasn't a good father in life, or a good husband. But he became a provider in death. It was the best thing he could have done under the circumstances and it helped me bury some of the shit he put us through."

My voice lowers from shame and maybe something more. "I haven't had the best experiences with women. In my defense, our father sucked."

"I know," Allie says. "That doesn't mean you can't have the happiness your mother always wanted for herself."

Of all the things Allie could've said, this one belts me the hardest. I don't let it distract me. There's a point to the story that I still need to make. "I think there are kids who've been hurt that dream of fighting their fathers. Some may even enjoy doing so. I didn't. But some good did come out of it." My knuckles skim her lower back. "It showed the man who hurt us that we were no longer going to take it."

Her gaze drops before I finish. She knows where I'm going with this.

"Allie," I say. "It's time to tell those who hurt you to stop."

CHAPTER 18

Allie

This coffee shop is the trendiest in town. Modeled in the early 90's after the TV show *Friends,* with its own artsy twist, I almost feel like I'm in L.A., rather than South Street where shops sell everything from cheesesteaks to super-sized phalluses.

I adjust my position on the well-worn couch in the small seating area designed to mimic a cozy living room and check my emails. The light streaming in through the window makes it a little hard to read the screen, but I manage.

As per his request and Seamus's encouragement, I'm meeting Andres. I like that Andres chose a public locale. As much as I think Valentina is aware of our meeting, I'd never want anyone to question my ethics.

I take a sip of my Americano, my go-to drink when I need to get piles of work done on very little sleep. Seamus and I fell asleep in each other's arms following our very long talk. Neither of us planned it. It just happened, keeping each other warm with our bodies instead of the spread of blankets beneath us.

It wasn't until the sun trickled through the stained-glass window, painting our faces in a kaleidoscope of blues and greens that we realized we'd slept until noon. It wouldn't have been a big deal if we both weren't hammered with work and late to client meetings.

"Oh, *fuck*," were his exact words. I grin. But I could be wrong.

The next week consisted of more O'Brien festivities and finally Finn and Sol's wedding. Finn and Sol haven't had it easy, but they're grateful and blessed to have each other. So, instead of walking down the aisle, they *danced*—the groomsmen and bridesmaids, too! Let me say, Seamus has some serious moves.

It was such a beautiful and fun wedding. I can't remember ever laughing as much as I had at a wedding, then crying just as hard when Finn and Sol exchanged their vows.

My phone buzzes twice, announcing two texts. One from Seamus, one from Mom.

Is the Queen of Hot Air and Darkness and her midget prince there yet?

You're meeting Andres? Does Valentina know? Do you really think this is appropriate?

I didn't have to check the names to know who said what.

A man in his early thirties sits down across from me. "Hi," he says. "Is this seat taken?"

I smile, thinking of Seamus and push back a curl behind my ear. It's time for another cut and Shaqwana was nice enough to fit me in. "It's not taken," I say. "But I am meeting someone momentarily."

He smirks. "Your boyfriend?"

I laugh, playing with the cuffs of my deep plumb blouse. "Definitely not my boyfriend," I say.

He smiles softly, his eyes skimming my outfit and maybe a little more. It's then I realize this very attractive man is checking me out. "It looks like you're almost done with your drink. Can I get you another?"

Since Seamus waved his wand, I've been surprised by how many men have approached me on the street, in restaurants, even at the shoe store where I bought these new heels. I'm still not used to the attention, and I'm not certain I want to be. "That's very kind of you," I say. "But I'm seeing someone, and I don't feel comfortable accepting a drink from another man."

He nods. "I understand." He seems to want to add more, but then he stands, straightening the jacket of his suit. "Have a good day."

"You, too." Wow. He sat down *just to speak to me*. I watch him walk out at the same time Andres appears with Valentina. The man holds the door open for them, but he doesn't seem to notice Valentina. Instead, he turns back briefly to smile at me.

My gaze drops and I blush from the attention he showed me, but also because I wasn't prepared to see Valentina.

Andres didn't select his place. She did. They walk in, her arm circling his. The barista with a tattoo sleeve of fairytale characters pauses in the middle of handing out drinks, as the laughter and jovial conversations drifting in the air lower to a murmur.

Everyone is looking at Valentina in her red floral spring dress and how the skirt flutters behind her with every step. My sister is striking. She always has been. It saddens me in a way that Andres looks like a stooge merely trying to keep up. He's dressed in a light green cashmere V-neck sweater and freshly pressed tan slacks. He has his head up, attempting to match Valentina in height. But in those platform heels, she towers over him.

Valentina's smile lights up the room. She waves, her enthusiasm appearing genuine and further highlighting her ethereal presence.

"Trophy wife," a man in the corner booth mouths to his friend, causing him to crack up.

If I didn't know them, I'd assume the same thing. For the life of me, I can't understand what Valentina is doing with him, and perhaps what Andres is doing with her, too.

Valentina clutches Andres's arm as she nears, pulling him closer to her when he sees me and his eyes widen.

"Allie," Valentina sings, bending to kiss my cheek. I don't bother standing, but I do return her affections. She releases her hold on Andres and steps aside, allowing him through. Like Valentina, Andres bends to kiss my cheek. I jerk away before he can make contact. His face reddens, my response clearly offending him. Perhaps I should feel bad, but I don't. I have my limits.

Valentina beams, ignoring my dismissal of Andres. "Look at you. I can't believe how much you've changed. You look . . . different."

I'm not convinced she likes my new style of dress or my hair. "Sexy in business without being slutty," Seamus calls it. I don't know about that, but I'm overjoyed with my new wardrobe and that Seamus likes it.

My talk with Seamus the other day took a lot out of us, but when he walked me out to my car and he hugged and kissed me sweetly on the lips, I fell so much more in love with him.

"Are you still with us?" Valentina asks.

"Sorry," I offer, setting my coffee down. "My mind was elsewhere."

"On Seamus, perhaps?" she asks, her smile oddly feline.

"Yes," I admit, the heat that claims my face validating my words.

Valentina sits on the couch across from me and crosses her legs, so perfectly poised I'm tempted to check the area for cameras. Andres sits on an extra wide chair to my left.

It surprises me that he doesn't sit directly beside Valentina. The twinkle in her eyes tell me she already knows what I'm thinking and is happy to put my concerns at ease. "Andres and I have a meeting with our wedding planner. It's the only reason I'm here." She laughs when I tilt my chin. "Allie, you don't think I'm here to make sure you keep your hands to yourself, do you?"

I pucker my brow, tasting a pang of what feels like resentment. "That's nothing you have to worry about, I assure you."

"I'm not worried," Valentina adds sweetly, her gaze flickering over me.

My instincts warn me to move away from her, but I don't stop holding my ground. She doesn't sound nasty, nor does her expression give anything close to it away. But I feel it directed at me like a shove.

Valentina continues to analyze me. "Did you wake up in a bad mood?"

"No, why?" I ask, noting how she's attempting to turn the tables to resemble prey and not the predator.

"You seem, I don't know, perhaps bitter is a good word," she muses.

I turn to Andres, mulling over whether he's responsible for this ambush. This is a man I once knew so well, whose statements I could guess before he made them. I can no longer tell what he's thinking. He could be nervous, sad, or possibly nonplussed, waiting for what comes.

I cross my palms over my knees and turn to face Valentina. It's the position I often assume when I'm meeting with clients for the first time. It's nonthreatening and reflects the honest person I pride myself in being.

"Why do you think I'm bitter?" I ask.

I'm not certain what I say or do to cause Andres to sit beside Valentina. He's just suddenly there. Seamus did something similar a few weeks ago when we went to a dive bar with his family to eat the best pierogis ever made. A man stepped in front of me on my way to the restroom. I didn't feel Seamus approach. He materialized with his arm around me, leading me forward and around the man who seemed interested in more than the pierogis. But where Seamus stood close, Andres sits away, keeping a good foot of space between him and Valentina.

Valentina's eyes darken. "Andres and I are in love, Allie. We never planned on it, it just happened."

"That's not entirely true," I point out, cutting off her undying declaration of devotion. I look to Andres. "That day, you said you had to do research at the lab, and that you'd be gone all day. When you came home, you told me you spent the afternoon with Valentina, who no one realized had flown in from France. That took a great deal of planning, even though you're not willing to admit it."

Andres regards Valentina as if waiting for her response. "It wasn't like that, exactly."

"Yes, it was," I say.

Valentina smiles. "It was a long time ago, Allie. It would mean a lot to us if we could move on."

Andres looks to Valentina as if searching for permission to speak. I'm glad he does. It's another reminder of why we never would have worked out. I want a man. Not a spineless slug.

"You hurt me. Both of you. It didn't end with that day."

Valentina's laugh cuts me off. "My goodness, Allie. You're not wasting any time are you? Going right for the throat, I see."

Again, she's trying to come across as the victim. "I have a client meeting in an hour. If we could get on with this, neither of us have to be late for our appointments."

I was worried that I wouldn't be able to keep my voice neutral or that it would shake inconveniently, making me appear weak. For now, it's hanging in there, and so am I.

Neither reply, both watching me, I suppose expecting the Allie they've known, the one who merely sits quietly and agrees. She's gone. It didn't take new clothes or a haircut. "Does anyone else have anything to say?" I ask. "An apology for the way I was treated, perhaps, or are we just here so you can tell me to get over it?"

The answer swirls like a mini-cyclone when neither respond. Wow. They're really not going to say, "I'm sorry," ever.

"You didn't get what you wanted," Valentina says, instead. "I know it hurts."

"No, you don't," I say. "You weren't the one betrayed, the one cast aside. You merely swept in and swept out the way you always do, Valentina." As I speak, I find myself addressing Andres. "The way you'll keep doing for the rest of your life."

Andres knows what I mean. He isn't stupid, his face pales slightly as I affirm his darkest fears. "He's not coming back to you," Valentina explains slowly, so my poor pitiful mind will understand.

"I don't want him to," I say, barely believing I have to spell it out. "I want someone who shows me respect, and a sister who won't consider me so far below her that my feelings don't matter."

"I've never mistreated you," Valentina replies, her voice as soft as the gaze she perfectly conjures. "The only thing I'm guilty of is finding my soulmate and acting on my feelings."

"You're a liar," I say. "And so are you, Andres." I stand. "God, I can't believe I was stupid enough to meet you. You'll never change."

"I never meant to hurt you, Allie," Andres says, keeping me in place when I stand. He rises slowly. So does Valentina, except for the first time, he doesn't seem to notice her there. "I know what you did for me. I'll never be able to thank you enough. For the support. For everything, but I . . ."

The momentary surge of courage abandons him as easily as he abandons me. His shoulders slump, giving me a glimpse of a broken, lonely man. Andres's accomplishments and wealth mean nothing now. He takes a step back, sitting slowly.

His response and actions don't seem real, too exaggerated and almost comical. But no one is laughing.

"You weren't enough for Andres, Allie," Valentina tells me, her voice and stance so graceful it doesn't fit the words she says or the ones that follow. "In every way Andres needed, you weren't enough of a woman for him."

The air leaves my lungs, the room, creating a vacant hole. Valentina has returned me to the place where all my insecurities lie in wait and my fears are realized. No one sees me here, no one hears my words.

A place I've allowed her to rule for far too long.

"You're right," I say, glancing up at her. For the first time, Valentina doesn't seem so tall or beautiful or perfect. She's a very flawed human being who hides from the world with a pretty smile and prettier face. "He needed a bitch and that's exactly what you gave him."

"Allie!" Andres says, choking out my name.

"I won't be a bridesmaid in your wedding," I say, ignoring him. "You don't deserve even that. Take the dress and give it someone who is more than happy to ignore everything you pretend to be. I'll be in the back row, wishing you happiness and hoping by some miracle of God you can pull off this façade."

Valentina squares her jaw. Again, it's only Andres who speaks. "You used to be such a sweet girl."

"The sweet girl became a woman who won't be mistreated by anyone, anymore," I lift my purse and phone and walk away, my steps measured and not hasty or slow.

"Allie," Valentina calls to me.

I should know better than to stop. "You'll never be able to hold on to Seamus either. You're simply not enough."

I glance over my shoulder just long enough to meet her in the eye and say what I say. "Watch me."

CHAPTER 19

Seamus

Melinda leans in close, whispering all the naughty things she wants to do to me. Ordinarily, this is the time I grab her hand and we head for my truck to do said naughty things and probably more.

So then, why the hell am I staring at my beer, full to the neck and wondering how Allie is doing? Her meeting with Tweedle-bitch and Tweedle-dumbass was earlier. Then she was showing newlyweds a house in Doylestown and rounding up her assistants, who listed ten houses this week. I know she's thorough and needed to go through a few contracts, but it's been hours since she texted.

I called Valentina a bitch, she said.

Good, I wrote, even knowing what doing that must have taken. *What did you call Andres?*

I'll talk to you about it later, she said.

She hasn't, though. It doesn't take a genius to know Allie was, and maybe still is, upset.

I take a pull of my beer. It's warm. I hate warm beer. I secretly blame that shithead Andres for it. If Andres had been a douche to begin with, Allie would have realized she could do better sooner, and I wouldn't be in the situation I'm in.

Damn, I'm worried sick over Allie and barely aware that Melinda has unbuttoned the top of her red blouse. The color would look great on Allie, and holy shit, doesn't that revelation give me one hell of a pause.

"What's the matter, Seamus?" Melinda asks. "You suddenly turned virgin or somethin'?"

"Huh?"

I better start paying better attention. Rumor has it, Melinda stabbed the last guy she was with in the stones. I think it was her ex-husband. In Melinda's defense, her ex always was a prick.

"I asked if you were a virgin."

She had to go there. Now I have to protect my manhood and reputation and all that. "Honey, you and me know that's not true."

"Then what is it?"

"Rough day," I mumble. I reach into my back pocket and check my phone for what has to be the ninety-eighth time since I sat down to have my beer.

"Are you waiting on someone else?"

"What?" I say, scrolling through Allie's last text and barely listening.

I'm not trying to insult Melinda. She's a decent person and hasn't missed one day of community service, from what I've heard. But I didn't come into the bar looking for a date. I came looking for . . . I don't know, something to do?

Ordinarily, I'd stop in to see one of my brothers or maybe even go to Wren's if I was desperate enough. But they're with their women and Wren is trying to get all the work done so she and Evan can have a decent honeymoon. Plus, had I stopped to see any one of my family members, I would've gotten, "What's wrong? Where's Allie? Did you fuck things up?"

I'm not prepared for questions, and I'm sure as shit not prepared to admit Allie is with her ex-lover. Alz needed to do this. Just like I needed to tell her what I did the other day. The way I threw my skeletons out there sucked pirate balls. Except there she was, giving my skeletons CPR or whatever, trying to make me feel better. I wanted to show her why you can't take shit from anyone, no matter who they are. If it meant me reliving some bad stuff from my past, so be it.

I roll the long neck in my hand. I had two choices. Sit at home looking at my phone. Or sit at a bar and look at my phone.

The change in scenery doesn't make me look any less pathetic and doesn't do anything to pick up my mood. I think I was here maybe five minutes before Melinda sauntered up to me. She flirted with Benji at the bar. Batted her new eyelashes at Anthony in the corner. Even gave a cute little wave to Ernie the Drunk. Ernie isn't really a drunk. He just pretends to be, so he doesn't have to go home to his wife. But that's another story.

Melinda remembered me from a barbecue Angus had last summer. She claims she was with someone else, and now they're not together, blah, blah, blah, her probation officer has hairy knuckles, blah, blah, blah and I need toenail surgery I can't afford.

I felt bad about her toenail and offered to buy her a beer. Next thing I know she's stroking the swell of her breast like the winning lottery ticket is buried beneath the skin.

Melinda slaps me across the arm. "I asked, if you're waiting on somebody?" Her scowl locks on my phone. "All you keep doing is checking your phone. You should be looking at these." She points to her chest. "I just got 'em done. A decent man would at least try to cop a feel."

A few months ago, I would have given them a squeeze to make her feel better. Hey, they even look the same size, unlike last time. Now, I can't psych myself up for it.

Jesus, what the hell is happening to me? When did I have to psych myself up to feel any woman's rack? It's like, one of my favorite things to do in the world, ever since Sabrina Guzman grabbed my hands in the back of her father's Chevy and placed them on her double D's.

My phone buzzes. I straighten when I see a text from Allie.

Hey. Are you there? She asks.

Yeah. You okay? I type.

No. It was awful. Strangely, cleansing. Ugly. Then ugly again.

Sounds about right, I type. *You want me to kick his ass?*

No.

Her ass? I offer. *I could send Wren. She owes me for pastry duty.*

I think she's smiling, but wish I could be sure.

No. That's okay. Just wondering what you're up to, she replies.

At Tonelli's having a drink. I don't mention Melinda. Melinda is nice enough, like the rest of us maybe just trying to find someone for at the night.

I don't quite finish what I'm thinking. Probably because one night is no longer what I want.

Do you want to come over? Maybe have some wine and watch terrible movies on NetFlix? Allie suggests.

I grin, realizing how good that sounds. *I'll be there in twenty.*

I drop a few bills on the table. It's more than enough to pay for my drinks and Melinda's. It's also enough for her to pay for another guy's drink if that's what she wants, except that's not how she takes it.

She stands, adjusting her new rack before tugging on her jacket. "I have to pick up my kid at my ma's by midnight." She pulls her long hair out from where it's tucked behind her jacket. Are you gonna be a gentleman and drive me back or are you going to be a prick like the last guy and make me fucking Uber it?"

"I'm headed out on my own," I say, trying not to sound like an insensitive asshole. "But if you need a ride, I could drop you off at your ma's."

"It's only nine," she snaps. "Are you seriously not taking me back to your place?"

"No, but like I said, I can give you a ride, so you can be with your kid."

She nails me in the chest. It's a good hit. I wasn't expecting it. It might even leave a bruise.

"I don't want to be with my kid. I'm with my kid every night of the week, unless his father has him. This is *my* night. You hear me, Samuel? My night to have a little fun. So either have it with me, or I'll have it with someone else."

A couple months ago, I would have taken her up on her offer and not even bothered to correct her on my name. We would have left laughing and had a good time. Tonight, I'm not laughing. I feel sorry for her. Melinda is lonely and looking for something I can't give. Probably because I'm lonely, too. But I'm not alone around Allie.

"Sorry, Melinda," I say. "Hope you find what you're looking for."

"My name is Nanette," she says, ripping the cash off the table, her boots stomping against the floor as she heads back toward Benji. I drop another twenty down and head out straight to Allie's, wishing Nanette well and hoping Allie is okay.

Allie's smile lights up the entire doorway when she answers. Her teeth are gleaming and so are her eyes, no matter that it's clear she was crying. That offer to kick Andres's ass? She should've taken me up on it. I wrap my arms around her and lift her in a bear hug.

"You want to talk about it?" I ask, setting her down.

"Not really," she says. She backs into the townhouse, letting me through and locking the door.

"Yeah, you do," I say, kicking off my work boots and leaving them by the door.

Allie is in a pair of black sweatpants that hang low on her hips and a black tank. I watch how her hips sway as I follow her into the kitchen. "Maybe, but some people aren't worth talking about."

The T.V. is on and there's some chick flick playing, an already opened bottle of red wine and two glasses placed on the table in front of the cream-colored coach. "You want a beer?" she asks, laughing when she sees I already pulled a Yuengling out of the fridge.

I crack it open and place it next to the wine glass. "Wine?" I offer.

"Yes, please." She busies herself in the kitchen as I fill her glass halfway.

My feet slide a little across her wood floors. I reach for a few paper towels and utensils, falling into our routine, even though I can't remember when exactly we established that routine.

Allie scurries around the gourmet kitchen, from stove, to counter, to oven, back to the stove again. She reminds me of a squirrel, going from spot to spot the way she does. But I'm not attracted to squirrels. What I am is head over heels for Allie.

The night when she kissed me in bed, I thought maybe it'd lead to something more. Not sex. Not by the way those lips met mine. But for something other than friendship. That kiss had a lot of heart to it, sealing her emotions and mine where they couldn't hurt us.

I never planned to tell her anything that personal, this soon, especially something I've never told anyone. But now that I did, I feel like I can tell her anything, except maybe how I really feel.

Allie grins from where she's arranging roasted vegetables around a bowl of ranch dressing. "Don't panic. It's not all healthy," she assures me. "I also have boneless wings and potato skins in the oven. You're hungry, aren't you?"

Like I'd ever tell the sweet thing no.

"There's always room for wings." I point to her. "That shit should be written on a bumper sticker, maybe some fortune cookies, too."

She grins, but there's a splinter of sadness shadowing her eyes. It does something to me and I don't just mean wanting to pound Andres into scrapple. I want to hold her and kiss her, too. My problem is, if I cross the friend zone, there's no going back. I'll lose my best friend.

I reach for the hot tray she pulls out of the oven, leaving her to carry the lighter stuff and head to the living room. We arrange the food like we always do, hot food closest to us, cold just behind it, our drinks directly in front.

We fill our plates, Allie with the veggies and a boneless wing, me with everything so she doesn't feel bad. "Tell me what happened," I say as we settle down.

She does, and it's worse than I thought. I'm pissed and proud. Pissed by the shit Valentina pulled, the pussy moves on Andres's part (shocker), but damn proud of Allie for not just telling Trashy Tina she won't be a bridesmaid, but for telling her off. But there's something else I hang onto. Not so much what Valentina said about Allie not being enough of a woman for Andres, but how Allie took it.

"Why does this thing bother you so much?"

Allie looks at me. "Is this a serious question?"

I hold out a hand. "I get the obvious. Andres and Valentina screwed you when they screwed each other, ultimately giving you the shaft. I'm not saying it shouldn't hurt. What I want to know, specifically, is why it bothers you. I've seen him, Allie. He's nothing to brag about. And if it weren't for the bills he made, your sister wouldn't be bragging about him either."

Allie grows quiet in way that breaks my heart. Those large brown eyes of hers filling up with sadness. "Did you love him?" I ask.

"Yes." She pauses. "No." She shakes her head. "I thought I did. Love is supposed to be forever, isn't it? It's supposed to border on obsession. The kind of emotion you feel even in the person's absence, right?"

Well, damn. If that's the case . . . I clear my throat. "Sure."

She tilts her head slightly, causing those big curls to sweep along her cheeks. I don't realize how hard I'm staring until I realize how hard she's staring back. "Have you ever been in love before, Seamus?" She seems afraid to ask, even though she does. "In the way I just described?"

"Nope." Until maybe now. Holy *shit*.

Whatever she catches on my face makes her laugh. Awesome. Still, it fills the void Andres and Valentina seemed to have created. "I used to think love was bull," I admit. Something musicians filtered into their songs to romanticize the lyrics and make the song more than it was."

"What about now?" She gathers her knees and tucks them against her, using them to rest her chin. It's not a deliberate pose. But it sums up Allie. She's guarded, protecting herself from harm, but showing enough of her face to prove she wants to let others in.

"I started to believe it with Killian and Sofia. We always joke he's loved her since before he got pubes. They spent years apart, without talking or seeing each other. But it's like you said. You never forget someone when it's real. No matter how much time passes, they remain in here." I give my temple a tap. "That was them. That was Kill and Sofe."

I finish off my potato and a few wings, giving Allie time to take in what I tell her. "It wasn't love" she finally admits.

I take a long pull of my beer and wipe my mouth. "So then, what's really bugging you?"

"I can't help thinking I did something wrong," she says.

"How so?" She rubs her hands, keeping quiet. "Come on, Alz. It's me. If you can't tell me, who can you tell?"

"It's because it is you that it's hard to say," she says, and like a light switch being flicked, her blush appears.

"Eh, so tell me anyway.

Allie scrunches her face and rubs her hands again. "I think if it hadn't been Valentina, eventually it would've been somebody else."

"But Andres looks like a cartoon character," I remind her. "Not   the cool kind like Bugs. More like Porky Pig and Yosemite Sam had a baby. But it wasn't a cute baby. It was like they got drunk and angry-fucked."

I'm trying to get her to laugh so she's not so nervous and just puts it all out there, but all she does is blush again. "I don't think I was good enough in bed," she blurts out.

"Sure, you were." I swallow down another potato skin.

"How can you tell?" she asks.

"It's easy." I try the roasted zucchini. Hey. Not bad. "Show me your fuck face."

Her jaw slowly falls open. "What?"

"You heard me."

"I'm not sure I know what it means," she stammers.

Allie looks . . . scared. The hell? This can't be the first time she's hearing this. I take another look at her stunned face. Except that yeah, it is.

"S'all right. I'll explain." I take another pull of my beer and spill the facts of life. "Men don't want the same face you make when you serve them milk and cookies, unless you plan to do something naughty with that cookie."

"Naughty?" she asks.

I hold out a hand. "We'll get back to the cookies. Men want their women to make them feel like they can't get enough of them in the sack. That desire needs to be reflected in a woman's face."

"In the *fuck face*?" Allie clarifies.

It's the first time she's ever really cursed in front of me. I'll admit, it's a little distracting and kind of hot. But onward and upward. "Yup. The better the face, the more the man is going to feel like an Alpha King taking on the universe, and the more he's going to make you beg for it. So go ahead, let 'er rip."

"Have you lost your mind? I can't make that face, with you, *here*." She looks around like someone else is watching or taking notes on this very important conversation.

"Why not?" I give her a wink. Women like that. She blushes. See, told you. "I thought we were friends?" I remind her.

"That's not something a friend asks another friend to do," she says, taking two very hard swallows of her wine.

"A real friend would," I counter. I lean forward. "On the count of three, show me your best face. Ready?" I wait for her to take another sip of her wine and put it down. "One, two, three, *go*!"

I don't think she's going to do it or even try. She looks down on the floor and then back up, pretty much with the same expression she had when she first looked down minus reddening cheeks. "I'm trying to help you, Allie. You have to at least try."

She points to her face. "That was it."

I lower my empty beer. "It can't be."

"It is," she insists. She hurries into her powder room and returns with a hand-held mirror, working hard to keep her features the same. "What's wrong with this . . . look?"

I rub my jaw when she plops down next to me. "There's no nice way to say this," I begin.

Allie lets go of whatever the hell that face was. "There never is, Seamus."

I ignore the dig. "The best way to describe what you showed me is the way I look when I'm trying to decide if I want fries or chips with my cheesesteak." I lift up my hands in surrender. "No offense."

She places her mirror on the table and folds her hands on her lap. "How am I not supposed to be offended? You basically just told me I'm terrible in bed and have no way of properly expressing my pleasure."

"That's the problem, you still think it's about you."

"It's not?" she asks.

I scoff. "No. It's like I told you. A man wants to feel like a sex god in bed, no matter how bad the sex is."

Allie tilts her chin. Damn, she looks good. "Just to be clear, the women you're with make you feel like you're doing everything right, even though perhaps you're doing it all wrong?"

I stare back at her, confused. "No, I'm doing it right. In fact, I'm probably the best these women will ever have." My shoulders sag. "It makes me feel bad, you know? To ruin these women for all others. Those poor bastards that follow, it's like they never stood a chance."

Allie sighs, clearly torn between banging her head against the wall and putting my head through it. "Congratulations, I'm thrilled you're so very awesome in bed. I'll be sure to say the rosary on behalf of all those women you ruined and their poor, pitiful men."

I place my hand on her knee. "It'll mean a lot to them."

It's taking all I have not to crack up. I don't quite stop my smirk and neither does Allie, making it all worth it.

"Let's try this again," I say. "You ready?"

CHAPTER 20

Seamus

"No," she croaks.

"Why not? No one is looking."

"It's not that," she says, shrinking inward.

"Come on, what are fuck faces among friends?" Her eyes narrow. "Believe it or not, I'm only trying to help."

"I know," she says, growing flustered. "I'm just not certain I can do this. It doesn't feel natural and I-I-I don't want to force things."

I spread out on the couch. "Allie, mind blowing orgasms are not natural. They're the result of fuck faces and don't let anybody tell you differently."

"Um," she says, or something like that.

"I'm going to teach you a lot tonight," I tell her. "Some of it you may not be ready for, but they're things you need to learn. Men will always make you feel good if *they* feel they're rocking your world. The more a man sees your pleasure, the harder they're going to give it to you. You understand?"

"Yes," she squeaks.

Hell, is it hot in here or is it me and Allie? "I'm not trying to brag here," I say. "But what I've seen in women's faces have helped me become the animal I am in bed."

"I figured," she says, swallowing hard.

"Ah, yeah," I say, my attention zoning in on her full lips. "Because I'm confident, I see those faces staring back at me every time I take a woman to bed, giving me even more confidence. It's a win-win situation. Two confident people in bed equal multiple orgasms. Repeat."

"Come on, Alz," I say when she doesn't. "Class is in session and I'm your hot teacher. Repeat after me, two confident people in bed equal multiple orgasms."

She shakes her head awkwardly and trips through each word. "Two confident people in bed equal multiple orgasms."

"That was a decent first start. Now, be a little more confident, and let me have it. Give me your best 'I'm ready to come' face."

She covers her heart, gasping.

"That wasn't it," I say. "Was it?"

Her mouth opens and closes several times.

"Shit," I say. "Now you just look like a fish. Did Andres do things to make you look like that in bed? Fucker, I should kick his ass."

"I wasn't trying!" she yells. "That was me trying to work through what you just said."

"Which part?" I ask.

"The part about *coming*," she says, whispering the last word.

"Where are you going?" I ask.

"Not that kind of coming," she says, covering her face.

I cough into my hand.

"You're laughing at me," she accuses, since I very much am.

"No, baby, I'm laughing with you, because you're so damn cute."

"Fine. Just . . . fine." She shakes out her hands. "Okay, here I go."

She squints her face, opening and closing her eyelids, fast. "Do you have something in your eye?" I ask.

"No," she says, like she can't believe why I'd think such a thing.

"You sure? There's gotta be something in there."

"There's not," she insists.

I look real close. "Then what the hell are you doing?"

"Batting my eyelashes."

"What the hell does that mean?" I ask.

"You told me to act seductive. I'm trying to be seductive like women are in the movies. And in the movies, they bat their eyelashes."

"Women don't do that shit," I tell her. "You want to be seductive, take off your panties and throw them at me. I'll be sure to catch."

Once more, there goes her jaw falling open. "That can't be it, either," I say. "Tell you what, I'll give you points by the way you hang your mouth open like that. Like you can't believe *how good* it is. Now give me a little bit more with the eyes."

"The eyes?" she asks. "Why? You just said women don't bat their eyelashes."

"'Cause they don't. You want to flutter them."

"Flutter them?" She frowns. "Wasn't that what I was doing?"

"Hell, no. You were squinting and hiding the lust in your eyes when you should have been working it." I make a circle motion around her face. "These babies don't lie."

"I'll bet," she says, not meaning one damn word.

"Try it again. Flutter, don't squint, and crane your neck," I tell her. "Like you can't possibly keep still by the amount of pleasure blazing through you, like your head is going to shoot off your shoulders like a cannonball."

"A cannonball?" she asks.

It's like arousal is a completely foreign concept to her. "Your head doesn't actually shoot off," I explain.

She almost laughs, except then it's like she's suddenly shy again, rubbing her hands against her black sweats.

"Seamus, I don't know about this. Don't get me wrong, it's really nice of you to help me out, but I've almost forgotten what it's like."

I don't like how lost she appears. I take her hand, hoping to settle her fears. "Forgotten what what's like?"

Her gaze falls to our hands. "To feel a real man touch me," she says.

Every word lands on my chest like falling stones. She doesn't hold my gaze, but I'm still watching her, realizing just how much she's missed out on.

"The most physical contact I've shared with a man these past few years has been a solid handshake, usually from a client."

"A handshake?" I ask. "From some guy in his eighties?"

She smiles softly. "Sometimes they're as young as sixty."

"Oh, good. I was worried there for a moment."

I kiss her hand when she laughs. I'm not sure where this might go tonight, but I'm ready for it to go somewhere if she is.

"As I was saying," she says. "It's peachy keen you want to help me with my romance issues but—"

She stops when I hold my hand up. "See, that's kind of your first problem. We're not talking romance, were talking about moving furniture, ripping clothes off with teeth, and forgetting your confirmation name."

"Oh," she says.

"Damn right," I assure her. "Peachy keen is not a word that comes up when you're in the zone. You hear what I'm saying? You want words that go with that face you're trying to make. So, no golly gee, no wowzers—nothing you'd say during mass when you see the altar boy carrying the offering trip over his Goddamn robe and send the body of Christ scattering down the aisle." I blow out a sigh. "In my defense, I had a little holy wine before show time."

"Mm," she says.

"It's time to take that leap, Alz. Time to show me what you want from a man, and how bad you want it." I open my arms wide. "So, tell me what you're going to say. Those dirty, *nasty*, freaky things you said in your head when you did go at it. It will help with the fuck face. It will help bring that navy ship into port and allow the lucky bastard in bed with you to give you all the explosions his missiles can muster. Let me have it." *Cause I need to believe you want more than my friendship.*

"I can't give you the kind of facial expressions you seek," she says, watching me carefully.

If I didn't feel stuck in the friend zone before, I feel it now. "Why?" I manage.

She wrings her hands. "I'm not positive I've had an orgasm before."

"You mean with Andres?" I scoff. "Not exactly a shock there, Alz."

"I mean with anyone."

"Come again?" I ask, certain I misheard.

"An orgasm," she says.

"I know what it is," I make a flipping motion with my finger. "I mean the other part, about you not being sure if you've ever had one. That can't be right."

She buries her face in her hands. "Look, I know you could probably make any woman orgasm with just a flex of your muscles and a wink of those darling baby blues."

"Well, I don't know about that," I admit. I frown when I realize how upset she is. "What's wrong?"

Her voice is barely a whisper. "I'm having a hard time," she says. "These issues and experiences. I've never had anyone to discuss them with."

"You do now," I say. I'm trying to make her feel better, but now it's like she wants to cry.

"All right," she says. "Fine. I'll tell you." She turns down the T.V. "I'm not sure I've had an orgasm. Ever."

It's like she's ready to crawl under the table. "I can't blame Andres for leaving me," she adds. "Like you said, had I made the appropriate faces, he would have been more confident and improved his technique."

"He has a little dick, doesn't he?"

It might take everything Allie has not to kick me in the face. "Does it matter? I was always told size doesn't matter."

"Two things," I say, holding out a finger for each for emphasis. "One, only men with small dicks say that. And two, what woman in her right mind thinks a rowboat is better than a Navy ship packing plenty of ammo?"

"Well, when you put it that way…" she says.

I move closer to her when she curls forward. "Allie, I wish you could see what I see when I look at you. You're a woman any man would be lucky to have."

Through eyes shimmering with tears, she smiles at me. "I wish I could believe you. But Andres did have me and he cheated. Not with a stranger. With my sister."

"I know. But did you ever think it wasn't about how Andres felt, but how Valentina feels?"

She cocks her head. "What do you mean?"

I glance around her townhouse, how nice everything is, how clean, how loved. "Alz," I say. "Look at where you live. How much did you drop on this place, three-quarters of a mil, maybe more?"

"Something like that," she admits, her gaze sweeping over my face.

"Bills you earned with hard work that Valentina was too lazy to commit to. Valentina didn't go to college. She could have, but she didn't. Instead, she went to Paris, leaving you to spend years earning a degree. It gave you a one-up Valentina didn't want you to have. So would marriage and a family with Andres. So, what did she do? She knocked you down a few pegs by taking Andres, then making you think you'd never have anything better."

Allie purses her lips together, listening, saying nothing.

"Think about it," I say. "Valentina didn't run away with Andres. She ran around Europe until those modeling contracts dried up. When was the last time you saw her on the cover of anything? Or heard about her at all, besides shit she fed your family?" I'm not saying this to Allie to make her feel better. I've had my suspicions and Googled Valentina. The most recent post about her was almost three years ago. "Valentina is only back because Andres has the money to support her lifestyle. You know it. I know it."

I'm sure Allie will argue with me and almost kiss her when she doesn't. "That's possible," she says, giving what I say a lot of thought. "I almost didn't graduate. I was so upset when I learned she and Andres had slept together. With one blow, that world I'd so carefully constructed blew up in my face and my sister was the one who flipped the switch."

"Yeah," I say. "Which is why I think you should move on from them both. Today was one hell of a start."

She squeezes my hand. I don't realize I'm back to holding it. It's nice, especially in the silence that follows. I let her have all the time she needs, preparing for more talk about Andres and Valentina, but grinning when that's not what comes.

"Okay, Mr. Alpha Male," she says at last. "We've established your prowess. Can we perhaps work on mine?"

I chuckle and scratch my head. "Oh, yeah, this is about you, isn't it?" She rolls her eyes, laughing. "Okay. If you want great sex, make the man want to give it to you. Show him you like what he's doing so you get more of it. That's where the fuck face comes in. It's not enough to make noises—you make noises, right?" I don't really want to know, but it's like I have to know.

"I guess."

"You guess?" I ask.

"Do whimpers count?"

"Depends on how loud," I ask, biting my tongue so I don't beg her to demonstrate. I know it's wrong that Andres and all the needle-dicks that followed never gave Allie anything good. But I can't say I feel that bad about it.

"Will you show me?" Allie asks, her voice an octave higher. "So I may have a better idea?"

"I don't whimper," I admit. "Unless the cookies are hard and stale."

Her jaw pops open again. "That was a joke, Alz," I assure her.

Allie shakes out her hands. "Show me yours. Your . . . face. Please."

Man, do I love the way she says please. "Watch and learn," I say.

I dive deep into my memories. Back to the last time I had sex, going on about six months ago. Shit. Was it that long ago? I look back at Allie and how sexy she looks. Guess it was.

The bartender was tall, big rack, and flashy; everything I like in a woman. I focus hard, trying to remember her face. I frown. I'm bad with names and remembering women, but I should be able to remember enough of her face during the act to conjure my own expression.

My eyes partially close. I remember grabbing her ankles, holding them up so her toes pointed toward the ceiling, and plowing deep. My skin starts to prickle with heat. But instead of long dark braids fanning across the bed, short bed-tossed curls gather around Allie's face beneath me.

My head pops up and my eyes fly open to meet Allie's dead on. "Wow," she says, breathless.

"Yeah, *wow*." I clear my throat so harshly it makes me cough. She pats my back when I fall into a fit of coughs.

"Are you okay? Here, let me get you some water."

She rushes into the kitchen. It should be a good thing and give me time to calm my shit. Instead, it gives me a perfect view Allie's round Latina ass bouncing along. If this was anybody else I would just lean back and admire the view, knowing what's coming next.

Instead, I'm struck dumb. Our terms didn't include fucking. I can't do that to her. She's not a woman I can sleep with and then walk away. We still have another wedding—two if we go to Valentina's. I don't want to screw this up with sex. Christ, I want more from Allie, but I want her to want the same thing, not long for something she thinks she missed out on.

Allie returns with a cool bottle of water from the refrigerator. I stop coughing, taking a sip when she offers it. Allie is like that, constantly giving, even when things should be all about her.

I take another few gulps of my water. As I watch her, I realize she's not watching me. Her gaze drifts toward the television, where a couple is crying, telling each other goodbye. Great, that's not what I need to see or anything.

"Seamus, do you think if I would've been better at expressing what I was feeling in the bedroom, Andres wouldn't have looked elsewhere?"

"No."

Allie seems surprised. "Why?"

I don't hold back. "Because no matter how much money Andres waves around or what a big shot he is with the government, he's still that same little prick who was never good enough to make the football team, the guy that most women ignored, and who was never anything special."

I take a moment, trying to find the words so she doesn't think I'm saying things just because I don't like him. "Valentina . . . I'm not sure what he feels about her. Not really. From what I've seen, she's just another FU to anyone who ever put him down. He was never going to be homecoming king, but he made sure everyone knows he fucked the queen."

The way Allie regards me tugs at my heart. "I'm sorry," she says. "I just think for all the things I did wrong in bed, Valentina did the right ones."

"I'm not sure what kind of faces she makes in bed," I admit. "But I guarantee they're not real. He's a loser, Allie. He always will be." I scoot closer, even though there's a part of me that warns against it. I skim a hand across Allie's cheek. "You're not and it's about time you had someone better."

Her landline rings, because why the hell shouldn't it?

"Just ignore it," she says, when I turn in the direction of her kitchen.

She moves closer to me, her gaze warming.

"I will," I murmur.

I lean in as her voicemail picks up. "Alegria. Pick up. Pick up the phone now!"

Allie's mother's voice rings with devastation. I think someone is dead or dying. Allie thinks the same, rushing toward the kitchen.

"You broke your sister's heart!"

Mamacita's voice echoes, bouncing along the tile lining the kitchen wall. The accusation and fury behind it slow Allie's steps.

"Tell her she broke your heart," another woman yells, her aunt I guess.

"She let down the family," yet another woman yells. "All of us."

"This was your sister's big day," Mamacita screams, cutting off another voice that tries to chime in. "The day I've waited for that *you never gave me!*"

Mamacita is in hysterics, the way she's breaking down is bordering on crazy. Holy shit. *This* is what Allie puts up with?

"All you had to do was pretend. You could pretend for a few hours to be happy for me, for your family—"

Allie lunges at the receiver, turning it on and abruptly cutting off the speaker. "Enough!" she yells. "You will not treat me this way. You won't. Don't call. I don't want to talk to any of you."

She disconnects, her hands shaking so badly, she can't house the receiver back on the base. When she finally does, she clutches her hands against her chest, staring at the phone as if waiting for the shrieking to resume.

My arms wrap around, pressing her back against my chest. "I'm . . . I'm sorry. They . . . I'm sorry."

I don't have to see her sweet face to know it's wet with tears. I kiss the top of her head and lead her back to the living room where the wine and what's left of the food remains.

I sit her down beside me, keeping my arm around her as I flip through the channels and find a really stupid movie to watch.

Allie did something brave today. She put her sister in place only to be rewarded with shit she didn't deserve.

She curls into my chest, a place I don't see anyone else belonging. We watch God-awful movies and we fall asleep. It's what friends do. Friends, and maybe a man who wants more.

CHAPTER 21

Allie

I pause at the bottom of the stone church steps. Perhaps, that isn't the best description. Stop dead is a better term. Seamus stands at the very top, laughing and joking with his brothers. They're all in pinstriped gray pants with a hint of a dark silver sheen. Tails adorn their black jackets, while dark gray vests cover their pristine white shirts and the base of their dark silver ties, except for Evan, whose tie is white. They look great. All of them. But it's Seamus I can't take my eyes off.

I took an Uber to the church since Seamus's duty as a friend and groomsman compelled him to arrive early to stand with Evan as part of his family. "It's gonna suck if God strikes me down or sends a nun to beat my ass with a ruler," he said, when he admitted he hadn't attended confession since his confirmation.

"You survived Finn's wedding," I remind him.

"I think the Benjamin I dropped in the donation bin helped. But Benjamins only get you so far with God," he reasoned.

It was great to hear him laugh and catch his grin. The other week, before my mother and aunts called, I thought we were taking that step that extended past the close friendship we share. But although we've continued to spend time together and pose as a couple in front of his family, it's like the opportunity was lost. There have been no more kisses, nothing more than hand holding and hugs, even in the company of his family. I hated him seeing me so angry and, in a way, so weak. It's altered the direction I thought we were taking.

Still, he insisted I obtain a ride here so he could take me home after the reception.

"You're my date, remember?" he said with a wink. "The least I can do is take you home."

I wouldn't say no to Seamus if it means spending time with him, especially when he looks as good as he does now.

Seamus doesn't see me watching him. Perhaps it's better. More than once he's caught me taking in his face, his hearty laugh, and, more often than not, his terrible inappropriateness. My man is not really my man, no matter how well we've pulled off this masquerade. But with every day that passes, I wish that he was.

Seamus is a sweetheart and a loudmouth. Someone whose politically incorrect persona has earned him death glares everywhere we go. That doesn't mean I've regretted our time together. Even if it's just for pretend, I'm honored to call him mine.

As much as Seamus and his brothers complain and made fun of the British style tuxedos they'd wear on Wren and Evan's wedding day, I've never seen a more stunning bridal party and Finn and Sol's party was unbelievably spectacular.

"Fuck you, Angus," my English gentleman calls out, nailing his eldest brother on his shoulder. "You passed out in front of the Virgin Mary that night."

"That was Finnie," Angus insists.

"It was not," Finnie argues. "I fell asleep in the manger and all youz damn well know it!"

"Then who the hell stole the camel?" Declan asks.

Everyone looks at Seamus when Curran hooks a thumb in his direction. "What?" he snaps, growing defensive. "I had him back by New Year's."

My smile widens. I love Seamus. I wasn't supposed to, but here I am wishing he would love me in return.

Finn, his face still beaming from his romantic honeymoon in the Swiss Alps, nudges Seamus a millisecond before he sees me.

Seamus' eyes widen at the sight of me in my turquoise cocktail dress before a big grin lights up his face and he hops down the steps.

"Hey, Alz, I didn't see you there, baby."

He lifts me into an embrace, making me laugh. Perhaps he's overdoing the girlfriend/boyfriend project in front of his family. I don't mind. It's more than he's done these past few weeks, and I welcome his touch like I do my next breath.

Seamus lowers me carefully, lifting my arms and making a show of taking me in. "You look beautiful," he says, keeping his voice low so I only hear him.

"And you look amazing," I say, meaning my words and desire for his kiss.

"I clean up good, don't I?"

"Yes, you do, my love."

The last part was a bit much based on how he guarded he becomes. He gathers me to him, whispering low. "That was pretty good."

I want to tell him how much I mean it, but the distance he's kept as of late reminds me I can't. I wait for him to say something, anything that may give me an indication he's willing to give us a chance. "You look nice," he says, instead.

"Hey, lovebirds," Curran yells from the top of the stairs. "Either get a room or get inside. It's getting close to go-time and we're going to have half the city to seat." He's holding his daughter Clodagh, the skirt of her pretty flower girl dress draped over his arm. She tucks a small rose from her basket behind her daddy's ear, earning her a kiss on the cheek that makes her giggle.

Seamus makes a face. "I have to do my job. But before I forget, could you give Evan's ring to Sofia? Sol is the matron of honor, but she has a lot to do back there. Sofia is in charge of handing the ring to Father Flanagan to bless. Wren forgot the ring at the house and I had to drive back and get it."

He holds out a square velvet ring box and opens it. "Nice, huh?" he asks. "It's platinum with gold mixed in."

I start to tell him how lovely it is when his brothers break out laughing. "Oh, man, Seamus," Killian hollers from the steps. "I thought you were proposing."

Angus laughs, his entire chest shaking. "We all did. Don't be giving me the big one this early in the day. I'm already going to lose my shit when I walk Wren down the aisle."

Molly, Angus's fiancée for the past twenty years, appears out of nowhere, the skirt of her beautiful silver bridesmaid dress flowing as she smacks Angus's arm. "What's wrong with youz?" she asks, her shrill voice sending the brothers scattering. She adjusts her large breasts beneath her "V" neck bodice. "I can hear you cursing all the way to the altar. Calm down before I send your mother out here."

An obedient silence befalls the entire area, giving our faces a moment to cool. Out of all the things his brothers could assume, why in the world would they jump to a proposal? I have this awful feeling we've played our roles too well, and worry what's going to happen when he tells them we're only friends even though I've dreamed of becoming more.

Seamus is worried, too. "I'm sorry," he says. "They shouldn't have said that."

"It's okay," I insist. I want to tell him I don't mind, but that doesn't sound right either.

He sighs. "They shouldn't make assumptions, you know?"

"I know," I say, growing a little sad.

Seamus closes the lid to the ring box and sets it in my palm, placing my other hand over it. His gaze shimmers with sadness, in spite of his small smile. "Will you take it back for me?" he asks. "And tell Wren I love her?"

The devotion that reflects in his features melts my heart and brings me back to the moment. "Don't you think it would be more appropriate if Molly does this for you?" I ask. I motion to where she's standing at the top of the steps arguing with Angus.

Seamus shakes his head slowly. "No, I want you to do it."

I nod, keeping my mouth shut so I don't admit that I would do anything for him. "Okay. I'll take good care of it," I say, instead.

He presses a kiss to my cheek, allowing it to linger before stepping back. "Hey, Mol," he yells without looking at her. "Could you take Allie back to see Wren? There's something she needs to tell her for me."

I expect Molly to offer her services on my behalf. She's an official bridesmaid. I'm merely the "girlfriend" to one of the groomsmen. For some reason, Molly doesn't bat an eye at the request. "Sure thing, Seamus. Come on, dolly," she says, motioning to me to follow.

My small purse smacks against my hip as I hurry up the steps. I don't want to anger Molly any more than I want to feel the wrath of Mama O'Brien. Molly is a woman capable of snapping me in half with as much effort as she's walking in those heels.

"I have to warn you," Molly says. "Wren isn't in the best mood on account of Mary Therese still isn't here yet."

Mary Therese is an O'Brien. I went to school with Mary Therese. She's very . . . nice . . . and as tough as the O'Briens come. I still remember her beating up a girl from my chemistry class who was twice her size after the girl accused her of sleeping with our teacher. "We've only made out like six times," Mary Therese screamed at her. "You trying to call me a slut?"

"I didn't realize Mary Therese was in the wedding," I say to Molly.

Molly rolls her eyes. "That's 'cause Mary Therese missed everything she was supposed to show for. But what can you do? Wren didn't have enough girlfriends and Mary Therese was the only woman she didn't have to worry about banging Seamus."

"*What?*" I ask.

Molly puts her arm around me and gives me an arm hug that shakes me to my core and makes me lose my balance. The fact that Molly could probably press two-hundred pounds is the only thing that prevents me from landing on my face.

"That was before, sweetie. Or like Wren and the rest of us call it, BSWU. Before Seamus Wised Up," Molly explains. "Dear God and every virgin on the planet, you wouldn't believe what it was like before you came along. It's like Seamus lost a bet with a higher power and all Cupid could do was launch arrows into skanks and prison escapees. You hear what I'm saying?"

"Yes?" I say, too scared to argue.

"Anyway, no one can find Mary Therese, not even Uncle Abner and she's his daughter. I think Aunt Ruthie is really going to kill her this time, but hopefully she'll wait till after Wren's honeymoon, otherwise I think it'll be bad Karma."

"I can see that," I say, realizing Molly expects me to agree with her.

Molly half grunts, half growls. "I told Wren she never should have picked Mary Therese. But Wren was desperate to have a bridesmaid accompany Seamus. She would've been better off hiring a prostitute, but then we had to still worry about Seamus, you know?"

"Ah . . ."

"Come on, Allie," she says. "We better hurry before we give Wren another reason to lose it in front of the priest."

She's already half-dragging me down the aisle, and I almost break my ankle when she hauls me up and behind the altar. Bless Molly's heart. For a curvaceous woman, she has the agility and speed of a stallion. "I'm surprised Wren didn't prefer to dress at her new house. She and Evan were over the moon when Angus's crew finished construction ahead of schedule."

"Yeah, she was real happy about it," Molly says, her long red curls bouncing along her back with how fast she's moving. "But she wanted to spend her last night at Grammie's with us girls. She thought it would be a nice tribute, kind of like how Seamus made the statue of her and Evan from Grammie's dead tree."

"Mm-hmm," I say, remembering said statue.

"Not to mention Wren's real superstitious about her and Evan seeing each other before the wedding. It was nice. We watched movies and looked through pictures of the family." She slows as we reach the long corridor. Even from this end, I could hear the chatter of women's voices further down the hall. "Hey, why weren't you there? You disappeared before the rehearsal dinner wrapped up."

I don't want to talk about the meeting I had with my mother and aunts. Valentina didn't attend. Something about visiting a producer she knew in New York. It was better, though. Like Seamus suggested, I saved the voicemail and played it back to family. They seemed shocked by how hateful and crazed they sounded. There were a lot of tears, but more understanding than I expected.

As a compromise, I promised to attend Valentina's wedding. In turn, they promised not to badger me if I left early or to expect my presence at any other Valentina event. I phoned Seamus when I arrived home. He wasn't happy, but he listened, making me smile and laugh until it was time for both of us to say goodnight.

"I had a family function to attend," I explain.

"That's right, your sister's getting married at the end of the month." She frowns. "I saw a write-up about it in the paper. Valentina was . . . never mind."

"What, Molly?" I say, clasping her arm before she reaches the door.

"It's nothing," she says.

Like everyone else I've ever met in my life, I was expecting to hear a comment about Valentina's superb intellect, charm, or sophistication. I don't have that impression from Molly. She seems hurt.

"You were going to say something about Valentina," I say, watching how she quiets. "It's okay, you can tell me. I won't be upset or judge you."

The term judge seems to bother her more than anything I say. Molly watches me closely. I almost expect her to gloss over things, but she doesn't. "Valentina was never nice. Not to me. Even then I was a big girl, and she reminded me every chance she got."

"That's awful," I say. "I never knew she was like that." Was I used to Valentina's pettiness first hand? My goodness, yes. But I always envisioned her driven to win everyone over to her side. I didn't realize she only sought the approval of those she deemed worthy of her time.

I want to hug Molly. Out of all the O'Briens, she and Angus were the first to invite me to dinner at their home. The first to say welcome, you're one of us now. I'll never forget either of them for that. "I'm sorry for how she made you feel," I say. "You didn't deserve that."

Molly smiles and rubs my arm. "Don't be, honey. You're nice and you're with our Seamus. That's all that matters."

Molly means to be kind, but I wish there was more truth to her statement.

She stops in front of a very dark and ornate door. I grew up in this church and like the O'Briens, I was baptized here and received my first communion and confirmation. I'd never visited this part of the building before. But then, it does belong to the brides.

"Do me a favor," Molly says. "Don't say anything about Mary Therese. She's a whore and a little bat shit crazy. But we love her."

"I won't say anything," I assure her.

"Thank you, honey." She pauses with her hand on the door and looks at me. "We haven't had much time to talk, but I want to after all the festivities wrap up. I mean it when I say we're all glad you and Seamus are together. You're everything he never knew he needed." Her smile fades a little bit. "I only hope good things for the both of youz."

"Thank you, Molly," I say, a pang of guilt hitting me hard. "I really hope things work out for us, too."

Molly raps on the door. "Who is it?" Sofia asks gently.

"It's me, Molly, and I got Allie with me."

Sofia opens the door carefully, her body shadowed by the dimness of the hall. "Hi, Allie," she says, tossing a nervous glance behind her.

"Is that fucking Mary Therese?" Wren yells from inside.

"Um," Sofia says. "Wren is—"

"Pissed," Molly finishes for her.

Sofia tries to smile. "She's a little stressed," she admits.

Molly walks in. "It's just me. I have Allie with me."

"Allie?" Wren asks.

Oh, no, perhaps I shouldn't be here. "I'm sorry to intrude, Wren. I have a message from Seamus and—"

"You're not intruding, Allie. Come on in," Wren says.

I open my palm and whisper to Sofia. "I also have Evan's ring."

Sofia places her hand over her heart. "Wonderful. Thank you, Allie. Wren," she says. "Allie has the ring."

"Well, at least I can count on Seamus," Wren grumbles.

Sofia opens the door, allowing us in and revealing the luminous gowns of the bridesmaids. Silver silk dresses alternate from sweet like Sofia's beautiful strapless, A-line skirt design, to more elegant like Tess's off the shoulder and straight skirt design, or as sensual as Melissa's halter top and flowing skirt, reminiscent of Marilyn Monroe. The material is the same, but it seems Wren took the time to select a style that matched her bridesmaids' personalities. Yet as beautiful as these women look, no one quite compares to Wren.

A loose, large braid pulls Wren's long ebony hair away from her face and gathers around the wave of neat, large, and graceful curls, cascading down the open back of her gown. A silver comb, adorned with diamonds and pearls fastens into the braid, holding the cathedral length veil everyone is doing their best not to step on.

Wren's dress isn't flashy or loud, but no one will miss her. The best way I can describe her dress is poured white silk. Sleeveless with a cowl neckline, the material gathers around Wren's amazing figure, flaring out in a trumpet cut and into a train as long as her veil.

I think Wren was going for subtle. Instead, she became the bride for the ages. She epitomizes everything I would want to be, lovely, elegant, and unforgettable.

"Wren, you look incredible."

"Thanks. Shaqwana did a nice job with my hair."

I wave my arms. "I mean everything. You're breathtaking."

Wren isn't shy or reserved, so it's sweet how she glances down and smiles softly. "Thank you. I just want Evan to like it."

"Oh, girl, you have nothing to worry about," Sol says, making us laugh. She bounces around the room, the ruffles in the skirt of her spaghetti strap dress make *wooshing* sounds. She kneels down, handing Tess's oldest daughter a teddy bear dressed in a flower girl dress. "This is from Auntie Wren and Uncle Evan," she tells her.

"What did they get Mateo's son as ring bearer?" Tess asks.

Sol laughs. "A stack of video games."

I approach Wren carefully. "Seamus wanted me to tell you he loves you."

Wren nods, again, glancing down and smiling softly. "I love him, too. I was going tell him when he walked me down the aisle. This was supposed to be the perfect day, you know? I can't believe Mary Therese isn't here."

"Worst case scenario, Angus and Seamus can walk down the aisle with Molly," Sofia suggests.

"We can't have that. It will leave us with thirteen adults. That's not a number I need on my wedding day. Bad omen, you feel me?"

As if in cue, we all cross ourselves. Call us crazy. Call us superstitious. Call us Catholic.

The clock strikes eleven thirty and we know time is running out. The tension shoots through the roof and everyone starts fussing over Wren, although she very much doesn't appear like a bride to be fussed with. I start to leave when a cell phone rings.

Sol shoots across the room, everyone growing silent when she answers it. She waves frantically at Wren. "It's Mary Therese... she says she wants to talk to you." "Sol practically trips over herself getting to Wren. Wren lifts the phone. "Where are you? Are you coming? . . . What? . . . *What*? . . .The hell? . . . Mary Therese, are you kidding me right now?"

Wren disconnects, flinging the phone across the room. "Mary Therese isn't coming," she announces to the room.

We all collectively gasp. "Where is she?" Tess asks, adjusting the silver sash around her daughter's waist.

"Are you ready for this?" Wren asks. "In Vegas and apparently married. She thought the guy was a manager at CBS. Turns out he's a manager at CVS. She's freaking out, trying to get it annulled, even though they spent the night banging like grizzlies in the woods with cymbals."

Wren looks at Sol. "I told you she'd pull something like this." She points to the dress hanging in the corner. "Why do you think I wouldn't let her hang onto the dress and the shoes? She's so irresponsible I thought she'd damage the dress and lose the shoes." She glances around. "But this . . . what the hell am I going to do with one less bridesmaid?"

"Maybe Evie would be willing to sub in?" Melissa offers.

Wren shakes her head. "Mary Therese is skinnier than an ostrich neck. Evie's pregnant and her baby bump is twice as big as it was a few weeks ago. She can't fit into that thing. It's a size two and . . ."

Her voice fades and it's as if she's suddenly remembers I'm here. Like the domino effect, all eyes are suddenly on me. "What size do you wear Allie?" Wren asks.

"Ah, six. Four on a good day," I say.

Sol leans into Wren. "That could work."

A big smile forms across Wren's face. "So, Allie. What are you doing for the next hour?"

CHAPTER 22

Allie

Wren didn't really ask me to be in her wedding. She more or less told me that was the plan. I was terrified to tell her no. It's not that I don't want to help. It's that I don't want to place Seamus in an awkward position. It's bad enough his brothers thought he was proposing. The look on his face? He wasn't embarrassed. He was mortified. Yet, here I am, getting ready to walk down the aisle with him on my arm.

Sol spins me around by the shoulders. She has a few inches on me and gives me a little shake. "What's wrong? You look scared. Are you scared? Don't be scared."

"Ah."

She points at the double doors, seconds away from being opened by Finn and Killian. "All you're doing is walking in. That's all you have to do—stop looking so terrified. You look awesome. You walk down—Oh, my God you're shaking—stop shaking. Oh, wait, that's me. Anyway, Molly is first, then Melissa, then you. Wren's having the guys walk forward from oldest to youngest—Jesus, Allie, you're sweating."

"Is Allie all right?" Wren calls from the back. It's taking most of her bridal party to fan out and straighten her train.

"Totally," Sol answers for me. "She's just excited."

"Oh, that's so sweet," Sofia says.

"When you get to the altar, bow, then take your place in front of the statue of the Blessed Mother. The one by herself, not the one of her holding Jesus. Got it?"

"Yes?"

"I'll be right behind you," Tess assures me, passing me a bouquet of fire and ice, pale pink and silver roses.

Wren's bouquet must have every shade of pink rose known to the floral kingdom. From pink so pale it almost looks white, to fuchsia so brilliant and bold, it's a Technicolor masterpiece of nature. Aside from the thick, white ribbon wrapped around the rose stems to maintain the bouquet's circular shape, there are no other frills, no other flowers, nothing. Just Wren in all her magnificence.

"Allie, are you okay?" Melissa asks.

"I can't breathe," I admit.

Mary Therese was as skinny as Wren claimed. She also didn't have much in term of cleavage. The dress is wrapped around my body like plastic wrap, and my girls are barely staying behind the plunging neckline of the halter top.

"I'll unzip you a little—Oh, *shit*," Sol says when my breasts pop out. "Here, *here*." She slaps my hands away when I try to tuck them back in. "I have them." And yes, she does, keeping them elevated as Melissa hurries to zip me back up.

"You can breathe after the ceremony," Sol says. "All you have to do is get through the next hour. Do not pass out. Promise me you won't pass out."

"I promise," I say.

What else can I say? Mary Therese made Wren's wedding all about herself, running off to an impromptu trip to Vegas because she missed Wren's bachelorette party. She lost all her money and her new husband doesn't make enough at CVS to buy her a plane ticket home. It doesn't look good for Mary Therese, and it won't look good for Wren if I don't stand by her. Hell will freeze over before I ruin her day.

Finn and Killian open the doors as the first chords of *Pachelbel's Canon in D* begin to play. This version, with a pianist and large ensemble of violinists, cellists, and children's choir is more akin to the Tran-Siberian Orchestra's Christmas version, the exception being the choir is to sub out "Christmas night" with "special night."

Molly proceeds ahead, her steps graceful and in time with the music. When Molly is about a quarter of the way down the massively long aisle, Melissa follows. I wait for Melissa to reach the same place Molly did before I begin my descent. Either I misjudged the position or Sol thinks we're running short on time. She encourages me forward with a slap to my ass. Oh, yes, she's an O'Brien now.

I right myself carefully, my bouquet of roses poised just above my belly button and my arms bent slightly as instructed. I will not be the one to anger the bride or the matron of honor. I want to live.

My smile is subtle, happy and respectful. I ignore my fears about tripping over the hem of my dress. If anyone notices that I've gathered it up beneath my flowers and am dragging the rest, no one reacts, beaming when they see me.

In addition to being a rather daring and adventurous member of the O'Brien clan, Mary Therese is a few inches taller. It doesn't matter that I couldn't fit into her shoes. No one will see mine as long as I don't land on my face.

From the altar, the O'Brien brothers march forward one by one. From what Wren said, they're to stop in front of their designated pews. Wren wouldn't pick between her brothers or her mother. Each member of the family will take their turn walking her down the aisle.

Angus is the first I see, his smiling cherubic face widening when he passes Molly and gives her a subtle pat on her ass. I can't see her face, but I don't doubt for a moment she's returning that grin.

Declan is more suave, winking at Melissa with all the charm he's known for. They hold each other's gaze as they close the distance between them, exactly as all newlyweds should. Miles is showing improvement thanks to the technological advances Evan's company developed. I pray

Miles wins his battle with cancer, and that Declan and Melissa spend a lifetime building on the adoration they share now.

I catch my first sight of Seamus as Declan passes me. No one, it seems, told him I was subbing in for Mary Therese. Either that or he very much likes how I look in the dress. My cheeks flush as I watch his jaw hit the floor.

He's openly gaping at me. "Jesus *Christ*," he mutters, banging his hip into a pew when he reaches me.

"*Oh*," a few people say over the ricochet of loud gasps.

I keep my focus in front of me. In addition to not pissing off the bride, I won't be the person who breaks formation.

I reach the altar and bow, smiling when I look to Evan. Dashing and refined are just two ways describe him, handsome and dignified are two more. He doesn't seem to notice me, so gripped with emotion and captured in this moment, his full attention and broad smile stay in the direction of the double doors, waiting with anticipation for the first glimpse of his bride.

I'm overtaken by the joy Evan emanates, my eyes welling as I take my place beside Melissa, in front of the appropriate Virgin.

One by one, the remaining bridesmaids make their way down the aisle, and the groomsmen reach their posts.

Mattie appears, his head up as he carries the silver pillow, his toothy grin lighting up the entire church. The girls walk just a few feet behind him. Little Clodagh follows dutifully behind Fiona, who is focused, if not determined, to spread the petals in her basket better than any flower girl ever has.

I almost laugh. They're so cute. I'm not certain what their parents promised them, but the children make excellent time, allowing Sol to take her position at the altar just as the extended melody finishes in a whisper of sound.

To my far left, and beneath the stained-glass depiction of Christ rising, the first of four women dressed in Celtic gowns of gold, green, and red begin a delicate acapella version of *Danny Boy*. One by one, their voices ranging from soprano to alto, take over each verse, gradually and seamlessly blending in perfect harmony.

"Oh, God," Tess whispers, her voice breaking.

Like Tess, none of the brothers were expecting this tribute. Their stunned faces and the way they exchange glances reflect as much. And if they were determined not to cry, all is now lost. Anyone can see what this song means to them.

Wren appears, her train and veil flowing behind her. She reaches Angus first, hooking her arm through his. Whatever she says to him has the big guy falling apart. We're already crying quietly, but when Melissa, who can so masterfully read lips, tells us what Wren said to Angus, I'm certain none of us will make it through the ceremony in one piece.

"Thank you for being my strength," Melissa says, repeating Wren's words.

Declan tenses as Wren nears. Wren doesn't disappoint. "Thank you for being my hero."

Declan swipes at his face, but there's no hiding the tears that flow.

Wren reaches Seamus, who's working to slow his breathing and keep it together. I think he'll be okay until Wren tells him. "Thank you for being my protector."

Down the line she goes, blessing and honoring each brother.

"Thank you for being my virtue," she tells Curran, smiling even as he weeps.

Killian, appearing so small at this moment despite his immense size, holds out his arm when Wren and Curran stop just behind him.

Wren pauses, still smiling through the feelings her kind words evoke. "Thank you for teaching me compassion," she tells Killian, taking his arm. "Your heart's my favorite thing about you."

Finn is the brother standing closest to us. But again, Melissa has to tell us what Wren says. "Thank you for being my courage," she tells him. "I love you, Finnie."

It's the first glimpse we have of Wren's splintering composure. Still, she smiles as Finn swallows back a sob, allowing him to lead her to the last O'Brien who remains.

Wren extends her arm to entwine around her mother. But as the two women reach the last step that separates Wren from marriage, Wren unleashes the emotions she held in.

"Thank you, Mama," she says. "You were the best mother and father we could have."

Tears stream down the women's faces. Wren bends, her long, slender arms wrapping around the tiny woman who gave her children all her heart possessed.

Mama releases Wren slowly, both women smiling through their tears. As the last verse of Danny Boy completes in a delicate echo of voices, Mama places her beloved daughter's hand in the hand of the man she prays will love Wren for eternity.

"Hello, darling," Evan says, his British accent as rich and bold as the adoration his words carry.

Wren's eyes glisten with the fresh start of tears, her elation matching his. "Hey, Bossman," she tells him.

As the bride and groom hold each other for the first time as the husband and wife they are about to become, all that remains is love and peace in its purest form, and a family's dream come true.

CHAPTER 23

Seamus

Here's the thing about Catholic weddings. They're serious. Dead serious. Even under the happiest circumstances there are rituals involved. Rituals we have to follow or else be damned to hell for eternity.

Wren had a mind-blowing ceremony, I'm not going to lie. Shit, it's been two weeks and my brothers and I can't talk about it without choking up. That tribute Wren did—the one where Danny Boy himself ripped out our hearts only for Wren to place them back in our chests—was epic, her way of saying, "I was the only girl, but all of you helped me become the woman I am."

All that said, her wedding followed the rules. Finnie, who also kicked us in the nuts with his vows, broke every last rigid tradition and Father Flanagan let him.

Out of all of us, Finnie had it the toughest. It didn't matter how hard we tried to protect him. We couldn't save our little brother. That's all right. He saved himself. He and that incredible woman he danced down the aisle with was the rock he needed.

Declan and Melissa, they had an intimate wedding. I don't think I've ever used the word "precious" in my life. I'll make the exception for them. They made something sweet out of circumstances that downright suck. But Valentina and Andres? What the fuck is this shit?

We walk through the foyer of the Montana Elite. God help me, Allie's hand in mine is the only thing keeping me in this circus filled with clowns.

I'm not joking. There are fucking clowns doing flips near the entrance.

"I guess she wanted a circus theme," Allie says, eyeing the aerialists twisting down from the ceiling on giant pieces of fabric.

Like me, she's probably hoping to heaven and back they don't land on us. Jesus, that woman's just holding that shit with her teeth. "Yeah," I agree. "Nothing says, 'I love you,' better than a freak show."

Allie covers her hand with her mouth, a choked squeak lodging in her tiny throat. It's cute, not that she looks that way. Allie is slamming it tonight, putting all the uptight B-list celebrities we're walking past to shame.

There's that redhead, what's her face? The one who used to be on that hit show until she shaved her head and mailed the pieces to Charlie Sheen. Babe, Charlie's already nuts. Why give him something else to lose his shit over?

Oh, and there's Deanna Bernstein. Former top model turned animal hater. You have to hate animals to wear a dead flamingo wrapped around you. A few of the hot pink feathers that make up her skirt flutter to the floor. "She must be molting," I say.

"Seamus, stop," Allie says through her smile. She's trying not to laugh. But she's not trying hard enough. I'm just getting started.

The former model turns, eyeing us with her nose turned up as she strokes the bird's beak, its neck wrapped around hers like a choker.

"I don't think she likes your dress," I tell Allie. "Told you, you should have worn that dead panda—"

Allie yanks me ahead. In truth, if I dug in my heels, she couldn't make me budge. But I'm starting to laugh, too. It feels good to laugh with my lady, and it feels even better to stand here as her man.

I'm in the dark tux and gold tie I wore as a member of Finnie's wedding party. Allie's in a strapless dress that falls just above her knee. I'm not sure where she found this sexy little number, but the subtle gold tone matches my tie to a tee.

She sees me eyeing her, glancing down and coming to walk beside me when she feels she's put enough space between me and the bird killer. "I hope you don't mind that we match," she says.

"I wouldn't want it any other way," I assure her.

What I would like another way is us, except I'm not sure how to make *us* happen.

This whole thing started out as an arrangement, this little agreement so we'd get what we needed. But Allie, being the amazing, fun, and smart woman she is . . . what can I say? She was just what I needed, even though I'd never pictured myself with someone this perfect.

When I saw her in Mary Therese's dress, I knew I was done for. But it's like everything I thought I should say didn't come out. My brothers had to go and think I was proposing—and then announce it, too! I was sure Allie was going to bolt. So instead of holding her in my arms like I wanted to at the end of the ceremony, I held her at arm's length worried she'd dump me right there. We had fun. We danced up a storm. We went home. Separately. Yeah, we've had dinner at my place and hers. But's it's like we've reached a standstill. Some place where friends, *just friends*, hang out.

Allie jumps when some asshole, his body painted in green scales, spits fire just a few feet away from her. I snatch her to me and point at the guy. "You set my woman on fire, I'm going to rip off your tail and shove it up your ass."

"I'm a professional," the man in a speedo with lizard parts sticking out between his butt cheeks says, all offended-like.

"You're going to be professional with a tail sticking out of your ass," I warn.

Allie hauls me away from the black and white stand the guy's perched on. Dragon dude scowls, but damn well moves back, leaving some space between him and the guests.

We pass a woman dressed in a plain brown dress that hangs to her ankles and a long white apron that's not that much shorter. Her face is painted like a porcelain doll. And, yeah, it's as creepy as it sounds.

She steps out from behind an old-fashioned peanut cart and smiles, offering us a paper bag. "Would you like some peanuts to feed the elephants?" she asks, attempting to fake an Irish accent. "They're in the garden just past the solarium."

Allie and I exchange glances. "Perhaps later?" Allie says, sounding about as dumbstruck as I look.

"Oh," creepy doll lady says. "Now is the prime time to feed them. The zoo is coming to collect them within the hour." She drops her voice. "They want to avoid the giant beasts stomping any drunks who may try to ride them later."

"I'll bet," I say.

"Thank you, anyway," Allie says.

As we make our way further in, the crowd of forgotten stars grows more pronounced, fighting to draw the attention of the camera crews that have arrived. Most are local stations, except for the reporter from one of those sleazy entertainment shows.

"Let me guess the caption," I say. "Valentina Mendes rushes down the aisle with secret elephant love child growing in her cavern of desire."

Allie grins. "That's enough out of you," she says.

"The hell it is," I say. "How 'bout, Rhinos, monkeys, and gazelles cause mass destruction at bizarre vampire-circus style wedding?"

"Seamus."

"Hot local carpenter saves all."

"Seamus!"

"Swings through curtains a lá Tarzan."

She throws back her head, laughing.

"With sexy Jane in gold dress. Footage at eleven."

Allie nudges me playfully, laughing at my stupid remarks. She stops laughing as more of the freaky shit comes into view. Man, I don't know where to look to catch any hint of normal.

We pass a bearded lady telling fortunes. A little person on a bike doing tricks. Like the clowns near the front, the aerialists, and the lady with the peanuts, their makeup is a combination of Goth meets Bride of Frankenstein.

"Valentina must have spent a fortune," Allie says.

I huff. "No, Andres did."

"Yes, he did." Allie isn't jealous. She sounds confused. Like me, she probably can't understand the why of it all. I get Valentina wants to show off and be remembered. But the best way to describe this whole thing is unnecessary. Then again, I'm talking like someone with nothing to prove.

"Seamus," Allie says. "You know what's odd?"

"Ah, everything?" I ask, motioning around this hot mess.

She turns her head in the direction that we came. "I've seen who's present, but I haven't seen who *should* be present."

"What do you mean?"

"My relatives, my cousins, my family. No one is here. I don't even see Andres's family in attendance and his family is almost as large as mine."

I shrug. "My guess is Valentina has them stowed someplace reserved for family or close friends."

"I hope," she says. "But knowing Valentina, it would make more sense to have them mingling here so she can show off her success and who she knows."

"But it's not real success. It's Andres's."

"I know," she adds. "Look . . . I'm not trying to pretend to know Andres. Especially when I've determined I never really knew him. But this is the exact opposite of anything that resembles his former persona. If he had a Star Wars theme wedding, yes, as nerdy as it sounds, it would fit. This doesn't make any sense. It's completely foreign from anything he may have wanted."

"That's because he probably didn't want it. I give them six months," I say, not bothering to whisper. I give Allie a one shoulder shrug when she looks at me. "It's for show, Allie. Just like their marriage."

"I know," she says, sounding sad.

"Why does it bother you so much?" I ask.

She smiles a little when I tickle her chin. "As much as I don't believe they're in love, I wanted to be wrong."

My arm slips around Allie's waist as the crowd thickens. I angle my body, shielding her against the slew of drunks. Women in top hats, black and white makeup, skimpy outfits, and fishnets pass us with silver platters piled with drinks. Even more pass us with empty glasses. The so-called elite guests are taking advantage of the free booze and the reception hasn't even started.

"Did you hear me?" Allie asks.

I practically snarl at the idiot and his date who stumble forward, leading Allie away until we're almost to the large hall and the crowd thins. "Sorry," I say. "I didn't hear anything. I was too busy trying to keep you safe."

"Thank you," she says. She quiets and adds, "I never wished Valentina or Andres harm. As much as I find their actions distasteful and selfish, I really hoped they could somehow be happy."

"Why?" She tilts her head, evidently questioning why I'd ask such a thing. "I get that you're a good person, but even good people have their limits."

I tug on her hair when she averts her gaze to the floor. Like some kind of magical gesture, she grins. "I suppose if they were happy and managed to have a long and wonderful marriage, their actions would be worth the hurt they caused me."

"I don't agree," I say. "If roles were reversed, neither would wish the same for us."

"Us?" she asks.

Okay. This is it. "Yeah, Allie. Us."

Some skinny guy in even skinnier pants, dressed like a ring master and wearing enough makeup to shame a drag queen, clears his throat, interrupting a moment I've waited too long for.

I'm not bothered about the makeup. Hell, it's a free country. He can do what he wants. I'm bothered by the interruption and the next few words that fly out of his mouth.

"Would you like a dove?" He lifts the bird he's holding and shoves it in my face, proving this isn't a joke, and that yes, he is an asshole.

"To eat?" I ask.

I don't think this guy is going to get many men like me in here. For that, and probably more, he's grateful.

His eyes round, but he recovers quickly. "No, sir. The bride and groom are offering doves to release as opposed to the exhausted tradition of throwing rice.

I give Allie a look that says, "Can you believe this crap?" A look I have no doubt she'll be getting a lot tonight.

"No, thank you," Allie says, taking in the row of white birds cooing behind their wooden cages.

"They don't peck," the dude assures us.

Like that's the damn problem.

"And you don't have to hold them. You just have to write a note, wishing the bride and groom well," he tells us. "We'll tie it to the dove's foot and send the message into the heavens."

See? There's that look again.

I glance toward our right where another woman in a gothic clown suit offers the Channel Twelve news anchor a sacrificial dove. The animal rights activists should be all over this place. Where the hell is PETA when you need them?

"It would mean a lot to the bride and groom," ring master guy insists when we try to walk away.

"Looks to me like most of the crowd would have preferred to throw rice," I say, pointing to the two sole doves with notes tied to their legs.

"Very well," Allie says.

The guy steps aside, making a show of presenting yet another she-goth clown behind a small ornate podium. She straightens a ribbon of paper and reaches for a black quill. "What would you like the note to say?" she asks.

"Don't shit on the bride," I offer.

Allie snatches my hand, trying not to laugh when she sees me trying to do the same. "How about, wishing you well?" she recommends, instead.

"That's it?" the ring master asks.

Now, I'm really annoyed. "If you don't like it, you can go with my first suggestion."

"Wishing you well works, sir." He adds the "sir" when I glare at him. Maybe I shouldn't. Maybe I should feel sorry for him. Seriously, what does he tell his family every Thanksgiving when they ask him what he's up to? "The usual. Dressing up like a freaky ring master and playing with pigeons. How's Uncle Lou? I hear he's got gout."

"Why don't we head in?" Allie suggests.

"If that's what you want," I say.

It's a good idea and maybe it will give us time to talk and—holy *shit*! We're inside of a circus tent.

This isn't an ordinary tent. The ceiling goes up a good fifty feet. The large hall is only partially lit, which is odd. Considering the size of the lightbulbs crisscrossing above us, there should be enough light to get a tan. As it is, there's barely enough for guests to find their way to their seats and not fall on their faces.

Each chair is covered in alternating fabrics of black and white, and tied with the opposite color ribbon. I take in the tightrope running from one corner to the other and a trapeze configuration opposite it.

I don't see a net. Not a good sign. "Maybe we should hang outside and feed the giraffes."

"Elephants," Allie corrects, but she isn't looking at me. She's looking further down the aisle where several women are clutching a crying woman.

I don't recognize Mamacita. Allie does, releasing my hand as she hurries down the aisle. "Excuse me," she says.

Mamacita is hunched over, the tan dress she's in causing her to blend in with the background.

"Mom, what's wrong?" Allie asks, bending to speak to her crying mother.

I reach them, holding back to give them some privacy, but close enough to have Allie's back. I wait to hear something about Valentina jumping ship on Andres. I don't expect what comes next.

"They're ignoring your mother," one of Allie's aunts says.

"Who's ignoring her?"" I ask.

They look up at once, appearing to notice me for the first time. Instead of bristling like a pack of porcupines, like Allie's family usually does around me, they seem relieved to see me.

"Everyone here is ignoring her," another aunt answers. "Either they don't believe she is the mother of the bride or they don't care."

Allie frowns. "Are you speaking of the guests, the staff, or . . ."

"Take your pick," another aunt bites out, causing Mamacita to cry harder.

Allie shakes her head like she doesn't understand how anyone could do this. Probably because she'd never treat anyone this way.

"We were left out of the planning and arrangements from the start," the oldest aunt says. "We tried to understand. It's in Valentina's right to refuse us. But your mother . . ."

"I just wanted to help," Mamacita says. "I was worried Valentina might need something done or handled. But she hasn't talked to me in weeks and didn't let me attend any of her fittings or meetings. This isn't like her."

Sure it is. Mamacita's just never been on the receiving end.

The aunt with the silver hair who looks the most like Mamacita wrings her hands. "Every time we've asked to speak to someone in charge, or tried to speak to one of the attendants, they've ignored us. The one man who didn't demanded to see our invitations. Even then, he still wouldn't help us."

"They won't tell us where Valentina is," the first aunt says. "We don't want to bother her. Your mother just wants to help her dress and offer a blessing."

Mamacita looks up. I didn't feel bad for her when I first met her. She was being mean to Allie and too busy kissing Valentina's ass to see how hurt Allie was.

I feel sorry for her now. Mamcita's face doesn't carry the cockiness I'm most familiar with. She's pale in this light, but there's more. This isn't a woman who's offended. This is a woman who feels abandoned by her child. "It's like they've been instructed to keep us away and silent," Mamacita says. "There's no other explanation."

Allie's aunts step aside when she kneels and places her hand on her mother's shoulder. "The wedding theme was a bit of a surprise."

"To us too," one of the aunts says. "Valentina wouldn't speak a word about it to anyone. Did you see the clowns?"

Allie's gaze softens, recognizing her family's unease, but mostly her mother's embarrassment. "Mom, have you considered that perhaps Valentina wants everything to be a surprise? Something special for you and everyone to remember?"

Allie is saying all the sweet things good daughters should. But Valentina isn't the good daughter Allie is. Today proves as much.

The lights flicker off and on, alerting the guests it's *Showtime*. Allie reaches for a tissue from her purse and wipes her mother's eyes. "Don't worry, Mommy. It will be all right," she says. "Let's get you cleaned up so everyone will see your smiling, pretty face when you walk down the aisle."

"There's no need." The aunt with the gray streaks in her hair clasps her hands, her lips pursing in reflection of her anger. "Your mother won't be walking down the aisle," she says. "Valentina won't let her."

CHAPTER 24

Seamus

The circus extends into the ceremony. I just don't mean the theme, I mean all the crazy. The moment everyone finds a chair, the lights go off, causing people to gasp with confusion or gasp out their "What the fucks?"

"If Valentina rides in here on a zebra, we're out of here," I mutter.

I'm trying to get Allie to laugh, but she barely cracks a smile. Instead, she looks to the row in front of us where her mother is struggling to get it together. It's just a taste of what Allie has put up with all these years, but it's still a bitter pill to swallow.

The regular circus lights don't come back on. Instead there's an explosion of gold and whirling lights as Britney Spears's *Circus* erupts from every direction.

The trapeze performers cut loose. "Oohs and Aahs" surround us. I'm not sure where to look until two "dragons" spit fire on either side of the aisle, pulling our attention toward the entrance.

There's no procession. Not in the traditional sense. The aisle becomes a runway for the first bridesmaid in this fashion show from hell.

"Christ," I mumble, blinded by flashes of what seems to be an army of photographers and the dragon's stupid fire. Orange and yellow flames spew as the bridesmaid strikes a pose and the trapeze people flip over her head.

I have to give it to the model. She doesn't blink, keeping that deadpan expression even though she has enough hairspray to catch fire or to die by gravity if one of those swinging bodies crashes on top of her.

The next model struts forward, striking a different pose as more fire and more flipping erupts. It goes on and on. Every model is close to six feet, their dark purple dresses long in the back, short in the front, and tight around their skeletal frames.

The last model appears. My guess is she's the maid of honor based on the tiny matching top hat pinned into what has to be a two-foot wall of hair. "So, was that the dress you were going to wear?" I ask Allie.

Allie raises her brows, taking in the statuesque brunette. Man, it's like all the models were cloned in some twisted up fashion lab. "Funny you should say that," Allie says. "I wasn't told about the runway walk. Valentina bequeathed me the honor of carrying the end of her train. My dress was the same color and fabric of the tent, and the exact duplicate of what my mother is wearing."

I don't think Allie means to be as loud as she is, but her aunts hear her and so does her mother. The dress Allie's mother is wearing is better suited for an eighty-year-old woman who's given up on life. Long-sleeved, boxy, with some sort of fishtail at the bottom, Mamacita isn't dressed to look good. She and Allie were dressed to make *Valentina* look good.

"You did yourself a favor by not being a part of this," I say. "It's like a wannabee Tim Burton threw up in here."

"No," Allie disagrees. "Valentina did me a favor by making me not want to be a part of it."

She sure did. I wonder how Allie and Trashy Tina could be cut from the same cloth. There's dumping on someone, and then there's this. "Can I ask you something?" I ask, playing with her hand.

"Of course."

"How much did you shell out for that dress?"

Allie shakes her head. "You don't want to know."

The club remake of *Circus* slows, alternating into a bed thumping, throaty beat as the maid of honor takes her position in the front,

We stand. Here comes the bride, and God-Almighty, look at her.

I don't want to flat out say Valentina is naked. But Valentina is pretty much naked.

What looks like the same material they make women's hosiery from flares out to create Valentina's gown. Don't worry. Whoever designed her dress was nice enough to bedazzle all the important parts with small diamonds. Valentina's nips, happy place, and butt crack are well concealed. Oh, and look at that. As a bonus, the diamond-studded top hat she's wearing covers her head, nicely

"So, do you think it'll be a Catholic ceremony?" I whisper to Allie.

Allie turns slowly to me. I can't be sure what's more wide open, her eyes or her mouth. I'm going to go with eyes. She starts to say something, but she's cut off by applause—not by Valentina's mother or aunts, they're too busy crossing themselves—almost every person in attendance is on their feet, clapping like this is the greatest moment ever. And it is.

For Valentina.

"She . . . I can't . . . Oh, my God," Allie says. "I was going to be behind her."

"Behind her behind? Yeah, that sucks," I agree.

"Why would she . . . *my God*," Allie says, watching the way the twirling lights cause Valentina's nipples to sparkle.

"We should have fed the giraffes," I remind her.

Allie doesn't bother correcting me this time, gasping when Valentina strolls past her mother and aunts without acknowledging them. I think my woman still can't come to terms with how selfish Valentina is being. But Valentina isn't done yet.

Valentina reaches the altar where a strong man wearing little more than gothic tattoos and a smile steps forward to preside over the ceremony. I didn't even notice Andres appear. The strong man dwarfs Andres, making Andres appear shorter than he is, yet somehow drawing more attention to Valentina in their collective nakedness. Never mind, the guy's wearing some kind of man thong. My bad.

Andres is dressed like a ring master, top hat, funky jacket, even a whip cinched to his side. But instead of looking like he's a part of this whole thing, he looks out of place and more like the little guy in the Monopoly game.

I shit you not, conjoined twins resembling crazed Mad Hatters step forward, each holding a velvet pillow with the wedding bands.

There's not much to the vows. Just the standard, "Do you take him. Do you take her," plus the "I do's." Not that it stops the epic climax.

Cannons on either side of the stage explode, erupting glitter in conjunction with the start of Madonna's *Ray of Light* and the doves flying across the room. The conjoined twins are flippity-flopping down the runway. Oh, and look at that, there go the trapeze and dragon guys again.

One by one, the models strut down the aisle, following the conjoined twins. It allows Valentina to bask in the attention a while longer. Applause, hoots and hollers, and cheers of "Bravo, Bravo" are everything Valentina wanted and something she can't get enough of.

As the newlyweds begin their walk down the aisle, I expect Andres to gloat. Just a little. After all, he got the prom queen and the last laugh at everyone who considered him a loser. So then why does he look over at us? Specifically, at Allie and the way I'm holding her against me.

Probably because Valentina was the only one who really got what she wanted.

And Andres damn well knows it.

CHAPTER 25

Allie

We sit down to dinner, the feel of Seamus's hand in mine giving me strength to remain in place. To my surprise, Valentina sat us in the middle of the ballroom, almost directly in front of her and Andres. She hasn't spoken to me. Worst of all, she hasn't spoken to my mother or aunts. I can't see them from where we're sitting, and I can't be sure they're still here.

My poor family. As rude as they were to me, they've always counted on Valentina's attention. Now, they don't even have that.

"Do you want to dance?" Seamus asks. "The tigers are all gone."

"True," I agree, squelching a smirk.

The theatrics didn't end when Valentina and Andres walked down the aisle. We were escorted to the reception and given 3D glasses. As Valentina and Andres took to the dance floor for their first dance, tigers raced around the perimeter of the room and leapt over our heads while lions jumped through hoops of fire on the dance floor. It was all part of the show. We couldn't see the animals or the fireworks exploding around us without the glasses. What we could see was the awkward dance between the bride and groom.

Valentina wrapped her arms around Andres, curling her long body into his dwarf figure, as if she is as in love with him as she so adamantly claims. Andres stiffly followed suit, his blank expression reflecting only his numbness.

I wondered briefly if the 3D showcase was to distract the audience from the deportment of the newlyweds. Regardless, I saw them, the entire experience churning my stomach.

Seamus, bless his perpetually famished disposition, ate his surf and turf with enthusiasm. "Mm. Good steak," he said. I barely touched my salad when it was served and only had a few bites of my lobster.

"You sure you don't want to dance?" Seamus asks. "It'll give us something to do besides hang with these assholes." He smiles and waves when the guests at our table look up.

I ignore the glares and look toward the empty dancefloor where that odd carnival style music continues to play. "This isn't exactly my jam," I admit.

"How do you know it's not mine?" he asks.

I laugh, not knowing what I would have done without him these past few months, especially tonight. I don't know anyone at the table, but they seem to know each other. No one bothered to speak to us even when we said hello. Well, except for one woman who asked me how I knew Valentina.

"She's my sister," I explained.

The group exchanged glances as if they didn't believe me. "She never mentioned she has a sister," the woman said.

That was the last bit of conversation we bothered initiating. Well, unless you count Seamus's "asshole" remark just now.

"I'm not trying to be a dick," Seamus says. "But how much longer do you want to stay?"

In all honesty, I could leave right now. But I adore the feel of his arms around me and I'm not certain I'll feel them any other way tonight. "How about we leave after one dance?" I ask. "To a semi-decent song, I mean."

Seamus has been more than patient, wonderful, and kind. The deadline for our agreement ends tonight. I want to hang onto my make-believe boyfriend a while longer and in any way I can.

He smiles softly, his blue eyes sparkling in the candlelight. "All right. We'll do whatever you want."

By some miracle, lights illuminate the dance floor and real music, sweet, *slow* music begins to play. I turn to Seamus, grinning. "Imagine that," he says. "They're playing our song."

It's not really our song. It's merely a slow song that couldn't have come fast enough. As we rise, I glance at Valentina. She's left her table and is laughing with her bridesmaids and a man I believe is a producer. Andres sits by himself, drinking what appears to be scotch.

Married for less than an hour and he's already miserable. I don't want that for me. I want something better. I look up at Seamus and the way he holds me as he guides me forward.

I want Seamus. God help me, he's everything I desire.

The song the band plays is one I remember from college, Snow Patrol's *Chasing Cars*. I always felt a strong connection to the words, they're so lovely. But as Seamus wraps his arms around me and his broad chest draws closer to mine, those lyrics become that much sweeter, fragile, and sexy.

We melt against each other in a way we haven't quite managed, ever. It's not forced, it simply happens as if this might well be our final goodbye.

I don't want to say goodbye. I want to welcome something better. Something real that has nothing to do with our families and everything to do with us.

I lift my chin to better see him, smiling wider when he returns my grin.

"This is nice," he says, his hands wandering from my waist and further down.

I swallow hard. "Yes," I agree, wishing I could find words that mean more.

He curls forward. I think he means to kiss my mouth, instead his warm breath reaches my shoulder and his lips touch my skin. My breath hitches and the tips of my nipples tighten. This is it, my moment to kiss Seamus for real. Not for others to see, but for us to experience.

As Adele's *Someone Like You* begins I find my courage, only to be denied.

"May I cut in?"

I'm stunned to see Andres beside me, the heavy glass that holds his drink clutched tightly in his hand.

"No," Seamus answers for me. His anger is palpable, surging his body temperature.

Andres laughs, bitterly. He glances down, staring at his almost empty glass, but when he looks up, I see it, the true extent of his misery. "Please, Allie. *Please*," he says.

I'm troubled by how lost he seems, how utterly demolished he appears.

"I don't want him touching you," Seamus says, his response surprising us both.

"Allie, please," Andres begs. He's no longer looking at me, he's staring down at the floor as if he wants to be buried far beneath it.

It's disturbing and hard to witness. I'm not a cruel person who can simply walk away from anyone hurting. Seamus knows it, not that it makes my words easier to say. "I think I need to," I tell him.

Seamus isn't happy and I can't blame him. Yet he releases me, watching Andres closely as he moves forward.

Andres drops his glass onto the tray of a passing server, this one dressed like a demented Harley Quinn. He walks toward me, reaching for my hand and placing his arm around my waist.

"Stop," I say when he attempts to draw me to him. "That's as close as you get to hold me."

He regards me as if struck, but nods, keeping several inches between us. I didn't sense Seamus's approach until I see him back slowly away to the edge of the dance floor.

I try to offer Seamus a reassuring smile. He doesn't return it. His warning glare is fixed on Andres.

The space that separates Andres and I, and the first awkward moves we make to the music, are more akin to middle schoolers at a 70s dance. We must look ridiculous to those watching, but I don't care. There's only one man I want against me.

"You look gorgeous," Andres says.

If he expects me to thank him, that thank you doesn't come. I don't find his remarks on my appearance appropriate, especially now that he's married to my sister and with Seamus standing mere feet away.

"I didn't understand what you were doing with him," Andres says. "I didn't want to believe it at first. You being with someone like that, and him being with you."

"How dare you?" I say. "You don't know anything about us."

It should be absurd that I'm growing this defensive about a relationship that doesn't really exist. Still, Andres has no right.

"I'm not trying to insult you, Allie, or him. But you're smart."

"So is Seamus," I tell him flatly.

"But you're also good. You have morals. Jesus, do you have any idea how many women he's fucked?"

"Oh, my God, Andres. You have so much nerve bringing up who *Seamus* has had sex with!"

Andres squares his jaw, quieting. I'm not certain he considered this perspective until I pointed it out. But he should have.

"I'm sorry," Andres says.

"You should be. Seamus means everything to me," I say, the truth sharpening my tongue.

A line of red rims Andres's eyes. "I mean, I'm sorry about everything."

This is the moment I once spent months dreaming about. The one that never came, and that he never bothered with when I needed it most. But the peace I thought his apology would bring doesn't arrive.

"You're drunk," I say. I'm not certain he is. I just don't believe him.

"I'm not, Allie," Andres insists. "It's something I've wanted to say long before this. But how could I? How could I ask for forgiveness after everything I did to you? Valentina was every guy's fantasy. One I never thought I'd get to live out."

"You're living it now." I only point it out because it's clear, he wants a refund.

"I know," he says. He shakes his head, his expression breaking as silence stretches, filling the broad space between us.

"You know I told you, you looked gorgeous?" he asks what feels like minutes later.

I barely nod.

"I didn't just mean tonight. Allie, you were always beautiful. I'm only sorry I never told you."

I break away from his hold, disturbed by the outpouring of emotion the very night he married my sister. I start toward Seamus, stopping in place when I see Valentina licking her lips and dragging Seamus down to her for a kiss.

CHAPTER 26

Seamus

I'm barely listening to Valentina yap away, too busy trying not to storm forward and ram my fist in Andres's face. I don't like the way he's looking Allie. It's like this dimwit finally realized what he let slip away.

It takes Valentina digging her claws into my neck and trying to kiss me for me to notice she's still there. "What the fuck?" I ask her.

She tilts her head, appearing confused. "What's wrong?" she asks. "Don't you want to dance with the bride?"

Wow. She's good. To anyone watching, I look like the asshole being mean to the bride on her wedding day.

Allie steps between us. "What are you doing?"

I start to tell her nothing. That her witch of a sister was pulling this crap on her own. But Allie isn't asking me. Nope. She's staring right at Valentina.

Andres, who looks like hell, because that's where he'll reside from now on, edges forward. Valentina places her long, skinny arms around him, cuddling him close as if he means everything to her even though anyone can see he doesn't. He's a prop she'll pose with as long as this charade of a photo shoot lasts.

"Just talking to your beloved," Valentina says, keeping her voice sweet. "Well, at least as long as he sticks around."

"Shut up, Valentina," Allie tells her.

Allie's reply shocks the shit out of me. I'm ready to fist bump my woman. Except Valentina isn't done digging her claws.

"I know it's not real," Valentina says. A glimmer of evil casts along her eyes, darkening the soft, angelic innocence she's playing up. "The woman at the bakery told me Seamus didn't know who you were. That no matter how you were throwing yourself at him, reminding him of all the events you'd attended together *and* all the work you'd done for him, he didn't remember you. But he remembered me." Her smile widens. "Didn't you, Seamus?"

Holy shit. Cara Maria sung like a canary. She must have seen and heard a lot more than we thought. I should have known Cara would do something like this. She wasn't happy when she showed up at Finnie's reception to personally deliver the groom's cake. I blew her off when she told me her and her man were separating, too busy wondering where Allie had disappeared and how bad I wanted her beside me.

Allie's bruised expression meets mine.

"Hot," Valentina says. "That's how you described me. Or was it smoking?" She looks at Allie. "Do you remember?"

Allie's breathing way too fast, fighting back tears I know aren't far from falling. Christ. I'd never hit a woman. But for the first time in my life I wish I *was* a woman, so I could knock Valentina on her ass where she belongs.

"You're right," I say. "I didn't know Allie. I couldn't have picked her out of a crowd, would've passed her on the street and not thought twice. But I know her now."

Allie teeters slightly when I take her hands in mine, her gaze dropping. The music switches to *Purple Rain,* which I fucking hate. Not because it's not a great song. But because it's about something special that comes to end.

I don't want Allie and me to end. Not now. Not ever.

I clench my jaw at the way Allie regards the floor with shame, like it's all over and everyone will know we never really belonged—that our families will realize we were too pathetic to find anyone worthwhile, even though we maybe wanted to.

The thought of losing Allie destroys me, like a knife slicing my heart open, every emotion bleeds out of me—*everything* I feel when I'm with her. Pain, want, love, and maybe hurt. It's all there, even though I never realized a woman would be capable of doing this to me.

My body trembles, riding out the tension and tightening every muscle I have. That's how I'm sure what I feel is real, and how I know I've finally found the one.

I just need the right way to tell her.

"You changed me, Allie," I tell her. "I fell for you. More than once, I fell hard." Her hands shake or maybe it's me. "From the first moment you really smiled at me, when all the piles of your hair lay in chunks on the floor, to those little moments when you showed up at my place to make sure I had a decent meal and that I was happy, to the day I bared my soul to you."

I've been quiet lately. Maybe too quiet. For a moment, I'm silent again. The realization of what I feel is awesome and all that shit it's supposed to be. But it's also scary as hell. No one ever tells you that piece of it. No one ever says hey, you're going to doubt everything she feels. You're going to wonder if you're good enough for her and what the hell she really thinks of you.

I tried to show her what she means to me earlier, when I bent to kiss her bare shoulder. She gasped, surprised and showing me actions alone aren't enough.

"I . . ." Allie says, except nothing more comes.

She's still not talking. Not like I need her to. So, I go for it, placing the final piece that's missing.

"I love you, Allie," I say biting out the words. "I just need you to love me, too."

Her slender shoulders rise and fall, her composure dismantling. I've said too much. I lift her chin, wanting to see what secrets I can unlock in that pretty face. God, I'm not expecting what I see. Her beautiful eyes meet mine with only sadness. She doesn't want me. Not like I want her.

Valentina's slow clap snags our attention. "Cute," she says. "Brilliant, even. It's a shame we know it's not true."

Allie releases me, her steps purposeful as she stops in front of Valentina. "I don't care what you believe or what you don't." She meets her square in the face. "I just need you to know if you ever touch Seamus again, you're dead to me. Even more than you are now."

Valentina's shock, no matter how brief, shows through her phony exterior. She knows Allie isn't messing around.

I can't imagine ever saying that to one of my sibs. But I can't imagine Allie not saying it to Valentina. It's not mean or heartless. It's self-preservation.

Valentina was a sister Allie could have gone her entire life without. There was never a kind word, soft touch, or well-meaning intention. She tossed Allie aside from the start, failing to recognize how much Allie loved and needed her.

Allie walks toward me, unable to meet me in the eyes. "I want to go home," she says, her voice distant. "Will you take me?"

I put my arm around her, wanting to spare her from all the nasty looks and judgement cast in her direction, although I can't be sure this is where my arm belongs. Allie didn't say anything about us. Not really. All she did was face-off with Valentina.

It was a good thing. But not enough for me and her.

We stop at the table just long enough to get Allie's purse, walking out of the reception hall without a word to anyone. The dark circus theme is still going strong, guests laughing and taking photos with the bearded lady and contortionists in skin-tight black suits.

We stand beneath the awning in silence, waiting for the valet to pull up with my truck. Lightning splits the night sky and a downpour of rain starts all at once. I shrug out of my jacket, using it like an umbrella to cover Allie, our feet pounding against the deep puddles as we race toward my ride.

Shitty end to a shitty night. It's what I'm thinking, but don't say. I crank my engine and blast the wipers, pulling onto the busy road.

I catch a glimpse of the Montana Elite in my rearview mirror. It takes all I have left not to roll down my window and stick out my middle finger. I don't think I'll ever be able to drive past that snooty place without spitting a curse at it.

"Are you all right?" Allie asks, her voice trembling.

I crank the heat when I see how bad she's shaking. "Fine," I say, but not much more.

The world falls into darkness, the only spot of light shining on Allie and all the memories we've shared. All our talks. All the time with my family. All those nights we've spent alone. No matter how hard I tried, it wasn't enough. *I* wasn't enough.

I shouldn't be pissed. I did my job. I made Allie find the confidence lurking just below the surface. I helped her realize her inner beauty, the one that's always been there, hidden beneath all those cruel comments her family threw at her.

Most of all, I gave her hope. The one thing she didn't have enough of when we met.

In return, she gave me friendship. In a period full of wedding cakes and walks down the aisle, watching those I most love begin their forevers. It's what I most needed.

So why am I so upset? Why am I so angry and in this much pain?

My grip tightens around the steering wheel. Maybe because as much as I want Allie happy, I wanted to believe she could be happiest with me.

Thunder crashes and lightning follows, dropping sheets of rain I can only barely see through. I mutter a curse when we reach Allie's neighborhood and the only available spot is almost a block down the street.

"Wait for me," I say, cutting my engine and slamming down my parking brake.

The moment she's tucked beneath my jacket, I shove the passenger door closed. We take off down the walkway, the amount of rain falling creating small rivers deep enough to splash against my knees.

The roof above Allie's front porch barely shields us as she fumbles with her keys, each second that passes intensifying all the bad feelings I don't want to feel. When she finally opens her door and steps inside, I can't take it anymore.

It's not just what I'm feeling. It's me not being able to kiss her goodnight or wake up with her in my arms. It's not knowing if we'll share another meal, take in another movie, sit down to another brunch with my family.

I'm not taking what I said to Allie back. It's true. All of it. But if she's not willing to act, I can't force it. She has to want to want me, and maybe need me, too.

The heels of my dress shoes strike against the concrete steps. I was in a rush to get Allie safely inside, but I'm not in a rush to get home. My jacket, the one I used as our makeshift umbrella, slaps against my side as I lower it, the amount of water it absorbed adding to its weight. It shouldn't be so hard to hold it up. But everything is that much harder now.

"Seamus?"

I stop at the bottom of the steps at the sound of Allie's voice and glance over my shoulder. She's just inside the threshold, her dress sticking to her soaked form and her curls plastered against her face. She's out of breath, like she just ran several miles instead of a small city block.

"Yeah?" I ask.

"Did you mean what you said?" she asks. "When you told me you loved me, did you mean it?"

My chest rises and falls with each harsh breath. It shouldn't hurt to breathe. Except here I am, barely able to contain everything Allie means to me.

"I meant every fucking word."

Her eyes flicker with the start of tears. "I *really* needed to hear you say that."

I don't remember charging up the stairs. I'm just suddenly there, yanking her into my arms and crashing my lips against hers.

Allie clings to me, moaning. I barely manage to kick the door closed and lock it before she tugs my shirt free of my waistband and I tear open the back of her dress.

Our hands are clumsy. Our bodies and clothes so drenched, we have to peel away layers of heavy fabric. Every tug, every article of clothing that hits the floor, makes it all worth it.

Allie's naked body slides against mine. She's freezing, shaking, and wet. Damn, so wet, the tips of her breasts hard and grazing my chest. I drag my hand down to her stomach and between her legs, seeking her warmth. She grunts when I slip my fingers over her center. I circle slowly, my lips sweeping over her throat and my teeth taking small bites.

I'm trying to take things slow and not overwhelm her. But she likes what I'm doing and doesn't want me to stop. Her tongue gives my earlobe a generous flick before her teeth nip at my chin. It doesn't hurt. Everything we're doing feels right.

"More, baby," she whispers. "I want you so much."

I push my finger inside her, her thighs locking around my hand and her pelvis rocking to match the movement of my palm as I quicken my pace.

Whimpers, quiet and reserved at first, morph into louder and needier. I kiss my way down her neck, fastening my lips around her nipple. One gasp. That's all I allow her before my hands shove apart her thighs and my mouth secures her throbbing core.

She writhes, gasping from my contact and lifting her leg to give me better access. I shove my face deeper, her soft pained voice begging me not to stop.

Allie's back slams against the wall, her hips creating a wild beat as she peaks. Guttural sounds break through on a scream as I pull on the soft flesh, savoring every taste.

She curls forward, pressing me closer.

My erection strains, slapping against her leg. I'm painfully hard, ready to enter her. But I've waited for this moment for too long. I'll be damned if I rush it. Every touch, every quiver, every gasp of pleasure she emits—*everything* is what I've wanted.

Tonight, Allie is mine. I'm going to make sure she fucking knows it.

One orgasm follows the other, her body convulsing.

"I need to get down," she stammers, her voice shaking as another climax draws to an end. "*Please.*"

I lower her leg carefully and rise, worried I did too much. Her entire body is rattling. She looks scared. "Baby," I say, clasping her face gently.

She drops to her knees. I think she's falling and I try to catch her. I'm not prepared for her to plunge me deep into her mouth or for the strength of her sucks.

Heat encases me in a rush and I lose my damn mind.

I grip the doorway to her sitting room to keep upright, my face scrunching when I see those large, brown eyes watching me. She strokes me slowly, taking deep, hearty pulls with her mouth.

My fingers thread through thick curls, fisting her hair to keep us in place.

Moans stir from the back of her throat as that familiar tightness spreads across my lower back and into my groin. My head falls back, the cords on my neck stretching enough to snap.

This isn't how I want to come. I need to be inside her.

My hands reach beneath her arms, hauling her up in one quick motion.

I swear when I break her strong seal. I mean to carry her to bed. We barely make it onto the couch. Her back bounces off the cushion and her legs land over my shoulders. I ease my way in, carefully stretching her and just short of falling apart when I finally make my way inside.

I start slow, not wanting to hurt her, but when her face mirrors all the lust and love spreading across my features, I no longer take my time.

Each thrust, each pound, captures everything I've held back. It's not until her face flushes and her back bows and I start to come that I remember the one thing I shouldn't have forgotten.

I pull out, slumping forward as I finish between her breasts.

Our breathing is nothing more than ragged spurts of air. That doesn't stop me from kissing her. "Sorry, beautiful," I tell her. "I should have used something."

She smiles, her irises flickering with the remains of her pleasure. "It's okay," she says. "I'm on the pill."

That can't be right. "Since when?" I ask

This time when she smiles, there's no hint of sex behind it. There's only that warm smile she's flashed me so many times before. "Since I realized I love you, too."

My eyes round, but my shock quickly vanishes. "You love me?" I ask.

"Yes," she admits.

"I love you, too," I tell her, and spend the rest of the night proving how much I've needed her.

CHAPTER 27

Seamus

We finally make it to Allie's bed around dawn. We don't get much sleep. That's all right. This is what I've wanted, to wake up beside her, not as her friend, but as something more.

The corner of her white sheet barely covers her round ass and the comforter is somewhere near my thigh, I think. I don't care enough to look. I'm too busy watching Allie sleep.

We're lying on our stomachs. While I'm tired as all hell, I don't want to sleep. Not right now. Instead I want to look at how Allie's full cherub lips press together and how her large dark curls fall along her face, covering one eye.

As much as I don't want to wake her, I can't help stroking her hair away to better see her pretty face. Her eyes don't open. Not right away. The first thing she does is smile.

"Hi, babe," she says.

"Hey, beautiful," I murmur.

Her thick row of lashes flutter open, revealing eyes glazed with exhaustion and all the happiness I sense surging through me.

"Is this the part where you kick me out?" she asks.

"Depends, are you going to pull a knife on me?

She grins. "No."

"Are you due in court?"

Now, she's laughing. "No, not today."

"Then you we have another hour. Besides, it's rude to kick you out of your own place." I pull her to me. "I'm classier than that and as an FYI, it feels good not to have to escape through a window."

Allie laughs, her head falling against my arm, her smile fading. "So, we happened, huh?"

"Yeah," I agree. "Took you long enough."

"I was thinking the same thing about you." She gasps. "I mean, I practically threw myself at you."

"Mm, no," I disagree. "Throwing yourself would mean me finding you in my bed naked. And before you try to argue, I gave you access to my house and my bed and no, I wouldn't have objected."

"You did give me your key," she agrees. "But I didn't want sex to ruin us. I wanted something better."

"Maybe what we were pretending to be?" I offer.

She quiets. "Yes," she admits.

Allie shakes her head. "I was so worried last night that everything you did was for show. That you were playing that final role to protect me from Valentina."

"No," I tell her. "That was me being real and telling you how I feel." I frown. "You realize Valentina went out of her way to find Cara Maria and get her to tell her everything she heard?"

"I know," Allie agrees.

"What kind of person does that, takes that much time to find the goods to hurt someone else?"

"Valentina," Allie answers simply. She drops her chin as if remembering all the crap Valentina pulled last night. "I don't know how or when Valentina became what she is. What I do know is my life is better without her. I always wanted to believe she was as good as my family claimed, and that perhaps I was in the wrong for being so jealous. But when she did what she did, I stopped believing."

"You mean her cheating with Andres?" I guess.

She laughs without humor. "I didn't want to say his name," she admits. "He doesn't belong in bed with us."

"Damn right, he doesn't," I mutter, making a face.

Allie doesn't return my sour expression. "As much as I haven't considered Valentina a good person for a long time, I still hoped to salvage something between us." She sighs. "That hope completely vanished when I saw her try to kiss you."

"Just so you know, I'd never allow that to happen," I tell her.

"Thank you," she says.

I take a finger and sweep it down the curve of her neck and down her arm. Allie shudders. I never knew how ticklish she is, but I found out last night and can't wait to discover more.

"When did you realize you liked me?" she asks.

I didn't realize I was smiling until that smile dissolves. "I don't know exactly. I thought you were cute from the start."

"From the start?" she asks, lifting her head. "You mean from the day we met at the bakery?"

"Yeah. Why do you find it so hard to believe?" I ask when she frowns.

Allie doesn't answer. I suppose she doesn't need to. She's never realized how amazing she is. "The more I got to know you, the more I liked and wanted you."

"Why didn't you say anything?" she asks.

I smirk. "Why didn't you?"

She shakes her head. "Seamus, for someone like me, I did a lot to demonstrate how much I cared for you. But I think it comes back to what I said. I didn't want merely a physical relationship. I didn't want to be another woman you slept with and then moved on."

"You could never be that," I assure her.

"I didn't know that," she admits. "But it remained my biggest fear. I can't imagine my life without you . . ." She crinkles her nose. "Sorry, was that too much?"

"Not at all," I admit.

It's good to hear her say everything I've thought about and everything that follows.

"I worried constantly about what would happen to our friendship if I told you how I felt. It no longer became about me having a date to my sister's wedding. I wanted it all. I just wasn't sure I'd get to have it."

My hand curls around hers. "You have it now and I'm not going anywhere."

The Darth Vader ring tone announces Mamacita's call. Allie groans. "I'd better get that," she says.

I follow her when she drags her body across the bed, my fingers dancing along her spine as she answers.

"Shhh," she says to me.

"You saying you don't want your mother to know I'm in bed with you?" I ask, nibbling on her ear.

Allie laughs and answers the phone. "Hi, Mom," she says.

"Valentina's gone," she says.

Allie sits up. "What do you mean gone?"

"Andres showed up to the brunch by himself. He told us Valentina had to leave for Europe with the producer who was there last night. Something about Valentina getting her own reality show where she designs elaborate weddings for millionaires and films the results."

Allie glances over her shoulder to see if I'm listening. I snort, letting her know I heard everything. All right, that explains the freak show. This wasn't just about Valentina's wedding ceremony. It was about what the ceremony could do for her career.

Damn, she must have been planning her return to greatness for months, not caring what it cost her, and especially, Andres.

The pride I expect in Mamacita's voice, that one that should come from her very extraordinary daughter getting an extraordinary opportunity, is noticeably absent. Mamacita isn't stupid. She knows what Valentina did.

"Would you like to come to the brunch?" Mamacita asks. "Andres is gone and the whole family is here. We'd love to see you."

Allie looks at me before speaking. "I can't, Mom. I'm with Seamus."

There's a brief pause and I'm sure as anything Allie's mother will rip me apart. Instead her voice splinters and there's no doubt in my mind Mamacita is crying. "Seamus really loves you, doesn't he?"

"Yeah. He does," I reply, pulling Allie on top of me.

Allie says a quick goodbye and disconnects.

It doesn't take long for me to get hard or for Allie to ride me. I sit up, pulling her hair back, exposing her throat and her tightening nipples.

I kiss her neck and suck on the tips of her breasts, rewarding the increasing speed and sway of her hips. Those sounds she makes, I've heard them all night and want to keep hearing them.

I flip her onto her knees when she finishes, her nails raking into the sheets. I think she's close again, but her back straightens, pushing into my chest. She cups her breasts as I thrust wildly.

Valentina and Andres may be over. But me and Allie have only just begun.

Epilogue

Allie

My hands are full as I walk in from the garage and into our kitchen. I place the mail on the quartz counter and our take-out on the center island. It's been a long week and I'm ready for a nice quiet evening and plenty of alone time with my love.

Still, I take a moment to admire the kitchen. I'm thrilled with the cabinetry. Seamus did a magnificent job with the details, adding his own personal touch, like always.

I hit the button to the intercom. "Hey, honey. Where are you?"

"In the shop," his voice calls.

Of course he is.

"You coming?" he asks, sounding rushed.

Quick shuffling ensues. "I'll be right there," I assure him, wondering why he sounds nervous.

I push open the French doors, the stained glass that decorates them another piece of artwork Seamus can take credit for. The construction is almost complete. But thanks to Seamus and my own decorating touches, this house became our home long before we moved in.

My heels dig into the soil of our large back yard. I shouldn't have worn them out here, but I miss Seamus and am anxious to see him.

My mother gave me an earful about Valentina on my drive home. As much as Valentina's career received that reboot she sought, it hasn't spared her from the tabloids or the mud flung her way. There are stories swirling around the gossip magazines about her affair with a director and the uncompromising position she was found in with a married duke.

"I'm so embarrassed," my mother told me.

Unfortunately, Valentina isn't embarrassed enough. Her marriage to Andres was annulled less than month after they exchanged vows. She was linked to the producer of her wedding show for a while, but then came the director and the duke after that.

I slide open the stable doors that lead to Seamus's shop. He usually leaves them open so the sawdust doesn't overwhelm him, especially on beautiful spring days like today.

Seamus looks up when he sees me, frowning.

"How come you're not naked?" he asks. "I haven't seen you since last night. The least you could do is walk in here naked."

I laugh. "The last time I did that, you yelled at me."

"That's because I was slicing through lumber at the time." He stretches, his gray T-shirt riding up and giving me a glimpse of those abs I should see more of tonight. "You hear any machines on?"

"No."

He strolls to me, his hands immediately seizing my backside and giving my cheeks a squeeze. "Then you should be naked."

We start to kiss, but he abruptly pulls away. I'm not certain why. I'm usually the one running out the door to escape that sexy body and those wandering hands.

I pout. "That's all I get?"

He grins, appearing shy. "I want to show you something."

Seamus's fingers thread through mine. He leads me to a small object covered with a towel beside a larger object covered with a sheet. He pulls the towel off the smaller subject first.

"Here it is," he says.

"Oh, my goodness," I say. "You finished it."

The statue is about three feet tall, depicting a mother and father cuddling their child. "You think Killian and Sofia will like it? I feel bad I didn't finish it in time for Logan's Christening, but I wanted to get it right. Between Angus and Molly finally tying the knot and all the other things with the family we had going on, I ran out of time."

"They're going to love it," I say, gushing. I step forward, analyzing the detail. "This is from what's left of Grammie and Pop-Pop's tree?" I ask.

Seamus crosses his arms, again his face reddening. "That's right."

I look at the large item with the sheet covering it. "Then what's that?" I ask.

Seamus turns around. "That thing? Something else I've been working on, but it's not quite done. Want to see it?"

I adjust the collar of my navy dress. Seamus is very particular about the artwork he creates, never wanting anyone to see or judge until they're perfect. "Only if you want me to. I know how you feel about the things you most care about."

"I know you do." His gaze softens. "Which is why I'd like you to see it."

Seamus walks forward and lifts the edges of the sheet, pausing and taking a deep breath before the big reveal. I can't quite see his latest project until he takes a step back and permits me forward.

Like the rendition of the family he created for Killian and Sofia, this statue is an abstract, the base secured to a granite slab where the male is kneeling. The male's hand stretches out, holding the hand of the woman he clearly loves.

Tears fill my eyes when I hear Seamus shuffle behind me. As I turn, I find him on his knee, holding out a blue velvet box, those tears spill and I'm not sure how I'll get them to stop.

Seamus opens the box, revealing a princess cut diamond ring. "The only way to finish this masterpiece is for you to say yes." He swallows hard, his eyes shimmering. "I love you, Allie. You are my life. Will you marry me?"

Of course, I say yes, signaling the final O'Brien receiving his happily ever after.

This book contains excerpts from *Let Me*, *Crave Me*, and *Feel Me* from the O'Brien Family novels as well as *Inseverable*, from the Carolina Beach Series by Cecy Robson. The excerpts have been set for this edition only and may not reflect the final content of the final novels.

Let Me

An O'Brien Family

Novel

by Cecy Robson

CHAPTER 1

Finn

I see the strike coming at me a split second before it connects with my skull. My head snaps back from the force, the crowds' hollers resonating like a muffled cry in the distance. It was a good punch—lightning quick with enough impact to knock most guys on their asses. But I'm not most guys.

You hit me, I'm only going to hit you harder.

My right hand shoots up, blocking and smacking away the kick gunning for my ribs. I pivot out of the way, again, and again, and again, avoiding Easton's arms and legs as they come at me. He's fast, strong, with a six inch reach advantage. But he's too eager to take me out and not pacing himself like he should. Already he's breathing hard and it's just the start of the second round.

I take my time to figure him out, planning each move, searching for that opening I need. Do I take a few bashes because of it? Sure. It's part of the job. But believe it or not, it's part of the job I look forward to.

Those punches and kicks remind me that I still *feel*, that I'm still human. And that for now, I'm still alive.

"Oh!" some drunk behind me yells when my uppercut finds Easton's chin.

He staggers back, swiping the blood oozing from his lip,

yet he keeps his grin. He's trying to make like it was a lucky shot. That it won't happen again.

Like me, Easton needs to win this match. And if he does, he'll move up to the top ten, making him a contender for the UFC Lightweight title.

Talent aside, the guy's a raging asshole, and so are the idiots in his training camp. They've been trash-talking since the moment I agreed to this match. I didn't really care and laughed most of it off until they got personal and took it a step too far.

Again he nails me in the head. It's not as hard as it was last time which tells me he's getting tired. Does it hurt? I guess.

But let's say I'm a guy who's used to pain.

Easton grins. He thinks I'm afraid of him. He thinks he has me where he wants me. But fear is an emotion I don't allow myself to entertain. Fear gets you hurt and rips you apart till you think there's nothing left.

I dodge out of reach. He scowls and takes another swing. This one gets close enough to my jaw to create a breeze that whips across my skin.

"Finn," my brother Killian barks from the side. "Take him out *now*."

He's worried about me. So is my family. But now's not the time to think about them. I keep my hands up as I edge away, letting Easton think I'm backing down, that I'm tired and need to catch my breath.

I sidestep when he lunges forward, avoiding his next swing and use the momentum to drop my head and nail him in the temple with a roundhouse kick.

Like I said, Easton's fast.

Too bad for him I'm a little bit faster.

The kick is my signature move, as natural for me as the next breath. He goes down like I planned. But in the Octagon you don't stop just because your opponent collapses like timber. You charge forward. You show him what you're made of. And you prove just how tough you really are.

That muffled screaming, isn't so muffled anymore. The crowd loses their shit as I pounce, my blows nailing Easton in the face until the ref's arms hook beneath mine as he hauls me off. I back away, my fists up because I already know I won.

I should do a back flip or some crazy shit to incite the crowd. This is it. My time has come to own it. But the good things aren't as great as they can be. Not with the memories that haunt me. And not with the anger they stir.

Killian rushes in as the medic wipes down my face. I'm bleeding from the punch Easton caught me with at the beginning of the round. I didn't think it was that bad, but the way the ringside medic is pressing the towel against my head clues me in the gash isn't closing like it should.

"I'm going to have to stitch you up, Fury," he mumbles.

"I figured," I tell him.

Kill pats my back. "Good job," he says.

Maybe he believes it, but I don't miss the concern in his voice. He thinks I took too many unnecessary hits. I can't really argue, seeing how it's true.

He doesn't understand that I don't feel those strikes the way I should. Hell, I don't think I've felt anything the way I should in a long time. Not like I used to. I try to tell myself that maybe that' a good thing. That numbness is better than pain. But I'm not so convinced anymore, and neither is my family. I try to shrug it off like I'm fine. Except given the way they've been eyeing me, I'm not fooling anyone.

I'm scaring everyone around me. And it sucks. Not only because I don't want them scared, but mostly because I don't know how to stop it.

"The referee has called a stop to this match at two-minutes and forty-nine seconds into the second round," the announcer begins. "The winner by TKO, Finn 'The Fury' O'Brien."

The crowd screams and pumps their fists in the air when my hand is raised. I take the few seconds I need to thank my sponsors, my camp, and my brother, because that's what I'm supposed to do despite the fog clouding my senses. I wish that disconnect had something to do with all the hits I took, but deep down I know that it doesn't.

I'm back in the locker room before I know it getting stitched up, too many people talking at once. God, I barely hear their questions or my responses. But they're there and somehow I make it through.

"I'm worried about you, Finnie," Kill says when everyone piles out.

"Don't. I'm not drinking tonight. I'm headed home," I assure him.

"That's not what I mean," he says. He's sitting in a fold out chair, his arms resting against his muscular legs. "I think you need to talk to someone."

I stretch out my arms. By now they're so tight, they pull against the bones. "I am. I'm talking to you."

I don't have to see him to know he's shaking his head, or that he's looking sad, disappointed, and maybe something else, too. "I'm not who you should be speaking to," he says. "Not for what's going on in your head."

"You're enough," I say, even though I know it's no longer true.

"Finn," he begins.

I don't wait for him to finish, leaving the changing area and heading toward the showers. "Go find Sofia and Wren," I call over my shoulder as I strip out my shirt. "See if they're up for some dinner."

I don't remember peeling the rest of my clothes off. That numbness I've been feeling too much lately claiming me like a mist until it fully engulfs me. Fuck. It's like I've stopped living even though for the most part I think I'm still alive.

I lean against the tile with my arms spread, allowing the water to beat against my back. It's too hot. I should turn it down, but I don't bother. Eventually, like everything else, the sensation fades.

I'm not sure how long I'm in that position. A few seconds? A few minutes? But then Easton and his trainer Yefim are suddenly there. "You got lucky, O'Brien," Yefim calls out, taunting me with his thick eastern European accent.

Shit. Like all the trash talk before the fight wasn't enough.

"Did you hear me, you pussy?" he fires back when I don't answer. "Did you hear me, you goddamn coward?"

Coward? Fuck you. It's what I think, but not what I say,

focusing instead on the streams of water that gather along my feet before they swirl into the drain.

It doesn't help. The rage that's building, the one I only manage to barely keep in? It stirs in my gut like a heavy pot filled with hate, sin, and all the curses my Ma would still beat my ass for saying.

"What're you doing?" Yefim asks.

His voice is closer, he's drawing near. It doesn't matter that I'm standing here naked. He wants to be next to me. I shudder, that feeling I keep buried drilling its way up.

"I know about you," Yefim says, not bothering to keep his voice low. "But everyone knows, don't they? Even if you don't want them to."

My body shakes a little more, but it's not from the cooling water. It's from his words and all that anger they trigger. *Don't do it. Don't go there.*

"You like to keep it a secret. Don't you, pussy?"

Yefim laughs when I keep my trap shut. He thinks I'm backing down, just like Easton did before his face met the mat. "He's crying," he calls out to Easton. "What? Not so tough now?"

That's where he's dead wrong. Every muscle I've conditioned serves a purpose—to take down those who fuck with me. And right now, Yefim is seriously fucking with me.

"You like to pretend that it's girls you like, don't you?" he says. "But that's not true, is it? Oh, no, that's not true at all . . ."

I raise my chin, knowing that someone's not leaving without bleeding, and I've bled enough tonight.

Yefim kicks at my calf. "What? Nothing to say? Can't speak without your boyfriend here?"

"Boyfriend?" Easton asks, laughing. "No fucking way."

"Yes. Way," Yefim insists. "Didn't you know this little pussy takes it up the ass—"

I punch him so hard, I feel his teeth crack against my knuckles. For someone with decades of boxing experience he never saw me coming. But I see Easton flying at me out of the corner of my eye. I toss him over my shoulder, slamming him hard onto the ceramic tile floor. Like in the octagon, I throw myself on top of him, my fists colliding against his skin.

Voices rush forward, telling me to stop. A woman screams, but I don't stop fighting off the bodies trying to grab me, breaking through the arms wrenching me back. I need to hit him—I need to feel my fists meeting his face—I need to feel *something*.

God damn it. I need to feel alive.

I don't want the pain.

I don't want the terror.

But once more, it's all I feel.

Crave Me

An O'Brien Family

Novel

by Cecy Robson

CHAPTER 1

Wren

I drop the keys in Mr. Esposito's hand and smile. He stares at them in his open palm like a precious gift, because to someone like him who's worked hard all his life, it very much is.

"Thank you, Wren," he says, meeting my smile. "I never thought I'd own a new car. Let alone be able to give one to my son as a gift."

"You deserve it, Mr. Esposito," I tell him, shaking his hand. "And so does your son for getting into Drexel. Tell Antonio, hi for me—Oh, and be sure to have someone take his picture when you hand him the keys." I motion to my office behind me. "I want to add it to my memory wall."

"I will." He presses his lips tight as if considering what to say. "Your father would be proud of you," he tells me. His soft brown eyes take in the massive dealership, fixing on the sales board displaying my current rank at number one. "Very proud."

I hold onto my smile as he walks toward the brand new candy apple red F-150 hugging the curb, ignoring the brutal January wind that sweeps in when the doors to the lot zip open. Mr. Esposito pauses when he opens the driver's side door. I had the boys in the back place a bow on dash like I do for all my customers. I think it's a nice touch, and a way to thank them for their business. Mr. Esposito tosses me a grin over his shoulder. Maybe it's the wind slapping against his face, or maybe it's because he's just that touched, but I catch his eyes glistening with tears.

Slowly he slips inside and grips the wheel, his widening smile lifting his deeply worn features.

The moment he pulls away, my smile vanishes. "Your father would be proud of you," he'd said. He meant it as a compliment. Mr. Esposito has always been nice like that. But instead of giving me the warm fuzzies, that familiar pang tugs at my insides.

My heels click against the bleached white tile as I cross the showroom. The phones ringing off the hook have me turning toward the finance department. It's been a nasty winter with all the snow we've been hit with, but I can't say it's been bad for business. One of the secretaries waves to me as she hurries to answer the phone. I wave back, not that she seems to notice. She starts writing as she takes the first call. Yeah, it's going to be a busy week. But busy means work, and that's something I've always been good at.

My eyes narrow when they fix on Oscar looming over Penny. Penny is smart, and an overall good person. She's young, and hasn't been here long, but she's trying, and I know she has it in her to succeed. Too bad Oscar is stomping on her success, luring customers away from her every chance he gets.

"You snooze, you lose," he tells her, pegging her with one of his more sleazy grins.

Penny was making headway with the guy who walked in, until Oscar shoved his way between them and baited him away, making Penny look like she didn't know what she was talking about. If I hadn't been busy with Mr. Esposito, I would have stepped in. Nothing gets me more than men who target those they think are weak.

"Wren!" Suze calls from behind the counter. "You have a call."

"Okay. Send it through to my office," I yell. I rush across the last few feet of the showroom, but not before I make sure Oscar steps far away from Penny.

The phone rings one, twice, before I slam the door behind me with my foot and reach across my desk and put the call on speaker. "Erin O'Brien," I say.

There's a brief pause before I hear, "Hi, Wren."

Shit. My stomach twists the way it always does when I hear his voice. "What do you want, Bryant?" I ask, digging out my cell phone from my desk drawer.

"I miss you," he says.

"Do you miss hitting me, too?" I fire back.

I'm talking tough. It's what I do. Too bad I don't feel so tough right now. Not when it comes to Bryant. A familiar sense of dread sends a chill down my spine, reminding me what happened the last time I pissed him off. I hit the record icon on my cell phone, hoping to catch him saying something I can use against him. But the damn thing beeps, and for all Bryant is an asshole, he's not stupid.

"Are you recording me, pretty girl?" He laughs when I don't answer. "Now, why would you do a thing like that?"

"Because I don't trust you, because you hit me—oh, and because you're an asshole."

"I don't know what you're talking about," he says, keeping his voice easy. "I'm just returning your call. You keep calling me so—"

"That's a lie," I say, my face heating with anger. He knows I'm recording him and trying to switch things around. "Don't call me again. I want nothing to do with you."

I hang up the phone. It's been months since I last saw him, months since he last put his hands on me. But just when I think I'm rid of him, he reminds me he's still there.

I could call the police. The problem is, he is the police . .

Evan

My Jaguar skids, again, again, and again, fighting to keep pace with the other drivers insane enough to travel the Blue Route in this weather. Chunks of wet snow smack against my windshield. My wipers squeak against the glass as they race to keep my line of sight clear when another vehicle cuts me off, pelting my windshield with more ice. My current struggle with life and death does not evidently discourage Ashleigh from barking messages over my Blue Tooth.

"Yodel called again, Evan. They want you to reconsider."

"No," I reply, cutting my steering wheel toward the left when my car veers right. "We're representing Mellon, their biggest competitor. It's a conflict of interest to supply both companies with the same technology."

I mutter a curse when the minivan in front of me slams on their brakes and I narrowly miss ramming the bumper. And I suppose, because we're in Philadelphia, the City of Brotherly love, the woman rolls down the window, permitting snow into her vehicle just to wave an irate middle finger at me.

"Rich Bitch loser," she cries out.

I rub my face. Bloody hell, why am I here again? Before I can finish the thought, Ashleigh reminds me.

"Evan, we're at risk for financial collapse. The company needs the revenue."

"Not at the expense of our ethics," I counter.

True, my company is at risk. But it's due to poor business practices, such as the ones Ashleigh suggests I entertain. I understand she learned these tactics from my predecessor, but he was a conniving snake—which is why he's currently serving time for embezzlement and I had to leave London to rebuild my father's dying empire.

"What about your eleven a.m. with the V.P. of County General?"

"Have Anne and Clifton start straight away. I emailed them the presentation last night—"

"Do you really think they're qualified?" she interrupts.

I open my mouth to insist that they are and to remind her I'm her superior, not the other way around. But I'm not oblivious to what she tells me. Anne and Clifton are fairly new and not at the level I'd prefer them to be. Nevertheless, they're learning fast under my tutelage and the only ones from the original staff I trust.

"Evan," she presses.

"Ashleigh, Anne and Clifton will handle it. That's my final word." I disconnect, swearing as I take the ramp and practically slide down sideways.

Another proud Pennsylvanian sticks his head out the window. "Get a real car, fucker," he hollers.

I rub my face again, tired and frustrated. I didn't arrive home until three this morning. It wouldn't have taken as long had I been driving a vehicle capable of enduring this ungodly weather.

I glance up, releasing a tense breath when the sign for the Ford dealership I researched comes into view. Saving iCronos will take me time. Time I can't spare driving a Jaguar on roads better maneuvered via dogsled.

My car slows to a stop in front of the massive dealership. The combination of the vehicle I'm driving, along with the expensive suit and coat I'm wearing, command attention. The moment I step inside, a young woman with dark spiky hair hurries over. "Good morning, sir. I'm Penny," she says. "Welcome to Ford Nation. Are you interested in acquiring a new vehicle?"

She seems young, but eager, a respectable attribute. Yet no sooner does she finish speaking than a man about my age steps in front of her, adjusting the jacket of his gray suit. "I got this, P," he tells her. "Get us some coffee, will you?" He holds out his hand. "Hello. I'm Oscar Nelson. Welcome to Ford Nation."

My frown bounces from his hand to the young woman whose face is now bright red with humiliation and possibly more. "Are you his assistant?" I ask her.

"No," she answers. "I'm a car sales representative—"

Oscar speaks over her, but it's the sound of quickly approaching footsteps that causes me to turn. A woman with a pinstripe jacket and matching skirt hurries forward, the quick motions of her long legs causing the edge of her skirt to brush above her knees and swing her hips seductively. Long hair flutters like streams of ebony smoke, revealing a staggeringly beautiful face better suited for my wildest fantasies.

I spent the first five years following the completion of my doctorate in either a lab or boardroom packed with men in alternating stages of balding, and these last nine months trapped in a building working a minimum of eighteen hour days. I haven't had the opportunity or time to meet women. But if I'd known she was out here, I'd have spared a moment.

Good . . . God.

I don't realize I'm staring until she stops directly in front of us and juts out her chin. "Problem?" she asks Oscar.

Oscar straightens to his full height. "No. I was just showing Mr. . . ." He motions to me. "My apologies, what's your name, sir?"

"Jonah," I say, returning my attention to the stunning young woman. I offer her my hand. "Evan Jonah."

Full pink lips lift into a dazzling smile that resonates in her deep blue eyes and lights her creamy white skin.

"I'm Erin O'Brien, but I go by Wren," she says. She shakes my hand with a firm grip, releasing me to guide the smaller woman forward. "How can Penny and I help you today, sir?"

"I'm afraid my vehicle isn't equipped for this weather and I am seeking a better alternative, possibly a truck or SUV," I reply, doing all in my power to keep my focus on her face.

"Then you've come to the right place. Penny, will you show Mr. Jonah—"

"Evan," I interrupt, mentally kicking myself for morphing into a fourteen year old boy the moment my eyes locked on this woman.

"Okay, Evan," she says. "Penny, please show Evan the latest members of the Ford family."

"Of course, this way, sir," Penny answers with a grin.

I reluctantly follow behind Penny. But as we reach a black Explorer my gaze trails back to Wren. She and Oscar have moved away from the showroom and closer to the rear offices. Yet it does little to muffle their exchange.

"What the fuck was that?" Oscar snaps.

My spine stiffens. I storm forward, ready to demand he apologize for using such foul language in the presence of a lady.

"You being a raging asshole," Wren replies.

I'll admit, her response gives me pause. And she doesn't stop there. "Look, I know you have to compensate for your less than average-sized dick. But that doesn't give you the right to mistreat Penny or pounce on every client she approaches. That's bullshit and you know it."

"Um, perhaps a truck will be more to your needs," Penny says, motioning to the opposite side of the dealership and away from the heated conversation.

I don't typically involve myself in affairs that don't concern me, nor do I interact with women who speak in such a manner. But it's not simply Wren's colorful vocabulary that captivates me, it's her strength and desire to defend her small friend.

"Where the fuck did you hear that?" Oscar responds. "I don't have a small dick."

Of all his possible retorts, this is the one he chooses?

"Suze," Wren calls over her shoulder in the direction of the finance counter. "What was it you said about that night you went out with Oscar?"

The woman behind the counter scowls and holds up her pinky. Wren smirks. "Looks to me like you should have called her back." She pats his shoulder. "My condolences to your man parts."

She starts to walk away, stopping when she realizes I witnessed their encounter. Instead of making a quick escape or pretending I didn't hear them, she walks toward me with her head raised. "Sorry about that, Mr. Jonah—"

"Evan," I clarify as she reaches me.

Her smile stirs one of my own. "Evan," she repeats, lifting a hand toward her friend. "I see Penny is taking good care of you."

"Um, maybe you can take over," Penny says. She edges away, aware how taken I am with Wren.

Wren tilts her head. "I don't want to step all over your pitch," she says.

"You're not," she responds. "I'll take the next one. Honest."

Wren waits for Penny to leave before turning to face me. She considers me a moment, but then motions back to the Explorer. "This is the latest model in Ford luxury," she begins. "Comfortable, secure, capable of meeting all your commuting needs, and packed with plenty of toys."

I follow her as she leads me around the vehicle. The ease of her speech and relaxed posture demonstrate a confident woman who knows her job well. I question her about the vehicle's basics first: mileage, warranty, and safety features, before testing her intelligence further. She doesn't disappoint, explaining everything in detail down to the engine's construction, adding to my growing attraction.

"Would you like to take her for a ride?" she asks. She punches my arm affectionately, the motion only briefly luring my attention away from her delicate features. "This way you can see how smoothly she handles the road and ask, 'Wren, how did I ever survive without a Ford?'"

"I'd like that," I answer, my deep voice quieting. This woman who appears more elite model than sales representative knows exactly what she's doing. "Very much."

"Good," she says, pointing at me. "You'll wonder how you ever got along without her."

As I watch her walk away, I start to wonder that myself.

READ ON FOR AN EXCERPT FROM

Feel Me

An O'Brien Family Novel

by Cecy Robson

CHAPTER 1

Melissa

I stare at the nameplate perched on my father's desk: *District Attorney Miles Fenske*. It proclaims his position, allowing those who read it a glimpse of what he's accomplished. Yet it's only a glimpse. It's not a true representation of all he is, or all he means to me. The nameplate is cheap, unlike the generous soul who stares back at me with the same loving expression he's held since the first moment I saw him.

What are you thinking, Melissa? He signs to me, moving his hands in beautifully fluid motions.

We're alone in his office. He doesn't need to sign to keep our conversation private. He could whisper, and I would still be able to read his lips. But he knows I'm more comfortable communicating with my hands, probably because American Sign Language is one of the many things we learned together. As a child I considered it our very own secret language, something he and I could share away from the hearing world.

That you're making a mistake, I sign back.

My comment earns me a smile, but I can see his concern, despite the crinkles around his eyes that deepen when he grins. "You're going to have to trust me," he says aloud.

I let out a breath. He knows I trust him. How could I not?

I was brought to the Lehigh Valley District Attorney's

office when I was about six years old, after my biological mother had attempted to sell me in exchange for drugs. My mother probably thought it was a brilliant plan. Being born with profound hearing loss, I couldn't speak, couldn't communicate, and couldn't understand. Which meant, I couldn't tell anyone what was about to take place.

My primal instincts ordered me to run, that I was in danger, so I did—thank God I did. I kicked and fought, dodging the hands trying to grab me, and scurrying out of my window.

To this day, I remember the way the cold metal grating of the fire escape felt against my bare feet, and the way my mouth struggled to form what I thought were words as I banged on my elderly neighbor's window. Miss Lena, the lady with too many cats and twice as many grandchildren, yanked me into her apartment when she saw me. She called the police, but by the time they arrived, my mother was gone. I never saw her again.

Not that I regret it.

I was placed in foster care, confused and frightened about what was happening and certain I'd eventually return "home". Instead, I was brought before the young Assistant D.A Miles Fenske. He was supposed to handle my case, dispose of it, and move on. He was never supposed to welcome me into his heart. Yet that's exactly what he did.

"Melissa," he says. His words aren't clear—not as clear as they can be, my hearing aids can only do so much, but I hear enough to sense the emotion in the way he speaks my name. "Why are you so sad?"

I raise my chin. "Declan O'Brien will never be the man you are. He's not the right D.A. for this position." I shake my head. "He belongs in the Trial Unit, Arson, Fugitive, anywhere else but where you've placed him."

"I know you don't like him . . ."

I raise my brows.

". . . and that your first encounter wasn't a positive one . . ."

"That's because he was an asshole," I mumble.

He chuckles. "I assure you he deeply regrets what he said. But Declan is smart, quick, and kind."

I don't agree. Not completely. Is Declan intelligent? Brilliantly so, and absurdly astute in court. With short wavy blond hair and a dashing grin that lights his blue eyes, he's also gorgeous, and he knows it. But is he kind? I'm not so sure that he is. "He'll never be the man you are," I repeat.

"I'm not asking him to be. I simply want the best person for the job, someone who will help the victims who need him most."

"That's what you claim. But he doesn't have experience handling delicate cases where offenders often inflict irreparable trauma."

"No, but as the head of Victim Services, you do," he offers with a knowing gleam.

My nails dig into the wooden armrests. "If you're trying to hook us up, I'm going to be seriously mad at you."

The edges of his mouth curve. "I'm only asking you to help Declan as he transitions into his new role. This new assignment won't be easy on him."

"Because he doesn't want it. He wants to be the head of Homicide." I stand with my hands out, pleading. "Daddy, please reassign him. The Sexual Assault and Child Abuse Unit is not where someone who seeks glory belongs."

My voice trails as I catch a glimmer of his pain. "Daddy?"

At once, his face scrunches, flushing red only to grow alarmingly pale. I race around his desk, clutching his shoulders to keep him upright as he grips his side and beads of sweat gather along his receding hairline.

It's only because he lifts his bowed head and a healthier shade of pink returns to his cheeks that I'm not screaming for help and dialing 911. "Daddy?"

He offers me a weak smile and pats my arm. "I'm all right," he says, leaning back in his chair.

"No, you're not," I say, my eyes stinging. His light blue dress shirt clings with sweat along his arms and plump midsection. He's not well. My father is . . . *sick*. "What aren't you telling me?"

His hand slowly eases away from his side. For a moment his eyes search my face, as they've done a thousand times throughout my life. "The doctors discovered new tumors along my colon," he finally says. "They're planning to resection my bowel and dispose of the affected area with the hope of avoiding chemo this time around."

Very carefully, I straighten, despite that my heart has all but stopped beating. My father was diagnosed with colon cancer years ago and barely survived the aggressive treatment. If it's returned, now that he's older, and not as healthy . . .

"When were you going to tell me?" I ask, struggling to keep my voice clear as it shakes, my fear likely worsening my speech impediment.

He sighs. "Friday, over dinner."

To give me the weekend to absorb it, no doubt. "And your surgery? When is that?"

"A few weeks." He frowns as if debating what to say. "I'll be out of commission for a while. In my absence, Declan will lead the office as acting District Attorney." He looks at me then. "And I ask that you help him, regardless of your feelings toward him."

Declan

"This isn't where I fucking belong." I'm beyond pissed, and started typing my resignation letter at least six times today only to delete it. Yet for as much as I don't want to head the Sexual Assault and Child Abuse Unit, I'm not a quitter. "Fuck," I mumble, dragging my hand along my face. "*Fuck.*"

My brother Curran crosses his arms over his chest, not caring how it creases the shirt of his Philly PD uniform. But then Curran doesn't care about shit like that. "It's still a promotion, Deck," he says. "You got this D.A. spot straight out of law school and have made more of a name for yourself than most douche-bag attorneys ever will." He holds out a hand. "No offense to the douche-bag attorneys of the world."

"That's my point. After all I've accomplished, I should be the one leading the Homicide unit."

I shove away from my desk and pace. When Miles gave me these new digs, I thought it was just the start of all the good things coming my way. When he assigned me a county car and a personal secretary, it only reinforced that my hard work had paid off. I was on my way …until I wasn't.

"I spent months dismantling a mafia empire, Curran."

"I know," he says. "I was there."

"I brought down a major crime boss—and his second in command, and his third."

"Yup. Saw that, too," he agrees.

"I received international attention—the trial of the century, the media called it—and for what? To be shoved someplace I don't belong."

"Why don't you think you belong there?"

Out of all my five brothers, Curran is probably one of the biggest ball busters. But he's not messing with me now. He's being serious.

"Do you want to hear about babies and women being hurt? Day in and day out?" I ask. "These are the cases I'm going to be dealing with."

"Someone has to do it, Deck. It's the right thing."

"I'm not saying it isn't. I'm only saying I may not be the man for the job. This shit's disgusting, what these low-life assholes are capable of."

"Is this about Finnie?" He huffs when I straighten and don't answer. "Christ," he mutters.

As easy as that, my brother nails it on the head. For all he sometimes pisses me off, my brother isn't stupid. "Finnie didn't deserve what happened to him," I say, feeling my anger burn down to my gut.

"Of course he didn't," Curran snaps. "No one does. But as his brother, you owe it to him to put monsters like the guy who hurt him away."

I sit back in my chair and rub my jaw. "I don't know if I can."

Our youngest brother was sexually assaulted by a

neighbor when he was ten. It screwed with his mind. What he doesn't realize is we've all suffered, too—not like he has—of course, not like he has. That doesn't mean we don't hurt for him or haven't spent sleepless nights worried about him.

Nothing bad was supposed to happen to Finnie. He was the baby. The one who counted on us. The one we were all supposed to keep safe.

With this new assignment—hearing stories like Finnie's on a regular basis?—God *damn* it. "I don't think I can do this," I say yet again.

"Deck, you have to, man."

A knock on the door interrupts us. I know who it is before I even ask. "Come in," I say, assuming my attorney pose because for now, I have to. For now, I'm a professional. Even though all the Philly boy in me wants to do is rage.

My boss, Miles Fenske walks in, followed by his daughter Melissa. Miles smiles warmly, nodding my way.

Mel? What can I say? She's the one person who's never been taken by my charm. Today's no different. Unlike the other females who work here, from interns to attorneys, she doesn't meet me with a grin, doesn't flash me a little leg, doesn't pretend to flirt. Brown hair, brown eyes, creamy skin, with a steel-hard exterior, she walks in with her hips swinging, her bright red dress hugging her hourglass figure, her full lips pressed into a firm line, and her unyielding stare meeting mine.

She doesn't like me. Not that I blame her. Too bad this is the one woman I can't seem to get out of my damn mind . . .

Inseverable

A Carolina Beach Novel

by Cecy Robson

Prologue

Callahan

Three days.

That's all I have left until this shit ends.

Three days shouldn't feel like forever, not compared to the eight years I've bled to the Army. Thing is, good men have been killed in less time. In as quick as a blink, a squeeze of a trigger, or a small breath right before a grenade blows is all the time it takes to shove someone right out of life and well into death.

That's what makes three days as long as it is. Three days is plenty of time to die.

My eyes tear when the wind picks up and shoots grime through the small hole of my lookout point. This blown out piece of cinderblock is only big enough to allow me a view of the street below, but not so small I don't get smacked in the face with more filth. The tarp flaps above me as I spit out another layer of the dirt-sand mix spackling my teeth. Christ Almighty, I need a swig of the water resting near my elbow. But my thirst, like everything else has to wait.

I have a job to do.

I adjust my hips against the cracked cement of my bed, bathroom, and home all rolled into one, thankful that the agonizing ache stretching over the lower half of my body has settled into a now familiar numbness.

Out of all the points I'd scouted, and all the accumulated years spent in this position, I should be used to it. And in a strange way, it should almost be home. Yet nothing ever has been home.

But in three days, maybe something finally will be . . .

I shove my thoughts away and breathe as my fellow Rangers stalk along the street. It's then I see them, a mother and daughter walking straight toward my team. Less than one city block separates them from the men counting on me to keep them alive.

The hell? How did they get past the other sniper unreported? Rogers is new on watch. But the quick paces these two are taking should have clued him in that something's up. I train my scope on their faces; their expressions are blank, unreadable. 'Cept that's not what keeps my attention.

The little girl can't be more than five. So why the fuck isn't her mother holding her hand? I lift my radio and bark a warning, dropping it beside me as I lock my scope dead center on the woman's head.

The radio crackles and Modreski chimes in, yelling at his team to hold their positions. He asks me what my plan is, knowing if something's caused the short-hairs on my neck to rise, he and the boys damn well need to listen. But I don't hear him, with a breath and a squeeze of the trigger, I leave a kid without a mother.

Just beneath the sleeve of her *abayah*—the dress completely covering her body—I see it, a detonator that would trigger the explosives likely strapped to her chest. A few Rangers I know—Simons and Boreman, rush forward. I start to mutter a curse, pissed at her for making me shoot her in front of her kid. But the curse lodges in my throat when I see the kid isn't looking at her mother lying next to her dead. She's watching my advancing team as she lifts the detonator clasped tight in her hand.

Chapter One

Trinity

"Trin! You coming?" Hale calls.

Even over the steady hum of the ocean, his deep voice cuts through the small opening of our lifeguard station.

"I need five more seconds," I yell back, my thick southern accent drawing out each of my words.

"That's what you said nine minutes ago," he complains.

"But I didn't mean it last time," I holler back.

I grin because even though I can't see or hear him, I know he's chuckling, no matter how much he's trying to hold it in. I hurry and finish writing the schedule on the white board and cap the dry erase marker, before tossing it in the small cup holder to join the rest.

No sooner do I reach for my beach bag and throw the sandy thing over my shoulder than the office phone rings.

Most people would run away, ignoring it, after all by now it's seven thirty and way after closing. But I've always been one of those goody-goody responsible types—you know the ones the teachers assign as classroom monitor and who always turned in her library books a day early? What can I say, I'm all about a good time.

I lift the receiver before it finishes ringing. "Magenta Groves Beach Resort, lifeguard station seven, this is Trinity speaking. How may I help you?"

"Trin. Screw the whiteboard and get in the damn car!" Hale yells through the receiver. I whip around as his voice echoes behind me, as well as through the phone. He hops up the steps as he disconnects, laughing like that was the best prank ever.

"Why did you do that?" I ask.

"Because I knew you'd stop to answer the phone, even though the rest of us have been waiting on you."

I pretend to scowl, but don't quite manage. Me and scowling don't go hand and hand. Life's too short to wrap your mind around everything that's wrong with it. So I grin, because that's something I can do and do well.

"You think you're so smart. Don't you?" I ask, placing the phone back on the charger.

"You forgot good-looking," he says. "But I'll let it slide on account of I'm modest, too."

I laugh, but don't argue—at least about the good-looking part. We've only been back at Kiawah for a week, but already Hale's wavy blond hair has bleached significantly and his skin tone deepened to a light bronze. His steps are slow and purposeful as he crosses the small space separating us and stops in front of me.

"Let's go, Trin," he says, hauling me along. "You've done enough for the day."

I readjust my bag over my shoulder, and follow him out of the office, the usual bounce to my walk kicking in despite my heavy bag.

"Here. I'll take that," Hale offers, reaching for my bag.

I step just out of reach, knowing he has his own stuff to carry. "I've got it, big guy," I tell him.

"You sure?" he slams the door behind us. I stare out to the beach where a young couple is chasing after their little toddler as Hale fumbles with the lock.

"I'm sure," I reply, my attention staying on the young family. "Hey, Hale, you know how I always mind my own business."

"Nope," he says, leading me forward.

"Well, this time I can't," I continue, ignoring his comment. "For your own good, I have to tell you that this maybe your last chance to do something about Becca. The summer hasn't quite started, but it won't be long before it's gone."

"Yeah. I know," he mumbles.

"And?" I ask, turning back to him.

He tugs on my long ponytail. Unlike Becca, my best friend in the world, I'm neither tall, blonde nor leggy. My hair is as black as midnight in winter, and I'm just barely five feet three. And where her eyes are light and striking mine are a dull brown. But I do have something my bae doesn't have. Freckles. Y'all feel free to envy me at any time.

"Well?" I press. "You going to do something about that girl or aren't you?"

He shoves his key into the pocket of his long red lifeguard shorts and glides the sunglasses perched on top of his head back onto his face. "I guess we'll just have to wait and see," he tells me.

His smirk widens into that grin of his—the one capable of sizzling panties like coals over a fire. I shake my head. "Boy, between that smile of yours and that face it's a wonder Becca's not running to you rather than away."

He flings his arm around my shoulders as our feet dig through the sand. "Now, sugar, I'm sure I don't know what you mean," he says, keeping his grin in a way that tells me he's lying.

"Come on. You can have anyone you want. And if it's Becca, you need to act fast before those girls slapping each other just to lie their beach blankets near your post lead you astray and down a long dark path of sin, sex, and STDs."

"Is that so?" he asks.

"I'm just watching out for you," I say, stepping with him onto the gray weathered steps leading to the lot. "It's the kind of friend I am. You know, the kind who likes to pretend you're still a virgin and not the manwhore you've become."

He laughs hard enough to shake us both as we reach the edge of the pier. Ahead of us in the sandy lot, Sean, Mason, and Becca look up from where they've been waiting for us.

Mason's dark skin glistens with sweat, likely from having dragged all the heavy equipment we weren't using back into the shed. But he's got the muscle and the stocky build for it. Poor Sean has the endurance to swim a few miles and back, but his long-limbed body is better suited for reaching things the rest of us can't, and his personality is best for those who don't mind the occasional dip in the gutter and can appreciate his not-always brilliant remarks.

But of course it's Becca Hale hones in on.

I can't blame him. Becca is leaning against the Jeep, poised like Miss America and as alluring as Miss Universe.

"What the fuck's taking y'all so long?" she yells.

But that mouth of hers makes her all Becca, so does that smile that pulls Hale closer.

"You know how she gets," Hale hollers, hooking his thumb my way. "Had to get the floors waxed, the office dusted, and mend that sea gull's broken wing before setting it free."

"You did all that shit?" Sean asks, moving forward. "Man, and here I was thinking you were just working on the schedule."

Mason who tends to be the most serious among us just shakes his head and laughs, because that's what we all do around Sean.

Becca backs away toward the driver's side, keeping her grin as she points to our boys. "Alex Pettyfer, Nathan Owens, Channing Tatum, y'all got the back," she tells them. She grabs my bag and tosses it onto the floor of the passenger side. "You, get to ride with me, cutie."

I almost ask to switch with Alex Pettyfer, aka Hale. But I've known Becca long enough to know something's up.

So I hop in the front, barely snapping my seatbelt in place before she shifts in gear and tears out of the lot.

We catch the road leading out of the resort. Mason tugs on my hair just like Hale had, just to say "hi". Like most men I meet, he thinks I'm cute. As in a kid sister or a BFF cute. Not cute as in, "hey how about you let me rip off your thong with my teeth?" You know what I mean? The kind of "cute" that really matters.

I've pretty much resolved myself to BFF status, even though I wish I could be more.

Hale, whether because of what I said, or because he realizes time is running out for him to make a move, leans in between the seats, his attention fixed on Becca. Unlike me, that's not sand filling out the cups in her swimsuit.

"Hey, Becks, how about we catch dinner Tuesday after work? Maybe even a movie?"

Becca's wild hair—highlighted in alternating shades of blonde and blonder—slaps around her gorgeous features as she grins. "I don't know. The boss may not like me dating a co-worker." She looks at me then. "Isn't that right, Boss?"

I crack up. All my lifeguards can do whatever they want during their time off. But these four in particular? These four that have been my friends since before any of us learned to read, swim, or cuss. I know they're a good bunch. I know they have my back. For all we joke, the minute their toes dig into that smooth white sand, it's on.

I perch my legs up and over the dash and cross my arms behind my head. "As your fearless leader, I hereby let that be your call, ma'am."

Okay. Maybe I'm not so fearless. And "leader" is a pretty loose title considering all I do is run a few drills each day and make sure everyone has a shift.

"I'll think about it," is all Becca tells him.

Hale is a good guy. Good enough to slink back and give her space. Like all my male besties, he's had a crush on Becca since he hit puberty and his male parts saluted her in celebration. Capable of stirring erections with a single glance was Becca's super power. Mine is the ability to make people snort drinks through their noses at my jokes. I adjust my head beneath my hand after another glance at my beautiful friend. We all have our gifts, and if mine includes making others smile, I can't complain.

Her grin widens as she takes the road that leads to Your Mother's Coconuts, better known to the locals as "Your Mother's". Once off the resort we're no longer lifeguards expected to abide by the rules. We're just fresh college grads ready to run amuck, do some skinny-dipping, and partake in all the fun our young selves demand.

In less than a minute, Becca is screeching to a halt at the far end of the half-filled lot. It is a quarter to eight on a Friday and our work week is done. With a hoot and a few hollers, our buddies jump out the back, rousing the other lifeguards who beat us here to do the same.

"Where the hell have y'all been?" the new girl calls out. "I'm thirsty."

Sean holds his hands out. "Then what're you newbies waiting for? Order up the first round."

"Us?" she asks, looking at her friend. "*We* have to pay?"

"Damn straight, yeah," Sean says like it's obvious. "Everyone knows virgins always buy the first round. Ain't that right, boys?"

The rest of my team, even those loitering on the outside deck, start chanting "virgins, virgins, virgins," pumping their fists in the air.

"Aw, hell," her friend says. "Come on. Let's go get our cherries popped."

They walk in, but we don't follow. Becca's made no move to slip out so I know she means to talk. I smile softly. "What's up?"

She looks to the ocean, where the waves sweep in to bathe the sand with all its salty heaven. But I doubt she really sees it, even though like me, Kiawah is a part of her. She crinkles her nose and then takes my hand. "Last summer," she says.

"Yeah, last one," I answer quietly, knowing how she feels because I'm feeling it, too. I squeeze her hand, my tone mirroring all the emotions fluttering inside me. "Time to grow up, right?"

"I wish we didn't have to," she mumbles, keeping her stare on the sea as if trying to gather some strength from it. "You still serious about applying to the Peace Corps?"

I was hoping we didn't have to have this conversation any time soon, but I've kept things from her long enough. "I applied over winter break, Becks."

Her mouth slowly falls open. "I told you to wait—to not do something drastic just because of what those doucheheads did to you."

The "doucheheads" she's referring to are Hunter, my ex-boyfriend, and Blakeney, my ex-friend. They once held my heart, until I caught them in bed and they ripped it from my chest.

Her words chip away at me. Not because I'm not over Hunter, or Blakeney. I am. I'm just not over their betrayal. I could never hurt anyone I claimed to love or called a friend. But they didn't feel the same.

I try to smile, knowing Becca needs my reassurance. But I can't quite manage this time. "You know I've always talked about going and serving. Ever since I was little."

"So you're telling me, if he'd stayed faithful and been a real man instead of a little bitch—if you'd agreed to marry him like he kept talking about—that you still would have signed up to join the Corps? Come on, Trin. Finding him fucking Blakeney was like a pen being slapped in your hand, forcing you to sign on that dotted line."

"No, it wasn't," I insist.

I don't want tonight to be about the bad things of the past. Not with the five of us together after too many months apart. But here we are, focusing on things I've tried hard to forget. "Becks, as much as I thought I loved Hunter, and as much as I believed that he wanted to marry me, I realize now we never would have worked out. I'm going into the Peace Corps, exactly like I've always planned. But knowing who he is—who he *really* is—he wouldn't have waited for me, and he sure as anything wouldn't have joined up just to be with me."

Even through her sunglasses, I can tell Becca's eyes are narrowing. "He's still a douche head, and so is she."

"I won't argue with you about that," I tell her. My head falls against the seat rest. Do you want to know something about Becca? She's sweeter than maple syrup and about as kind as people get. Until you hurt someone she loves. I'm among the lucky few she loves. But it's because she loves me, that she reacts the way she does.

She pushes her sunglasses up to her head, pegging me with enough disappointment to make me ache. "When do you leave?" she asks.

"September. But I won't know my placement for another few weeks." I answer so softly, I'm not sure if she hears, but her tensing posture assures me she does. "Daddy used his connections at the UN and arranged it so I'd have time to take my boards and have one last summer here with all of you."

"So from Princeton to the Peace Corps. From rich kid, to just another volunteer. "She sighs in that way she does when she's trying not to cry. "Nice," she says, not that she means it.

My attention falls to our hands and to how hard she's holding me. "It's the right thing to do, Becks," I tell her.

"Helping people *is* the right thing to do. Signing up for twenty-five months with no way out, that's above and beyond." She shakes her head. "Hunter and Blakeney are assholes for what they did to you."

They are. But she needs to know that's not why I applied. "Becks, it's time to grow up and move forward, and to do the things we've always planned."

"What if I don't want to?" Her voice splinters and tears glisten her eyes. "What if none of us do? I don't want life to go on without the five of us together—you, me, Sean, Mason, and Hale—especially you, Trin."

Like me, she wishes she could stop time, and that somehow things could be different. But somethings can't be helped, and this is one of them.

Her parents and mine had offered to send us backpacking across Europe, but we chose to come back here. Back home to spend one last summer doing what we loved, and to pretend to be forever young, forever free of life's demands, forever friends. As I look to my pseudo sister, I swallow hard and hope that the latter stays true.

Tears trickle down her cheeks, causing my eyes to sting. But Becks doesn't need me crying with her. Right now, she needs my strength, and maybe a little of my humor.

"*Trin, Becks*!" Sean hollers from the deck. "What the hell? We've got shots waiting and horny women who can't wait to have a piece of me."

"Sorry!" I yell, hopping out of the jeep. "Becca dared me to spell my name across her belly with my tongue and I couldn't refuse."

Instead of taking it for the joke it is, Sean freezes. "No, shit," he says.

Becca doubles over, practically falling out of the driver's side seat. I hurry around to steady her and lead her forward. Sean continues to stare at us, his eyes clouded with whatever dirty thoughts are swimming through his mind as we stumble into Your Mother's.

My laughter fades as I look to where the rustic blue double doors open up to the rear deck. But I'm not staring at Hale as he points to his raised shot glass filled to the rim, or at Mason who's smiling politely at the women admiring his muscles. And my, I barely notice Sean shooting past us.

I'm too busy gaping at the smoking hot bartender with the Army Ranger tat inked to an arm as thick as my thigh.

Holy Baby Jesus in a manger sleeping on a bed of hay.

"Hmm," Becca says in a purr. She leans in close to whisper in my ear. "Who do we have here?"

Brown strands of wavy hair spill around his strong features and startling light eyes, and a thin beard lines a jaw I could probably pound horseshoes on. If I knew anything about horseshoes. Or horses. Or, pardon me, what was my name again?

Not to be rude, or inappropriate—I do have morals, after all—but that tight blue shirt stretching across his broad chest is one pec flex shy of ripping in half. Or me ripping it in half when I straddle him.

"You want to straddle him?" Becca asks, a delighted gleam fixing on her face.

I look at her, realizing I spoke out loud. "No?"

She busts out laughing. This time, she's the one dragging me forward. "Come on, Trin. Time to have fun."

We stroll toward the hot guy. Or as I call him, 'my future baby daddy' because for the first time in too long I'm looking—we're talking full-out gawking—at a man. He has my attention and whether he means to or not he's not letting go.

I smile his way, not because of what he looks like, but because I can't seem to help myself. I think maybe Becca smiles at him, too. But "sex in a tight T-shirt" isn't impressed by her charm, and he sure isn't captivated by mine. He scowls—as in *scowls*—which of course earns him a wink from me.

Hey, sticks and stones, or whatever, I'm going to get this guy to smile. Even if it's clear he doesn't want to smile at me.

Photo by Kate Gledhill of Kate Gledhill Photography

Cecy Robson is an author of contemporary and new adult romance, young adult adventure, and award-winning urban fantasy. A double-nominated RITA® Finalist, Winner of the Gayle Wilson Award of Excellence, and a published author of more than twenty titles, you can typically find Cecy on her laptop or stumbling blindly in search of caffeine.

www.cecyrobson.com

Facebook.com/Cecy.Robson.Author

instagram.com/cecyrobsonauthor

twitter.com/cecyrobson

www.goodreads.com/goodreadscomCecyRobsonAuthor

For exclusive information and more, join my Newsletter!

http://eepurl.com/4ASmj

www.ingramcontent.com/pod-product-compliance
Lightning Source LLC
Chambersburg PA
CBHW030600170726
48283CB00002B/403